Michel Bussi is the author of many bestselling novels, including *After the Crash*, *Black Water Lilies* and *Never Forget*.

He is one of the most successful French authors of all time, with millions of copies sold internationally and over a quarter of a million in the UK alone.

Vineet Lal studied French at the University of Edinburgh and Princeton University. He has translated several well-known French authors, including Guillaume Musso and Grégoire Delacourt, along with a number of books for younger readers. He lives in Scotland.

*Also by Michel Bussi*

After the Crash
Black Water Lilies
Don't Let Go
Time is a Killer
Never Forget
The Other Mother

# The Red Notebook

## MICHEL BUSSI

Translated from the French
by Vineet Lal

WEIDENFELD & NICOLSON

First published in Great Britain in 2022 by Weidenfeld & Nicolson
This paperback edition published in Great Britain in 2023 by Weidenfeld & Nicolson
an imprint of The Orion Publishing Group Ltd
Carmelite House, 50 Victoria Embankment
London EC4Y 0DZ

An Hachette UK Company

First published in French as *On la trouvait plutôt jolie* by Presses de la Cité

1 3 5 7 9 10 8 6 4 2

Copyright © Michel Bussi et Presses de la Cité, un département de Place des Éditeurs, 2017
English language translation copyright © Vineet Lal 2022

Extract from *The World of Yesterday* on p. 225:
Stefan Zweig, *Die Welt von Gestern*, Stockholm 1942, © Williams Verlag Zurich
Translated from the German by Anthea Bell, © Anthea Bell 2009, published by Pushkin Press 2011

Extracts from 'The Graveyard by the Sea' on pp. 259, 261:
Paul Valéry, 'Le Cimetière marin' in *Charmes ou poèmes*, © Éditions Gallimard 1922
Translated from the French by David Pollard, © David Pollard 2017

A CIP catalogue record for this book is
available from the British Library.

ISBN (Mass Market Paperback) 978 1 4746 1325 5
ISBN (eBook) 978 1 4761 1326 2
ISBN (Audio) 978 1 4761 1327 9

Typeset by Input Data Services Ltd, Somerset

Printed in Great Britain by Clays Ltd, Elcograf S.p.A.

MIX
Paper from
responsible sources
FSC® C104740

www.orionbooks.co.uk
www.weidenfeldandnicolson.co.uk

*For geographers, friends and colleagues,*
*who explore the world*

❁

'What's wrong, Leyli? You're pretty. You have three lovely children. Bamby, Alpha, Tidiane. You've done very well for yourself.'

'Done well? That's all just for show, all that. Hot air. Oh no, no, we're no perfect family. Not us. We're missing one key thing.'

'A father?'

Leyli gave a gentle laugh.

'No, no. We can easily do without a father, or even several fathers. All four of us.'

'What are you missing, then?'

Leyli half opened her eyes, like a Venetian blind letting a ray of sunshine filter through to light up a dark bedroom, turning the dust into stars.

'You're really quite inquisitive, cher monsieur. We barely know each other, but you still think I'll tell you my deepest secret?'

He said nothing in reply. The slatted blind in Leyli's eyes had already closed again, plunging the room back into darkness. She turned towards the sea, and blew out her smoke to blacken the clouds.

'It's more than a secret, Mr Nosy Parker. It's a wicked curse. I am a bad mother. My three children are doomed. My only hope is that one of them, maybe just one of them, will break the spell and be free.'

She closed her eyes. He continued to press her:

'Who put this terrible curse on them?'

Thunder rumbled behind the closed shutters of her eyelids.

'You. Me. The whole world. No one's innocent in this affair.'

❁

1

# The Day of Anguish

# 1

The barge slipped silently below the number 22 bus.

Leyli, her forehead pressed against the window, two rows behind the driver, watched the huge pyramids of white sand pulling away, carried along by the flat-bottomed boat, imagining that someone was making off with the local sand, and after they'd taken the rest, they'd steal the beach as well, one grain at a time.

The bus crossed the Canal d'Arles à Bouc and continued up Avenue Maurice Thorez. Leyli's thoughts drifted along at the same languid pace as the barge. She had always pictured this canal as a seam that was coming apart, and the town of Port-de-Bouc as a bit of land floating slowly out towards the sea, now separated from the mainland by a twenty-metre-wide strait. By an ocean tomorrow.

That's plain silly, Leyli reasoned to herself as the 22 joined the bypass – the four lanes of the N568 and their non-stop flow of cars isolated Port-de-Bouc far more from the rest of the world than the well-behaved, tree-lined canal where only the odd lazy barge meandered its way along. It wasn't even 7 a.m. yet. The sun was up but had still only opened one murky eye. Through the bus window, the pale headlights of the vehicles cut across the reflection of her face. For once, Leyli thought she looked pretty. She had made an effort. She had woken up more than an hour earlier to braid her hair with multicoloured beads, strand by strand, just as her mother, Marème, used to do in Ségou, by the river, during those summer months when the sun burned everything; during those

5

months when she had nevertheless been deprived of sunlight.

She wanted to look attractive. It mattered. Patrice, or rather Monsieur Pellegrin, the employee who was dealing with her case file at FOS-HOMES, was not immune to her colours. To her smile. To her zest for life. To her Fulani roots. To her mixed-race family.

The 22 drove along Avenue du Groupe Manouchian, passing the Agache housing estate.

*Her family*. Leyli raised her sunglasses and spread the photos delicately on her knees. If she had to touch Patrice Pellegrin's heart, these snaps were as vital a weapon as her charm. She had chosen them with great care, photos of Tidiane, Alpha, Bamby, as well as the apartment. Was Patrice married? Did he have children? Was he easily influenced? And if he was, did he have any influence himself?

She was getting closer. The bus crossed the retail park, weaving its way between a massive Carrefour hypermarket, a Quick burger outlet and a Starbucks. In just a few months, since her last appointment at FOS-HOMES, around a dozen new signs had sprung up. So many copycat metal cubes, and yet each instantly identifiable at a glance – the white horns of a Buffalo Grill, the orangey flower of a Jardiland, the pyramidal roof of a Red Corner. On the iron-and-glass frontage of the multiplex, a gigantic figure of Johnny Depp as Jack Sparrow stared at her; for a second, the reflection gave her the illusion that Johnny had the same beaded plaits as she did.

Everything here looked exactly the same. Everything looked exactly like everywhere else.

The 22 headed back down towards the Canal de Caronte, between two seas, the Mediterranean and the lagoon of the Étang de Berre, then turned into Rue Urdy-Milou, where the FOS-HOMES offices were located. Leyli looked at her reflection one last time. Her ghostly self in the glass mirror was gradually fading in the faint light of day. She had to convince Patrice Pellegrin that she wasn't like all those soulless places, those everywhere-and-nowhere places – she who, like them, belonged to here, there and everywhere too.

She had to convince Patrice that she was unique, it was as simple as that. Incidentally, the more she thought about it, the less certain she was that this guy at FOS-HOMES was even called Patrice at all.

# 2

Bamby was standing opposite François.

The skilful interplay of mirrors in the Scheherazade room at the Red Corner produced multiple viewing angles, as if a dozen cameras were filming her and projecting her image onto the walls, the ceiling, from behind, from the front, from below.

François had never laid eyes on such a stunning girl.

Not for twenty years at least. Not since he'd stopped criss-crossing the world and treating himself to Thai and Nigerian prostitutes for just a few dollars – girls who could have ended up as Miss World, had the accident of birth not left them on the wrong side of the tracks. Not since he'd settled down, with Solène, Hugo and Mélanie, and had a house built in Aubagne. Not since he'd begun putting on his tie every morning to go and check the Vogelzug accounts, and now hardly ever went overseas on business. Never any further than Morocco or Tunisia these days.

François calculated the months in his head: he hadn't cheated on Solène for more than a year. He'd become faithful almost without realising it. At Vogelzug, among the passion flowers fighting the cause of illegal migrants, he had few opportunities of seeing girls dressed as sluts, showing off their curves and flaunting their breasts.

And even fewer of holding those breasts himself.

The girl who was undulating gently in front of him was called Bamby. A Fulani name. She was twenty-four, had the body of an African princess and was writing an anthropological thesis on

7

patterns of human migration. She had contacted him quite by chance; he was part of a sample group of fifty professionals involved in migration management who made up her body of research. Fifty hours of interviews captured on a voice recorder . . . including one conducted with himself, a one-hour monologue apart from a few prompts, carried out in the Vogelzug offices.

Bamby had seemed captivated by his journey. François had laid it on a bit thick – the beliefs, the activism, the soul-searching ever since the carefree days of travelling light had given way to those of experience, the prime of life, success, seduction. She'd made him read over his words, by email, before they met again a fortnight later, a restrained, well-mannered evening of discussion, without a voice recorder this time. Nevertheless, they'd allowed themselves a long embrace before parting. *Call me if you want . . .*

The charming doctoral student had called him back. She was snowed under with work. Her thesis, tutorials to prepare for uni, no room for a boyfriend, this simply wasn't the right moment, so let's save some time.

A stroke of luck: François shared more or less the same view of things.

Let's save some time.

A rendezvous here, at the local Red Corner.

Barely had François entered the room than he lay down on the bed, faking a sudden bout of lethargy brought on by the three miniatures of vodka he'd drunk in the bar below the themed rooms. Saving time? It had taken the pretty young thing several hours to let herself be tamed.

Bamby crouched down near him, without false modesty but with a disarming tenderness. She confined herself to caressing him, just below the nape of the neck where the hair turns soft and fluffy. She was wrapped in a traditional African wax-printed pagne, the colour of the sun. A slim-fitting dress which hugged her body, reaching down to her ankles but leaving bare the upper part of her bosom and her brown shoulders. A little silver pendant disappeared under the elasticated border of the golden material.

'Is that a bird?'

'An owl. Do you want to see?'

The pretty doctoral student slid the African fabric downwards, very gently. It seemed as if a curtain were dropping, slowing for a second on her curves, then falling to her waist. All at once.

She had nothing on underneath . . .

Her breasts sprang out, magnificent, almost unreal; the little owl lay quivering in the valley.

The sun-coloured garment floated over her lower back, brushing against her navel, clinging on to her hips. Bamby stood up again, letting her finger skim down François's neck, running into the top button on his shirt, then down, down to the flies on his jeans. The little minx had decided to drive him crazy!

She could only just have been a little younger than his daughter. This didn't shock him. François was aware he was still attractive, silver-haired, reassuring. He knew how alluring money was, too.

Did money have anything to do with all this?

Bamby was swaying softly in front of him. Smiling. Acting like a butterfly that's likely to flutter away at any moment. François forced himself deep into his thoughts, losing himself, so as to calm down, not fling himself too quickly on this girl, remain in synch with her rhythm. Would Bamby accept money? No, of course she wouldn't. The simplest thing would be to see her again. From time to time. To treat her like a princess. The occasional present. A restaurant. A more elegant hotel than this suburban Red Corner. He adored these girls who enjoyed the double privilege of being beautiful and intelligent. He had noticed that – contrary to appearances – somehow that made them kinder than the others, because they arouse so much jealousy that they feel obliged to become your exemplary best friend so as not to end up being attacked. Obliged to learn to be modest as a means of survival.

Angels, which few men have the privilege of touching.

*He has a soft voice, he likes talking. He likes to hear himself talking, more than anything.*

*His wife is called Solène. He has a little one-year-old girl. Mélanie.*

*A little scar forms a comma under his left nipple.*

François's state of arousal intensified as Bamby came closer, slipping her fingers under his shirt, undoing two buttons, lingering on his nipples. She fondled him for a long while and, for the first time, allowed him to place his hands on her breasts, for a few seconds, before she recoiled very slightly, as if burnt by the physical contact.

Or as if she still wants to play, was François's preferred reading. Bamby stared at him defiantly, then turned around deliberately slowly.

'I'm going to get a glass of water.'

François's hands felt like orphans, but it was his eyes' turn to be dazzled. Patience, he argued silently to himself, there will be something for each sense. Sight was the first to be favoured. As she walked across the room, Bamby let the sun-coloured wrap slip sensuously to her feet.

She had nothing on underneath.

Neither above the waist, nor below.

She moved away, passing in front of a stained-glass window, unleashing a stream of colours onto her skin.

A second later, Bamby was walking back, holding a glass of water, giving François a full-frontal view which left him breathless.

'Do you like it?' whispered Bamby innocently.

François sat up against the pillow. That was his secret with women. To never play the conqueror. Even less so when he was certain of having won.

He gazed at her adoringly, the way you accept a present you've hoped for so much that you pretend you don't deserve it.

'*Ma belle, ma si belle, mon hirondelle*, what the hell are you up to with an old fogey like me?'

'Hush, François.'

Bamby moved towards him. She was wearing nothing but a hijab which covered her hair. When they had first met, the headscarf had surprised François; it jarred with the rest of this liberated student's personality. It added to her ambiguity. Bamby drowned out his question in a peal of laughter.

'Don't you think I'm prettier like this?'

Of course, this divine temptress was right. The hijab prevented you seeing the oval shape of her face, concealing her round cheek-bones in shadow, like a frame that focuses your gaze more clearly on the highlight in a painting, two eyes tapered like olive leaves, two iridescent, milky-white boats sailing through the mascara night, between the reed lashes, carrying two jet-black pearls glistening with honey.

A fragrance tinged with spices filled the room. Hidden speakers were churning out a constant stream of corny Middle Eastern-sounding tunes. François felt anxious – perhaps there were cameras watching?

Bamby was swaying her hips very slowly, barely even moving to the rhythm of the music, leaving François to fantasise that, as soon as she'd made up her mind, it would be over to him to make her naked body vibrate. That she'd be nothing more than an instrument in his hands, an exceptional instrument which only a few select virtuosos were allowed to play.

'You love me because I'm beautiful.'

Bamby had a voice that was almost childlike. Not husky, not that gravelly voice you found in female gospel singers.

'I don't know you enough yet. To know the rest.'

'Close your eyes, then.'

François kept his eyes wide open.

Slowly, Bamby removed the scarf from her head. Her hair was long, black, braided.

'I want you to love me with your eyes shut.'

The young girl climbed onto the bed. Sweeping aside all prudish distance in one stroke, she straddled François's chest with her thighs, lifted her breasts to the level of his eyes, then her vagina to within a few centimetres of his stubble. Every inch of Bamby's skin exhaled the scent of *wusulan*, the incense Malian women use to perfume their clothes and hair, and to oil their skin to bewitch their lovers.

'Pleasure me. With your touch. Just your touch.'

Fine. François was more than happy to play along. This was not the first time he'd be making love blindfolded. He'd often found himself doing it, with Solène, at the beginning. Then it had stopped. That was why he was here, for that and that alone. He closed his eyelids. Bamby tied the headscarf around his eyes, and François, now unable to see, fumbled around, trying to reach the areolae around her nipples with the tip of his tongue, to feel the weight of her breasts in the palm of his hand.

'Behave yourself now, Mr Suit-and-Tie!' said Bamby in her irresistible little-girl voice.

Her delicate hand closed around his wrist, as if prising a naughty boy's fingers from a tin of sweets.

*Click.*

At first, François was confused. His instinctive reaction was to try to pull off the blindfold covering his eyes. Impossible – first one wrist, then the other appeared to be shackled. In a fraction of a second he realised that, after tying the scarf, Bamby had placed him in handcuffs while pretending to play a kinky little game. The handcuffs must have been prepared in advance, he assumed, attached to the bars of the bed, behind the pillow.

This girl had planned everything. Fuck . . . what the hell did she want from him?

'Be a good boy, *mon petit* Casanova,' continued Bamby, 'the game has only just begun.'

*He dreams of living in a house above Marseille, in Aubagne. He has found a plot of land, at the foot of the Parc de la Coueste. He likes to call women* mon papillon, mon hirondelle, ma libellule.

*He loves wusulan, he refuses to touch me if my body isn't perfumed with it.*

*He is demanding, sometimes even violent.*

François remained hopeful as Bamby finished unbuttoning his shirt, as she brushed her body against his, skimming over him with her scent. It was only a game! Even more of a turn-on.

What on earth could the girl want? He had nothing to feel guilty about. He had no more than two hundred euros on him. To blackmail him? Well, she could bloody well take a hike! But in fact, now that Mélanie and Hugo were adults, that would give him a good excuse to leave Solène. He'd almost managed to put his mind at ease now, to relish finding himself like this at the mercy of this sublime girl. At forty-nine, he never put himself in danger these days, not any more, he had reached a point of equilibrium which felt so reassuring . . . until he felt the pain in his arm.

A jab! In a vein. That bitch had injected something into his blood!

François panicked, tugged at his handcuffs, considered shouting for help, even though he knew these goddamn rooms had padded walls, soundproofed so lovers could enjoy their intimacy without comparing the intensity of their orgasms with those of their neighbours. And on second thoughts, Bamby hadn't injected him with anything at all. It had simply felt . . . as though something were being sucked out. This girl had taken some of his blood!

'It won't be long,' whispered Bamby in a calm voice. 'Just a few seconds.'

François waited. A long while.

'Bamby?'

No one replied. He thought he heard crying, but that was all.

'Bamby?'

He was beginning to lose track of time. How many minutes had he been here? Was he alone in this room? He really had to call for help now – too bad if they found him like this. Too bad about the embarrassment, the shame. Too bad about the explanations he would have to give. Too bad if Solène's peaceful little world fell apart. Too bad if Mélanie discovered Papa was sleeping with a girl her own age. A girl he knew nothing about, really. Perhaps she'd been manipulating him all along with her tale of a doctorate, a sample group and an interview? Now that he thought about it, this girl was far too hot to be a PhD student . . .

He was about to yell when he felt a presence by his side.

He tried to focus, to identify Bamby by the scent of *wusulan*, but the spice-laden perfume filling the damned Scheherazade room infused everything; he strained to listen for the sound of footsteps, for breathing, the rubbing of a pendant on bare skin, but the never-ending solos, played on the *oud*, made it impossible to hear anything at all.

'Bamby?'

François sensed nothing more than a little pain in his wrist, barely a scratch, less painful than if he'd cut himself shaving. He only understood when he felt the warm liquid running down his right arm.

With all the precision of a barber, someone had slit the veins in both wrists.

# 3

In the long corridor, the chairs positioned in front of each door reminded Leyli of those endless hours spent waiting during parent–teacher meetings, first in primary and then secondary school. Often, she was the last to arrive, took the last appointment of the day, found herself waiting alone, for more than an hour, before being dispatched in two minutes flat by an English or maths teacher equally desperate to get home. Bamby, Alpha, the same story each time. Alone in the corridor, like this morning.

The FOS-HOMES offices wouldn't open for half an hour, but they had let her in without asking any questions. Before 9 a.m. and after 6 p.m., in the shiny glass offices you found in the business districts, black women were identical ghostly figures. Indistinguishable. Leyli was anxious to be the first in the queue. It was barely 8.30 a.m. when, as she sat on one of the chairs, the lift doors slid apart and Patrice Pellegrin suddenly appeared before her.

'Madame Maal?'

The FOS-HOMES advisor came towards her down the corridor that led to his office, looking surprised, as though he were walking along it for the very first time.

'Madame Maal? Apologies, I don't open for another thirty minutes!'

Leyli's expression made it clear this wasn't a problem – she had plenty of time, he didn't have to make any excuses.

Nevertheless, Patrice Pellegrin fumbled for his words.

'Um, er, OK, so sorry, back in a sec, I'll just get myself a coffee.'

Leyli flashed him her prettiest smile.

'Would you get me some croissants?'

Pellegrin came back ten minutes later carrying a tray laden with two espressos, a bag of pastries, two bottles of fruit juice and a basket filled with butter, jam and fresh bread.

'Seeing as you're here, do come in. You can share my breakfast with me.'

Clearly Leyli's smile, the warm colours of her African tunic and her beaded plaits had done the trick. She wasn't brave enough to tell Patrice that she drank litres of tea but never coffee. Insolence was a weapon to be used sparingly.

She dunked her croissant in the black liquid, hoping its soft spongy layers would soak up everything in the cup. Through the office's huge plate-glass window, they had an unobstructed view over Port-de-Bouc – the tower blocks crammed onto the peninsula, the retail parks linking them to the mainland, the tentacles of the breakwaters floating on the sea. The streetlamps were going out, traffic lights were flashing, apartment windows lighting up.

'I like to be up before everyone else,' said Leyli in a soft voice. 'When I arrived in France, I did my first cleaning job at the top of the CMA CGM tower in the Euroméditerranée district. I was up there every night. I loved it. I felt as though I were watching over the city, seeing it wake up – the first windows lit up, the first pedestrians, the first cars, the first passers-by, the first buses, all those lives beginning again and me about to go to bed, the opposite of the rest of the world.'

Pellegrin gazed dreamily at the panorama for a moment.

'I'm on the other side, over towards Martigues, in a bungalow. I can't see any further than the thuja trees that surround the house.'

'At least you have a garden.'

'Yes . . . And in order to enjoy it, I've got to leave really early in the morning, before all the roads get clogged up in Marseille. I get here ahead of time to slog through the files.'

'Except when a tenant rolls up to get on your nerves.'

'To keep me company!'

Patrice Pellegrin was a chubby forty-something and possessed the reassuring self-confidence of a married man, a guy whom a girl won't readily let go once she's found him, and who's borne him a kid or two very quickly to be sure of hanging on to him for ever. A guy who, when he's chatting sweetly to a girl, isn't necessarily coming on to her.

'I live over there,' said Leyli, pointing at the eight white towers of the Les Aigues Douces area which stood lined up facing the Mediterranean, like sugar dominoes.

'I know,' replied the advisor.

They carried on talking for a few minutes while they finished their breakfast, and then Pellegrin took a seat behind the desk. He got out a file and invited Leyli to sit down in front of him. They were separated by the desk, a hideous thing in a light shade of pine. Playtime was over.

'Now then, Madame Maal, what can I do for you?'

Leyli, too, had her files ready. She spread out a series of photos of her apartment for the FOS-HOMES employee, giving a running commentary as she did so.

'I'm not telling you anything new, Monsieur Pellegrin, you know as well as I do that the one-bedroom apartments are all the same, no matter which block you're in: twenty-five square metres, kitchen-living room, bedroom. How do you expect the four of us to fit inside?'

She stuck a few photos right under Pellegrin's nose – her sofa converted into a bed each night, the children's room where Bamby, Alpha and Tidiane all slept. Their things scattered around or piled up – clothes, school notebooks, paperbacks and toys. Leyli had spent hours staging these apparently impromptu photos, to ensure there was enough mess for Patrice Pellegrin to be aware of the urgency of the situation, and sufficiently little to prove she was still a good mother, well organised, school things neatly sorted, clothes folded, a spotless interior when it came to cleanliness. Just one issue, Patrice. We're packed in like sardines.

Patrice seemed genuinely concerned.

Outside the window, the sun had suddenly risen above the tall

17

corrugated-iron silhouette of the multiplex and now flooded the room with its rays, like a solar clock announcing that the city's offices were now open. Almost without thinking, Leyli pulled some dark glasses from her bag. Glasses in the shape of an owl, two perfectly round lenses connected by an orange beak with two little pink pointed ears on top. They made Patrice smile.

'Is the sun bothering you?'

He went over to lower the blinds, without asking for any further explanation. Leyli appreciated the gesture. Often, when she wore a pair of glasses from her collection in even the mildest of sunlight, ones costing five euros at most, she sensed others wincing in discomfort; aggressive people took her for a poser, manic depressives for a woman who was deeply unhappy. Leyli didn't hold it against them. Who could have suspected the truth?

Pellegrin, on the other hand, seemed to view it as nothing more than an amusing eccentricity. As soon as the office was plunged into semi-darkness, Leyli lifted her dark glasses up again.

'I quite understand, Madame Maal. But . . .' (His eyes fell on a tall column of files in assorted colours, a pile consisting purely of applications for council housing.) 'But I've got hundreds of families in the queue already, just like yours.'

'I've found a job,' said Leyli.

Patrice Pellegrin seemed genuinely delighted.

'A permanent job, at the Heron Port-de-Bouc,' she continued. 'Cleaning the bedrooms and breakfast room, everything I love doing! I start this afternoon. If you find me a bigger apartment, now I'll be able to afford it. I've got an employment contract. Would you like to see?'

She held out a sheet of paper. Pellegrin left the office for a few seconds to make a photocopy, then handed it back to her.

'I'm not sure that's enough, Madame Maal. It's certainly a point in your favour but . . .' (He stared at the stack of files once more.) 'I . . . I'll send you an email as soon as I have any news.'

'You said that before, the last time. And I'm still waiting!'

'I know . . . er . . . ideally, how much space would you need?'

'At least fifty square metres . . .'

He wrote everything down on a piece of paper. Without batting an eye.

'In Les Aigues Douces?'

'Or anywhere else – I really couldn't care less, as long as it's bigger.'

Pellegrin continued taking notes. It was impossible for Leyli to tell whether her request felt a bit surreal to the advisor. He reminded her of a father solemnly writing down a list of over-the-top Christmas presents asked for by his child. Pellegrin finally looked up.

'Not too hard, then, living at Les Aigues Douces?'

'We've got the beach, and the sea. That helps us cope with the rest.'

'I understand.'

Patrice seemed genuinely moved. He tried to avoid looking at the tower of files again; it was becoming a nervous tic. Perhaps he pulled the same old trick on every tenant, and those goddamn folders contained nothing but blank sheets of paper.

He quite understood, he understood completely. He sounded like the kindly, well-meaning complaints manager of a prestigious store who'd been transferred to a council housing estate. Leyli tortured her beaded plaits by twisting them around her fingers.

'Thanks. You're a good guy, Patrice.'

'Um . . . my name's Patrick. But it doesn't matter . . . You too, Leyli, you're—'

Leyli didn't let him finish.

'You're a good guy, but on balance, I'd have preferred to run into a bastard! Sure, I'd have given him the same old charm routine, but at least he'd have had the nerve to move my case to the top of the pile, he'd have shoved a rocket under the admin team, stood up to his boss. You, you're too honest. Basically, it's a bloody shame I just happened to be landed with you!'

Leyli had delivered her tirade with a disarming smile. Patrick Pellegrin froze for a second, his pen hovering in the air, wondering if she was joking, then burst out laughing.

'I'll do my best. I promise.'

Patrick seemed at least as genuine as Patrice. He got up and Leyli figured she had to do likewise. He stared briefly at the owl glasses perched on his client's forehead.

'They're so you, those pretty glasses, Madame Maal. You arrive before dawn. You can't stand the sun. Are you a night owl?'

'I was. I have been, for a long time.'

He saw a veil of melancholy descend over her eyes. As the Mediterranean sun blazed overhead, Patrick Pellegrin pulled up his office blind again to welcome the long daily queue of tenants, while Leyli lowered her owl glasses onto her nose and left.

❁

Patrick Pellegrin closed the Leyli Maal file, and was just about to add it to the stack of a hundred-plus other files to be reviewed in three days by the joint commission, for at most only a dozen or so vacant apartments, when his arm stopped abruptly in mid-air.

Leyli Maal's application had no chance of being successful for months to come, not even with this new job! Yet Patrick was reluctant to place it among the others. It felt as if that amounted to filing Leyli Maal away in the anonymity of hundreds of other single mothers, women of African origin sweating blood and tears to raise their families, to find a home, a job, to make ends meet.

Leyli Maal was unique.

Patrick was thoughtful for a moment, looking down at his cup of coffee, now empty, and Leyli's, where a vile grey sponge was bobbing around on the surface, surrounded by soft crumbs.

Leyli Maal was in a class of her own.

For starters, mused Patrick, Leyli Maal was beautiful, wasn't she?

Yes, indisputably. She was sparkling, quick-witted, disarming beyond your wildest dreams, but Patrick could sense, beneath the sequins in her eyes, the weight of years riddled with misfortune, below her rainbow tunic a weary body which no longer revealed itself to any man.

Was he imagining things? Impossible to be sure, but he was haunted by another question. *Was Leyli Maal genuine?*

Through the window, he saw her taking her place at the Urdy-Milou bus stop, waiting, standing, for a few minutes, then getting onto the 22, as packed as a cage stuffed with battery chickens.

He carried on watching, following the bus until it disappeared around the corner with Boulevard Maritime, unsettled by his feelings of confusion. He felt an unexpected sense of complicity with this simple, unpretentious woman, he could even have fallen in love with her very easily, and yet, without knowing why, he was convinced that Leyli hadn't told him the truth.

Patrick continued watching the lorries moving along the Canal de Caronte for a moment, then closed the Maal file again. Another ninety-nine files would be dumped on top of it before the day was over.

# 4

Commandant Petar Velika absorbed every detail of the Scheherazade room with a mixture of dismay and disgust. The naked man lying on the bed – stiff, cold, drained of blood – seemed to be carved from stone, as white as everything else was now red: the bed sheets, the Persian rugs, the once golden-brown hangings attached to the walls. The commandant's eyes lingered on the arms handcuffed to the frame supporting the canopy.

'Jeez. Holy shit . . .'

Petar Velika had, however, seen more than his fair share of crime scenes, and even more that weren't elaborately staged like this. Having fled Tito's Yugoslavia at fifteen and left half his family in Bjelovar, he'd enrolled at police college when he was just twenty and taken only a few months to build his reputation as a tough cookie and a leather-clad toughie. Thirty years later, most of them spent recovering bodies all over the Marseille metropolitan area, things had not got any better.

'He took more than an hour to bleed to death,' said Julo beside him.

'Oh?'

'Going by the cuts to his wrists, I'd say he lost between fifty and sixty millilitres of blood per minute. If you extend that to an hour, it's easy to do the maths – that makes three thousand six hundred millilitres, namely half the body's total blood volume, the moment when organs begin to fail one after the other.'

Velika was already only listening to his assistant with half an ear. They'd foisted this guy on him, a decent enough lad, twenty-three years old, fresh out of police college. He wondered what could have driven such a bright kid to ask to be assigned to a team as utterly hopeless as the one he was in charge of. *Julo Flores*. A police lieutenant who was considerate, polite, fast, knowledgeable, almost impossible to offend and even gifted with a certain sense of humour. In short, everything to wind him up!

Nodding to his assistant every now and then, Commandant Velika watched the other two cops bumbling around the Scheherazade room. The illusion of having been teleported back in time was perfect: a sort of ritual killing committed in the caliph's palace, punishment meted out to a eunuch who'd dared place his hands on the vizier's favourite concubine. The scent of spiced incense filled his nostrils. No one had turned off the harem-and-bazaar music still pumping out of invisible speakers, as you might instinctively do. The cops stomped around, crushing the woollen carpets with their boots, their Lumilite torches scraping against the porcelain bowls and vials of argan oil. The Scheherazade room certainly lived up to its name – you'd easily have believed you were in the heart of the souk in Baghdad.

'Can I open the window?'

His question was directed at Mehdi and Ryan who were busy taking fingerprints.

'Um, yeah . . .'

Velika pulled back the curtains and pushed open the shutters.

The magic fizzled out in an instant.

The window looked onto a concrete yard and a storage area for wheelie bins and skips. The exotic music was drowned out by the sound of gulls in the air, and lorries and buses streaming relentlessly along the main road. He turned his head and his eyes alighted on the signs at the neighbouring retail park: the Starbucks, the Carrefour, the multiplex. Johnny Depp's dreadlocks were on full view, a massive five metres by four. The Mystic Middle East had evaporated in the fumes belching from exhaust pipes. No minarets stood opposite, merely the towers of apartment blocks and the silos at the port. The caliph's palace was nothing more than a cube of corrugated metal. A miracle of modernity.

'Boss,' said Julo gingerly, standing just behind him. 'This is Serge Tisserant, the manager.'

In front of the commandant stood a man of about forty, wearing a tie, looking like a guy who flogged sofas or fireplaces for a living – the kind who's a walking-talking marketing brochure.

'Perfect timing,' said Petar, glancing around at the crimson-stained wall hangings. 'So, tell me a bit more about how these Red Corners work – feels like they've been popping up all over the place, these last few years?'

The commandant smiled as he watched Julo, standing behind them, taking notes on a rectangular tablet hardly any bigger than a paperback, ultra-thin, a gadget meant to replace the paper that Velika was in the habit of scattering everywhere like confetti.

'It's a brand-new concept in hotels,' replied the salesman.

'Tell me more.'

'Well, it's a franchise that's expanding, pretty much all over the world. You have a bar on the ground floor and rooms upstairs. The principle's based on, um, I suppose you'd call it self-service. The guest simply needs a bank or credit card to open their bedroom door – it's as easy as paying a toll on the motorway. Guests are billed by the quarter-hour, then the half-hour, then the hour. The charge only goes on your card when you leave, like in a car park. A few minutes later, one of our housekeeping ladies turns up to clean everything and the room's free to book again. No reservations, no names, no room service. Like any normal hotel, you see, Commandant, but more convenient.'

Petar's eyes wandered over the ornate Ali Baba-esque decor of the room again.

'Yeah ... I guess. But still, the furnishings, the look of your rooms – it's not exactly what you'd find in a budget hotel, right? Like a HotelF1?'

Tisserant's face was a display of impeccably mastered professional pride.

'That's the other innovation at Red Corner! We've got themed bedrooms. Have you had time for a tour? We have the Luxor room, the Taj Mahal, the Montmartre, the Caravanserai, the Venetian—'

The manager was apparently set to reel off the entire promotional leaflet. Petar cut him short. Julo must already have downloaded all the marketing bumph.

'Tailored for each hotel? But you've got precisely the same rooms in all the Red Corners across the world, haven't you?'

Mr Glossy Brochure puffed himself up again.

'Exactly the same! The same thrill of travelling to exotic places, the same change of scenery, wherever you are on the planet.'

Petar noticed this seemed to amuse Julo. Even pique his interest. After all, perhaps it was the ideal concept for romantic young people on measly salaries? For his part, he was staggered by this sort of cardboard cut-out decor. Why not a Vukovar room while they were at it? In the Scheherazade room, meanwhile, the two cops carried on bustling around ineptly. Ryan was trying to saw through the handcuffs to take away the body.

'Are there cameras in the rooms?'

'Are you kidding?' said the salesman, who mastered less well the role of the mortally offended small-scale craftsman. 'All our rooms guarantee the strictest anonymity. Secure, private, soundproof . . .'

Ah, thought Petar, that ability to say 'our' which you find in employees of a company that's going to replace them in less than six months.

'And outside?'

'We have three cameras in the car park and one in front of the door – they film round the clock.'

'Fine, we'll check . . . And if you don't mind (he stared intently into the salesman's eyes), would you kindly turn off that bloody screeching! It's like the frigging *Arabian Nights* in here!'

'I'll try,' spluttered Tisserant. 'Um . . . All the mood music's controlled centrally too.'

'Well then, ask Sydney, or Honolulu, or Tokyo to kill the sound!'

❀

Finally, the music in the room had fallen silent, the body had been removed, the scent of spice had dissipated and most of the cops had slipped away. Petar was leaning against the window ledge, the only place in the room to sit apart from the mattress which had been transformed into a blood-soaked sponge. The commandant turned to his assistant.

'I'm all ears, Julo. I'm sure you've already interrogated a dozen websites, and hacked into his social media, and you know all there is to know about this poor guy.'

Lieutenant Flores merely gave a little smile.

'Got it in one, Commandant! The victim's called François Valioni. Forty-nine. Married. Two kids. Hugo and Mélanie. He lives in Aubagne, Chemin de la Coueste.'

Petar had lit a cigarette, and blew out the smoke in the direction of the retail park.

'You're bloody fast, Julo. Fast and precise. I'm gonna end up believing in the virtues of this fucking big data lark.'

The lieutenant blushed, and paused for a second.

'Um . . . well, to be honest, boss, it's mainly because I found the victim's wallet in his jacket.'

Petar burst out laughing.

'Excellent! Good, carry on, what else?'

'A weird little thing. It was Ryan who noticed it, a needle mark on the right arm, but this wasn't any old jab. Someone . . . someone took some of his blood!'

'What?'

'While he still had some left, of course.' (Petar appreciated his assistant's touch of black humour. Thanks to his influence, the kid was gradually starting to loosen up.) 'In all probability, his killer took some of his blood using a kit before slashing the veins in his wrists.'

Julo produced a clear plastic bag containing a needle, a small test tube and a cotton bud soaked in blood.

'A gizmo that costs fifteen euros – we found it in the bin. You can find out your blood group in less than six minutes.'

Petar threw his cigarette butt out of the window. It landed among the condoms scattered around the Red Corner's rubbish skips.

'Hang on, Julo, let's get this straight. So this guy, François Valioni, willingly enters the Scheherazade room, most likely accompanied by his future killer, and lets himself be handcuffed to the bed. Then his murderer takes some of his blood, waits for the result, bleeds him dry and buggers off, leaving behind a halal corpse.'

'You could sum it up like that.'

'Fuck . . .'

Petar took the time to reflect before he carried on, with a heavy dose of irony:

'Perhaps we're dealing with a guy who's looking for a blood donor. It's urgent, a matter of life and death. He tests a potential donor, and when the blood doesn't match, he flips out and bumps him off. What's Valioni's blood group?'

'O+,' replied Lieutenant Flores, 'like more than a third of the French population. Or else it's a remake of *Twilight*.'

Petar frowned, taken aback.

'It's a vampire story,' said Julo.

'Oh, really? And you couldn't have said *Dracula* like everyone else? Right, we'll start by asking the external cameras what they've seen. The person who came into this room with François Valioni must be a girl. I can't really see this decent family man venturing in here with his boyfriend.'

Julo Flores remained standing in front of his boss. He produced two more little clear bags.

'We found these in Valioni's pockets too.'

Petar leant over to examine both of the exhibit bags and their contents. In the first, he could see a red band, made of plastic, perforated, the kind you'd fasten around your wrist in an all-inclusive hotel. He spent longer musing over the second, which contained . . . six little shells. Six virtually identical shells – oval, white, opalescent with a pearly sheen, three centimetres long, split down the middle by a narrow, serrated opening.

'I've never seen that kind of shell on the beaches here!' said the commandant. 'Mystery number two. Where could our nice Monsieur François have picked these things up?'

'He travelled for work, boss.'

'Did you find his diary too?'

'No, but there were some business cards in his wallet. François Valioni manages the finance division of a refugee aid organisation, Vogelzug.'

Petar Velika's world-weary attitude suddenly switched to one of keen interest.

'Vogelzug, you sure?'

'I can show you his business card, and the photo on his company ID, and—'

'No, it's OK, it's OK . . .' (Petar Velika's curiosity had turned into eagerness, tinged with unease.) 'Leave me alone for a bit, I just need to take stock of things . . . Here, get me a coffee at the Starbucks next door.'

Lieutenant Julo Flores, initially surprised, paused, and then, realising his superior wasn't joking, left the room.

As soon as his assistant was sufficiently far away, Petar Velika checked he was alone, then took out his phone.

His hand was trembling slightly.

*Vogelzug.*

It couldn't be a coincidence.

He looked again at the apartment blocks, the port, the industrial zone, and on the other side, close by, the marina. A mix of abject poverty and oodles of cash.

Shit. And plenty more to come.

# 5

'Can we have some more Coke, Grandpa?'

Jourdain Blanc-Martin nodded. He wasn't going to deprive his grandchildren of Coke, or indeed anything else, and especially not on their birthday. He was standing in the fifth-floor conservatory – an airy, glass-walled space that housed a swimming pool – holding an espresso, with the children playing a little further away.

Everything was going smoothly, at last.

He'd arranged a birthday party for his son Geoffrey's twin boys, Adam and Nathan, as Geoffrey had been left on his own, his wife having gone off to Cuba for two weeks. Jourdain was a little reluctant to admit it, but he'd been more stressed about sorting out this party than organising the Frontex symposium, to be held in three days' time at the conference centre in Marseille. More than a thousand delegates. Forty-three participating countries. Heads of state, CEOs . . . It was as if all this energy devoted to migrants no longer really interested him. It was probably time for him to hand over, permanently, to Geoffrey, the eldest of his three sons, before settling into a deckchair and watching the sunset over Port-de-Bouc. To sip a coffee which hadn't been brought to him by a secretary. To hear children's laughter other than via the speaker of a taxi's hands-free kit.

The party was going brilliantly, like a dream in fact, but then again he'd paid through the nose for it. Five party hosts for fourteen kids, all of them classmates from the Montessori les Oliviers school.

Their parents were hardly on the breadline, but he'd still left them open-mouthed with a welcome by the pool on the fifth floor of his villa, La Lavéra, which looked out over the Golfe de Fos, Port-Saint-Louis-du-Rhône, as far as the edges of the Camargue and the beaches of the Pointe de Carro. *No need to bring anything,* the invitation card had said, *no presents, just your swimming gear.*

Fountains of fizzy drinks, pyramids of sweets, showers of streamers and confetti. A Bacchanalian feast for the very young.

The sound of violins playing Barber's *Adagio for Strings* floated up from Jourdain's right pocket: the ringtone on his mobile. He didn't answer. Not now. He was blown away by the party hosts and their ingenuity. A young lad was playing Peter Pan, a rather cute-looking girl was Tinker Bell, another girl was a Native American, and all the kids had been dressed up as pirates. A large inflatable island was moored in the centre of the pool, guarded by a dozen or so plastic crocodiles. The children were on air beds, paddling their way between the harmless reptiles to reach the island and retrieve the gold chocolate coins strewn across its surface. It was obvious they were loving every minute.

Jourdain turned his attention away from the pirate crew for a second to gaze at the panoramic view from the conservatory. Due south stood the towering apartment blocks of the social housing development – one of those high-priority urban projects – in Les Aigues Douces, the area where he had grown up. Down below, a few hundred metres from the high-rise blocks and overlooked by his villa, Port Renaissance – Port-de-Bouc's marina – stretched out before him. An unrestricted view of his yacht, the *Escaillon*, and the *Maribor*, smaller and more feminine, which belonged to his daughter-in-law.

Just a few hundred metres, and yet two worlds with nothing in common. Hermetically sealed. He had taken fifty years to move from one to the other. It was what he was most proud of – to have made his fortune less than a kilometre from the apartment block where he was born, to have climbed every step of the ladder without going into exile, to be able to look down on those tower blocks whose shadow had crushed his childhood, just as a prisoner might buy a house next to the jail where he'd been locked up so as to better savour his freedom.

'Can we have some more Coke, Grandpa?'

'As much as you like, darling.'

Nathan was on his fourth glass. He already looked nothing like his twin brother. He was putting on a kilo a year. It was an easy way of telling them apart, even though Geoffrey kept mixing up his sons half the time. Geoffrey was travelling the world for Vogelzug, only coming home every third Sunday to kiss the kids and sleep with his wife, Ivana, a dazzling Slovenian who was less interested in her children's toys than her own, her little luxury yacht and her F-Type Jaguar, who'd end up cheating on Jourdain's big lumpish idiot of a son, convinced that her husband was unlikely to win the prize for self-restraint in various Hiltons and Sofitels around the globe.

When Jourdain had created his organisation, in 1975, there were barely fifty million people on the planet who'd been displaced for reasons linked to work, or war, or poverty. That figure had exceeded a hundred and fifty million by 2000, and the curve continued to grow exponentially. What other raw material, what source of energy, what financial investment could boast of such a steady rate of growth over the fifty previous years? He hoped his nice-but-dim little Geoffrey, with responsibility for the entire organisation resting on his shoulders, had better things to be doing than having it off with prostitutes.

Barber's *Adagio* played on, relentlessly. Jourdain headed for the terrace, as much to get away from the children's screams, which were becoming unbearable, as to answer the phone. Peter Pan and Tinker Bell hadn't managed to control the six-year-old monsters for more than twenty minutes with their aquatic treasure hunt. These well-behaved little kids, empowered by their Montessori education, were taking their roles very seriously indeed, whacking each other senseless with foam swords, scattering sugary Haribo strawberries in the water like myriad drops of blood, and turning the marshmallow skewers into mini-harpoons to burst the poor innocent crocodiles, or spear the gold chocolate coins on the island.

Jourdain closed the glazed door of the conservatory behind him, and read the name on the screen of his phone.

*Petar Velika.*

What the . . .

'Blanc-Martin?'

'Speaking.'

'It's Velika. I know you don't like me calling you on your personal phone, but—'

'But?'

Jourdain stared into the distance at the tip of the peninsula. It jutted out into the sea as far as the end of the jetty, opposite the Fort de Bouc, practically closing off the harbour.

'We've got a corpse on our hands. You're not going to like this. He's a high-flyer, one of your top execs. François Valioni.'

Jourdain dropped onto a teak deckchair, which almost toppled over. The screeching of seagulls mingled with the muffled shrieks of the children behind the French window.

'Go on.'

'He was murdered. We found Valioni this morning. Blindfolded. Handcuffed. His veins were slit. In a room at the Red Corner.'

Jourdain instinctively turned his head towards the retail park in Port-de-Bouc, even though you couldn't see it from his terrace. He had spent tens of thousands of euros on reforestation, so the view to the north of his villa would be of nothing but the maritime pines lining the Canal d'Arles à Bouc.

'Do you have any leads?' he asked.

'Even better. They've just brought me the footage from the security cameras.'

At the other end of the phone, Petar Velika screwed up his eyes, trying to analyse the pixellated image: a hijab obscured most of the girl's face as she stared into the camera outside the entrance to the Red Corner, then turned away almost immediately, as if to leave a clue that was intriguing, but not enough to go on.

Nevertheless, he remained upbeat:

'You can clearly see Valioni going inside with a girl. A really stunning girl.'

Jourdain walked even further away, checking that no one was standing nearby, that no Captain Hook, Smee or Native American chief had emerged from their make-believe land behind glass.

'Well then, you identify her, you track her down and you lock her up. If she's left you an image of herself, that shouldn't be difficult.'

Petar qualified his statement.

'She ... she was wearing a Muslim headscarf, an odd sort of headscarf with an owl pattern ...'

The concrete parapet was more than a metre high, but Jourdain Blanc-Martin felt himself drawn towards the void.

'Are you sure?'

'About that, yes.'

Jourdain's eyes skimmed across the apartment blocks in Les Aigues Douces – all alike, built like the towers of a white citadel facing the Mediterranean. Like an unfinished fortress whose walls had seemingly never been erected.

Blanc-Martin was mulling things over in his mind. A headscarf with an owl-pattern print. Blindfolded. Slashed veins.

A really stunning girl ...

A queasy feeling in the pit of his stomach told him she would strike again, she would carry on killing, spilling blood.

Until she'd found the man she was looking for.

# 6

As she was about to exit the stairwell, Leyli groped around for the timer to put on the light, using the only hand she had free. Her hand slid over the peeling paintwork until it reached the switch on the seventh-floor landing of Block H9 at Les Aigues Douces.

Leyli winced at the sight of the cracked tiles, the rusty handrail, the patches of damp and mould which had left blisters along the skirting. FOS-HOMES had repainted the front of the blocks the previous summer, but apparently there hadn't been enough paint left for the stairwells. Or else, she thought as she looked at the hearts, skulls-and-crossbones and genitals spray-painted on the walls, the council had set up a committee to discuss the preservation of the graffiti, a testament to the urban artistic heritage of the early twenty-first century. What was she complaining about? In a few millennia, people would come to visit her landing just as they visited the Lascaux caves today. Leyli loved thinking positively! After all, her little charm act might work its magic on Patrick Pellegrin and he'd unearth that dream apartment, perhaps an email was already waiting for her . . . fifty square metres . . . on the ground floor . . . a small garden . . . fully fitted ki—

'Madame Maal?'

The voice, which was more like a piercing cry, was coming from the floor below. A girl's face appeared on the staircase, twenty steps lower down. Kamila. That was all Leyli needed right now!

'Madame Maal,' repeated the girl. 'Could your kids please turn

34

down the music? Some of us in this tower are trying to revise. Just so we can get the hell out, some day.'

Kamila Saadi. Her downstairs neighbour. A psychology student. In her third year, like Bamby. As a matter of fact, Kamila did everything like Bamby. Through one of those strange quirks of fate, Kamila had arrived in the building two years earlier, having been placed there by FOS-HOMES. The social housing agency was trying to put them all up at Les Aigues Douces – students, the retired, the unemployed, the poorest of the poor from other areas who didn't have the option of refusing and who added a semblance of diversity. Before they cracked up and left.

Kamila had recognised her upstairs neighbour among the six hundred and fifty other female students who were crammed, along with her, into the psychology lecture theatres at Aix-Marseille University. For a whole year, they'd taken the same bus, the 22, revised the same subjects, shared the same kebabs. Kamila and Bamby had done everything together, but Kamila hadn't done it quite as well. Kamila and Bamby looked like each other – the same long hair, whether braided or straight, the same slender black eyes with glints of hazelnut, the same olive-coloured skin – but Kamila wasn't quite as pretty. They had sat the same exams, but only Bamby had passed her end-of-term assessments with distinction. They had dated the same boys, but it was Bamby who'd gone out with the cutest. Their beautiful friendship had slowly turned into an ugly jealousy. And to think that when they first became friends, Leyli had been afraid that Bamby might move in with Kamila, that her floor might become the girls' ceiling.

'Keen'V,' continued Kamila, labouring the point. 'Canardo, Soprano – no thanks, I'm way too old for all that.'

And Gaël Faye, added Leyli in her head. Bamby really liked Gaël Faye. And Maître Gims, whom Tidiane adored, or Seth Gueko, Alpha's favourite, or – depending on the time of day – Jean-Jacques Goldman, Daniel Balavoine, Renaud. Leyli would listen to Radio Nostalgie at full volume while she was ironing. At night, working for her bosses, she wore earphones, but at home she wasn't about to forego the pleasure! When you've only got twenty-five square metres to live in, music's the only way of making the rooms feel bigger.

On Kamila's landing, the opposite door opened to reveal a man of around fifty whom Leyli had sometimes bumped into on the stairs. He appeared to have only just woken up and was wearing a crumpled T-shirt, the kind you slip on in the morning to go to work and don't bother taking off when you collapse into bed in the middle of the afternoon. His face was as wrinkled as his T-shirt, and his two blue eyes, which were clear and bright, still seemed to be lost in their dreams. A beard was devouring his chin and neck, while a few sparse hairs fought bravely against his baldness. The T-shirt clung to the bulging curve of his belly.

'Well,' said the neighbour, 'I didn't hear a thing.'

He gave her a knowing smile. Goodness me, thought Leyli as she recalled Patrick Pellegrin's smile from earlier, the male race was certainly excelling itself this morning.

He smiled at Kamila the same way.

'I head off to work at 6 a.m., I sleep here all afternoon. If the music were too loud, *ma belle*, I'd have heard it.'

He had a strange, rasping voice, as if he'd been shouting too much. It made you less inclined to contradict him, let alone force him to repeat himself. Kamila shrugged and slammed the door of her apartment. The stranger climbed the stairs and extended his hand to Leyli.

'Guy. Guy Lerat.'

And at the same time, he grabbed the two bags of shopping clutched in her hands. Yoghurts, cut-price cakes, fake Nutella, a whole load of junk food bought at the Lidl to fill up the fridge. Guy stood on the doorstep, looking sheepish, while Leyli searched for her keys and opened the door. She felt rather moved by this big timid hulk who wasn't brave enough to venture into her home.

'Please come in.'

He seemed hesitant.

'Just up to the fridge, that's all . . .'

He placed one foot on unknown territory.

'So is it true, then?' asked Leyli as she took the bags from his hands. 'The music doesn't bother you?'

'No idea,' he replied in his croaky voice, 'I sleep with earplugs on!'

Guy's eyes twinkled mischievously, and Leyli burst out laughing as she thought about Kamila's fit of pique. That pesky little so-and-so was sure to find a way of taking revenge.

'I work on the machines, you see, at the refinery, down at the oil terminal. They've done the calculations, we're getting more than a hundred decibels in our ears, all day long. All very well, you know, having ear defenders, but we've still gotta talk to each other. Fucked up our voices it has, the whole damn lot of us. They say it's because of the noise, and we believe them, and they keep assuring us it's not asbestos, which is something, I guess. But they'll probably tell us it's something even shittier between now and retirement . . .'

Leyli nodded sympathetically, went into the kitchen and began putting away the shopping while Guy looked round the apartment, which consisted of just two rooms. He first took a peek into the tiny bedroom, whose door opened straight onto four bunk beds. It felt like a weird sort of room where the child had seemingly changed bed every five years, without letting go of the previous one. On the first were scattered some soft toys, a Buzz Lightyear, a model of the *Millennium Falcon*, comics, football sticker albums and books on Greek mythology; on the one above, covered in a green, yellow and red duvet, posters of African reggae singers, trainers and a carton of cigarettes took pride of place; on the one beside hung two bags, through which you could make out lacy blouses, fuchsia tops, pairs of sequinned shoes. The last bed was completely empty. Not even a quilt on the mattress. Bare and dirty. As if reserved for a child yet to be born. Guy wondered why, given how crammed in they were, the other three children hadn't colonised the fourth mattress too.

'Would you like some tea?' asked Leyli.

Guy said nothing, but turned away from the bedroom, as if caught red-handed.

'Don't look at the mess,' continued Leyli. 'Three kids, all in there, can you imagine? Tidiane's ten – have you seen the pile of books he brings back from the library every week? The complete opposite of his brother, Alpha.'

Her gaze fell on the top bunk.

'Alpha and school . . . It's all very complicated . . . I pushed as much as I could so he'd stay on until sixteen, but for the last two years, apart from music, his pals and sport . . . I'm not worried about him, mind you, Alpha's streetwise, he'll always manage to worm his way through. He just needs to stay on the right track.'

Leyli was choked with emotion, her voice quivering. Guy carried on listening.

'And Bamby, well, she's going to be twenty-two. She's just got her psychology degree. She's not sure whether to look for work or carry on studying, but finding something in psychology, well . . . She helps me with little jobs all over the place.' (Her eyes drifted across to the portrait of her three children which hung in the living room. Tidiane snorting with laughter, Alpha's head rising clear above the two others, and Bamby, staring into the lens with her big doe eyes.) 'She has no problem finding a job as a waitress in those bars down on the beach. Now then, some tea?'

Guy was still somewhat reluctant. He took a step towards the main room. The sofa was impeccably neat and tidy, and he guessed that was where Leyli slept by converting it into a bed. A small table, four chairs, a computer, an ashtray. Most striking of all, however, were two quirky features which were impossible to ignore. Firstly, a big wicker basket crammed full of sunglasses of every shape and colour. Then there were the figurines. Dozens of owls placed just about everywhere around the room. Made of wood, glass, terracotta.

'My own little collection,' said Leyli, beaming proudly. 'There's a hundred and twenty-nine of them, exactly.'

'But why owls?'

'Oh, so you like them too? Are you a night owl as well?'

'Mmm. A *dawny* owl, more like.'

Leyli smiled again and walked towards the steaming kettle.

'Cup of tea?'

'Another time.'

Guy took a step towards the door. Leyli pretended to take offence.

'You do know it's terribly insulting to turn down hospitality from a Fulani woman! They've found explorers in the desert butchered with machetes for a lot less.'

Guy squirmed uncomfortably. He seemed increasingly ill at ease. His eyes had settled on the framed picture above the computer. A sunset over a river – probably an African river, judging by the dark shadows of the dugouts and the huts.

'I'm joking,' said Leyli. 'What's bothering you?'

'Nothing . . . it's just that . . . I'm not used to it.'

'Used to what? The mess? Kids? Owls? To a girl as rich and sexy as me coming up to you, and inviting you back to her luxury hotel for a glass of champagne?'

'Used to Africa,' said Guy.

He was almost out of the apartment, standing by the door and nervously toying with a loose piece of tile with his foot. Leyli froze, the kettle in her hand.

'Wow, I didn't see that coming. Kindly explain, dear neighbour.'

Guy seemed to summon up all his courage at once. His words poured out in a stream that almost felt aggressive.

'Do I need to spell it out for you? I spent my youth between Vitrolles and Gardanne, I've been slaving away for thirty years, working on the docks at Port-de-Bouc, three-quarters of my mates are *pieds-noirs*, or the sons of *pieds-noirs*, we spend the weekends shooting ducks in the Étang de Berre, we all vote for the same party, it's the right sort of party, about as far to the right as you can go, do you get me . . . ? Look, you seem really nice, I've no problem with you, even less with your kids, but . . . fuck, how can I put this . . . I'm not really the kind who mixes with Arabs—'

'The Fulani aren't Arabs.'

'Darkies, wogs, ragheads, Bin Ladens, call 'em what the hell you like.'

'Ah, so you think I'm a Bin Laden, do you? Righto, hop to it! Sit yourself down on that pouffe – here, take this cup, and mind you don't burn yourself.'

Guy shrugged in annoyance, but he was no match for Leyli's infectious energy.

'You rescued me from that bitch Kamila, so you really can't turn down my cup of tea. And besides, I'm celebrating a new job. My first permanent contract for three years. I start this afternoon.'

As Guy was taking a seat, she took down the painting of the sunset over the river using her free hand. She cast one last glance over to the kitchen, around the living room, then her eyes lingered on the children's room. She felt reassured.

She hadn't left a single clue lying around. She'd made no mistakes of any kind. This fear always haunted her, gnawing away inside, whenever she let someone into her home. She had to think about everything all of the time, about every little detail, leave nothing to chance, arrange everything exactly as it should be. Inviting a stranger inside allowed her to be sure that you wouldn't notice anything. Apparently, this shy neighbour, this big cuddly bear apologising for being racist, had no inkling whatsoever.

Leyli pulled forward a chair and sat down opposite Guy.

'This is Ségou,' she explained. 'In Mali. That's where I was born. Now sit back and listen . . .'

## LEYLI'S STORY

### Chapter One

Ségou – because I suspect, my dear neighbour, that you've never heard of it – is a small town two hundred kilometres from Bamako, but more than five hours away by bus, via a big tarmac road which seems destined never to leave Bamako, as if the city were expanding faster than the speed of the cars, even though they eventually do reach the desert to be swallowed up by its vastness. But Ségou, above all, is the river: the great Niger River, almost wider than the town, almost a sea. We lived in a hut in the potters' district, near the river. My mother and father made pots, vases and earthenware jars with clay from the riverbank. They were sold to tourists, in the hotels. Before the 1991 revolution, though, there weren't many tourists, so more often than not you had to sell them to travellers.

Most of the activity in Ségou, Guy, revolves around the dugouts, the pirogues. The ones that belong to the fishermen, the ones that head down the river to Mopti or Koulikoro. But their main function, in Ségou, is to cross the river. There's no bridge across the Niger, no bridge for thousands of kilometres. As a result, people are constantly going from one side to the other with their food, their money, wood, stones, bricks, animals, and on each side of the river, especially on the Ségou side, there's a huge permanent market with donkeys, dogs, people selling all manner of things, sometimes even camels when a Tuareg ventures as far as there, and then the children all crowd around as if they'd never seen one before.

When a pirogue arrives, it's over to whoever's the fastest to try flogging a piece of jewellery, or some pottery, cigarettes, condoms, any old thing in fact . . .

And the fastest, that's me! The boys might have run faster with a football, but when it came to throwing myself into the water and wading through it until it was up to my breasts, carrying my bag over my head and smiling, laughing, shouting – yes, Guy, I was the fastest, the most daring! I used to sell more pottery than all of my cousins put together. The people crossing the river knew me, they enjoyed seeing me diving, splashing around, thanking them, catching the CFA francs they would throw as they passed by, and watching me slip them into the purse hung around my neck. From the ages of six to eleven, I was the little princess of Ségou beach, the little darling of the pirogue-men, the little sweetheart of the fishermen who would offer them bottles of cold water, dates to chew and kola nuts to munch, their ray of sunlight as they used to call me, the little bare-footed pedlar-girl, already in the water when folk thought I was still on the riverbank, already back out again while the rest could barely bring themselves to get their knees wet. Half girl, half fish, more tireless than the tide.

The red blotches appeared one April morning, a fortnight before I turned eleven. To begin with I noticed little spots on my stomach, like leech bites, then bigger patches – on my legs, my back, my buttocks, they went up as far as my growing breasts. Then the blotches began to join together, like stains eating away at a piece of cloth. Papa took me to the community clinic, behind Ségou's cathedral. The doctor, a Frenchman dressed in a jacket and trousers made of the same material as tent canvas, who'd been living there for thirty years and still didn't

41

seem used to the heat, examined me and reassured me. It wasn't serious, nothing more than an allergy – hardly astonishing, given all the filth floating around in the river, they really ought to ban children from swimming there, and women from doing the washing, and animals from pissing in it. A simple skin reaction to the putrid, polluted water, but nevertheless he would much rather I went to Bamako, to the Gabriel Touré Hospital.

Once I got there, I had some tests done and a woman came to see me in my white-painted room. She had a lovely, kind smile which scared me. From the window in my room, I could see Kouluba Presidential Palace just opposite, and the university which I would never attend. After speaking to my father at length, the lady came to explain that I'd caught a disease because of wading in the river. A skin disease. It wasn't serious, it was easily cured, the red blotches would disappear by themselves, but only on condition I didn't go swimming in the Niger again and, more importantly, that I didn't expose myself to the sun. The allergy had weakened my epidermis; I was suffering from an acute case of nettle rash, and adding the sun on top of all that risked leaving me scarred for life. 'You just need to wait for your skin to heal on its own,' said the nurse as she handed me a little piece of card, printed with a grid in blue ink, 'you need to wait at least three months.' And she slipped the tiny calendar between my fingers, along with a grey pencil, so that each evening I could colour in the day that had just passed.

At first, I couldn't quite grasp what three months would be like, much less what 'not exposing myself to the sun' could possibly mean. It only hit me when I got back to the hut. Papa, who'd been trying to make me laugh all the way home by tickling me with the baobab leaves that women sold at every stop, had phoned ahead to Ségou. Maman and my cousins had prepared a hut just for me, with cushions, big sheets and furniture made of woven wood fibre. My father had hidden away a doll bought at Bamako market, which he only gave me when I entered the hut, along with a doll's tea set made of clay which he had modelled himself.

'You'll have to stay here for almost a hundred days, my little princess.'

Apart from the door, the hut's only opening to the outside world was a big round window, a hole cut high in the wall. All my toys and clothes were laid out in the far corner. In the shadows.

'We'll take care of you, Leyli, we'll all take good care of you. A hundred days will go by so fast. Very soon you'll be able to run again, play with your friends, run faster than the antelopes. Even faster than Chiwara!'

Did that mean I had to stay locked up in here?

Eventually, everyone left and I found myself alone in the hut, with my only instructions being to avoid the shaft of light which shone through the round window, forming a bright circle on the earthen floor. I kept on shifting my meagre possessions around, in synch with the slow progress of the blazing sun.

That was the first day. After only a few hours, I was already bored to tears.

How could I possibly have imagined, at that moment, that those three months confined to my prison of clay would become the three most wonderful months of my life?

But just as life never gives you anything without asking you to pay something back, how could I ever have suspected that those three months would also be the cause of such misery, for the rest of my life? My curse for having wanted to find happiness.

43

# 7

'What do you want to drink, boss?'

Lieutenant Julo Flores was standing in the queue at Starbucks, his phone glued to his ear. Commandant Petar Velika replied in a voice that was part astonishment and part irritation.

'I haven't changed my mind since you left, sunshine. A coffee, like I said!'

'Sure, boss, but that's not gonna get me very far.'

An awkward silence took the place of the answer Julo was expecting. The lieutenant felt like a teacher who's just asked a pupil a childishly simple question, yet the kid still doesn't understand what it means. He tried his best to explain as diplomatically as he could.

'I'm at Starbucks, boss. They're not exactly, um, short on choice. Do you fancy a Guatemala Antigua? An Organic Ethiopia? A Kati Kati Blend? A —'

The attempt at conciliation was a dismal failure. The commandant exploded before Julo could finish his list.

'Bloody hell, lad, just sort it yourself! Christ, when I feel like a coffee, I go into a bar and I order an espresso without asking the owner if the beans were picked in Mozambique or ground in Nepal!'

'OK,' said Julo, quietly conceding as he hung up, 'I'll do my best!'

Julo hadn't set foot in a bar for years, but on the other hand he adored Starbucks – that mix of generations all waiting patiently,

44

students for whom a meal only really existed if it were served on a tray, tie-wearing execs bolting down their breakfast with one hand while tapping away constantly, grandmothers choosing their tea and muffins with a truly delightful lack of urgency. The queue was moving slowly. Julo studied the list of coffees with no idea of which he'd choose to take back to his boss. Petar Velika intrigued him. Julo always had difficulty making choices, always needed proof, always needed to consult large amounts of data before constructing hypotheses; he felt like a powerful, efficient computer, but only capable of programmed reasoning.

Petar, conversely, operated on instinct. He couldn't care less about objective analysis but could spot a significant clue at a mere glance; he didn't give a damn about psychological theories, but was able to drill into a suspect's personality in just three words. Julo too would have loved, like Petar, to be able to take on an investigation with amateurish zeal, as a gruff cop rather than a busy little ant – to be able to slam head first into puzzling crimes with nonchalance, screw things up without turning a hair, and flatly deny everything in order to land back on his feet.

Finally, a girl with a ponytail sticking out of her green cap took down his order with a big smile.

*Stéphanie.* It was written on her apron, above her left breast.

'Sorry, we're really busy. It'll be a short wait.'

Julo loved the girls who worked at Starbucks as much as the coffee chain's Banana Nut Loaf.

'No problem, Stéphanie,' he replied, smiling back at her.

Nowhere else but in a Starbucks would Julo have allowed himself to call a server by her name. It was a matter of reciprocity. He knew the little ritual, the question the charming young lady was going to ask once the order was taken.

'Your names, please?'

While the employee was writing 'Julo' and 'Petar' on the cups, the lieutenant sat down on a nearby bar stool, turned on his 4G tablet and placed it on his knees. An enlarged photo of a shell was displayed full screen. He had a few minutes to start getting into the life of molluscs. A few seconds later, he was already so absorbed by the subject that he didn't look up when Stéphanie called out the names of two customers in a loud voice:

'Bamby. Bamby and Alpha. Two coffees. Ready!'

❀

'He's quite hot, that guy with the tablet on his knees.'

Bamby took her eyes off the man perched on the bar stool near the tills and watched her brother set down the coffees.

'He's a cop!' said Alpha.

In order to sit down, he had to try to fold his massive frame, wedging his knees between the stool and the table. Alpha was more than one metre ninety. He'd already reached that height at the age of fifteen, when he was nothing more than a tall, gangly vine, and had spent his entire adolescence lifting weights at the gym, swimming in the sea and carting boxes around in the local warehouses, purely to make the transformation from weakling to towering colossus. Mission accomplished. At seventeen, Alpha had turned into an impressive athlete. Ninety kilos of muscle, two powerful thighs concealed under baggy joggers, and pectorals proudly on display in a tight-fitting sleeveless T-shirt.

'How do you know?'

'I just know, that's all. And you'd better stop checking him out, believe me.'

Bamby did as she was told. Her brother was right, even though she thought the young cop was cute, and even though he hadn't looked up when their names had been called out. She turned around, took her brother's hands and looked straight into his eyes.

The pressure began to subside.

After a long silence, she released her fingers and unfastened the pendant she was wearing. She placed the triangle of black ebony on the table. Among the Fulani, the tip pointing downwards symbolised femininity and fertility. Alpha did the same with the pendant he had around his neck, completely identical but with the tip pointing upwards, the sign of masculinity, the two testicles and the phallus. He overlaid his black triangle on his sister's, forming a six-pointed star.

Their black star. Their only goal. Their sole objective.

'I'm not sure I can do it,' said Bamby.

Alpha took his sister's hands and held them between his own, his enormous hands still warm from having brought over the two cardboard cups.

'We don't have a choice. We're like feathers. Carried by the wind.'

Bamby was shaking. Alpha came closer and hugged her tight. A heavyweight cuddling a flyweight. Yet Alpha knew his big sister was stronger than he was. Always had been.

Bamby stared deep into Alpha's eyes.

'Of course, little brother, we can't turn back now. Tonight we set the monster free. But . . . but you're the one I'm worried about.'

Alpha straightened his black triangle with the tip of his finger so the star was perfect. He paused to sip his coffee before saying very softly:

'We've discussed all the details, we've stacked all the odds in our favour. We're like astronauts, piloting a rocket into another galaxy. All we have to do is carry out our plan to the letter.'

Alpha wrapped his arms around Bamby's shoulders and held her tight against his broad chest for several long seconds.

'I'm so proud of you, little sis.'

'We'll be cursed,' whispered Bamby.

'We're cursed already.'

Bamby grabbed her own cup in turn. The hot liquid flowing down her throat felt like lava devouring wild grass in a fallow field. Would a scalding-hot shower have the same effect on her skin? She forced a smile.

'Two doomed little feathers? Two grains of sand tossed around by the harmattan? Two grains of pollen floating through the air, before falling at the base of the very flower they came from?'

Alpha laughed.

'Not always, Bamby. Not always. Some pollen grains can travel hundreds of kilometres before finding their flower, they don't care about walls, or seas, or borders.'

Bamby was well used to Alpha and his speeches. In a few seconds, he would come out with the scientific name for wind pollination, anemophily. She hated it when her little brother started acting the intellectual. He had a hang-up about education – a rebellious attitude to all scholarly authority – and made up for it with his grandiose theories, masking his lack of culture by spouting Wikipedia. It was a weakness common to all hunky, good-looking boys. Wanting to play the wise guy. The eternal problem with Alpha was thinking he was cleverer than everyone else, when in fact he was simply physically stronger. She let out a barely audible sigh which didn't escape her brother's attention. He had to keep from laughing out loud.

'OK, *ma belle*, I'm boring you with my stories. But just wait a couple of minutes, yeah? I've got someone coming. Someone who'll explain it better than me. Just need to . . .'

He looked over to the policeman who was still hunched over his tablet, as if the cop posed some kind of threat. Bamby followed his eyes, somewhat perplexed. She felt tired. The coffee was making her feel sick. Her voice grew drier.

'What if our plan doesn't work? What if we end up in jail? What if we don't survive? This time Maman will be left alone for ever.'

She placed her hand on the black triangle, as if to break up the star. Alpha held her back.

'We're doing all this for her, little sis. For her. Don't forget that.'

'And Tidiane?'

'I'll explain it to him.'

There was a long silence. It was broken only by the girl behind the counter, yelling like a bingo caller announcing the lucky winners:

'Julo and Petar. Two coffees? Ready!'

Alpha signalled to his sister to keep quiet by pressing lightly on her hand, just while the cop put away his tablet, grabbed his two coffees and headed towards the door. When he passed in front of them, Bamby turned away, then looked up again to ogle his cute buttocks. He'd barely stepped outside when a black man came in, older than Alpha but almost as tall. His head was shaved, apart from some fuzzy grey hair on his temples.

'Bamby, this is Savorgnan.'

Alpha explained in a few words that Savorgnan was an illegal migrant. Savorgnan came from Benin, a tiny French-speaking state

48

wedged right up against the Nigerian giant. Benin was one of the poorest countries on the planet, without oil reserves, without any tarmac roads – just a port in the south which allowed you to escape by sea, and a forest in the north where you could hide before crossing the desert to get here. Savorgnan had arrived two months earlier, accompanied by his cousins from Cotonou – Bola, an IT specialist, Djimon, an architect, Whisley, an Afro-zouk musician, Zahérine, an agronomist. The embrace between Alpha and Savorgnan seemed to drag on for ages. Bamby felt it was all a bit contrived. She looked down at their two black triangles sitting on top of each other. Alpha too would have to flirt with both good and evil if they were to reach their star. Walk on a tightrope. Sell his soul.

'Savorgnan's left his wife and two children behind,' said Alpha, as if it were the ultimate sign of courage. 'Babila, Safy and Keyvann.'

Bamby couldn't help reacting. She glared at Savorgnan.

'So you've abandoned your wife and kids to come here illegally? And you think that somehow makes you a hero?'

Alpha was annoyed, and was about to stop his sister mid-flow, but Savorgnan restrained him. He radiated the gentle aura of an African saint.

'What is your dream, *ma belle*?'

Bamby fell silent, taken aback.

'Um . . .'

'Well, my dream's all about words. I read. I write. That's all I do, all day. But I don't just dream of becoming a journalist, or even an editor, a columnist, a novelist. No, *ma belle*. I want to be the best. Win the top literary prize. It's the Goncourt or nothing!' (He roared with laughter.) 'Whisley the guitarist, he'd like to become a Presley or a Marley. Because the names sound the same! And Zahérine – now he's more realistic, he simply wants to be a researcher in agronomy to tackle famine across the world, or in Africa at least, starting with Benin. But you haven't replied. What is your dream, my princess? You must have one, surely.'

Just one? thought Bamby. Dance? Music? Fashion? The arts? Meet a Prince Charming? Become a millionaire and buy her mother a palace? Travel round the world?

'I've got . . . quite a few . . .'

Savorgnan slipped on some little squarish glasses which made him look even more intellectual.

'Everyone has dreams, Bamby. And what's important isn't making them come true, it's simply being able to believe in them. To believe anything's possible, that you'll get a lucky break, even a tiny one. When you're born in Benin, when you've got to stay in Benin, in Cotonou or Porto-Novo, you bury that sliver of hope. You chuck it into the ocean for good. Out of ten million Beninese, why wouldn't there be little Zidanes, little Mozarts, little Einsteins? Why wouldn't the Beninese also be born with that seed of talent? But can you name me just one Nobel prizewinner from Benin? Or an Olympic medallist? Or even a single Beninese actor? You see, Bamby, we just want our share of the dream, that's all!'

'Even here,' replied Bamby, spluttering out her words, 'even in France. You know, that sort of dream—'

'I know. They're a rare breed, true dreamers. Treasure hunters. The stubborn ones, the ones who don't merely accept what they've been given. The nutters who believe in their destiny. In my town, Abomey, there were five of us who decided to leave.' (He burst out laughing again, gulping down the coffee Alpha had brought him in one go.) 'The West believe that if they don't barricade themselves, the whole of Africa's going to turn up on their doorstep. Daft thing to be scared of, if you ask me! The vast majority of the population want to stay where they are, where they were born, with their family and friends, as long as they've got more or less what they need to survive. They're satisfied with that. There's just a handful of crazy folk who'll give it a go, who'll take a chance. You've got, what, a hundred thousand to two hundred thousand migrants trying to cross the Mediterranean each year, with fewer than one African in every ten thousand, and they're talking about an invasion?'

Alpha tugged at Savorgnan's sleeve as if to signal they had to go. His brother had put on his sunglasses and slipped on his leather jacket, precisely the outfit required of a small-time gang leader. The Beninese refused to move.

'You'll always have those lunatics,' he said, staring at Bamby, 'the

50

ones who're ready to risk everything to see what's happening on the other side of the water. On the far side of the mountain. Do you see what I mean, Bamby? Odysseus, the Golden Fleece, Christopher Columbus . . . The ones who're born with that quest in their blood. A few years ago, when scientists were looking for candidates to go off to Mars, in the certain knowledge they'd never return to Earth alive, they still found thousands of volunteers.'

Alpha stood up this time. He glanced around them, on the look-out, as if the survival of the group hinged purely on his vigilance. The one who knows it all, who's ahead of the game and makes split-second decisions. Bamby smiled. Once again, her little brother was laying it on a bit thick.

'One last word, my friend. One last word.' (Savorgnan stared into Bamby's eyes.) 'Contrary to what everyone thinks when they run into migrants dressed in rags in the streets, it's not the poorest folk who leave, not the ones who've got nothing to lose. No, these are people who've got every chance of winning, these are champions, champions chosen by their families, valiant knights who've been given everything so they can return victorious.'

Alpha caught hold of his arm.

'Good,' he said. 'Champions they are, and it's thanks to champions like you that I'm going to win.'

He was about to say more, but Savorgnan stopped him.

'You can tell me about your plan later, my friend. Your foolproof plan. I'm not in the mood for that just now.'

He rummaged in his pocket, clenched his fist and placed a perforated green wristband on the table.

'Bola and Djimon got caught by the cops an hour ago. They'll find it hard to avoid being deported. Especially Djimon. With that scar right across his face, the cops'll be able to spot him easily. Six months of effort, flirting with death on a daily basis, just to end up back at square one.'

Alpha took the opportunity to regain control.

'That's just why we're going to work together, Savorgnan, both of us, to prevent all that.'

Bamby watched Savorgnan getting up in turn, Alpha slipping his arm around his shoulder. Her brother was acting all bossy again, a bit too big for his boots. Brute force is always a bad counsellor, she mused. The virile self-confidence that produces the butch guys we dispatch to do our dirty work, the penniless light brigade, battered by life and the first to charge, those fearless wannabe heroes whom we send on suicide missions.

Alpha hung the black triangle around his neck; Bamby did likewise, trembling as she did so.

'Good luck, little sis.'

'Good luck, Alpha. See you this evening. Maman mustn't suspect a thing.'

'Maman's very anxious that we should look like the ideal family. Don't worry about it.'

He gave her a confident smile.

'Take care, little brother.'

'Take care, Bamby.'

# 8

'Your coffee, boss.'

'Thanks.'

Petar Velika stretched out his arm without bothering to turn around and grabbed the coffee from Lieutenant Julo Flores's hand. A few more policemen were pottering around on the ground floor at the Red Corner.

'I got you a Kati Kati Blend,' said Julo. 'This coffee's in season. It tastes of lemon, spices and summer fruits.'

The commandant paused, his cup hovering just a few centimetres from his lips.

'You serious?'

'It comes straight from East Africa. It's one of a kind!'

Petar frowned and stared at his deputy with consternation.

'Would you prefer mine?' asked Julo. 'Caffè Verona. A fusion of Latin America and Indonesia, with a hint of Italian Roast.'

Petar glanced down at his dark beverage.

'The coffee of lovers,' said Julo. 'It goes well with chocolate and—'

He stopped suddenly, realising the commandant had his hand clenched around the coffee, as if debating whether to fling it against the giant screen that hung above the drinks vending machine. He glanced around the room. Everything at the Red Corner seemed to be automated. Doors, cameras, dispensers for alcohol, condoms, massage oils. Petar Velika settled for placing the cup on the table in front of him, before turning to the nearest policeman.

'Ryan, could you start the movie?'

The young police officer tapped on a laptop connected to the giant screen.

'I've no idea how they've done it,' said the commandant, 'but the boys have managed to get the security camera tapes to play on this TV. Take a seat, young man. The show's about to begin.'

They sat down on two pink-and-gold striped armchairs positioned around a circular coffee table in varnished wood. A few seconds later, the images filmed by the outside camera were projected onto the screen. Petar had had enough time to reset the film to the exact moment when François Valioni had passed in front of the security camera: 00.23. Valioni was walking along, looking relaxed, his arm wrapped around the waist of a girl a little shorter than him.

'Stop, Ryan!'

The image froze.

'This is the only time the girl looks at the camera,' said Petar.

Julo screwed up his eyes while his boss pulled a face as he sipped from his cup. Was this the only shot that would allow them to identify the woman who'd gone into the Red Corner with Valioni? Got our work cut out, thought the lieutenant. The girl was wearing a long, loose-fitting headscarf over her hair, which concealed most of her face in the shadow of its folds. The scarf made her partly unrecognisable; you could only make out two dark eyes which seemed to defy the future viewer, a mouth thick with lipstick, a slender, sharp chin. The first thought to cross Lieutenant Flores's mind was that this girl with the face of an angel couldn't possibly be the killer! An absurd gut reaction, which he tried to dismiss.

'It's weird, boss, isn't it? Staring into the camera like that, if she's indeed the one who slit Valioni's veins.'

The commandant hadn't touched his coffee. He was watching Ryan coming and going between the chairs, like a frenetic waiter bustling around with the cocktail menu.

'It only lasts half a second, Julo. And this little bitch is only showing us what she wants – she seems to know exactly what she's doing with her chador.'

'It's not a chador, boss.'

Petar's gaze fell on the headscarf.

'A niqab, if you prefer, or a hijab. Call it whatever you like, but—'

'Look closer, boss.'

The commandant turned around to his deputy, feeling annoyed. The kid was fast, efficient, smart. But just a tad too insolent.

'There's a pattern printed on the fabric,' explained Julo. 'It looks like owls. A subtle pattern of owls, in beige and ochre.'

'Yes, I saw that. And?'

'Well ... Owls on a religious headscarf, I'm not sure if it's terribly—'

'If it's terribly orthodox? Is that what you're getting at?'

Petar Velika spun around and called out to Lieutenant El Fassi.

'Ryan? According to the Koran, is that allowed, having little pictures on a hijab? Little flowers? Animals?'

Lieutenant El Fassi walked towards him.

'I've no idea! I last had Koran lessons at nursery school. Seriously, Commandant, would I ask you to reel off the names of the twelve apostles, just because you happen to be Croatian?'

Petar sighed.

'OK, Ryan, save us the sermon, will you, and make an effort.'

'If you pushed me, I'd say it wasn't allowed, but . . .'

The lieutenant examined the headscarf on the screen more carefully.

'It's still very subtle, though. If there were Mickey Mouses printed on it, that would be a different story. But this doesn't shock me, frankly.'

'Your theological expertise is mind-blowing, Ryan! We're cooking with gas now. Print me out some close-ups, will you – eyes, lips, nose, chin, anything we can use. With a bit of luck, that'll be enough to identify our praying mantis.'

There was one detail that made Julo uneasy. The way the girl was challenging the lens. As if everything had been carefully planned – working out the fraction of a second when the camera could focus on her, stealing a furtive glance. If she hadn't wanted to be spotted, all she had to do was not look up, remain hidden under her scarf.

The mysterious woman seemed to have deliberately left them a clue, a trace of herself, but one that was hazy, blurred, not enough to identify her. Like those serial killers in novels, thought Julo, who taunt the police by sending them letters. To help them when they were really stuck. Or to throw them off the scent?

'Even if we *do* identify her,' said Julo, 'that doesn't necessarily mean this girl's the murderer.'

Commandant Velika was leaning over his cup again. He looked up before replying.

'So she enters the Red Corner with François Valioni. They go up to the same room. A few hours later, Valioni is found tied up on his bed. He's bled to death. Not sure what else you really need.'

'Perhaps she was just acting as a pimp. As yet we've got no trace of her leaving the Red Corner, on any of the security cameras. Perhaps Valioni was still alive when she left him and his killer came to meet him afterwards.'

Petar had been listening, amused, to his deputy's hypotheses, before suddenly exploding with laughter.

'You're in love, my little Romeo! I'm Mr Impulsive, you're the scientist – and there you go chucking your crappy little theory at me, just because this girl's got big puppy-dog eyes, a heart-shaped mouth and the silhouette of a delicate little bird.'

The lieutenant blushed. This son of a bitch had to be both the sharpest and the slowest of all the cops in the squad. He coughed and drained his cup. Petar watched him with a look of derision.

Caffè Verona. The coffee of lovers . . .

Julo was looking for a diversion. He had a burning question to ask.

'Boss, cut the babbling, would you, and tell me about this organisation François Valioni worked for. Vogelzug. You seem to know all about it.'

The effect was immediate. Commandant Velika's beaming face gave way to a stern look, like a smiley turning its mouth upside down. He seemed unsettled to the point of emptying half of his Kati Kati Blend without even making a face. He limited himself to a few words of explanation.

'Vogelzug is one of the largest European organisations defending the cause of migrants. Several hundred employees across Europe and Africa. Vogelzug means "migratory bird" in German. Every year, apparently, more than five billion birds cross the Mediterranean without anyone asking for their passport or a residence permit. Do you get why it's their emblem? Vogelzug's based in Marseille, but you'll find branches all around the Mediterranean. Inevitably, this involves them working with customs, the police, politicians. They've established official agreements with Frontex, the European agency which manages Europe's external borders. Will that do, Romeo?'

'Perfect, boss! I'm going to do some digging. To try and find out just what our head of financial services was doing at the heart of all that. And please note that Romeo didn't waste any time while he was waiting for his Caffè Verona at Starbucks.'

He turned on his phone, which he set down in front of them on the coffee table. The shell they'd found in François Valioni's pocket appeared on the screen.

'I ran it through some image recognition software. I thought it would sit there, crunching away for hours and hours, and we'd find millions of images of similar-looking molluscs.'

'And?' said Petar, beginning to lose patience.

'Well, no. Not in the least. I had a result in just a few seconds. I found this little guy's twin brothers! Brace yourself, boss: this three-centimetre-long shell is a rare natural gem. One of the rarest in the world. You only find it in a few specific places on the planet.'

'In the Mediterranean?'

'Wrong! You'll find this shell's cousins in just the one spot: chilling on the beaches of the Maldives, south-west of the Indian coast. Just there, nowhere else! No doubt whatsoever, I've checked everything – the shape, the serrated opening, the colour.'

'What the fuck was Valioni doing over there? That's way beyond the area Vogelzug works in! Any news on the blood?'

'Steady on, boss. I only had a few minutes at Starbucks, while a charming young lady brewed you a love potion.'

Petar smiled as he looked down at his lukewarm cup of coffee, now half empty.

'But I've still got my little theory all the same. Needs some work. There's just the torn red wristband that foxes me, and—'

They were interrupted by shouting at the entrance to the Red Corner. A police van had just screeched to a halt. Two policemen got out.

'Petar, we've got some surprise guests in the van.'

Julo stole one last glance at the screen, at the girl with the head-scarf, as if snared by her eyes, then followed Petar towards the door of the Red Corner. A cop pointed to two Africans sitting in the back of the van. One of them, an elderly man, seemed resigned to his fate. The other had a long scar that stretched from his forehead to his chin, and his face, contorted with rage, was pressed to the window.

'Two illegal guys who were hanging around near the port,' said the policeman. 'No ID or papers. They were staring at the sea, as if they wanted to cross over again.'

Petar ran his hands through his dishevelled hair, then dropped his arms in a gesture of helplessness, as if to signify he had other fish to fry.

'OK,' he conceded, 'take them back to the station. We'll try and find out where they come from . . . So we know where to send them back to.'

The elderly man seemed lost in his thoughts. The other, the one with a scar, had started banging against the reinforced windows. It wasn't the man's anger that shocked Julo. Nor the indifference of the policemen. Over the past year, he'd gradually become used to not searching for that fine line between misery and violence.

It was the man's fist, squashed against the glass of the window.

An ebony fist, a pale-coloured palm.

And around the scarred man's wrist was a blue band, strapped tight against his veins.

# 9

The sun was poking its way through the plane trees on Quai de la Liberté. It was late morning, and the 22 was taking its time, passing the locals playing boules on the square, families coming back from the market, employees from the dockyard finishing their beers as they sat on terraces under the palm trees. As soon as you left the towers of Les Aigues Douces behind, and in the first rays of sunlight, Port-de-Bouc took on the appearance of a picture-postcard Provençal village. Leyli liked crossing the town sitting in the bus. Driving alongside the commercial port, catching a glimpse of the Étang de Berre and the brightly coloured facades of the Port de Martigues, crossing the retail park. She would be there in less than ten minutes. Leyli liked to be early.

She lifted up her ladybird sunglasses, which matched the red dress with black polka dots that she'd slipped on when Guy left, and then read the letter of appointment again.

Please report for duty as follows:
12.30 p.m.
Heron Port-de-Bouc
Allée des Bruyères
Écopolis Business Park

Spending part of the morning with her neighbour had spared her from thinking too much about this permanent job on which so much depended: the extension of her work permit, the hope of a bigger apartment. She had enjoyed seducing this big, lumbering bear who only had to leave his den between two long naps. A gluttonous bear, attracted by the merest whiff of honey, who'd suddenly found himself distracted, looking up to follow a colourful butterfly as it fluttered past. Guy. Leyli found a certain charm in him. His gentle eyes. His strong arms. His childish way of listening to her stories. Would he be brave enough to come back and knock at her door? He'd left his lighter and packet of cigarettes behind when he went back down to his apartment. A subconsciously deliberate mistake, a crude little trick, or plain absent-mindedness?

The Écopolis stop.

Leyli reread the letter one more time. She could no longer manage to control the anxiety that was choking her.

Please report for duty as follows:
12.30 p.m.

She wasn't afraid of work. Doing the cleaning in a hotel, in empty offices on some industrial estate or in a school dining hall, what was the difference? Her concern was purely about her future manager. For five years, she'd hopped from one thing to the next: a string of little contracts, temping work, a spot of moonlighting, jobs that lasted no more than a night, and seen dozens of bossy managers parade by. Almost all employees of some multinational, companies structured like a Russian doll – a head office perched on the other side of the world, from where revenue targets tumbled like a ton of bricks onto the tiny local branch of the cleaning business that lay under their control. Over time, she had come to classify these upstart managers into four categories, ranging from the least to the most dangerous. The real good guys, servile, all slimy and sugar-tongued, who applied even the worst rules with feverish obsession, explaining it was not of their making. The real bad guys, hired for that very purpose, and who made no attempt to hide it. The fake good guys – understanding, accommodating, a bit clingy – who acted all buddy-buddy to better mask their incompetence, and ended up sacrificing you to better protect themselves. And worst of all, the fake bad guys, those who didn't even see the hurt they caused, who took themselves seriously, who thought they were fair and impartial, like little apprentice gods, hoping each morning to be entrusted with a slightly larger galaxy to rule over.

The letter of appointment was signed by Ruben Liberos. Which category would the boss of the Heron fall into?

The bus dropped her at the entrance to the business park. The Heron had been set down just opposite. Set down, that was truly the impression this concrete cube gave – deposited there, rather than built. Then a small tarmac car park had been built next to it.

Ruben Liberos was standing in front of the door. That had to be him.

Leyli saw a tall, slim figure corseted in an immaculate grey suit. As she approached, she saw polished Italian shoes and darted trousers, perfectly ironed on the crease. Liberos had a long face, a high forehead covered with fine, almost vertical wrinkles, as if pulled taut by grey hair that was possibly combed back, or wet, or slicked with hair cream. He looks like a tango dancer, thought Leyli. An incongruous elegance compared to this hotel where you could sleep for fifty-nine euros a night.

Fake good guy? Real bad guy?

How far would she have to compromise to hold on to this job?

Leyli took three more steps across the deserted hotel car park. You would probably only sleep the one night here, arriving at midnight and leaving before noon. When she was within three metres of Ruben Liberos, she saw him examining the ladybird sunglasses perched high on her head, her beaded braids, her polka-dot dress, her sandals. Would he demand that she dress like a chambermaid? Black tights and a white apron? Leyli stood on guard, ready to promise, her eyes downcast, that she could wear a scarf, slip on some trousers, sweep her hair back in a chignon.

Ruben Liberos greeted her with open arms.

'Welcome to my palace, noble lady.'

Leyli stopped short in surprise.

Ruben glanced up at the sky and then back at Leyli.

'Did some great star in the heavens transport you here, my little princess of the sun? The last thing I ever expected was to welcome a rainbow fairy into my dusty cottage. Pray enter, my fair child, I beg of you, I shall attend to you in two shakes.'

Leyli thought the hotel manager was taking the piss. A guest was waiting at the reception desk. A salesman, judging by the sample cases at his feet. Ruben Liberos slipped behind the counter to hand over the bill in a grand gesture.

'Godspeed, valiant traveller, and I fervently hope your odyssey will lead you back to one of our verdant oases.'

Behind them was pinned a map of Heron hotels around the world.

'There are other humble hosts just as devoted as your humble servant, waiting for you in all corners of the world.' (He began to whisper, but loudly enough for Leyli to hear.) 'Let me share a little secret, my friend: under this discreet sign bearing a wading bird's name lies a secret passage connecting 1,823 identical lodgings. You fall asleep in Port-de-Bouc and wake up in Kuala Lumpur. You come down to breakfast in Valparaiso and find your bags in Tegucigalpa.' (He winked at the bemused salesman, slipping a Heron leaflet into his hand.) 'Even better than Harry Potter's Floo powder. Here? Somewhere else? You'll feel at home, wherever you go.'

The salesman disappeared across the car park, no doubt convinced that this speech was part of some communications strategy dreamt up by the Mondor group's marketing division. Thank goodness the team in his company weren't quite as bonkers. Ruben Liberos finally turned to Leyli.

'Sincere apologies for the wait, my pretty ladybird. Yes, I know, I'm a bit over the top, purely for business reasons – but isn't it fabulous to imagine that this insignificant cube of metal is just like thousands of other metal cubes on the planet? As if nomadic man, lacking the skill to teleport himself through space, had somehow managed to create multiple homes.'

Leyli felt like replying that this was not exactly her idea of nomadism, let alone that of the Fulani herders who criss-crossed the plains of Africa. Another time. Ruben placed his hand gently on her waist and invited her to look round the hotel.

A low-end hotel. Decaying. Ageing badly. Peeling lino, cracked ceilings, pitted mirrors.

'You shall do your utmost to make the mirrors sing,' declared the manager, almost apologising. 'Make our masterpieces dazzle again' – Liberos nodded at the poster of the Arles amphitheatre and Notre-Dame-de-la-Garde pinned to the wall – 'and—'

Ruben stopped. Another cleaning lady was walking towards them along the narrow corridor. A girl of Bamby's age. Mixed race, just like her.

'This is Noura, with whom you shall perform your broom ballet. Freestyle, of course, no compulsory moves. Sweep us off our feet, my dear!'

Noura passed by, indifferent. Leyli was surprised the girl didn't react, before realising, on hearing the crackle of electronic music, that Noura was working with earphones glued to her ears. Leyli remained with Ruben for another good quarter of an hour, touring the hotel. He compared the breakfasts, delivered pre-packed in tubs and stored in a cold room, to those served with fresh coconut milk at the Herons in Borneo; the view of the Étang de Berre, from rooms 207 to 213, to those from the Heron Port-Vila which opened onto the lagoon in Vanuatu. Ruben Liberos seemed to have already accumulated more than a hundred years of service, if you added up all the years he claimed to have spent managing hotels in every part of the world.

Leyli found him adorable, this tall, elegant man, so eccentric and so completely unhinged. They ended up talking in the corridor that ran alongside the rooms while Noura vacuumed the lobby. Nevertheless, when Liberos asked whether certain hours suited her, she was still on her guard. The 'fake good guy' category had been flashing away ever since she'd met this astonishing manager. Gifts from bosses always had strings attached.

'I've got . . . I've got two grown-up children,' Leyli finally confided. 'Alpha and Bamby. I'm not worried about them. They come home whenever they want. But I've got a ten-year-old boy. Tidiane.

When I'm working, my parents look after him, but I try to be there when he's around too, as much as I can. Especially in the evenings.'

'I'll see what I can do. That's a Galician promise. Or a Haitian one. Or maybe it's Phoenician? Your word of honour is worth the same, isn't it, no matter who you are?'

Leyli felt like trusting Ruben. Despite her heightened suspicion, despite the hundreds of hours spent with women like her who had told her, time and again, never to let her guard down, that cleaning ladies were ghosts and had to remain so. Appearing by magic at night, disappearing in the morning. Commuting on monochrome trains and buses.

Leyli so wanted to believe Ruben!

Reassured, full of enthusiasm, charmed, Leyli reached for the door handle of the nearest room. Before going home tonight, preparing their meal, helping Tidiane with his homework, she had enough time to estimate the size of the job, and then give Noura a helping hand.

Ruben held her back just as she was about to open the door.

'Whoa, not so fast, my sweet ambassador from the tropics.'

Ruben's voice had become agitated, as if he'd suddenly been overcome by fear. He stationed himself firmly in front of the door and tried to make light of things, but his tone left no room for debate.

'My beautiful child, this room is the chamber of secrets, and as yet you are not initiated. You must never, do you hear me, never open it – neither this one, room 17, nor rooms 18 to 23.'

# 10

Tidiane placed the ball precisely on the small pile of gravel, held it for a moment with two fingers to make it balance, took two steps back, took a deep breath while analysing the distance between Steve Mandanda's glove and the right-hand goalpost, threw a fake glance at the basement window opposite – purely to mislead the goalkeeper – and then with a sudden, crisp shot, perfectly curved, sent the ball flying into the top corner. Steve, meanwhile, hadn't made the slightest move, dumbfounded by the purity of the shot.

Tidiane performed a little dance before celebrating the goal, eyes closed, hands open and joined together, raised to the sky, forming a round cage to trap the sun. An act of celebration which millions of players around the world would repeat, when they'd long forgotten those of Pogba, Benzema or Usain Bolt. By the time he had waved to the crowd, the ball had already rolled to the other side of the courtyard. It couldn't go terribly far. The courtyard was a square, enclosed by four walls, one wall running along Avenue Jean-Jaurès, another along Avenue Pasteur, the third surrounding the university annexe. The fourth was his apartment block. Or rather, the one where Granny Marème and Grandpa Moussa lived.

The Poseidon building.

Most of the time Grandpa Moussa watched him from the balcony on the second floor. Tidiane didn't know much about the neighbourhood, just that it was called the Olympus Estate, and that the entrance to each building was named after a Greek god

– Apollo, Zeus, Hermes, Ares, all those weird gods from the stories Grandpa had told him. Names he could only half remember. His own gods of Olympus, the *real* ones, were those painted on the walls of Avenue Jean-Jaurès. Mandanda, obviously, but also all those footballers he'd never seen play but had heard so much about: Jean-Pierre Papin, Basile Boli, Marius Trésor, Chris Waddle . . . and of course, his all-time favourite, Zinedine Zidane, even though Zidane had never worn the OM jersey, the celebrated shirt of Olympique de Marseille.

Tidiane walked across to retrieve his ball from the opposite wall and placed it back on the gravel. Before the next kick, he straightened his jersey. It was Abdelaziz Barrada's. Granted, Barrada's portrait wasn't on the wall just yet, and he'd left Marseille to go off and play in Dubai, but according to his coach, he was far better at taking free kicks than Cristiano Ronaldo! And what's more, he'd been injured during the two years spent in Marseille. In any case, a favourite player isn't really something you can explain. Tidiane's favourite was Barrada.

'You coming up to eat, Tidy?'

Grandpa Moussa was calling from the balcony.

Tidiane wavered for a second, unsure whether to attempt another free kick. Finally, he decided to obey his grandfather, and carefully picked up his ball emblazoned with its lion-head logo. *Morocco. Africa Cup of Nations 2015.* It was Alpha who'd given it to him. His big brother was smart, the smartest of them all, forever dreaming up clever wheezes to get stuff you couldn't otherwise find, like this incredible ball. There couldn't be more than ten people in the world who had one, or so Alpha had told him. Morocco had been meant to host the Africa Cup of Nations, or AFCON, in 2015, but because of the Ebola virus, they had refused to let in players from other countries. As a result, AFCON had had to be reorganised in another country, Guinea-something (there are so many countries called Guinea in Africa!), and everything they'd made for AFCON in Morocco had to be chucked away. Posters, T-shirts, scarves, badges . . . and even footballs! Since then, his Morocco AFCON 2015 ball with its lion symbol had become his lucky charm, his little buddy, his cuddly-ball, as Maman used to call it. He played with it, slept with it, ate with it.

'You coming, Tidy?'

'In a sec, Grandpa.'

The courtyard of the Olympus Estate was perfect for football training, or even organising a match with a few friends from the neighbourhood. Not too big, enclosed like a city stadium, with walls high enough so the ball didn't go over too often. It had only two drawbacks.

The cellars and garages underneath, for one. The courtyard, and indeed the whole housing estate, had been constructed over a huge car park, as vast as a labyrinth based on what Grandpa had told him, like the maze where the Minotaur lived. If by chance there was a drain cover left open, or you were playing with a ball that was too small and went through a hole in the gutter, you were screwed. The ball was lost. Fortunately, this almost never happened.

But the main problem with playing football in the courtyard was the tall tree which stood smack-bang in the middle. An orange tree. In fact, some people called the neighbourhood the Orange Tree District. It seemed as though the houses, roads and schools had been built around it. The one in the Olympus courtyard was almost ten metres tall. Tidiane was only allowed to climb up it to a height of four metres, precisely as high as their apartment balcony. Grandpa Moussa had built a small hut in the tree using a few wooden planks and a net, and then stretched a rope between the balcony and the nearest branch. Tidiane would usually have his afternoon snack there, sent in a basket prepared by Granny Marème which Grandpa would pass over. Grandpa would smoke on the balcony and Tidiane would munch on his Prince biscuits.

Sometimes, when it was too hot and the sun was beating down so hard it melted the tarmac, Tidiane remained in the shade of the hut and Grandpa would tell him stories.

Like today.

'Grandpa, will you tell me the story about the sun?'

'The legend of the sun god? You've heard it a thousand times, Tidy.'

Now you see, Tidiane, your mother was about your age at the time, and she was stubborn, even more stubborn than you, almost! She'd caught a skin disease from swimming in the river, which meant she had to protect herself from the sun for three months. Your granny and I put your mother in a hut. The hut wasn't very big, but we did everything we could to make sure your mother wouldn't be bored. I made dolls from millet and sorghum seeds, clay animals, and little houses from woven banana leaves, and Marème sewed her some dressing-up clothes. After a week, Leyli, your mother, already had itchy feet. She was an antelope. She lived only to run barefoot in a cloud of dust. Granny and I had no idea what to do. It felt as though we were locking up a piapiac in a cage. A bird that would lose its gift of song, and the colour from its feathers, until one day it could no longer fly.

It so happened that, a few days later, some men from the village organised a trip to Bamako to present their grievances to their elected député who had never ventured as far as Ségou. I went with them. I had a little idea of my own. Once in Bamako, I left them and headed straight for the French Cultural Institute.

To borrow some books.

Your mother could read, Tidy, she was a good student, curious about everything, even though she infinitely preferred chasing butterflies through the fields to sitting on her school chair. They had a lot of books at the French Institute, but they weren't happy about me taking them so far away. Finally, after much discussion, they let me take out one book. Just the one.

*Tales and Legends from Greek Mythology.*

I, who'd never heard of Hercules, Odysseus or Zeus. I couldn't have imagined that one day I'd be living in a building called Poseidon on the Olympus Estate. Which goes to show, Tidiane, nothing ever happens by chance. Everything is meant to be. I came back to Ségou with my big white book. Leyli was still sulking. She didn't want to open it. So every morning, every noon, every evening before nightfall, I would read her one of the tales. There were about fifteen stories in the collection, and we got through them all in less than a week. Within a month, Leyli already knew all the stories by heart.

Her favourite was the eleventh Labour of Hercules – the one where

Hercules has to borrow Helios's sun-chariot to go to the western end of the world and steal the golden fruit from the Garden of the Hesperides, right under the very nose of Atlas, the Titan who carries the world on his back. It is said that this golden fruit was in fact oranges, Tidiane, and that the Greeks had no knowledge of such fruit. It is also said that, because of this legend, the great Moroccan mountain range is named after Atlas, and that Hercules sailed as far as Gibraltar, between Africa and Europe, where his pillars still stand to this day.

A few weeks later, I returned to Bamako. I managed to borrow some more books from the French Institute and placed them on a small wooden shelf at the foot of Leyli's bed. And your mother started reading. Straight away. Reading a lot. She often says today that those two months, when she sometimes read several books a day, were the most precious moments in her life. From then on, everyone in the village was aware of her predicament, and would help her, bringing her books from Bamako. She had books lent to her by French VSO workers, by the village teacher, by tourists heading for Dogon country. At the time, the French could travel freely in Mali, without their president forbidding it for fear they might be kidnapped.

Everything was going well, Tidiane. Your mother had found the best way to occupy the endless days when she was condemned to stay in her cage-hut: roaming the world through reading! Even I would never have thought it possible. That a restless creature of the wild could turn itself into a bookworm. Since then, it's all made sense. I've realised it was the same curiosity that drove Leyli to run, then to read, the same thirst, the same hunger, the same burning desire, but you're too young to understand all that, Tidiane.

Leyli devoured books all day, and yet every morning she reread the first story I'd brought her: the eleventh of the twelve Labours of Hercules. The golden fruit of the Garden of the Hesperides. She'd been fascinated by the sun-chariot borrowed by Hercules, the chariot of Helios which sped from east to west to the end of the known world, drawn by ten fabulous horses. They included Actaeon, the first rays of dawn; Asterope, who lights the first stars; Erythraeus, the sunrise; Phlegon, the sunset; Lampus, the brightest of the bright, who can only be seen at noon; Pyrois, the raging fire at the very heart of the sun . . . There's always a grain of truth in stories, Tidy – or so your mother believed.

Left alone in her hut, and with no other window on the world than the large round opening in the cob wall, Leyli – the moment she put down her books – tried to discover the secret of the sun. To follow the course of the chariot and identify each of the ten horses of the god Helios. Actaeon and Erythraeus in the mornings, Asterope and Phlegon in the evenings, Lampus and Pyrois when the sun was at its highest in the sky. Every day she would note the exact position of Helios's chariot by following the rays that filtered through the opening, then making small marks on the mud walls with her fingertips.

One morning, one of the first mornings of the third month, I found your mother lying on her mattress. For the first time she had no book in her hand, nor was she even staring at the round window. Her eyes were looking down into the shadows, at her finger marks on the wall. She simply said to me:

'My eyes are tired, Papa.'

I drove her to the clinic, shielding her body from the sun, covering her arms, shoulders and legs with large pieces of cloth. What an idiot I had been. The damage had been done. The evil had entered. The sun had sidled up to her, wearing a mask, like the devil disguised as a *griot*, a village storyteller. I hadn't been able to protect my little girl. Worse still, because of that book, I had let the demon into her room.

The doctor at the clinic took me aside and spent a long time trying to convince me.

'She's been staring at the sun too much.'

I didn't understand. All children in the world, all men and women, walk around and look up at the sky without fear of the sun burning their eyes. The doctor explained things to me by showing me a medical dictionary, so I could grasp how an eye works from the inside.

'The cornea is particularly sensitive to ultraviolet rays from the sun, but normally you don't feel any pain until afterwards. Just as with sunburn, you don't feel the heat immediately, but the corneal cells have already been damaged.'

I still didn't understand. Surely everyone should be affected then, if the sun were so dangerous. Everyone who goes out in broad daylight. Everyone who doesn't wear dark glasses. No one wears dark glasses in Africa.

71

'What do you do, Monsieur Maal, if by chance your eyes glance at the sun?'

I didn't answer the doctor. I didn't know what to say, Tidy. I was worried about your mother, but only worried, not desperate yet.

'You instinctively close your eyes, monsieur, because you're dazzled. That's what eyelids are for. Like an automatic door sliding shut. But . . .'

I was afraid of what he was about to tell me.

'But your daughter refused to close her eyelids. I don't know why, but she displayed an iron will. She fought the glare, often, very often. For a long time.'

'So what now, doctor? How long will it take? Will she be able to read again soon?'

I was anxiously counting the thirty days that remained, during which Leyli wouldn't be able to read or write. The doctor looked at me as if I were the last fool on earth, as if I were the kind of man who triggers disasters without meaning to, who doesn't understand anything until you've made things crystal clear for him.

'Didn't you hear me, Monsieur Maal? Your daughter didn't feel any pain right away, but her corneal cells had already been damaged. The process has already begun. Nothing can prevent it now.'

'Nothing can prevent what?'

'The onset of NPL.'

I didn't know what that meant, Tidy. The doctor must have realised, or maybe he felt a little sorry for me at that moment, so he explained it to me:

'No Perception of Light. Your daughter will go blind, Monsieur Maal. There's nothing you can do to stop it.'

# 11

When Commandant Petar Velika had taken up his post, he had been lured by the promise of year-round sunshine, a view of the sea, small-time crooks and big-time mobsters to keep him busy and, as the icing on the cake, a large forty-square-metre room as his office. Barely three years later, however, by means of some mysterious process to which only the French public sector held the key, his government department had asked him to share his office with his deputy. To reduce the number of police officers while simultaneously making police stations more crowded was indeed quite a feat – something that only the combined and co-ordinated action of the Ministries of Finance and the Interior could brag about having achieved.

For a year now, Petar and Julo had sat facing each other, each hunched over his desk, as in any open-plan office, be it a company's mailroom or accounting department. Something invented for women, thought Petar. A godsend which allowed them to chat all day. Men, on the other hand, needed privacy. Even more so, on this particular morning!

Commandant Velika had spread out dozens of photos of girls on his desk, all more or less naked. More, rather than less. All wearing make-up, some more, some less. Young girls, far too often. Not all of them pretty, some quite touching to look at, all a bit of a turn-on. The commandant was pulling the photos out of a large black binder: a comprehensive catalogue of all the city's prostitutes.

All manner of women: from the casual worker to the professional hooker, from illegal Nigerian migrants to independent high-end escorts. The file represented many hours of police surveillance and online research. A database that Petar was busy updating with dedication and a sense of professional duty.

'You getting there, boss?' shouted Julo from the far end of the room, hidden behind his computer screen.

Commandant Velika exchanged looks with his deputy. Julo's eyes were full of derision. The lieutenant seemed unconvinced by Velika's homespun method of identifying the notorious hijab-wearing girl from the Red Corner. *Go on, take the piss,* thought Petar, *but how do I know what pictures you're scrolling through on your screen?* Next to the photos of the prostitutes, the commandant had enlarged the image captured by the security camera, zooming in on the eyes, mouth and chin. Petar knew he had a good memory for faces, and if the girl who had taken François Valioni to the Red Corner happened to be on file, he would recognise her. Petar finally looked up to respond to his deputy.

'Making progress, son . . . I'll let you know as soon as I find your girlfriend's price list.'

Julo tilted his round head to one side of the screen.

'Cut the crap, boss. Besides, how can you be so sure this girl's a hooker?'

'You can see I'm right. You're already pleading her case!'

'Anyhow, while you've been getting your cheap thrills, I've moved on.'

'Oy, kid,' said Petar, turning another page in the black binder, 'don't you joke about the Holy Book! You do know that several generations of cops have had a bloody good wank on this old thing? Magic, this is. A book of spells. A loyal friend for all those evenings on duty, nights on watch, weeks of being on a stakeout without seeing their wives. Show some respect, boy!'

It was all Lieutenant Flores could do to stop himself bursting into laughter. Would he ever be able to achieve the detachment of his superior? That state of relaxation, as elite athletes referred to it. That ability to act without questioning yourself, to sweep

Tidiane looked at the window to the right of the balcony. The one that belonged to his room at Granny and Grandpa's. Which had been Maman's room, in the past.

'Not that one, Grandpa. I want . . . Maman's story.'

Grandpa paused for a moment to reflect. He had already told his grandson this story at least once or twice. Tidiane was a smart cookie. He had heard the tale from cousins, neighbours, friends. Playground truths can often do more harm than family secrets. Tidiane had got wind of the story – about the treasure his mother had found, the cursed treasure she had stolen and then hidden. About her being punished, even before she'd committed any crime. Her mother had been punished in advance, by a god who saw everything, even the future. The sun god.

'Again, Tidiane?'

'Yes, again!'

The boy knew that each time Grandpa Moussa would add fresh details. Even if Tidiane found it hard to believe this story about a village he didn't know, a country he didn't know, and a little girl he didn't know, who also happened to be his mother, it was his favourite. Because it was sad. So sad. The story about a time before his mother found the treasure and was saved. The treasure that he too would find, one day.

He sat wide-eyed and let Grandpa Moussa's soothing voice wash over him, like a lullaby.

## LEYLI'S STORY

### Chapter Two

Do you remember, Tidiane? Your mother lived in Ségou, a small town on the banks of the great Niger River, a five-hour drive from Bamako. She lived in a hut, like most of the people there. It was a normal house, except the roof was made of tin, the floor of sand, and the walls of cob, a mixture of earth, water, hair and straw. It's very strong, cob, as long as it doesn't rain. In Ségou, you see, it never rained. The sun, always that damned sun.

away the horror of a criminal investigation with self-deprecation?

'Go on then, Bill Gates, what have you found?'

'I've been through François Valioni's computer. Trawled through everything. It was a doddle – he didn't use an alias when he was on social media. What's really interesting are the private messages on his Facebook account. He was contacted six months ago by a girl, a so-called doctoral student in anthropology working on patterns of migration. Their early interactions are quite formal, all very business-like, but after their first meeting the PhD student seems to have taken a liking to Valioni. She suddenly loses her inhibitions, and increases her use of innuendo and explicit emoticons.'

'Emoti-what?'

'Smileys – little drawings if you like, smiles, winks, beating hearts, red lips blowing kisses . . .'

Petar sighed. Clearly not high on his list of fantasies.

'So, this is the girl who contacted Valioni, yes?'

'Yep. And what's really weird is that she seems to know a lot about him. As if she'd been spying on him. More than that, in fact, as if she'd been briefed about his tastes, his family, his job, his past. When you read back through all of their past exchanges, it's pretty obvious that Valioni fell into a trap. He wasn't chosen at random. The girl in the scarf came looking for him. She targeted him meticulously, following a carefully planned timetable to seduce him.'

Commandant Velika's eyes hovered over a tall blonde woman leaning against a lamppost, wearing a thick fur coat which only half covered her bare thighs. It was hard to guess what time of year the photo had been taken.

'All sounds a bit too easy, son. If this girl's plan was so well thought out, why leave so many clues behind, so any old geek who comes along can easily identify her?'

'She's not a doctoral student, boss. It's all phoney. The title of her PhD, her research, her enrolment at the university.'

'Surely you've got her name, at least?'

'Just her nickname. So, no. Nothing.'

'Go on, let's hear it anyway?'

'Bambi13.'

Petar had closed his black bible, having dutifully filed away every photo of every girl. According to the information Julo had dug up, they were not dealing with an escort hired to drag François Valioni to some isolated hotel, as part of a quick and sordid settling of a score – although Petar had seen a few dozen of those since being in post. Commandant Velika grabbed a chair and came to sit next to his deputy, facing the screen.

'No photos on Bambi13's profile, I suppose?'

'Yes, dozens. But not a single one where she's identifiable. On her Facebook page, she only posts pictures of her back, her feet, her arms, her hair, as if she were carefully trying to hide her face. Mind you, that's pretty common for women on Facebook, especially the really cute ones who don't want any hassle.'

'Mmm, yeah . . . except in this case, *she's* the one trying to pick up a guy.'

'The images must have been part of the plan to snare Valioni. Based on what we can make out, Bambi13 is young, tall, slim, and mixed race with dark skin. If she's indeed the girl in the headscarf caught on the security camera, she's not exactly one for swimming in a burkini. Half the photos are taken on beaches where she's posing in a bikini, or even lying on her stomach with her top off . . .'

Petar watched carefully as the pictures scrolled across the profile.

'Was Valioni really that stupid? Slightly obvious as a trap, wasn't it? A hot girl who hits on him, who's the same age as his daughter, who never shows her face but wanders around naked in the most heavenly locations, in every corner of the globe.'

'Um, not necessarily,' argued Julo. 'It fitted neatly with her character as a researcher on international migration. Apparently, the photos were taken in Sicily, Turkey, the Canaries, the Dominican Republic, Mayotte – in just about every hot spot where illegal migrants land up. I'll dig around, boss. Maybe she's let some little detail slip that will let us identify her, but . . . but there's something even stranger on Valioni's Facebook profile.'

To Petar's great regret, Julo left Bambi13's page in order to open François Valioni's. A family photo of the Vogelzug executive appeared, posing in front of the Calanques de Cassis. François had his arms around his wife and two children.

'Fucking hell,' said Petar. 'What with all these frigging social networks, we'll just end up trusting search engines to do our investigations for us. They keep boring us to death with RoboCop and the like, but the cops of the future will simply be software that interrogates suspects via messaging, arrests them with a tweet and locks them away just by terminating all their bloody connections. No need for prisons any more!'

'Look, boss,' said Julo, who didn't even seem to have heeded the commandant's tirade. 'François Valioni posted this photo on his Facebook page yesterday at 4.11 p.m.'

Petar leant over. He immediately recognised the dozens of blue fishing boats, the tangle of ropes mooring them to the small square port, the white kasbah and the old fort in the background.

'Essaouira? Jesus, what was he doing there? That was less than eight hours before entering the Red Corner and getting bled to death.'

'Bonus points, boss! Essaouira, no doubt about it. I looked up the distances between Essaouira and the nearest Moroccan cities with an international airport: Casablanca, Marrakesh, Rabat. Between three and four hours, and then you need to add two hours' flying time from Marseille. We know that François Valioni left the Vogelzug offices at 10 a.m., that's the last time witnesses saw him alive, which leaves a fourteen-hour window before he walked past the Red Corner security camera at midnight. That would just about work . . . Cutting it fine for a round trip to Essaouira, but that would work.'

Petar continued to scan the dozens of blue boats left stranded in the dry port.

'What the hell was he doing there?'

'Maybe it was a work trip, boss? A business meeting with a business-class ticket paid for by the company. We just need to ask Vogelzug. Seems like a long way to go for a romantic getaway, though.'

'Let's see, Romeo . . . Let's see. If you stuck the face from the security camera onto our fake student's body – and it's one hell of a body – that gives her plenty of physical assets, yes? Enough to convince the globetrotting Valioni to take her to the ends of the earth.'

Julo Flores did not react. Commandant Velika clearly seemed in no hurry to follow the Vogelzug trail.

'To the Maldives, for example,' he added. 'Where those bloody shells found in his pocket come from.'

'There's no record in his diary of a trip there in the last ten months. But give me a break, boss, I can't be everywhere at once. I'll deal with the exotic seafood later. I've put Ryan on the case. And there's the blood-sampling business too.'

Petar Velika stood up. He stared at the framed image in front of him, a blurred poster that owed as much to impressionism as it did to photography, depicting hundreds of pink flamingos splashing around in the waters of the Étang de Vaccarès, in the heart of the Camargue, a few kilometres from the Étang de Berre.

'Ah, the blood sample. That's right, Einstein, so you've got a theory about that too?'

'Yeah . . . but I got it wrong.'

'What did you have in mind? Remember, we ruled out the whole vampire thing.'

'Simpler than that, boss. I thought it was a test.'

'A test for what?'

'A paternity test!'

The commandant paused for a moment while he assessed the age difference between François Valioni and his supposed female murderer. Julo carried on.

'I thought that knowing the blood type of two individuals would tell you if there was a parental link. But I've been searching online and I've realised it doesn't work like that. Only DNA tests can do that.'

'Keep digging anyway,' said Petar, without taking his eyes off the flamingos. 'I quite like the idea that François Valioni scattered his seed in every refugee camp on the planet before settling down in Aubagne.'

Ryan and Mehdi walked past along the corridor. A few shouts could be heard coming from reception. In Arabic, as far as Julo could make out. This happened all the time. The bilingual cops were twice as busy as the rest.

'By the way, boss, those two illegals our colleagues picked up. Did they talk?'

Petar almost seemed to have fallen asleep in front of the picture of the flamingos in the lagoon. On one leg. He suddenly snapped out of his torpor.

'Tight as a clam, those two. Fortunately, just like our lady friends in the black book, the consulates have files, with copies of passports and visa applications. If you're keen to know, our two pals are called Bola and Djimon. Bola, he's the calm one, and Djimon's the excitable one, the guy with the scar. They're from Benin – from Abomey, north of Cotonou, according to colleagues at the embassy.'

'And we're going to send them back there?'

'Yeah . . . That's how it works, kiddo. They take weeks, months to get here, using cunning and energy you can't possibly imagine, and yet the moment they arrive they're sent straight back on the first available charter. Five hours in the air and they're home again. That's why, even if it's exhausting, repetitive, an endless battle, migrants will never win against countries that pull down the shutters. Because even if they pile up by the dozens in lorries, or by the hundreds in boats, it takes infinitely less time to send them home than it takes them to come. They're like ants that keep coming back to the biscuit cupboard. Once in a while, you wipe them away and forget about them. Careful now, I'm talking migrants here, not refugees.'

'What's the difference, boss?'

Petar looked at his deputy, somewhat amused. Julo guessed he'd often debated this on café terraces and that his argument was well honed.

'Nothing could be easier, kid! Refugees are the good guys, they're fleeing war in their countries, we need to feel sorry for them, we've got a moral duty to welcome them: France is the land of asylum!

The migrants, though, they're the bad guys, they want to invade us, they're only poor, that's all, but we've already got enough poor people here. Do you get it?'

'So we let refugees in, but not the migrants?'

'Tut-tut-tut, not so fast, my boy. France's *duty* is to welcome refugees, but our *instructions* are not to let them in! At least, those who don't have any documents – but as it's quite rare for dictators to stamp their visas, or to find a working photocopier in a bombed-out city, they've got to risk their lives and cross illegally. But once they've set foot in our country, well, bingo, they've hit the jackpot, they're saved.'

'Can't we send them home after that?'

'In theory. But it depends *where* they came from. We only send them back if they come from an SCO, a safe country of origin – that is, one that won't torture them as soon as they get off the plane.'

'So if I understand correctly, we won't send back anyone from Sudan as long as there's a war on, but we *will* send back everyone from Benin?'

'Got it in one! The poor have to be lucky enough to be living in a country at war to be able to stay here. We take in political refugees and boot out economic migrants. And don't you go asking me why we've got a duty to welcome a guy who's dying of fear in his home country, and not a guy who's dying of hunger.'

Lieutenant Julo Flores wondered how sincere his commandant really was. How involved he felt. Or just how disillusioned. He was pensive for a moment, but his reflexes were slow, and by the time he'd asked his question Petar Velika had already opened the office door.

'And the wristbands, boss? The blue ones, the ones they had on?'

His superior had already gone out.

Without replying.

He hadn't heard. At least, that's what Julo Flores assumed.

# The Night of the Owl

# 12

Leyli walked as fast as she could after the bus had dropped her off at the Littoral stop, in front of Les Aigues Douces. She walked across the deserted play area, across the pink gravel esplanade with its stunted trees, planted before the summer by the council, and climbed breathlessly up the seven floors of Block H9, scattering crumbs from the baguette she was clutching under her arm on every step. She finally pushed open the door to her apartment.

Alpha, Bamby and Tidiane were already seated for dinner. Plates, glasses and cutlery were set. The food laid out. Leyli threw her handbag onto the nearest shelf and dumped the bread on the table rather too abruptly. The three children looked at her without reacting. Leyli was annoyed. On edge. Not because of her new boss; Ruben Liberos was perfect, even beyond her expectations, an astonishing, surprising, seemingly benevolent guy – but disconcerting too, right down to the mystery of the secret rooms she hadn't been able to clean. No, Leyli was on edge because she was late. It was the fault of traffic jams she hadn't foreseen, of the bus having to crawl through a conurbation where all the offices closed simultaneously, as if people were not only forced to live and work in the same giant cities, but also forced to leave and return home at precisely the same time.

Bamby stared pointedly at the clock hanging above the sideboard.

*7.37 p.m.*

Her daughter had a face like thunder. Not a hello. Not a smile.

83

The cold mask worn by a teacher confronting a kid who returns from break a minute late.

'I was working,' said Leyli apologetically. 'I'm sorry.'

She tossed her sunglasses into the basket, sat down at the table and poured herself a glass of water. Her children's glasses were already full.

'Sorry,' she repeated. 'It was my first day at work. From 6 p.m. onwards, all the roads are chock-a-block. I'll plan things better tomorrow – I'll finish earlier, my boss has agreed.'

'No worries, Maman,' said Alpha, cutting himself a good third of a baguette.

Bamby, on the other hand, refused to shake off her stubborn look. Pretty as a picture, thought Leyli with amusement. Every man's dream. And yet, she felt sorry for the poor boy who would end up seducing her cute little dragon for real. He'd better be on time . . . and woe betide him if he forgot the bread!

Leyli helped herself to a portion of chicken tagine with couscous. As expected, her children hadn't waited for her, but they'd barely begun to eat. After all, Leyli thought, Bamby was quite right to be in a huff with her. It was Leyli who'd established this ritual, this sacred family tradition: having dinner together at 7.30 p.m. sharp. No television on, no radio.

Leyli had had to battle every evening with the two older children who always had better things to be doing – homework, friends to see, *no problem, Maman, I'll eat something later, I'll see what's in the fridge*. They had grumbled, Bamby even more so than Alpha, that they weren't babies any more, that they surely didn't have to be there on the dot, that something unexpected might crop up – but Leyli had stood her ground. Until such time as either of them had started a family of their own, it was their mother who would decide. They could do whatever they wanted during the day, see whoever they wanted, get up late, go out again later, but they would have their evening meal together. Leyli knew too many families where you only saw each other fleetingly, in the stairwell, where you lived side by side without ever communicating at all. Including families where there was a father too! So grumble if you like, my children, grumble away, but every evening we shall eat together. And at 7.30 p.m., because Tidiane's got school the next day.

Leyli had stood firm. She had won. She glanced briefly away from Tidiane, towards the bedroom. Her three children's clothes were scattered everywhere. Tidiane's ball had rolled off a shelf and ended up under the window, probably because of a draught, and knocked over the pot containing the ficus plant. Of course, no one had swept up. Leyli might have given in on the rest, on all the rest, but no one could take away her one and only victory. The Maals dined together every evening! Debating, laughing, talking.

Tonight, not that much.

Alpha's chair creaked as he rocked back and forth. Bamby silently got up to fill the water jug.

It was as if their mother's lateness had broken the spell. An almost unhealthy solemnity reigned over them. All this for a mere seven minutes? Leyli didn't dare think back to her own anger when her children were even less late. She kept the conversation going on her own. She told them about her day. The magic of family meals is that you always find something to say. Alpha looked preoccupied. Bamby looked tired, even though she was gradually lightening up. She was rather taken by the character of Ruben Liberos.

'So, did he really call you "little princess of the sun"?' she asked between two bird-like mouthfuls. 'You're losing the plot, Maman!'

She seemed amazed that there were so many Heron hotels in the world, that one could criss-cross the globe by simply hopping from one identical hotel to another, either to sleep there or to be its manager. Several times, Leyli noticed Bamby and Alpha trying to catch each other's eye. It was in their nature. Joined at the hip, that pair. But tonight it was far more than a glance of complicity. It was a look of secrecy. As if her lateness were merely a pretext for her daughter's resentment. Too preoccupied with the two older children, Leyli hadn't paid much attention to Tidiane. Unlike his brother and sister, his plate remained virtually untouched. He was faffing over a chicken tagine made by Granny Marème. Tidiane was dragging the meal out, twirling his fork in the couscous, which was now cold, taking care to avoid it spilling over the edge of the plate, so as not to incur his mother's wrath, while explicitly signalling that – in his opinion – the tiny grains of wheat were about as appetising as grains of sand.

'Tidiane, will you finish your dinner! Granny's been cooking for you all afternoon.'

Leyli was playing for time. She talked about her morning, and her visit to the FOS-HOMES offices, about her real hope of getting a bigger place to live thanks to the intervention of the friendly Patrick. Or was it Patrice? She had already forgotten.

'Seriously, Maman,' said Alpha, 'you've met no one but Samaritans today.'

Bamby rolled her eyes, then stared past her mother at the room with the four beds, as if to imply they were still living in the same miserable conditions.

'It's gone cold, Maman.'

Tidiane's fork had slipped. A constellation of couscous decorated the dark table. The chicken lay bathing in a sauce of turnips and courgettes. For a second, Leyli felt sorely tempted to give Tidiane a slap. It was the same tantrum every third meal. She finally came to her senses. Slapping her child? Impossible, of course. She had to show patience, time and again. Honestly! Why did overstretched mothers always have to show more patience than others? Tidiane still hadn't touched his chicken by the time Bamby grabbed her dessert. A plain yoghurt. It was only then that Leyli noticed her daughter was wearing more make-up than usual. She seemed in more of a hurry, too; in retrospect, perhaps that explained her irritation at her mother being late.

'Are you going out tonight?'

'Yes, I am. I'm meeting Chérine. We're working an extra shift at Happy Days – there's a party for the pharmacy students.'

Bamby was wearing a relatively modest outfit. A country-style skirt which came down to her mid-calf, a white shirt with a plunging – but still discreet – neckline which highlighted her tanned skin, a bandana covering her hair, her ebony triangle around her neck. Apart from the fact that her make-up was a little too heavy, her daughter's natural beauty was going to make her female classmates

– a whole class of future pharmacists – jealous beyond belief.

They wrapped up their meal a little after 8 p.m. Bamby left the table almost immediately. Leyli apologised to Alpha. She had ended up giving in on the tagine and allowed Tidiane to leave the table too.

'I'm going to put your brother to bed.'

'OK, Maman, take your time.'

She took her time. Tidiane, at ten, still clung to a six-year-old's elaborate routine every night: one minute to brush his teeth, more than ten for a story, two to give his cuddly-ball a long hug before tucking it away in the bed beside him, and a last, never-ending minute for a torrent of kisses, of pretend goodbyes, of *Maman, I've still got something to tell you*, of *Maman, I forgot something for my schoolbag tomorrow*, of *Maman, Maman, come back, just one last time*.

When Leyli left the room, a good fifteen minutes later, Alpha had gone out too. He hadn't even bothered to clear his place. All that was left of him was an empty plate, a full glass and some breadcrumbs.

Suddenly, Leyli felt alone. So alone. Almost an irrational fear.

For the first time all evening, silence had crept into her apartment. Leyli fought off this oppressive feeling. The feeling that nagged away at her every day, but never with such intensity as tonight. This meal was the last. The last she would have with all her children.

She felt like turning on the radio, to fight off the silence. She wasn't fast enough.

It might have been a coincidence, but the sound of *raï* music came wafting up through the floor. Kamila! That jealous so-and-so from the sixth floor had cranked up the volume as soon as Alpha and Bamby had left the table. As soon as she thought Leyli's son was about to fall asleep, to satisfy her petty desire for revenge.

Leyli wavered between going downstairs to bang on her door, stamping her feet . . . or doing nothing.

Do nothing, that was it! After all, she quite liked *raï*, and you couldn't hear it very loudly in her apartment, whereas it was probably belting out loudly enough to pierce your eardrums at Kamila's.

She was about to sweep up the soil from the ficus, before attacking the washing-up, when there was a knock at the door. Through sheer instinct, she glanced all around her. A panoramic sweep. The cluttered sink. The leaflets on the living-room table. The shelves bending under the weight of books. Her collection of sunglasses. Her collection of owls. The bedroom. The clothes left all higgledy-piggledy. Quickly, she looked to see if she had forgotten any detail, any tiny clue which might be her undoing.

She had no idea who was knocking. It didn't matter.

Every time someone came to visit her, she had only one thought, one fear, one obsession.

Keeping her secret.

himself to be calm. To think more clearly, to piece things together, to tune into the rhythm of his thoughts.

After wolfing down his kebab, shoving the greasy wrapper into the nearest bin and wedging the bottle of water between his knees, he turned on his tablet.

The beach was silent. Julo had always imagined he would meet the love of his life like this. At the edge of night. On a bench. In a park, holding a book. In just about any deserted place. Someone like him, a loner. A woman who was a bit of a spinster, with a whole series of little quirks that would make her charming and above all guarantee that she too would indulge his bachelor habits. For example, letting him have his breakfast and dinner in front of a computer, and letting him spend most of the day with it sitting on his lap.

Did they exist, women like that?

This certainly wasn't one of them.

The photos from Bambi13's Facebook profile were displayed on his screen. Julo took the time to go through the thirty or so pictures again, one by one, all posted in the previous few months, most of them before Bambi13 had contacted François Valioni. Even after a careful examination, there was nothing to reveal who the mysterious doctoral student really was. Neither clothes, nor jewellery, nor tattoos, nor any object that could be identified.

By typing *Bambi* into a search engine, Julo had obtained thousands of results, hundreds of Facebook pages, sometimes accompanied by a first name or surname, sometimes spelt *Bamby*; for the Bouches-du-Rhône *département* alone, *département* 13, *Bambi* or *Bamby* matched dozens of entries, mostly pets, but also girls, artists, companies. What could he glean from this pseudonym, which in any case might have been chosen purely to lead them up the wrong track?

In the distance, on the beach, a group of teenagers were approaching, laughing, playing football in the moonlight. Well, the boys were, at least. But the ball was merely an excuse for them to strip off their shirts and chat up the girls.

The wrong track? Julo continued to wonder about this while

scrolling through Bambi's photos, each more suggestive than the last. He was trying to think without being distracted by the caramel glow of her mixed-race skin. A lost cause! His gaze lingered on Bambi13 lying on her stomach, her face hidden under a straw hat, revealing the perfect curve of her neck, the narrow groove running down her spine, the gentle hollow in the small of her back. Another one, quick . . . Julo plunged into the swimming pool of a big hotel, a mojito in the foreground, the arms of a sun lounger in the background, and two bare suntanned legs, made endless by the perspective. One more. Julo's eyes traced the curves of a slim figure silhouetted against the beach like a shadow puppet, her open hands forming a chalice to catch the ball of fire hurtling into the sea in the distance.

The more the photos scrolled past, the more Julo felt uneasy. Not just because of the girl. Because of the setting, more than anything. There was something wrong with this series of snapshots.

# 14

'I really have to go, darling.'

Hanging up on Skype was even harder than hanging up a phone. Who would be brave enough to turn off the camera first? To make that move, in full view of the other, of leaning over to replace the absent person with a black screen.

Jean-Lou waited for Blandine to deal with it. As if to make her bear the burden of the silence, of the responsibility created by distance. Jean-Lou instinctively moved the presents he'd slipped under the coffee table closer together, so his wife wouldn't spot them through the webcam. Two large bags filled with top-of-the-range products from L'Occitane en Provence. Facial care products, Essential Water, home fragrances; Blandine loved the scent of lavender and angelica. They had been living in Strasbourg for almost twenty years, but she'd always felt nostalgic about the years they'd spent in Marseille. Nostalgic about the time he worked for Vogelzug. About the time he used to travel round the world. About the time when Jonathan hadn't yet been born.

Since being employed by SoliC@re, Jean-Lou had almost never had the chance to go back to Marseille. He'd managed to turn down, as far as possible, the business trips necessitated by his job as sales manager. He postponed, delegated, communicated remotely. But this time he hadn't managed to wriggle out of the conference for top-level sales representatives. So he would return to Strasbourg with his suitcases packed full of Provençal gifts. For Jonathan,

Jean-Lou had chosen a small model plane, an A380. Jonathan was twenty-one. Jonathan loved these kinds of toys. Jonathan had Down's syndrome. Jean-Lou and Blandine had dithered for many long weeks about whether to keep the baby or not. Blandine was against abortion, and her entire family, staunch Catholics, stood united behind her. Jean-Lou was in favour, foreseeing that a disabled child would put an end to their lives as globetrotting bourgeois-bohemians, or *bobos* as they liked to call themselves. A pair, in love, footloose and fancy-free.

Twenty years later, Jean-Lou could barely remember what his life had been like in the past – a life filled with hotels and drunken evenings spent with his colleagues from Vogelzug. Jonathan had transformed him. As if all the misery of the world had been distilled into this innocent little guy weighing fifty kilos, and Jean-Lou bore the entire responsibility. There was no longer any need to run around the planet in search of some utopian meaning to his life: he was needed at home. Every night. Simple as that. Jonathan was his whole life. Just as Jonathan's life boiled down to Blandine and Jean-Lou.

Jean-Lou stared at the black screen for several more long seconds, then finally looked up. The spacious lounge of the Radisson Blu looked directly onto the sea. It was the sole touch of originality in this hotel reeking of cold, impersonal luxury where he would have to sleep for two nights. For a moment he watched the ballet of boats in the old port. Calling home, seeing Blandine, talking to Jonathan had done him a power of good, a salutary pause to bolster his resolve. The resolve not to go astray. He had come so close to making the biggest screw-up in his life.

*His son will be called Jonathan.*
*He has Down's syndrome, he's only just found out.*
*Jean-Lou is kind, kinder than the others. Gentler. More tender. Different.*
*But he pays, like the others. He loves another, like the others. He hides, and rapes me, like the others.*

*He's more deceitful. Even more cowardly than the others. He only loves me because I don't look at him.*

*Because I will never be able to recognise him.*

At the far end of the lounge, the girl in the tight skirt and prim blouse with jet-black hair tied back in a chignon was sipping a glass of champagne. She gave him a knowing smile.

She got down from the bar stool, grabbed another flute and an ice bucket, and walked confidently towards him.

Faline. It had to be.

Pretty, very pretty.

Slim, elegant, brazen.

Far less shy than the messages they'd been exchanging for weeks had suggested. Faline was four months pregnant. Down's syndrome had been detected in her foetus during her ninth week of pregnancy. Jean-Lou was president of T21, the French association for helping children with Down's syndrome. Faline had contacted him via his personal email. They had communicated quite a bit. A little game of seduction with no consequences, until Faline had suggested they meet. Finally. In real life . . .

These two nights at the Radisson Blu were Jean-Lou's only business trip in months. He had suggested that Faline join him. Then he'd immediately regretted it. Then he'd reasoned with himself. Nothing would happen apart from a drink together. It was purely a test. A test to better prove his love for Blandine. To test the solidity of the impenetrable wall they had both constructed around Jonathan.

He had filled his nostrils with L'Occitane's Arlésienne eau de toilette. He could almost sense Blandine's presence. Faline's patchouli scent overpowered the Provence fragrances – almost brutally so, in a way he found displeasing.

'I've ordered a bottle of champagne and two flutes, as we promised.'

She placed them on the table and sat down on the low armchair opposite him. Legs crossed. High heels. Satin-smooth thighs. What on earth had possessed him to invite this girl, thirty years younger than he was? How was he going to get rid of her? Looking at her properly, she wasn't even really pretty. Too much make-up. Too sure of herself. Most probably used to the fact that a slightly sexy outfit, something tight-fitting, was enough to make boys of her age grovel in front of her.

'Are you all right?' asked Faline anxiously.

'I'm fine . . .'

Jean-Lou was kind, it showed. Everyone said so. As if no one were aware that kindness is merely polite hypocrisy.

They exchanged a few trite pleasantries, slowly emptying their flutes between long silences.

'I'm sorry,' Jean-Lou finally confessed, 'I'm less talkative in person than in writing. I think I got a bit ahead of myself and—'

Faline leant forward and pressed a finger to his lips.

'Shhh. Don't say anything. Let's not talk about the past. Let's talk about the future instead.'

'About the future?'

'Do you want me to predict it?'

Jean-Lou, taken aback, set his flute down in front of him while Faline took a small canvas purse from her bag and then, from the purse, pulled out around a dozen shells.

'My mother taught me divination. It's a Malian tradition.'

She threw the handful of shells onto the table, like a game of dice. They were all the same shape, rounded, no more than three centimetres in diameter, split down the middle like the inside of an apricot. Most of them were white, iridescent with a pearly shimmer, but others had subtle echoes of pink, blue and green. It was in these almost invisible hints of colour that Faline appeared to be reading his fate.

She tried to take Jean-Lou's hand, but he pulled it away.

'Ah, I see,' she began. 'A job you find less and less stimulating. Routine. Boredom. Responsibilities piling up, like a heap of mail you don't feel like opening . . .'

'Go on,' he said a little sneeringly. 'I'm warning you now, it'll take a lot more than that to impress me.'

Faline smiled.

# 13

Lieutenant Julo Flores watched as the waves came rolling in, dying away beside his bare feet and threatening his abandoned moccasins which lay thirty centimetres away. The night was warm, the sand barely damp, the moonlight subdued. The police officer felt comforted by the soothing tranquillity of early evening. He preferred to work late. He was always the last to leave the office, never before 7 p.m. By then Petar had already been gone for almost two hours to be with Nadège, his beloved hairdresser, a pretty fifty-something with blondish-white hair. Julo had then roamed around aimlessly for a bit before getting to the beach, wandering down endless streets, Avenue 11 Janvier and Avenue 2 Mars, in search of a kebab. These street names bearing some unfamiliar date always intrigued him, as did those carrying the names of anonymous heroes, long-forgotten ministers, executed activists, unfashionable writers. He had then walked along the wall of Avenue de la Résistance to reach the sea. He had sat on the beach plunged in twilight, enjoying the unimpeded view of the fort and its ramparts, which were bombarded with the regularity of a metronome by the beam from the lighthouse.

Julo liked these moments of slightly melancholic solitude. A solitude which was neither quite that of contemplative poets, nor that of gardeners. A sort of blend of the two. The soul of the artist, coupled with the handiwork of the craftsman. Julo liked to isolate himself, but not to do nothing. Quite the contrary. He isolated

'Give me your hand, Jean-Lou.'

'No . . .'

'The forecast will be less accurate, then.'

'Who told you I want it to be accurate?'

She winked at him, which he thought vulgar. She drained her glass of champagne before continuing.

'I see a woman too. Your wife. You love her. It's obvious.' (She was looking at a pair of the redder-coloured shells stuck together.) 'You're close, very close, you've never been so close. And yet . . .'

She fell silent. Jean-Lou held back from making the move she wanted. From extending his hand so she could grasp it. He waited. She stared at a shell with green reflections.

'And yet, Jean-Lou, you would like something to happen. Something to fall from the sky. Something that links you to your past, to everything you left behind. Something that connects you to yesterday without calling into question what you're experiencing today. A little thread of nothing at all, which will turn you into a whole man. Not merely someone who sacrifices himself for others.'

It was Jean-Lou's turn to empty his flute. He even considered whether to applaud.

'Well done. Honestly. Well done.'

He toyed with the shells with his fingertips. Then he left his hand on the table. Faline seized it as if it were a princely tip.

'Well played, Faline. You're right about everything. But I'd rather be frank with you. I'm not crossing that bridge. I'm not grabbing that thread.'

Faline's eyes misted over. Was she offended?

The more Jean-Lou looked at her, the more different she seemed from the pregnant, anxious, fragile young girl who had corresponded with him. No hint of distress. No cry for help in her body language. Nothing but pride on high heels.

'I'll do what I never do. I'm going to be frank. Straightforward. Cruel maybe. I'm sleeping alone tonight. I'll sleep alone tomorrow night. I'm not cheating on my wife. I'm sorry if our emails have been ambiguous. I just don't want to do it. It's got nothing to do with you, Faline.'

Faline looked up at him with amused eyes. As if all trace of disappointment had vanished at once.

'Bravo, Jean-Lou. Well done. You've passed the first test with flying colours. But . . . but I'm not Faline.'

'Sorry?'

The young woman gently took hold of Jean-Lou's hand, and directed it at the corner of the lounge closest to the old port. A girl was waiting, immersed in a book. She was wearing a long Western skirt and a white lace shirt. Her only jewellery was a black triangle adorning her neck. Her hair was hidden by an elegant russet-brown bandana.

'I . . . I'm simply her friend . . . Faline's shy. She doesn't have much confidence in herself. And above all, she was afraid you might be a serial womaniser.'

She let go of Jean-Lou's hand, which remained suspended in mid-air. Pointing at the girl in the scarf. She had turned her face towards him, looking at him over her shoulder. It was not just the position of her face that inevitably reminded Jean-Lou of the *Girl with a Pearl Earring*, nor the bandana concealing her hair. It was her eyes. Her immense, all-consuming eyes.

All the misery of the world distilled into one imploring look.

# 15

It had taken Julo some time to understand what was bothering him about the photos on Bambi13's Facebook page. He had been lulled by the gentle sound of the waves, allowing the sand from the beach to trickle through his fingers. Then he had dusted his hands meticulously before returning to his tablet.

It was a contrast that unsettled him.

Most of the time, the location of the shots was indicated on the page. Bodrum in Turkey. Lanzarote in the Canaries. Santo Domingo in the Dominican Republic. Lampedusa in Sicily. Ngapali in Myanmar. Almost always upmarket tourist resorts. Unaffordable destinations. But all of these paradise enclaves were located in close proximity to the world's major refugee camps. Was this a coincidence, or a perfectly set-up trap? Bambi13 had claimed to be a student who defended human rights, a militant adventurer, concerned about the agonising misery of displaced families in death camps . . . and had photographed herself as a feather-brained jet-setter. *Was it possible to reconcile the two?* Julo asked himself. Empathy for the misery of others along with a carefree holiday? Yes, of course it was. Indeed, it was the default attitude of just about any tourist in search of sun and exoticism.

Julo stretched his legs out on the sand and forced himself to stay focused. On second thoughts, it wasn't this contrast that troubled him about these pictures. No, his line of questioning was a lot more fundamental than these philosophical considerations. Bambi13 wasn't a PhD student in anthropology!

She had told François Valioni that her trips were paid for by her research laboratory, as part of her thesis, and that she was invited by overseas universities. But it was all a lie! Bambi13 was a twenty-year-old girl from a migrant background. So how had a girl of her age managed to afford all these holidays over the previous six months? So frequently? Where had the cash come from?

Julo couldn't imagine Bambi13 as a girl rolling in money, the spoilt child of some oil tycoon. Perhaps his intuition was linked to the '13' appended to her nickname? To what that said about her. The Bouches-du-Rhône, Marseille, the daughters of African migrants who clean luxury hotels more often than they stay in them. Perhaps his perception was simply based on that expression in front of the security camera? That look of defiance as well as resignation, that of a woman determined to follow a certain path despite not having chosen it. That look which had pierced straight through his heart. That bastard Petar Velika with his hair-salon psychology was spot-on. That look had overwhelmed him far more than the tanned curves of the faceless stranger. Not to mention the hijab with its subtle pattern of owls. Owls that seemed out of place on an Islamic headscarf.

The sea continued to nibble away at the beach, a few centimetres at a time. Julo sat back, still looking at his screen. He flipped the window to another file. Before leaving the office, he'd done a quick search on words associated with the owl. The ambivalence of differing views regarding this bird of prey had surprised him. According to some interpretations, the owl was seen as a bird that brought good luck. Or misfortune. The owl was presented as the symbol of wisdom, from Greek mythology to the present day, associated with the goddess Athena. Intelligent, clear-sighted, perspicacious, cunning. But the owl was also the familiar of demons, witches, the messenger of death. And above all, the owl was a bird of the night. Hidden during the day, able to see less well, it only came out at nightfall to hunt. To surprise prey lost in the dark when it alone could see, smell and hear. The owl killed its enemies in darkness. Its hooting announced the death of a loved one to the sleeping family. *Another coincidence?* wondered Julo.

The parallel with Valioni's murder was obvious. Too obvious?

In the distance, the teenagers had stripped off to go for a swim. There was nothing sinister about their shouting, but the sound made it hard for Julo to think any more. He felt annoyed. Almost always, he thought, girls and boys attract each other by making a noise, in nightclubs, by whistling, by beeping their horns, by laughing too loudly. Given his own love of silence, there was little chance of him finding a girlfriend!

Or perhaps he'd find some old, bespectacled night owl, just for him?

The polar opposite of Bambi.

He hadn't factored in the '13' in his head. Strangely, the name alone, Bambi, sounded more familiar, as if he'd already heard it before. Recently. Very recently.

No, that was patently daft. He dismissed the thought and turned off his tablet, reflecting on his boss's words back in the office: 'If you stuck the face from the security camera onto our fake student's body – and it's one hell of a body – that gives her plenty of physical assets, yes? Enough to convince the globetrotting Valioni to take her to the ends of the earth.'

Petar had hit the nail on the head.

Just as she'd seduced François Valioni, this mysterious girl had charmed him too.

Even though everything suggested that she was a killer.

And even worse, Julo had a strange intuition.

She was going to kill again.

The lieutenant stood up and took one last look at the teenagers. A little further away, beyond the lighthouse and the fort, a red dot was floating out at sea. It was probably a fishing boat returning to port.

# 16

Alpha kept his eye on the red dot as it grew larger and, as it drew near, split into a constellation of seven little red lights dangling from the rail of the fishing boat. He waited a good ten minutes for the trawler to pass behind the seawall, manoeuvre and dock. The fisherman was steering with one hand, with a long, hand-rolled cigarette stuck to his lips. He tossed the mooring rope to Alpha, who was standing on the quay.

'Seeing as Allah's put you here, tie her up.'

Alpha stooped down to lift the rope, which felt incredibly heavy. He stood up and read the name of the trawler on the hull.

*Arax.*

This was the boat he was looking for.

The fisherman was leaning against the rusty cabin door and seemed to relish this moment, when he could spit out his smoke without having it blown back in his face. He seemed in no hurry to talk. Alpha analysed the few details he could identify in the glow of the only streetlamp on the quayside. He thought he recognised a dove tattooed on the smoker's right arm. And etched onto the bow and the cabin was a sort of boat perched on a mountain. How bizarre. Maybe it was Noah's Ark?

'Are you from Armenia?' said Alpha.

The fisherman stared at him malevolently, then spat out his cigarette with diabolical precision into the few centimetres separating the hull from the quay.

'You know, there's guys rotting at the bottom of the Caspian Sea for lesser crimes. I'm Kurdish, lad, can't you tell?'

He opened his shirt and revealed a Hand of Fatima, tattooed between the hairs on his chest.

'We were born at the foot of Mount Ararat, we're all descendants of Noah! That's why we went into exile. To repopulate the planet, to help mankind reproduce and disperse. I'm telling you this to explain why I inflict all this back-and-forth on myself, across this fucking sea.'

During the fisherman's lyrical outpouring, Alpha had taken the time to tighten the mooring rope, making a great show of flexing his muscles. He stood up straight. His head was level with the cabin.

'I'm here on behalf of Savorgnan.'

The Kurd had already lit another cigarette. Clearly, he'd rolled a whole stash of them while out at sea.

'Sorry. Never heard of him.'

'A group from Benin. You picked them up two months ago. A musician, an agronomist who talks a lot, a guy with a scar . . .'

The fisherman scanned the deserted harbour around them, as if he feared some eavesdropper might overhear Alpha reeling off his list.

'OK, OK, I remember that trip. Who told you about my ark?'

'They did . . . and some other friends too.'

'And what did they say about me?'

'That you were legit.'

Visibly moved, the Kurd took a longer puff.

'Well, what can I say . . . If you can lend someone a hand . . . I was born too late to be a people smuggler during the war. You know the type, the kindly shepherd who helps Jews or Gypsies flee to Switzerland. So I make up for it any way I can.' (He banged the rusty cabin door with his fist to show how strong it was.) 'At least on the *Arax* they're safer than on an air mattress.'

Savorgnan had told Alpha how much a crossing on the *Arax* would cost. Between two and five thousand euros. The equivalent of business class on Emirates. He took care not to bring up this petty detail.

'I agree,' said Alpha. 'Helping our brothers to escape is a duty, not a crime.'

The Kurd broke into a wary smile.

'Your brothers, your brothers. OK, so you're blacker than me, but I know several of your brothers who'd let their little brothers from the south of the Sahara die in the desert, without too many scruples.'

Alpha nodded slowly in agreement. He'd been mulling over this for a long time.

'I've got a plan,' he said finally. 'A way to help our brothers. A plan that's simple and safe. I know too many who've died and—'

The sailor refused to let him finish.

'Don't bother, it's always the same old tune. "With me, you're sure to arrive safe and sound." That's what all the people smugglers say. So spare me the patter, will you? Don't worry, we'll never be anything but skippers. We're not responsible, neither for those who die, nor those who survive. We're neither heroes nor bastards. We're just doing our job.'

He sniggered before carrying on, too long for anyone not to guess that his next joke was probably one he rolled out time and again.

'I'm not sure if the guy who drove the train to Auschwitz was ever sued.'

Just a minute ago he'd been a Resistance fighter. Alpha guessed that the Kurd wasn't that great at history. The fisherman had abandoned the conversation to put away the crates of fish.

'Exactly,' insisted Alpha. 'I want to see your boss. The one who manages the shipments.'

Noah's descendant was busy scattering ice and salt on the sea bream and sardines.

'I've got a plan,' repeated Alpha. 'It could really pay off, big time. Much more than your little tub here. I've got a network in sub-Saharan Africa, I've got some great inside info and, more importantly, I've come up with a scheme no one's ever thought of.'

Alpha had stood up completely straight. His impressive physique suddenly blocked out the light from the single streetlamp. The Kurd cowered in the shadows, like a terrified lion on the day of a solar eclipse.

'You know, kid,' he ventured, 'there's already loads of ways to get across. And crucially, there's some big monopolies you really don't want to upset.'

Alpha had managed to extend his two-metre shadow even further over the *Arax* moored below the quay. Covering the etched Noah's Arks. Giving the tattooed dove goosebumps all over.

'Competition's my problem. Just call your supply manager, your logistics director, your stock manager, call him what you like, but tell him I want to see him tomorrow. At noon.' (Alpha paused for a second.) 'The Olympus Estate, at the foot of the orange tree, at the crossroads. Avenue Pasteur and Avenue Jaurès. He can't miss it. A scheme that'll pay off big time. If he wants a piece of it . . .'

The Kurdish fisherman had opted for prudent indifference. He was sorting his dying catch into crates. Two by two. Like a slightly dim-witted Noah, trying to save the fish as well.

'OK,' he conceded finally. 'I'll call him. After all, vocations ought to be encouraged.' (He stared at Alpha, and then spat his cigarette butt into the messy tangle of seaweed in the middle of the deck.) 'And then all that's likely to happen is me pulling you out of the sea, trussed up like a *saucisson*. Like food for the scorpionfish.'

# 17

Tidiane woke up with a start.

Sweating. Heart pounding. Astonished to see a glow behind the shutters.

A second before, he'd been blind. He was running through the labyrinth, feeling his way, bashing into the sides, into dead ends, orientating himself by the sound of his shins, knuckles and skull smashing against the walls. He had simply run after his Morocco AFCON 2015 ball, had followed it to the gutter, failed to catch it before it tumbled into the yawning black hole of the open drain, fallen down with it too.

Alive. Able to see.

Attracted by a glow, at the far end of the corridor.

The golden fruit.

It was the treasure. Golden fruit. The fruit of the giant Atlas. In the sky, the ten horses were pulling the chariot of fire, packed as full as a Mercedes-Benz on market day. Whole crates of golden fruit. Thousands of suns. He was about to grab one of the fruit. His finger had even touched it, or so he thought.

And then everything had gone dark.

No matter how wide he opened his eyes, he couldn't see anything.

He had been running, through corridors, dead ends, cul-de-sacs. Perhaps he wasn't blind. Perhaps the sun was still shining outside. Perhaps there was a light behind the door. Perhaps he would stop bashing into the walls, suffering, crying, he would stop feeling the blood, its warmth, its taste, without even knowing if it was red or not.

Perhaps.

He had heard the cry of the owl.

Tidiane's heartbeat was beginning to slow down. He had heard its hooting for real. Not in his dream, he was sure of that.

Under his window. It was the cry that had woken him up. It was the cry that had saved him.

Tidiane remained completely still for a long time, sitting on his bed. Clutching his football in his arms.

It was a dream, nothing but a dream. His ball was there.

He felt like yelling 'Maman', but he held himself back.

He was a big boy now.

In the room next door, the living room, he could hear music. Grown-ups talking.

A guest?

The owl had flown away. Chased away, perhaps. Or gone to save other children.

Reassured, Tidiane went back to sleep.

# 18

Perched on the seawall, Julo methodically brushed away the grains of sand stuck to his feet, clinging to his ankles, wedged between his toes, before slipping on his moccasins. As bachelors do! Three women jogged by along the promenade. They didn't seem to care about their sweat, the salty spray and the gravel under their trainers.

Julo watched them absent-mindedly as they ran past. His thoughts drifted elsewhere. He was savouring a tiny little victory, having just received confirmation of it by text: a key appointment for the following morning. He wavered for a moment, unsure whether to forward the message to Petar, then decided to let it go. He would surprise his boss. He would be back at the office by 10 a.m. at the latest, and wasn't even sure if the commandant would have arrived by that time. He preferred to handle this part of the investigation – the part concerning the blood sample – on his own for the time being.

He put on his shoes while examining the row of apartment blocks facing him.

What if the solution to this case lay within the confines of one tightly defined area?

He kept revisiting that figure 13 attached to the nickname 'Bambi' . . . The Bouches-du-Rhône had two million inhabitants – that is, almost as many as Slovenia, Jamaica or Qatar. A very large area indeed, but everything led back to Port-de-Bouc, and more specifically to the headquarters of Vogelzug, the organisation where

François Valioni worked. Petar remained evasive on the subject, but he navigated his way through the city of Marseille like an eel in the Étang de Berre, and had extensive experience of the Marseille metropolis – of its codes, its networks, its power-based relationships.

Julo, for his part, who had landed there from his native Basque Country, felt like a stranger. It was as if an invisible wall separated him from reality, the reality of Port-de-Bouc, a theatre where every-one crossed paths, spied on each other, played their parts while knowing the lines of the other actors. He was merely a spectator, unable to understand the silences, the unspoken words, the stage directions, the close-knit ties within the community – ties to your neighbourhood, or through blood.

He walked along the seawall towards a children's play park. *Blood ties* . . . He would start by focusing on those in the morning.

Julo took one last look at the row of council housing blocks in front of him, around a dozen white cubes, horribly dilapidated and yet blessed with a superb view of the sea. Strangely enough, the area reminded him of a satirical cartoon he'd seen in a newspaper a few months earlier: a property developer was trying to rent out a shithole of a place to some wretched family living in poverty. The property was in a slum just across from a stunning residential estate, separated only by a wide ditch. The agent was flogging this hovel using a simple sales pitch: *You're lucky, the view from here is a lot prettier than from the other side!*

Good point.

You couldn't argue with that!

Except, Julo thought as he walked away, there always comes a moment when you're no longer just satisfied with the view.

# 19

**9.33 p.m.**

Leyli had smoked a leisurely cigarette with Guy on the balcony, then left her neighbour in the living room – busy counting owls, sunglasses or tins of tea – and swapped her ladybird dress for a comfortable red djellaba which revealed only her ankles and a demure half-circle of bare skin around her neck. She placed the tea tray on the table cautiously, as if the echoes of *raï* from Kamila's apartment, like the aftershocks of an earthquake, might somehow disturb the scalding-hot surface of the tea.

Guy was sitting on a chair. He was looking around with a worried expression – at the painting of Ségou, the Dogon masks hung on the wall, the dining table that Leyli hadn't yet cleared, at Tidiane's ball and the spilt earth – as if wondering what he could possibly be doing in this apartment which was in such a bloody mess that he was afraid of disturbing it by touching anything at all. When Leyli had opened the door to her neighbour just under an hour earlier, she had been moved by the way he'd fumbled through his excuse, like a shy little boy babbling his words without even believing them himself.

'I . . . I think I left my fags at your place,' he had said, sounding like a smoker experiencing withdrawal symptoms.

Leyli had let him in with a big smile, had explained that Bamby and Alpha had gone out, that Tidiane was in bed, that he could stay a while if he wished, that she could heat up a portion of tagine for him, or make him some tea, that he could smoke at the window while she went to change out of her clothes which reeked of dirt and bleach, and that above all he should pay no attention to the mess.

When she had returned wearing her djellaba, she had savoured his discreet vertical gaze. Her dress was loose enough not to hug her curves but still emphasise her long, slender waist. Leyli felt a tinge of pride in wearing it with as much ease today as she had twenty years ago. Her downstairs neighbour, whose checked shirt stuffed into his jeans could barely strap in his belly, wasn't quite so fortunate. Leyli had settled into the sofa; Guy had remained by the window for a moment, before coming to sit down opposite her on a chair.

'Are you here for the rest of the story?' said Leyli, looking him in the eye.

She felt reassured. The hardest part was over. Tonight, her secret was well protected.

'But I don't know anything about you,' she added.

Guy played nervously with his fingers.

'Oh, me . . . There's a lot less to say about me than you. I was born in Martigues and I landed here fifty years later, less than ten kilometres away, imagine that. I've been working in the same company for thirty years. I kept the same woman for twenty years, and when she left because she was tired of cooking for me, of making conversation all by herself and listening to the sports channels all day long, I looked for another just like her, but I didn't find anyone. As women get older, they become more wary. You see, I'm really the kind of person who doesn't like change very much.'

'So what are you doing here, then?'

'I don't know, I'm—'

'Shall I heat up some tagine for you?'

'And then you'll do the talking on your own? Listen, if you just put on the sports channel too, I'd marry you straight away!'

Leyli burst out laughing. She loved his direct sense of humour.

'Even if I'm black?'

Leyli's djellaba had slid slightly over her shoulder, moved slightly up her legs. The striking contrast, cherry against chocolate. Guy let his gaze linger a little longer.

'You, though, you're different . . . How long have you been here? Four or five years? You're practically a kid. We never blame the kids, we blame the parents. Do you know why there are so many foreigners in Port-de-Bouc?'

'No.'

She headed for the kitchen with the dish.

'When I was a kid, in the seventies, after the shipyards closed, they announced that they were going to create the biggest industrial zone in France here, on the Étang de Berre, in Fos. The biggest, I swear. A gigantic affair, thousands and thousands of jobs in the coastal steel industry. It was a new thing. And as the empty land was in Port-de-Bouc, they started to build housing and bring in people from all over Europe, and loads more from Africa. More than ten thousand workers settled here, ready to work as soon as the factories arrived. Except that some guy in Paris finally decided the factories would never come. The Fos industrial zone was dead and buried, but the foreigners were already here. They stayed. That's the whole story. Since then, Port-de-Bouc's never been so aptly named . . . Now it really is the Port-of-the-Goat. Eid al-Adha's become a national holiday here!'

He burst into croaky laughter, like a scratched record, watching inanely as Leyli returned with the tagine.

'It's chicken,' she said, looking at him indulgently.

She detected something endearing in this man, without being able to define it exactly. His eyes? His voice? His awkwardness?

Guy held her gaze.

'You think I'm stupid? Racist? Macho?'

'All three, skipper.'

'Are you still going to talk to me?'

She laid the dish on the table.

'No, I'm going to educate you. Listen carefully . . .'

# LEYLI'S STORY

## Chapter Three

I went blind at thirteen.

You'll find it hard to believe, as all I feel today is a certain discomfort in the sun, and the need to wear dark glasses. But my collection of sunglasses isn't simply vanity, Guy, it's more than that – it's a reminder of that long period in my life. My Black Period, just as Picasso had his Pink and Blue Periods. How did I get my sight back? That's a long story. Another story, which I shall tell you later. Perhaps even more incredible than this one. But let's start at the beginning.

To this day, I still can't make up my mind. Was it a blessing or a curse to know that I was going to go blind, as the doctor at the clinic coldly told my father, as my father told me with tears in his eyes, the only time in my life I saw my father cry? A bit of both, I think. Going blind, of course, drove me to despair.

But being able to prepare for it was unexpected. I lived from the age of eleven to thirteen, more than thirty months, with the certainty that the dark would eventually win. Month after month, the days became shorter, the mornings and evenings darker. The lines on my notebooks became blotches, spider's legs, rivers of tar and then seas of ink. No matter how wide I opened my eyes, I was sinking into an endless night. It's a strange feeling, believe me, to see the world vanishing into nothingness, toppling over, disappearing while *you* still remain. It's almost the opposite of death, if you think about it.

So this is how I reassured myself. I played a gigantic version of Kim's Game – the one the Scouts play, from Kipling's novel. I blindfolded myself and had to remember everything. Those who were born blind were much worse off than me – they'd never seen the thousands of shades of colour, the grace of a butterfly's flight, the beauty of a smile on someone's face. If I were clever about it, my blindness would scarcely be a disability: merely a game of concentration. All I had to do was develop my four other senses, and my memory would take care of the rest. A meow, and I was following in the cat's footsteps. The scent of shea butter, and I was taking part in the joyful ablutions of the village women. During those thirty months I became a camera that recorded everything. I gorged myself on images, landscapes, photos, movies. All the magazines Papa could find me, all the reports shown on the TV at the Hotel Djoliba where they would kindly let me in to watch. My teacher, Madame Fané, used to tell me that I was becoming intelligent, more so than all the other young people in the village, that this was my chance, that I was building up my brain while the boys were building up their thighs kicking a ball. It was Madame Fané who first nicknamed me the owl, because the owl could see in the dark, because it was the favourite animal of the goddess Athena, the animal of wisdom. Of wisdom and war.

Then one day, when I was thirteen years, seven months and eleven days old, everything went black. Permanently. I had fallen asleep at night, barely able to make out the stars in the sky. In the morning, the sun did not rise. As black as pitch, even though in my head I could position each constellation with pinpoint accuracy. I've forgotten it all since then, Guy. Today, I'd be unable to tell you where Orion, Vega or the Unicorn are located. But at thirteen, I had the map of the sky – along with many other maps – imprinted on the inside of my skull.

Strangely enough, from the day I went blind, people around me started telling me I was beautiful. At first I thought it was to console me. But Maman would take my hand so I could feel my legs as they stretched, my breasts as they grew, my waist as it curved. My role models were the supermodels you found in magazines – Naomi Campbell, and especially Katoucha Niane. My mother would paint me a mental identikit portrait, telling me I was half lion like Tina Turner, half antelope like Whitney Houston. I found it hard to believe her, in fact I don't think I ever did – I wasn't as pretty when I regained my sight, and they didn't take photos in Ségou.

They said I was beautiful. Intelligent. And blind. Maybe being blind prevented other girls my age from being jealous of me. Maybe my beauty protected me from their pity. You can always find arguments against fate. I didn't feel any more unhappy than anyone else. Maybe I just refused to admit it to myself. I was already so vain.

Time passed. The rumours had been growing for years. I was just over seventeen when it became a reality: a dozen men and women from the village had decided to leave. Seven men and five women to be exact.

113

They had gathered the savings of most of the families in the area by the river – they were the youngest, the strongest, the most determined. They had to cross the desert first, due north, to reach Tunisia. Then they had to set sail from Tabarka to cross over to Europe.

I told Papa and Maman I wanted to go with them. It took me twenty-three days to convince them. Three of those who were leaving were my cousins. I could trust them. They would be my eyes, my arms, my legs.

My guides.

I would be their brains, their translator (I spoke better French than they did and I knew a little English and Spanish), their cartographer (I knew everything by heart: the towns we would pass through, the distances between them, the layout of the roads, the precise location of the oases). Everything was etched on my mind.

Their guide.

It took eleven days to cross the desert; we sailed for Europe, in a fishing boat, almost as soon as we reached Tabarka. The borders weren't as closely monitored back then. At least, on the way out.

We docked in Mazara del Vallo in the small hours of the morning. In Sicily. I hadn't stored many images of Sicily in my memory, just those from the film *The Godfather*, a photo of Etna, an engraving of Syracuse from the time of Archimedes. I could only rely on my imagination for the rest: Palermo, Marsala, the ruins of Agrigento and Selinunte, the island of Ortygia, the balconies of Taormina. During the last kilometre of the crossing we were escorted by customs officers in three patrol boats and, when we arrived in Mazara, the *carabinieri* were waiting for us. All thirteen of us were taken to a sort of camp, together with migrants who had arrived from all over Africa. We had to wait for them to go through our files. The next day, we fled. Not very far. Almost all my cousins from Ségou were caught again, one by one. It seems they weren't very good at hide-and-seek.

But I was.

I had stayed huddled up in a dark corner, motionless. That's how you always win at hide-and-seek. Without moving. Without speaking. Without even breathing. The impatient always get spotted. Fatia, my mother's niece, used to bring me food and drink every day, she managed to pinch what she could for us. Then, like the others, she ended up getting caught.

I stayed there.

Alone. In my dark corner. An abandoned apartment in the hills above the old town of Agrigento. One room. A toilet. The permanent smell of burnt iron and sulphur from the ceramics factory below. I knew I had only two options left. Get caught too. Or die in my hiding place. Starving.

I hesitated, but I think I waited as long as I could before I decided to choose the first option. I think I was waiting for a miracle.

And it happened. Believe me, Guy, it really did happen.

One day, the door to the hiding place opened.

I thought it was a *carabiniere*. A rapist (I'd been told so many times that men liked me). A thief (but what could they possibly steal from me?). A killer.

If he *had* come to kill me, I would feel a sense of regret: he had a gentle voice. Musical. Almost feminine.

I felt his hand being placed on mine.

*You don't need to be afraid any more, mademoiselle.*

It was a voice, words, that you wanted to believe.

I believed them, oh how I believed them.

Oh, how I believed in that miracle.

# The Day of Blood

# 20

Comfortably ensconced on his teak-wood terrace overlooking Port Renaissance in Port-de-Bouc, Jourdain Blanc-Martin was about to perform – with meticulous precision – each little stage of his breakfast ritual. A breakfast prepared by Safietou, an absolute gem who'd been in his service for nearly twenty years. A bowl of coffee on a linen placemat, a napkin and that day's copy of *Libération* folded into two impeccable, wrinkle-free rectangles, a bowl of red fig jam and a line of three sesame seed bread rolls, split lengthwise.

Jourdain Blanc-Martin watched as the Port-de-Bouc fish market began to empty in the distance. The refrigerated lorries were already heading back to Marseille while the trawlers carried on returning to port, passing a few yachts on their way out to sea. A sign that it was set to be a very hot day. One of those scorching days before the mistral, which was scheduled for tomorrow.

He checked his phone as Safietou placed his soft-boiled egg in front of him. Plunged into boiling water for exactly two minutes fifty-three seconds. Plus another seven to get from the kitchen to the terrace. He waited for her to leave before rereading the latest message, then put the phone to his ear.

'Commandant Velika?'

A breathless voice answered.

'Yes?'

'Jourdain Blanc-Martin.'

119

The voice became panicky, as if the mere mention of Jourdain Blanc-Martin's name were a wake-up call after too short a night.

'As it happens, I was just about to update you. We're making progress on the murder of François Valioni, good progress, but let's just say that . . .'

Using a spoon in his left hand, Blanc-Martin hit the top of his egg a little too hard. He was exasperated by the slavish haste of these minor bossyboots types. Petar was one of them, but then again you don't build an empire without loyal and zealous servants.

'I'm calling you about something else, Velika. Some trusted friends informed me last night that a petty criminal has contacted them. He seems to want to set up a network for illegal migrants. People's vocations appear to be flourishing at the moment. Won't be long before people smuggling becomes cooler than drug dealing, for the kids in the suburbs. Every kid with an uncle in sub-Saharan Africa thinks he can make a fortune by investing in an inflatable boat.'

'What do you expect me to do?' said Petar Velika anxiously.

'He's set up a meeting in the north of the city. I know the place and time. You arrest him, you scare him, you make him never want to do it again. In short, you do your job of prevention.'

'It's not that simple, Monsieur Blanc-Martin. We can't just bang the guy up, if we've got nothing to pin on him.'

Jourdain's ivory spoon sliced through the curved tip of the egg. Too fast. A few fragments of shell tumbled onto the milky white as the viscous yolk slowly trickled down the eggcup. Blanc-Martin despised that. He could have happily strangled the cop for that minor irritation alone. Breaking his egg to perfection every morning was like a yoga session for him. Relaxation in the movement. Precision in the impact. Refinement in the tasting. He began to extract the pieces of shell one by one, while forcing himself to put things into perspective. He wasn't about to turn into that caricature of a fastidious lord of the manor, capable of letting a badly broken egg ruin his day.

No, not him . . .

'You'll manage, Velika. You'll find something. Anything. The tyres on his scooter are flat, or he doesn't look like the photo on his identity card. Anything you like. Any pretext to give him a good lesson in morality.'

'It won't be very legal, monsieur, if we have no evidence, no witnesses.'

The zealous servant was resisting. Petar Velika didn't seem keen to play the neighbourhood educator. Clearly, Blanc-Martin was interrupting him. What could this cop possibly have to do so early in the morning that was more important? Blanc-Martin lifted the warm, yellow heart of the egg to his lips. He took his time sucking the spoon until it sparkled.

'Velika, I don't think you can complain about the tip-offs I've given you so far. Vogelzug is co-operating perfectly with the police, isn't it? How many of these bastards' networks would you have broken up without me?'

'Of course, monsieur. And without you, those illegals would be on the streets trying to survive by any means they could, but—'

'I'm going to ask you to go even further,' interrupted Blanc-Martin. 'You're going to stick that boy in jail for me, just for one night. I'll arrange for a few of his reformed big brothers to teach him a lesson in there.'

'I'll see,' said Petar reluctantly. 'I'll see.'

He seemed annoyed. Blanc-Martin could hear a noise in the next room. Velika wasn't the type to bring his sweetheart breakfast in bed, or devour croissants with his offspring on his lap.

'I trust you. Prevention, Velika. Remember that. We should invest everything in prevention. We have to root out the evil before it grows. Maybe a night in jail will keep this kid from spending his life there.'

He paused, and gently scraped the inside of the shell so all the white would come off and fall into his spoon, which was hollower and more pointed than an ordinary one, a spoon made of ivory, as silver made the egg taste bad. He turned and looked at the pool through the conservatory windows. His left hand was already un-doing the belt of his bathrobe while his right hand held the phone close to his ear. Blanc-Martin liked to swim a short distance – a kilometre or so – every morning before getting down to work.

'I have to go, Velika, the Frontex symposium starts in three days. I'm supposed to give one of the opening speeches, so do your job and spare me the details. Just wrap it all up, and get me the girl who murdered François before the big event starts. You've got her on camera, it shouldn't take a genius to track her down.'

# 21

The school was at the far end of the street, a long straight line edged with olive trees, cleverly planted to create a subtle interplay of shadows to combat the morning sun. Tidiane didn't mind leaping from shadow to shadow. Sweating, wearing shorts and a football jersey, he trotted along, schoolbag on his back, ball at his feet, able to dribble past the olive trees without even slowing down.

OK, an olive tree, even if it's not a hundred years old, is easier to fool than a Varane or a Kanté, but it still tries to tackle you with its sly roots sprawling across the pavement, or stretch out a hooked branch to pull at your jersey. Tidiane tried to take out the last defender with a masterly Marseille turn, but the ball slipped away, rolling a few metres further on.

With his nose glued to his own trainers, at first Tidiane saw only another pair.

Nikes.

Red with a black tick.

Gigantic. At least a size 47. They lifted the Morocco AFCON 2015 ball, juggling it with the left foot. Tidiane finally looked up.

'Alpha!'

The boy rushed into his big brother's arms. The giant lifted him two metres into the air.

'Surprise, Shorty! Now tell me, that wouldn't be my ball, would it?'

He had put Tidiane back down, and was holding the ball under his arm like a school monitor who'd just confiscated it.

'You do know it's a collector's item?'

'You bet I know, Alph . . . I'm never without it. They're all dying of jealousy!'

'Don't let anyone steal it, Tidy! If anyone bothers you, I've already told you, let me know.'

Tidiane knew he would never be as tall as his brother. As strong. Never have the same courage. Tough luck for him: they were brothers, by blood, but not from the same father. He had inherited everything from a short teacher with glasses. He had never seen him, but that's what he imagined based on what Granny Marème and Grandpa Moussa had told him. Not Maman. She never talked about it.

'I can defend myself, you know!'

'I'm sure you can, Shrimpy. Anyhow, I need you.'

Tidiane's eyes sparkled. His big brother needed him?

'After school, Tidy, right after school, you're going to run to the Olympus Estate and climb the orange tree.'

'Up to Granny and Grandpa's apartment?'

'Higher, Tidy. Much higher. I want you to climb as high as possible, so you can see over the buildings. I want you to be my eagle. I want you to be able to see the whole neighbourhood and warn me in case of danger.'

Tidiane was suddenly a little scared. He had never climbed higher than four metres in the orange tree. He didn't even know if he was afraid of heights. And what if Granny or Grandpa saw him? He didn't dare protest. He simply asked a question, while making an effort not to shake.

'What sort of danger?'

'Cops. Shady-looking guys. Anything abnormal.'

Tidiane wondered how he would spot the cops if they approached in plain clothes and an unmarked car. And more importantly, how he would recognise a shady-looking guy. There was no lack of them in the neighbourhood. He suddenly reacted on impulse, and surprised himself at his own audacity. It came to him intuitively.

Maybe he too, deep down, had some gang-leader blood; so they both got that from Maman.

'And what do I get?'

Alpha stared at him in astonishment, but Tidiane also saw admiration in his older brother's eyes. He felt as if he'd grown five centimetres all at once, not enough to grab the ball from under Alpha's arm, but enough to impress him.

'My respect, Tidy . . . A jersey signed by Barrada?'

Tidiane didn't seem convinced.

'You'll have to go to Dubai for that. And you? What do you get?'

'Money, Tidy. A lot of money.'

'We don't need any, we've already got Maman's treasure.'

'Do you know where it is?'

'Almost . . . I'm still looking. But I have a little hunch.'

This time it was Alpha's eyes that sparkled.

'That's good, Tidy, that's good.'

He tossed the ball to him.

'Take care of it. There's only three in the world like that. The other two belong to Messi and Ronaldo. So I care about this ball even more than I do about you.'

The next moment, Alpha had disappeared.

Tidiane wanted to be like him one day.

# 22

'Believe it or not, O Charming Stars from the Twinkling Skies of the Morning Calm, but I do happen to know Seoul rather well.'

Opposite Ruben, six Korean students, young women all dressed in identical Kyungpook University uniforms, were waiting for the hotel manager to finish telling his stories so they could pay for their rooms. Ruben spoke in a mixture of French and English which the students seemed to understand perfectly. They listened. Fascinated.

'At the time, I was running the Myeongdong Grand Hotel. Thirty-six floors, one thousand five hundred rooms, including the presidential suite where Park Chung-hee regularly came to sleep with one of his twenty-three mistresses. A different one every night.'

The students sniggered. Behind them, Leyli was waiting, a vacuum cleaner in her right hand, for the Asian guests to return the keys to their rooms. More amused than annoyed. She had started her shift at 9 a.m. The rooms had to be ready by noon.

'Do not be shocked, my little princesses of the dawn. I myself became the lover of the president's wife. She wanted to learn tae-kwondo and, as fate would have it, I'd been introduced to this noble martial art by General Choi Hong-hi himself. One contact led to another, and so there I was, reluctantly forced to honour the First Lady of your exquisite country, who seemed to have as much appetite as her husband's twenty-three mistresses combined.'

The Korean students, who according to the passes they were wearing had come to visit the port facilities of Port-Saint-Louis-du-Rhône, looked at each other, blushing. Leyli tried to interrupt Ruben. All she needed was the keys; the manager seemed ready to ramble on for ever.

'But I'm boring you with my tired old kiss-and-tell stories. Let's get down to business, *mes gourmandes*, I feel duty bound to ask you *the* indiscreet question, the one that embarrasses my colleagues all over the world.' (He left an ominous silence lingering in the air.) 'Have you raided the minibar? Champagne Deutz? Absolut vodka? Otard cognac? Hmm, my pretties, you would have been wrong to deprive yourselves.' (He gave them a knowing wink.) 'I shall turn a blind eye, and you won't say anything about my torrid love affair with your First Lady, will you?'

Leyli couldn't help but smile. Of course, there were no minibars in the rooms at the Heron. No frills, not even a pen or sachets of shampoo. She forced her way gently through the Korean women's blockade and headed towards the front desk.

'Even if this romance achieved public notoriety . . . You're too young, my slender gazelles, to remember these shenanigans, but some tactless reporter from the *Korea Daily News* put together a front page featuring a shot of your humble servant, with the trousers of his dobok down round his ankles and the First Lady of Korea busy adjusting the knot on his black belt; today, that photo would generate a billion views on Twitter, but at the time, the *Korea Daily News* had to settle for a circulation of 6.7 million. Poor old Park Chung-hee was forced to publicly defend the honour of his "official" wife, incurring at the time the wrath of his twenty-three offended concubines, and challenged me to a Haidong Gumdo duel on Dragon Mountain. My fencing skills being limited to a reading of *The Three Musketeers*, I preferred to flee to a destination which, alas, I have no time to tell you about . . .'

Behind him, the printer was finally spitting out the room bills. The students seemed disappointed to be leaving the Heron. As if to console them, Ruben handed out leaflets to each of the departing guests.

'Since you have to visit the biggest ports in the world, stop at the Heron Las Tablas, in Panama. My colleague Esteban Rodriguez will tell you how we travelled together in a shipping container along with thirty virgin Maasai girls, selected from all over Abyssinia for their beauty, who absolutely had to learn English during the journey in order to participate in the Miss Black America contest being held in the lobby of the Grand Hyatt in New York.'

Leyli gave up trying to attract Ruben's attention, and stretched out to grab the keys lying on the reception counter. She walked away without hearing Ruben's latest anecdote, one which made the South Korean women burst into peals of laughter.

Room 11.

Open.

Room 13.

Open.

Room 15.

Open.

Leyli moved methodically and energetically through the corridor, leaving the doors wide open, pushing her laundry trolley to retrieve the sheets and towels in assembly-line fashion.

Room 17.

Op—

Leyli heard Ruben's breathless footsteps too late. She realised too late that room 17 was one of the rooms the manager had forbidden her to enter.

She had grabbed the key along with the others — Ruben hadn't noticed at the time.

Leyli had already inserted the key. Turned the handle. Pushed the door open. Perhaps she could still have closed it again, or left it ajar and tried not to look in.

Yes, she could probably have known nothing. Seen nothing.

But she had heard them. Inside. And from then on, nothing in the world could have stopped her from opening the door even wider.

From entering room 17, since now she knew its secret.

# 23

'Julo's not here yet?'

Commandant Velika slung his leather jacket onto a branch of the coat tree with visible annoyance. The stand wobbled precariously for a split second before rebalancing itself in the nick of time, as if trying not to add to the boss's anger. The other policemen present in the office scarcely moved any more than the coat rack. The commandant's first name was particularly apt this morning. Petar by name, fiery petard by nature.

'Julo's not here yet?' repeated Petar, in disbelief.

Normally, Julo was the last to leave the office . . . and the first to open it the next day. A godsend, enabling Petar to indulge in one last frisky roll under the sheets with Nadège before rocking up at the office in the morning. Usually, it was just like going home at night and finding your wife all ready and waiting for you. Blinds up. Steaming coffees. Humming computers. Except that today, Jourdain Blanc-Martin had called him a few seconds before Nadège climbed on top of him. That had been enough to wind Petar up for the rest of the day. Seriously, he had to be bloody kidding, that Jourdain Blanc-Martin, perched at the top of his pristine ivory tower at La Lavéra with his army of St Bernards. Treat all the illegal migrants on earth with humanity, track down networks of people smugglers, scare off those who might turn into people smugglers and, in the same breath, find the person who'd murdered the director of Vogelzug's finance division.

'Where's the kid gone?' asked Petar anxiously.

It was Ryan who finally answered.

'He said he had to go to the hospital.'

'The hospital?' said Petar.

*Fuck!*

All he needed now was for his deputy to go and snuff it on his watch.

❀

Lieutenant Julo Flores was walking slowly through the sprawling gardens of the Avicenne Hospital, full of daturas and jasmines, towering over Professor Waqnine, the hospital's most renowned haematologist. Head doctor. Specialist in tropical diseases and immunology. Visiting lecturer at a dozen universities. A quiet, elderly, cultured guy, the kind who's close to retiring but has no desire to do so. He spoke as slowly as he walked. An educator who'd learnt how to make his knowledge accessible to the layman, from anxious patients to tightly packed crowds of students. The kind who's animated during a consultation and soporific in the lecture hall.

Waqnine had agreed to meet him between two other appointments, and had suggested they walk for five minutes in the grounds to enjoy the bright sunshine. He put on a little straw trilby, but in fact never left the shade of the paths in the wooded garden.

'Lieutenant, before I explain the relationship between blood and parental connections, I must make something important clear to you. The different blood groups – groups A, B, O, if you prefer – are not evenly distributed across the earth. These blood groups stem from the age-old relationship of humans to their environment. Their biotope, to be precise. From diet in particular, or from resistance to localised diseases. In the beginning – and I'm talking about prehistoric times – the whole of humanity belonged to group O. Groups A and B only appeared between 15,000 and 10,000 BC, in Asia, the Middle East and on the slopes of the Himalayas, and then followed the great migrations towards Europe, to give rise to group AB, the rarest, less than twelve centuries ago.'

Julo didn't dare interrupt the professor, but wondered why a question as basic as 'Can you deduce paternity from a simple blood test?' necessitated going back to the Jurassic period.

'Even today, despite the mixing of populations, blood types remain unevenly distributed across the planet. Thus, while all Native Americans were originally group O, you don't find any – or very few – representatives of group O negative in China. Conversely, greater biological diversity is found in Africa. For example, among the Fulani, they've identified a greater presence of group A, and fewer representatives of groups O and B, unlike neighbouring ethnic groups.'

Julo was thinking about the consequences of what the professor was telling him.

'Does that mean that from a blood sample you can work out where an individual comes from, geographically?'

The professor looked at him in dismay. Strolling around like this in the gardens of a hospital with a man in a white coat, Julo felt like a mental patient who hadn't realised he was the real subject of the consultation. Waqnine's sarcastic tone did nothing to reassure him.

'No, Lieutenant. What a ridiculous idea! Since prehistoric times, mankind has mixed a lot, you know. Building walls, that's very recent. And even if the most developed part of humanity feeds itself mainly on hamburgers, kebabs and pizzas, we have not yet detected any adaptation of Western man's blood system to this new form of nutrition.'

He savoured the effect of his apparently well-rehearsed joke, then suddenly became serious again.

'You see, Lieutenant, biological diversity in major migration hubs is in fact one of the greatest health challenges we have to deal with. Men and women of all groups can now be found in the world's major cities, but that's not the case for blood donors. Blood donation remains linked to psychological, social and even religious criteria. In concrete terms, there's a lack of certain types of blood in Marseille. Or in Paris. Or in just about any metropolis in the world. We spend a fortune on information campaigns targeted at certain populations.'

Professor Waqnine slowed down even more, seemingly lost in

admiration in front of a bougainvillea in flower. The search for rare blood, thought Julo. This was another lead that might explain the blood sample taken from Francisco Valioni's wrist before his killer slit his veins. He remained stubborn, however, about his first hypothesis.

'But, Professor, to come back to my original question: from a blood test, you can't deduce paternity. You can only rule it out?'

'Exactly. I've brought you something that will help you understand.'

Professor Waqnine took a sheet of paper from the bag slung over his shoulder.

'The complete table of impossibilities. You can examine this in detail later. It's not rocket science, as you'll see. Even the thickest of my students can usually cope with it.'

He sat down on a grey stone fountain and invited Julo to sit next to him.

'Look, this is a simple table, eight columns by eight rows, all blood types A, B, O, AB, both positive and negative, the father's blood in the columns, the mother's blood in the rows. The box represents the impossible blood types for their children. For example, two A+ parents, or about a third of the world's population, can't have AB or B children. Two O+ parents can only have O children. We can be even more precise for the rarer blood groups. Two AB+ parents, or 3 per cent of the world's population, can't have O children . . . In fact, there are very few parental blood combinations that can give rise to all possible blood groups.'

Julo kept his eyes fixed on the table.

'So, Professor, to sum up, if I know my blood type, and my mother's, I can deduce whether my assumed father isn't my father at all?'

The professor gave him an admiring look. Top marks! This was probably more to do with the doctor's pedagogical qualities than his student's intellectual ones.

'Well done, Lieutenant, you've got it in one. You will be able to say with scientific certainty that your supposed father *isn't* your father if you come across an impossibility in this table. But you'll never be able to say that he *is*. He's no more statistically likely to be your father than the millions of other men of the same blood group who walk the face of the earth.'

❀

Julo arrived at the office a little after 10 a.m. A few other cops, including Ryan and Mehdi, were walking up and down the corridors. Lieutenant Flores placed the photocopy of the blood group impossibilities chart on his desk and turned to Petar.

'So, I've made good progress regarding the mystery of the blood sample. What about you?'

'Zilch. I'm stuck on this migrant business. It's eating up all my time. It's eating up my men. While you're away playing Sherlock Holmes, I'm holed up here doing all the admin for the Ministries of Foreign Affairs and the Interior, fifteen embassies and dozens of organisations.'

Julo walked up to his boss's desk.

'The only thing I achieved this morning on the Valioni case,' grumbled Petar, 'was that I was allowed to put a man outside the Red Corner 24/7.'

Julo sat on the desk and looked at his boss in surprise.

'Do you think there might be another murder?'

'Yeah . . .'

'Why?'

'The flair, kid. All that staging. This girl challenging us with her eyes. This guy she sets out to trap online as if she's picked out her target. I could easily see your little love interest as a praying mantis. Don't you agree?'

Lieutenant Flores took the time to think. Velika impressed him. The same feeling had been gnawing away at Julo since the beginning of the case, but he would never have dared express it.

'Yes,' the lieutenant conceded. 'But why put a man in front of the Red Corner? If Bambi13 is to commit another crime, she's unlikely to risk going back there.'

Petar tapped nervously on his keyboard.

'Jeez, you haven't half got some questions, kid! When a bomb explodes in a bin, don't ask me why we post a man in front of it for a week, given you'd have to be dealing with the daftest of terrorists if they chose the same one twice.'

'Maybe because if some gormless terrorist did it, and we hadn't kept watch on the bin, it would look like the worst kind of incompetence? It's only human, boss. We'd always rather be accused of being overzealous than lax, right? That's the irony of the precautionary principle. The more our madness imagines absurd risks, the more our reason invents norms so they never happen.'

Petar stared at his deputy in amazement.

'You fucking little genius, you know I've had a mental block on that bin story for years, and you've just explained it like I was a kid in primary school.'

Julo shrugged, indifferent to the compliment.

'Elementary, my dear boss. In the meantime, your Sherlock Holmes will carry on having fun. I'd like to know more about those bloody wristbands, and what Valioni was doing in Essaouira, and those shells from the Maldives.'

'That can wait, Sherlock.'

Julo had already pulled off one sleeve of his jacket. He stopped.

'You up for stretching your legs?' asked Petar.

Lieutenant Flores had a nagging feeling that every time he broached the subject of Vogelzug, his boss deflected the conversation. Pure coincidence? His gaze wandered over Petar's belly, which was bulging out of his tight blue shirt.

'You suggesting a jog along the seafront?'

Petar leapt to his feet.

'Better than that. Arresting a lad whose career plan is making a fortune in people smuggling.'

'What's he up to, this kid?'

'Nothing!'

'What do you mean, nothing?'

The commandant was already slipping on his jacket.

'Don't try to understand, it's all about prevention.' (His eyes flicked up to the shield in blue, white and red that hung above the ceiling beam.) 'A sort of first cousin of the precautionary principle.'

Julo dithered over whether to follow his superior, even though it was clear that Petar would leave him no choice. Since waking up, he'd been doing everything he most hated about the job, one task after the other. Talking about blood all morning. About to carry out an armed arrest. Attending a little autopsy at the end of the day would make it a full house! His eyes automatically drifted across to his boss's computer screen. A photo of an African city was displayed in close-up. A flat, dusty city which looked as if it had been built on sand, without using concrete or tarmac.

'Where's that, boss?'

'Cotonou. In Benin. That's where most of the guys we nabbed yesterday are from. The embassy's screwing us around with the paperwork and—'

'Can I have a look?'

Julo was already leaning over the screen.

'You planning to spend your holidays there?'

Lieutenant Flores did not answer. One detail intrigued him. An almost surreal detail. At that precise moment, he thought he was the victim of a hallucination. In the Cotonou cityscape, which consisted almost entirely of low houses, sheet-metal roofs and scaffolding only a few storeys high, a tower, one single tower, dominated the city. Julo turned to Ryan, who was carrying two blue bulletproof Kevlar vests.

'What's that, Ryan, that tall building?'

The cop took a quick look.

'The BCEAO tower, I think.'

'The what?'

'The Banque Centrale des États de l'Afrique de l'Ouest. The bank for the CFA franc. Eight countries, millions of customers, the euro zone of West Africa, if you like . . . and the BCEAO towers are its cathedrals. The only skyscrapers in the capital cities. They dominate the landscape in Dakar, Abidjan, Ouagadougou, Bamako, Lomé, like a stark reminder to the starving of the power of money—'

The commandant interrupted Lieutenant El Fassi and turned, annoyed, to Julo.

'What's your latest idea, clever clogs?'

Julo didn't even look up. Leaning over the computer, he moved the mouse to zoom in on the photo. Cotonou's BCEAO tower appeared in close-up.

'Look, boss.'

Petar looked. So did Ryan.

*Jesus Christ . . .*

The two cops had the same wide, incredulous eyes.

Running down the BCEAO tower in Cotonou, you could make out four vertical white lines.

Julo zoomed in closer.

This time, the decorative elements adorning the seventeen floors of the concrete tower were perfectly clear. Four lines. Four times thirteen giant shells. The same ones. Exactly the same as those found in François Valioni's pocket.

There was no room for doubt. Those shells, a few centimetres in size and supposedly only found in the Maldives, were reproduced in around fifty sculptures, each a metre long, visible from everywhere in Cotonou.

'Shit,' muttered Petar, turning to the lieutenant, 'what the fuck's all this?'

'No idea,' answered Ryan, chucking the Kevlar vests at them. 'But if we don't leave for the Olympus Estate right away, we'll be late for our rendezvous.'

# 24

Ruben Liberos placed his hand on Leyli's shoulder.

Too late.

The door to room 17 of the Heron Port-de-Bouc was already half open. A dozen eyes alighted on Leyli, almost as surprised as she was.

Twelve big white eyes.

Four men, a woman and a teenager. One man stepping out of the shower, bare-chested, another bent over a guitar, two more looking up from their books. The teenager was sitting with his back to her, the woman was combing her dreadlocks. Leyli recognised her. It was Noura.

Africans. Sub-Saharans. Steam was rising from a teapot on the bedside table.

'My sweet princess of the desert,' said Ruben from behind, 'I bless my good fortune that you should be the one to discover my protégés.'

Leyli walked into the room. She tried to smile at Noura, but her housekeeping colleague's eyes slid over her without displaying any emotion whatsoever.

'Pray take a seat, my beautiful child.'

They made a space for her on one of the two beds in the room as Ruben launched into an explanation.

'The occupancy rate of my palace is precisely 58 per cent. I'm quoting reliable figures calculated by the big moneymen from the

137

Mondor empire. It rises to 87 per cent in the summer, and falls to less than 30 per cent in the winter. That represents on average twenty-seven unoccupied beds across thirteen empty rooms every night – a drop in the ocean among the more than five hundred thousand rooms made available worldwide by the empire. So, *ma belle*, do you really think Ruben Liberos could leave his doors closed while hundreds of homeless travellers sleep on the streets? I throw open my empty rooms to those passengers of the wind every night. For free, no strings attached. For a night. For a week. Just as you might share an overladen dinner table with a hungry neighbour.'

Leyli stared at Ruben, at his charcoal-grey suit, his black tie, his slicked-back greying hair. Who could possibly have suspected that his elegant bearing and impeccable clothes concealed the stuff of a resistance fighter? Certainly not his superiors at the Mondor chain, at any rate! The hotel manager continued to hold forth. Leyli had realised that his pseudo-megalomania masked a real shyness. A compulsive liar, a smooth talker, but this verbal diarrhoea served as a screen for his true nature. An everyday hero. It's easier to drown the truth in a sea of lies.

'For pity's sake, Leyli, don't look at me like that with your gazelle eyes, or I'll have to kick out all our friends straight away, just so I can share my palace of a thousand and one rooms with you. Your humble servant is merely doing his job as an anonymous member of staff, concerned about the reputation of the company that employs him. Putting up men and women in need of help, all over the world, even if the company's unaware of my . . . shall we say . . . little arrangements. In '78, I housed fifty-three Cambodian families in the Heron Hanoi for a month. In '93, at the Heron Kigali, I saved a hundred and twenty-seven Tutsis who—'

A short man, the oldest of them all, who was wearing thick glasses and practically swimming in a baggy pair of beige canvas trousers, interrupted him.

'There's never been a Heron in Kigali, brother.'

Ruben burst out laughing.

'Zahérine. You crusty old crab! You ungrateful little bastard. I put you up at the risk of my reputation, and you make me look like a fibber in front of the two most beautiful women Africa has ever borne on its soil.'

Leyli and Noura smiled.

Ruben carried on by explaining that he extended free hospitality to migrants based on the hotel's occupancy, which he usually only knew in the evenings. He never crammed people together. Only one family per room, one man or woman per bed, even though, when evening came, it was common for siblings or extended families to get together in the same room or in the lobby to chat, sing, play music.

'Or just to listen to Ruben Liberos's endless stories,' said the man with glasses, his eyes sparkling with mischief. 'That crazy old guy only takes us in to have a captive audience every night!'

Ruben burst out laughing again.

'I understand President Kérékou tried to assassinate you ten times, you old death-defying rat.'

He turned to Leyli.

'You already know the lovely Noura, who shares with you the responsibility of making this chateau dazzle like the sun.' (Noura granted her another icy look.) 'This is my friend. A dear friend. Savorgnan Azannaï.'

Savorgnan stood up. He radiated a mixture of wisdom from his blue-black eyes and feline strength from his gentle, almost feminine gestures. The magnetism you found in exceptional people, from Mandela to Obama.

'You're Leyli?' said Savorgnan. 'Leyli Maal?'

'Yes,' she replied, surprised.

'I met your daughter yesterday. Bamby. She has inherited your beauty.'

Savorgnan held Leyli's gaze. A look of friendship in which she read no ambiguity. A simple brotherhood. But she could also feel Noura's eyes digging into her back, sharp with jealousy. The girl was in love with Savorgnan. A silent lover, who probably hoped her physical signals did the talking for her.

'I know your son better,' continued Savorgnan, indifferent to

Noura's body language. 'I've met Alpha often. He's offered to help us. We're . . . we're thinking about it.'

Leyli felt reluctant to ask for more details. Savorgnan had left his last words hanging in mid-air, 'we're thinking about it'. She thought she detected an ellipsis, 'we're waiting to get a better idea', 'we're a bit wary'. She understood, without even knowing anything about what they were up to. Alpha was an ambitious and determined boy. Honest and loyal, but not one to let anyone but himself draw the line between right and wrong. Maybe because he liked to live like a tightrope walker on that line. Often with intelligence, sometimes with violence.

A brief silence enveloped the room. Leyli took the opportunity to scrutinise every detail of room 17. Crushed cigarettes in an ashtray, empty beer bottles and open pizza boxes, a few seashells in a glass bowl. Steam continued to rise from the teapot on the bedside table, a cup sat beside each man. A blue band adorned the guitarist's wrist. The one on the teenager's wrist was red. Zahérine wore none, nor did Savorgnan. Leyli noticed the ring on his third finger.

A wedding ring.

She realised that, apart from Noura and the teenager, all the occupants of the room were over thirty. Yet she couldn't see anything in the room to indicate the presence of a child.

'What about your families?' she asked.

Savorgnan raised his tea to his lips.

'We're all trying to bring them across. We've all just arrived, you know. Look, I'll show you.'

The Beninese took a photo from his wallet. He was posing next to a radiant girl with long, slicked-back hair and two children under the age of eight.

'Babila, my wife, she's a nurse. Keyvann, my son, he's crazy about trains. He dreams of driving a high-speed train one day. Safy, she's my little princess. She wants to open a fashion boutique, a hair-dressing salon, anything to help make women more beautiful.'

Noura stood up abruptly. She seemed to be struggling to cope with Savorgnan's tender look as he gazed fondly at his family. She grabbed a broom from the wardrobe, stared at Leyli and marched towards the door, clicking her heels conspicuously to make it clear she wasn't being paid to sit on a bed looking at pictures and drinking tea.

Ruben intervened gently.

'There's time, Noura. All the time in the world. The dust settles on our hearts faster than on the furniture.'

She shrugged and strode out. The atmosphere suddenly felt calmer. Leyli turned to Savorgnan.

'It's risky, isn't it, bringing them across?'

He smiled, talking as though he were the spokesperson for the other three men.

'Imagine, Leyli. Just imagine. Even if I got my papers. Even if I got a real job, with an official residence permit. Do you know how long it takes to get your family over here?'

Leyli remained silent.

'A lifetime, maybe. Getting a visa takes a few days if you're from Canada, or Switzerland, or Japan, but a lifetime is often not enough for an African family. Tell us your story, Darius. Tell us.'

The man sitting on the bed put down his book. He was about fifty.

'I'm here along with my brothers, but I'm not illegal. I've been living in France for seven years now. My wife and four children remained in Togo. I work in the warehouse for the Marseille Transport Authority, I earn one thousand two hundred euros a month, which is the minimum salary required to apply for family reunification at the *préfecture*. But there's a second condition for bringing your family here: you need to have a home with at least ten square metres per person, including children. I've been trying for years to find somewhere of at least sixty square metres, even if it cost me three-quarters of my pay. But who'd want to rent a two-bedroom apartment to a single man on the minimum wage?'

Savorgnan had pulled the table with its teapot into the centre of the room. They were all sitting on the two beds, like students putting the world to rights in a hall of residence. The oldest man, Zahérine, continued.

'The French are crafty. They don't *forbid* our wives and children to come – oh no, they open their arms to us, they love us *so* much that they want to welcome us properly. Then all the investigators have to do is decide there aren't enough rooms in our home for our family, or the plumbing's too old, the shower too cold, the attic too damp, the stairs too steep.' (Zahérine's eyes glistened behind his glasses.) 'Isn't that beautifully contrived, Leyli? Denying our families the right to live together, on the pretext that they deserve comforts they've never known – comforts they don't even expect to have?'

After a short silence, Savorgnan went one further:

'The investigators are appointed by local councils. What council would want to lumber itself with foreign families who don't even vote? They just pass the buck . . . Thirty-six thousand *communes* . . . The French state has smashed its human rights into thirty-six thousand tiny pieces.'

Ruben leant towards the bedside table in the centre of the room.

'To human rights,' he said. 'And to those who still believe in them.'

He produced a hip flask of Licor 43 from his pocket and offered some to the men. Savorgnan refused but the other three accepted.

'My dearest friends,' said Ruben, 'I raise my glass to the land of asylum that was France, to the land of asylum that welcomed me in '71 when I was fleeing Franco, that welcomed my Polish brothers in 1848, my Armenian brothers in 1915, my Russian brothers in 1917, my Portuguese, Greek and Cambodian brothers after me. To this land that was the first in the world to enshrine the duty of asylum to the oppressed peoples of the earth, in its constitution of 1793.'

He downed his cup in one gulp, then turned it over.

Empty.

Zahérine also drained his cup, then began opening his flies as he headed for the toilet.

'Well, I'm about to piss on this land that's managed to make itself so inhospitable, even to its French-speaking African brothers who still love it so much. This land that treats the three hundred thousand refugees who somehow survive in France as outlaws, while Spain, Italy or Germany give several million of them legal status.

Piss on this France that's growing old, that can no longer afford pensions and care for the elderly, that will ask its citizens to work until they're seventy, while right on its doorstep African countries don't know what to do with their idle youngsters.'

Zahérine disappeared into the toilet. Savorgnan put down his cup of tea and took over. He addressed Leyli as if she were solely responsible for the immigration laws. She didn't dare answer, though. It was rare, so rare, to bring up these issues. She lived with them but never discussed them. With anyone. Migrant workers like her were isolated. Got up early. Went home late. Wandered through deserted offices. Locked themselves in the silence of the first and last suburban trains. Had better things to worry about than philosophising. So far removed, thought Leyli, from the damned of the earth in her favourite novels, by Zola or Steinbeck, who stuck together, formed trade unions, marched in the streets. Today, migrants were a fragmented working class. So much easier to exploit. All this was running through Leyli's mind without her daring to express it. She listened.

'We don't come to steal the wealth of the French,' explained Savorgnan, waving his hands animatedly. 'Or even to ask them to share it. We come to create wealth, to work, become consumers, get married, have children. We just want freedom. What are they afraid of? That everyone will rush in if they half open the door? But what do they think might happen? The time for mass migrations is long gone! Almost no one can afford to travel any more. The poverty-stricken, the uneducated are confined to their own little patches of the earth. Dependent on the solidarity and support of their neighbours, unable to break free. If things come to the worst, they'll cross a border to an even poorer country to escape a war or famine.'

Sitting on the bed by the window, the guitarist, who was called Whisley, was playing softly, accompanying Savorgnan's long lament.

'Candidates for the great exodus are rare, Leyli. Those who cross entire continents are not hordes of starving people thrown onto the roads – they are the bold, the ambitious, the reckless, the desperate, the banished, the mad, the dreamers. The free. Almost never women. Rarely fathers. And, more and more these days, they are children.'

Savorgnan finally fell silent, looking down with misty eyes at the photo of Babila, Safy and Keyvann.

'The mad,' he repeated slowly.

Zahérine emerged from the toilet. Ruben took the opportunity to pour the rest of his flask into the cups in front of him. All the men took some, even Savorgnan this time. The teenager had backed away, as if indifferent to the conversation, and was humming, in Bambara, to the rhythm of Whisley's guitar.

'All countries in the world have signed the conventions on the rights of the child,' said Zahérine, turning to Leyli again for support, 'but as soon as we're dealing with some minor who's entered illegally, a kid who's likely to increase the public deficit because he'll have to be looked after until he comes of age, we stamp on his rights. We manage to find him a country to send him back to, or some temporary home, a make-do family, and failing that, we let him hang around outside hostels and let the street take care of his education. We deport him as soon as he comes of age, at fifteen, believing he's bound to be lying about how old he is.'

A long silence filled the room. Ruben turned his flask upside down but it was empty. The three Beninese drank the last mouthful from their cups. Leyli took the opportunity to stand up. Vacuum cleaner in hand. Zahérine held her back.

'You see, Leyli, our only strength is they'll never be able to do without us.' (He turned to Ruben.) 'I don't mean you, you old fool, you're just a little exploiter who eases his conscience by inviting us for a drink with nothing more than a litre of crappy Spanish booze to offer us.' (Ruben burst out laughing once more.) 'I mean *Homo megapolitas*, the beaming citizen who strolls around the planet's wealthiest megacities. *Homo megapolitas* will always need us to do the three Ds, as the Americans say: *dirty, dangerous, dull*. Who could replace us? Who would want to, as long as we're invisible? As long as we remain ghosts, but the streets of the big cities are clean in the morning, the bins are empty and the windows of their gleaming towers are always shining. As long as, when dawn breaks, those nasty little pests – without which no ecosystem could survive – scurry back into their burrows.'

Leyli took a step towards the door. Straightened her scarf. Her apron. She had had the courage. A long time ago. Her reserves had run out.

She left the room.

A few moments later, the noise from a vacuum cleaner drowned out the sound of Whisley's guitar. In the corridor, she bumped into Noura whose arms were full of sheets. The young mixed-race woman did not look up. Lost in the music crackling from her earphones, she didn't seem to register Leyli's presence, nor even hear the sound of the vacuum cleaner.

Leyli slid past her. A little phrase kept running through her head.

A fragmented working class.

# 25

Tidiane hadn't managed to climb to the very top of the orange tree.
But almost! He wasn't good at calculating in metres, so he was using
the Ares and Athena buildings as a guide. He'd hoisted himself well
above the second floor. He was sitting astride a solid branch. As if
to get closer to the sun, even though he was careful to remain in the
shade of the leaves; he wasn't as stupid as that idiot Icarus, whose
story Maman had read to him.

The most difficult thing hadn't been hauling himself up the tree,
but doing it without Granny Marème or Grandpa Moussa seeing
him. He had waited for the exact time when his grandparents sat
on the sofa to watch TV. It seemed Alpha had planned everything.
Alpha was smart! The smartest of all.

From his vantage point, Tidiane could keep an eye on all of
Avenue Pasteur and all of Avenue Jaurès, as far as the university,
and keep watch over the sea much further away, and if he looked
down between his feet, he could see the top of Alpha's head at the
foot of the orange tree.

*Whistle, Tidy*, Alpha had told him. *Whistle if you see more than
one car parking in the neighbourhood.*

Tidiane loved it when Alpha called him Tidy.

*Whistle and I'll hear.*

Tidiane couldn't remember if he knew how to whistle.

Tidiane felt as if he'd been waiting for an eternity when he saw
the two vans emerging from the roundabout on Avenue Pasteur.

First, he noticed that they were identical. Then that they were slowing down. Finally, that they had beacons on top. They weren't turned on.

Cops. Two police vans!

Fortunately, Tidiane calculated at lightning speed, it would take them a good two minutes to park, go around the Ares and Apollo buildings and reach the courtyard of the Olympus Estate. He tried hard not to panic. He put his fingers in his mouth, as Alpha had taught him the previous summer, as they'd sat on the quayside in the port and watched the girls in skirts go by. Tidiane had whistled. The girls had turned around, angry. Alpha had laughed, Tidiane had looked down. The girls had ended up laughing too.

A long whistle rang out, strident and powerful, so much so that Tidiane felt as if the branches of the orange tree were shaking.

He had succeeded!

He looked down.

Alpha hadn't moved.

The cops had been deployed all around. A rather short, stocky guy, sweating under his leather jacket, was in charge. There seemed to be six of them, but Tidiane might not have counted them all. They were starting to go around the buildings. If they entered both sides of the courtyard together, Alpha would be trapped.

Quickly, Tidiane let go of the branch in order to wedge his fingers between his lips again. Too fast. He could feel his legs slipping, scraping the rough bark of the orange tree. He thought he was falling. He had ventured too close to the sun, like Icarus.

He managed to save himself through sheer instinct, gripping the branch, pincer-like, using both hands. He regained his balance and leant back firmly against the trunk, cursing the precious second he had lost. The next second he whistled even louder, loudly enough to make all the birds in the area jealous.

Some neighbours appeared at the balconies of the Poseidon building. Because of his whistles, or because of the unusual flurry of activity caused by the police?

Alpha still hadn't moved.

Maybe he hadn't heard?

Maybe Tidiane hadn't whistled loudly enough?

Maybe he'd whistled too late, and Alpha had realised he was screwed . . .

These questions would remain in Tidiane's head for many long hours, many long days.

It was too late.

Alpha was screwed.

The cops were entering from every corner of the enclosed courtyard. Alpha was all alone against the trunk of the orange tree, like that first poor kid who gets captured in a game of cops and robbers – the kid no one's going to bother to come and rescue.

Tidiane was tempted to whistle a third time, but he knew it wouldn't change anything now. His brother had the cops in his line of sight. If he whistled, the cops would look up, the neighbours would turn towards him, Granny and Grandpa would come out too. Maybe.

Tidiane was now keeping a close eye on the balcony on the second floor of the Poseidon building, at the same height as his hut.

He didn't want Alpha to get arrested. But more importantly, he didn't want Granny and Grandpa to see Alpha getting arrested.

Why were the cops arresting his big brother anyway?

Was it to do with drugs? Weird, Alpha had always lectured him about that. But maybe he was just selling them, and not touching them himself?

Two cops were pointing their guns at Alpha, the fat one drenched in sweat under his leather jacket, and an Arab. Alpha didn't move. He simply raised his hands in the air.

This reassured Tidiane a little.

They were going to pick Alpha up, interrogate him, hold him in custody. His big brother was smart. Tomorrow he'd be out. If he'd let himself be caught, it was because he had nothing to feel guilty about.

As Alpha walked across the courtyard, handcuffed, flanked by two cops with blue bulletproof vests over their shirts, that was all Tidiane could think about. Alpha had let himself be caught. He'd done it on purpose.

The next moment he found himself thinking it didn't make sense, he was simply imagining it so he wouldn't have to admit he hadn't managed to keep a lookout, he hadn't whistled as he should have done, he'd been crap at the first grown-up job his big brother had entrusted to him.

Alpha was getting into one of the police vans. Without resisting.

The curtains on Granny Marème and Grandpa Moussa's balcony hadn't moved.

Tidiane was trembling all over.

He felt a huge knot in his stomach when he saw the identical vehicles disappearing at the end of Avenue Pasteur. An urge to burst into tears that was stronger than he was. Like when you can't stop yourself from peeing.

He would never be Tidy. Just Tidiane. A baby.

He would never be like Alpha.

If Alpha had let himself be caught, it was because he'd been willing to. Like in the movies. He had a plan. Alpha was smarter than all the cops combined. Alpha had told him he was going to make money, lots of money. Even more than the cursed treasure, the treasure Maman had hidden away.

# 26

The sun was rising over the sand dunes, the fine grain of their soft curves reminiscent of golden-brown skin. In these ephemeral desert hills you could make out the arch of a back, the contours of a bust, the roundness of a buttock. This was undoubtedly the intention of the anonymous photographer who'd created the poster that was pinned up in the breakfast room of the Heron Port-de-Bouc. A cloud of migratory birds was soaring away into the red sky.

After clearing up the stuck-on remains of croissants, butter and jam, Leyli paused, lingering on the poster for a few seconds. Almost through a reflex action, she put on her sunglasses. Round. Yellow. A happy smiley painted on each lens.

The room suddenly became darker. She hadn't heard Ruben Liberos approaching behind her.

'Really captures the Nubian desert,' said the hotel manager. 'All the travellers who feast here are transfixed by the sensuality of the dunes, and none of them notice the birds merging into the sky. Sacred ibises! Yes, another wading bird that migrates – just like our heron! A little in-joke which amused me . . . And also a little gesture of support for those poor ibises, once venerated in the Ancient World by the Egyptians, and today vilified in France, accused of being an invasive species which comes to steal the nests of other birds, destroying their eggs and killing the chicks – especially those of our very pink flamingos.'

'Is that true?'

'That's what they say ... A stone's throw from here, in the Camargue, like everywhere else in France, park officers – whose job is to conserve our natural heritage – are shooting ibises that try to migrate here, to our local marshes.'

They remained side by side looking at the poster, then Ruben turned to Leyli.

'My dear indefatigable sultana, could you possibly start your shift earlier tomorrow? Around 6 a.m. Just this once. Noura has asked for the morning off.'

Leyli paused to think. She lifted her yellow smiley glasses over her hair.

'I have to take Tidiane to school. Wake him up. Make him breakfast—'

'I understand, my princess, I understand.'

Ruben was not the type to insist. Leyli wasn't mad keen on doing Noura a favour, but she thought back to the conversation in room 17. A fragmented working class.

'I can work things out,' she finally conceded. 'Tidiane's grandpa will come and pick him up tonight after dinner so he can sleep at their place, and his grandparents will take care of him tomorrow morning. I'll text him.'

'Thank y—' Ruben began to splutter his gratitude.

The end of the word caught in his throat.

Leyli had turned pale. Her eyes were staring at the screen of her phone.

'Alpha,' she said. 'Alpha, my darling boy. He's been arrested. A few minutes ago. Outside his grandparents' apartment. My father saw him in handcuffs, being picked up in a van and—'

Ruben placed a hand on Leyli's shoulder.

'It's OK. It'll all be OK.'

Given his employee's distraught face, he tried to make light of the situation.

'He hasn't done anything wrong. The police will release him. At worst, if he's the victim of a miscarriage of justice, he'll manage to escape. Did I tell you, my anxious Penelope, how, in '74, I escaped from Bang Kwang prison in Bangkok, after a bizarre misunderstanding that—'

'Stop! Enough!'

Leyli had let out a scream. Tears dripped in tiny beads from her eyes, leaving dark marks running down her cheeks.

'Shut up, Ruben. Shut up.'

The hotel manager invited Leyli to sit down. They sat like this for a long time, in silence. Only Noura's footsteps could be heard, energetic and noisy. And Leyli, sniffling into the Heron-branded paper napkins Ruben had given her.

'I'm sorry,' the manager finally said.

'No, I'm sorry. I'm sorry for shouting. You're the kindest boss I've ever met.'

'That's what my female employees always say before I try to kiss them.'

Leyli smiled. Ruben was twenty years older than her. He wasn't being serious. At least, that's what Leyli made herself believe. Ruben had too much elegance for that, the elegance of shy, polite boys in secondary school. The fragile gentleness of men who are virgins.

'Then, after turning me down, they rarely get angry. They're rather flattered, and reassured to note that I'm not offended. So, almost every time, I become their confidant. Especially when it comes to desperate women! Did you know I was Marilyn's confidant when I was running the Palomar in west Los Angeles, just a few hours before her suicide? And that of many others. Jean Seberg . . . Dalida . . . Romy Schneider (he paused briefly) . . . Cleopatra.'

Leyli gave a faint smile. This time Ruben took her hand.

'Leyli, I suggest we skip the bit where I try kissing you, and you turn me down. You won't be cross with me if we dispense with all that daft foreplay between a girl and boy before they become real friends? Confide in me, Leyli. Confide in me if you want. Everyone thinks my favourite sport is telling stories. That's not true. I ramble on, I tell the same ones over and over again. What I like, more than anything, is listening to them.'

Leyli squeezed his hand even tighter. She waited for Noura's footsteps to fade away down the corridor.

'Then listen, my confidant. Listen, and never tell another soul.'

## LEYLI'S STORY

### Chapter Four

I was alone. Alone and blind. Hiding in that stinking room in Agrigento, in Sicily. All my friends, all my cousins from Ségou had been picked up again by the *carabinieri* and were going to be sent back to Mali. I had a choice between letting myself die or surrendering to the police, when the door opened and a hand reached out.

*You don't need to be afraid any more, mademoiselle.*

Adil.

His name was Adil Zairi.

All of the sentences he uttered after that contained the words 'too beautiful'. He was talking about me. Too beautiful to die. Too beautiful to stay here. Too beautiful for him not to fall in love. Adil repeated this to me dozens of times afterwards. He had loved me at first sight. With each passing night, he came up with other images – a sick little bird, an abandoned kitten, a beached mermaid – but he always returned to his starting point. My beauty.

Adil had been tipped off by the neighbours. He lived down below, he'd heard the rumour on the stairs, a woman was living on the third floor, neglected, left to fend for herself. Adil had come up to see.

He clearly hadn't expected me to be blind. He realised I couldn't see the instant I turned my blank eyes towards his voice. I think I fell in love with him very quickly too. Not just because he was the only lifeline in my dark night. Quite the contrary – I was wary, a tigress unmoved by promises, an owl frightened by a whisper. I think I fell in love with him because he had the strength to be humorous. He ought to have felt pity for me, and yet here he was, crawling around at my feet.

'Are you really blind?' he asked me straight away. 'Can you really see nothing?'

When I whispered a fearful 'Yes', he answered with the very last word I expected.

*Phew.*

I swear that's the word he used, Ruben.

*Phew.*

He said it again in his lilting voice, *Phew*, before adding: *You'll never see how ugly I am!*

I burst out laughing, but he wasn't joking. Not really. He returned to this often in the months that followed. He wasn't handsome, he said, so his only chance of sleeping with the girl of his dreams was if she were blind! He would run his fingers along my thighs, my breasts, my back, telling me over and over that they were perfect. I loved it. I also loved to stroke his face, which I didn't find any uglier than any other, his belly, which I didn't find any flabbier, his penis, which I didn't find any less hard.

Yet he'd said to me one night, 'If you regain your sight one day, then you'll leave me.' This was a few weeks after we met, and again I was sure he was joking.

Adil was French. He worked for an organisation that helped refugees, and he travelled extensively around the Mediterranean. I followed him everywhere. I waited for him in hotel rooms. I did nothing but wait for him – in Beirut, Nicosia, Athens, Bari, Tripoli. He would leave me in the morning after making love to me, barely even touching the breakfast which I'd then spend the rest of the day picking at, like a sparrow. He would come back in the evening. He spoke little. Curiously, it was I who would tell him about my day, during which nothing had happened, and talk about the cities I couldn't see, that I could only imagine – that I could only make any sense of – based on sounds from the street.

He spoke little and he loved me deeply. At least, he would often make love to me. Women tend to confuse the two. Not men.

One evening when we were lying in bed, in a room overlooking the port of Oran, while he was quietly reading the paper and I was listening to the cries of the fruit sellers on the waterfront, he paused.

'Listen to this, kitten.'

Adil never read me anything at all. He didn't like it. Yet I missed reading so much. I often thought back to my tales and legends from the hut, reciting them endlessly in my head. I would have loved Adil to read

154

me stories in the dark, as my father used to do in Ségou. Adil preferred to make love to me. That was normal: I was his. His woman. If we ever had a child, perhaps he would read those stories to our daughter.

'Listen, kitten.'

That night he read me a long scientific article which talked about corneal transplants, the operations that restore your sight. According to the article, this was increasingly common, both north and south of the Mediterranean. We then checked whether this operation was compatible with my blindness. It was indeed – it was practically a minor procedure. A few days in hospital.

I couldn't believe it. It was the sort of miracle I couldn't even imagine. It was as if I'd just been offered the elixir of immortality. I snuggled up to Adil. The mere fact he'd told me about this possibility was the most beautiful proof of love he'd ever shown.

'You're not afraid I'll leave you if I regain my sight?' I said, stroking his chest, slowly, so he'd understand how well I knew every inch of his body. Knew it by heart.

He kissed me.

'I lied to you from the beginning, my little bird. It was a trick to seduce you. In fact, I'm the spitting image of Richard Gere!'

I laughed, just as Adil often made me laugh, even though I had no idea what this actor looked like, this man I'd only ever heard about on the radio. My fingers carried on running down his chest. I think I knew the precise location of each of his hairs, and if he'd pulled out a single one I would have noticed. Then I asked that wretched question.

'How much does the operation cost?'

'Thirty thousand francs. A little less in Morocco, if you pay in dirhams.'

A fortune. Years of salary. And here was I, who'd never earned any money in my life . . . My fingers had reached Adil's penis. That night, he didn't have a hard-on.

'Let's forget it, darling,' I whispered, feeling upset. Shaken. 'Let's forget all about it.'

We never spoke about it again. In the weeks that followed, I left the room more and more often. Especially after dark. I would have dinner with Adil's friends or colleagues, or we would go to the bar together for a drink, to smoke a cigarette facing the sea. One evening, I think it was

155

in Sousse, when we went back up to our room, Adil held me tight in his arms. He smelt strongly of *boukha*, the fig alcohol from Tunisia. I didn't like it; I almost never drank – I felt lost, oppressed, vulnerable as soon as the alcohol anaesthetised my senses. My sense of hearing, my sense of smell.

'Sami thinks you're really beautiful.'

Sami was a French-Tunisian shipowner. He employed dozens of people. He was funny, rich, undoubtedly attractive.

'He . . .'

Adil hugged me even tighter before continuing.

'He's offered two thousand dinars to sleep with you.'

At the time, I didn't realise Adil wasn't joking. I laughed, and as usual Adil didn't push it. I forgot about it. He waited a few weeks before bringing up the proposal again. We were still in Sousse. Adil had found a permanent post in his organisation – he was working with the consulate on obtaining legal status for refugees. He barely told me anything about it.

'Sami asked me about you again. He's ready to offer you three thousand five hundred dinars.'

I was sitting on the bed. Through the window you could hear the seagulls flying around the boats. This time I knew Adil was serious.

'You're missing a golden opportunity, but I can't help it,' babbled Adil.

At the time I didn't get it. He had to explain.

'You can regain your sight, Leyli! It's as simple as that. You can get your sight back in a few months, maybe a few years. A corneal transplant costs a fortune, we both know that. But . . . but many men are willing to pay that fortune to sleep with you.'

I was crying. So was Adil. It was the first time.

'I want you to be happy,' repeated Adil. 'I want you to have a normal life.'

'I can't, Adil. I can't.'

He was silent for a long while.

'Do it for me then, Leyli. Do it for us. I want you to see my face one day, Leyli. I want to read in your eyes that you find me handsome.'

I did it for Adil. I swear to you, Ruben, I did it for Adil. For love. Everything was churning around in my head. If I regained my sight, I would no longer be a burden to him. His love was so overwhelming. Letting me sleep with other men, ignoring his jealousy for my happiness, my only happiness, my selfish happiness. Would I myself have been capable of such a sacrifice? No, probably not. I would never have accepted Adil sleeping with other women, even if his life depended on it. At least, that's what I thought.

I slept with Sami the next day. I did it three more times that week. Then Sami got bored, he went off to sort out some business elsewhere, but Adil offered me reassurance. I was so beautiful. He would find other friends, other colleagues, other neighbours, willing to pay.

He never used the word client.

He found them.

They paid.

How much exactly, I didn't know. Between my fingers, one banknote felt much like any other, and moreover Adil's friends usually paid up in advance. I tried to keep an account in my head, ten times a thousand dinars, twenty times fifty francs, thirty times a hundred dollars. I tried to calculate how long this hell would last.

Adil was jealous. I would spend hours stroking and reassuring him. *Your chest is firmer than theirs, Adil. Your nose is finer. Your skin tastes sweeter*. I insisted he arrange meetings for me with the same friends each time. That's what we called it, meetings. Just a few friends, the ones who pay well, I told Adil, but in reality it was because I preferred to be touched by men I knew. I hated giving myself to a stranger. I had to overcome an uncontrollable fear with each new encounter, whereas I learnt to tame the regular ones.

I talked a little, and above all I made them talk. I think that's what they preferred, deep down. Confiding in someone. Maybe I'm deluding myself about men – maybe they were only after my smooth buttocks and my breasts, which I could hardly believe could be as desirable as those of Naomi Campbell or Katoucha Niane, the only ones I could remember.

But one thing was certain, Ruben: even if dragging out the discussions was just a strategy to delay the moment when they would touch me, touch me again, they were talking to me all the same. Telling me about their lives. Their wives. Their kids. Their fears. Their loneliness. Like babies, after making love to me.

To begin with, I could remember everything. Then, when it all began to get confused, I tried to think of how I could help my memory. It was impossible for me to take notes, let alone read them back, so it occurred to me to ask Nadia. She was a waitress in the bar at the Hannibal, the hotel where most of the meetings were held. Adil had taken a large room overlooking the market – so I could hear the sound of activity all day long, he had said as he kissed me. It was because of this sort of thoughtfulness that I knew Adil loved me. More than anything. Despite my defiled body.

I asked Nadia to buy a small notebook, and sometimes, after the meetings, I dictated my lovers' confidences to her. They never shared their surnames with me, but I knew their first names, those of their wives, of their children, their phobias, their fantasies, their dreams. Nadia would write everything down and, when I asked her to, she would read it back to me. She liked to sneer at men, to ridicule them – she was raising her daughter, who was just a few months old, all by herself. She was the only one who shared the secret of the notebook which I always kept with me. It had become a kind of obsession. Since I would never know what these men I'd slept with actually looked like, I wanted to record everything about them.

I still have it. At Les Aigues Douces, under my mattress. I haven't taken it out in months. I don't know if I was right to reveal this secret to you, Ruben. To tell you about those dark years. I see the pity in your eyes. And yet, Ruben. And yet, despite everything you might imagine, the blindness and the prostitution were not the worst years of my life.

# The Night of Darkness

# 27

**7.23 p.m.**

> Surname: Maal
> First name: Alpha
> Date and place of birth: 20 May 1999 in Oujda, Morocco

'You're pretty tall for your age,' commented Petar, glancing once again at the personal records of the boy sitting in the squad's office. 'But apparently that doesn't stop you doing some bloody stupid things.'

Ryan was standing next to the commandant and had dressed for the occasion in an immaculate navy-blue uniform. So far, the teenager hadn't put up any resistance, neither during his arrest, nor during his journey in the van, and certainly not since being interrogated by the two policemen. But nor had he co-operated, any more than he'd resisted. He'd been as obedient as a teenager whose parents are pissing him off, and who responds via onomatopoeia, without ever losing the hint of a smile on his lips.

Petar and Ryan were striding back and forth in front of Alpha, who was sitting at the back of the room. Behind his computer, in the opposite corner, Julo sat watching. Listening. Not necessarily terribly focused on Petar and Ryan's monologues, which played out to the rhythm of Alpha's docile nods, and the occasional 'Yes' or 'No' wrenched out of him by way of punctuation to a comment ending in a question. Lieutenant Flores's eyes fluttered around, taking in the two cops, the suspect (suspected of what, he still didn't know), the poster with the pink flamingos of the Étang de Vaccarès and – behind the policemen – a large TV screen, hung on the wall of the opposite room and visible through a glass panel. The public servants, as compensation for doing overtime, had left it on.

Match night!

*Astra Giurgiu versus Olympique de Marseille.*

Julo had learnt on this occasion that OM were playing the second leg of an early-round match against a team from some charming little town in Romania lying along the banks of the Danube, on the Bulgarian border. At least football was helping him improve his geography! Alpha, when he wasn't nodding, was craning his neck to see. He was clearly more interested in the match score than the police officers' sermon.

*Prevention*, Petar had insisted, as if he were being paid by the number of times he slotted the word into his day. Prevention, that's all.

'Yeah, yeah, Commandant, whatever,' Julo had said, amused. The kid, who was almost two metres tall, was well aware that the cops had no evidence against him, not even a shred of dried weed found in his pocket. Just an allegation. Julo had reservations about the effectiveness of Petar and Ryan's little double act, however well-rehearsed it might be.

The commandant focused on the statistics. There was barely any room for one-man bands in the business – the competition was fierce, and incredibly so when it came to rookie people smugglers, just as it was for rookie drug dealers. He could name dozens of folk, young men just like Alpha, good-looking bodybuilder types with thighs and arms as thick as tree trunks who, thanks to a simple 6-millimetre bullet straight between the eyes, would never enjoy the full benefits of their annual subscription to the gym. Let alone a love life.

Ryan, on the other hand, playing the role of the priest, or perhaps the imam, invoked the elders. In short, appealed to morality, to the hundreds of families drowned in the Mediterranean since the start of the year, people who might be your uncle, your cousin, your sister, your father; he quoted celebrities who condemned these merchants of false hope, including Youssou N'Dour and a stream of rap, football and *raï* stars whom Julo didn't know.

Petar nodded, listened, and began again.

His boss's energy surprised Julo. He hadn't expected Petar to show so much compassion. It felt as though Petar were on a mission he had been ordered to carry out. A salesman who persists in flogging his snake oil to a stubborn customer – who refuses to buy it – simply because he knows the conversation will be recorded.

Strange . . . The suspect merely wriggled around on his chair every time Ryan and Petar moved, so as not to lose sight of the TV screen. Especially Petar, who was twice as wide as Lieutenant El Fassi.

'Alpha Maal! Are you even listening?'

Yes, he was listening. With all the attention of a teenager being told off by the headmaster, while staring through the window at girls passing by in the playground.

*Alpha Maal.*

Julo kept repeating this name and surname in his head. Some little detail had been troubling him for several minutes, but he couldn't quite put his finger on it. A connection with something he'd seen, or read, or heard, only a short time before, but which he couldn't remember.

Never mind. Julo leant over his computer. A huge shell was still displayed, full screen, along with the photo of the BCEAO tower in Cotonou. At least he had solved the riddle of the relationship between these shells from the Maldives and the banking system in West Africa. All it had taken was a few clicks when he returned to the office. The solution had a simple name, *cowries*, although this fact didn't get him any further in understanding why the shells were in Valioni's pocket. He needed to know more than what Wikipedia had to say. He would have liked to talk to Petar about it, but he didn't see how he could interrupt the class he was currently attending, and he didn't want to have to wait for the lesson to end. He continued trawling the internet and soon discovered the name of the top specialist on the subject. Mohamed Toufik. A university lecturer and expert in contemporary African history. Three books on colonisation and decolonisation, a ten-page list of articles in history journals, a Facebook page with all his scientific references, and an email to contact him. History teachers were no longer the ghosts lurking in archives he'd previously imagined! A few seconds later, he was sending an email to Mohamed asking for an urgent appointment, hoping the scholar was as responsive as he appeared to be well-connected online. Presumably, however, this academic still received fewer messages than a reality TV star?

The sound of a file being dropped violently onto a table startled him. Petar had just slammed down the weighty list of all gangland executions and score-settling since the beginning of the year.

'So, where do we go from here, Alpha Maal?' chanted the commandant. 'What are you going to do, if you're released back into the wild? Answer me a simple question, will you. Where do we meet next? In the morgue? In a fishing net in the middle of the Mediterranean?'

Julo continued to think his superior was overdoing it. However, another matter was preying on his mind. Overpowering. Elusive.

That first name, *Alpha*.

That surname, *Maal*.

If only Petar would stop yelling for a second, perhaps he could get his memory to work. He couldn't quite pinpoint this one specific memory, because he had the curious feeling of having read and heard both at the same time – of having read that surname and heard that first name, or perhaps the other way round. Yesterday. Yesterday, he was sure of it. A furtive double-memory.

Petar finally fell silent, Julo breathed, but in the next second, a dull brouhaha rattled the windows in the corridor. Petar left the room in a fit of pique, slamming the door behind him.

After less than ten minutes of play, OM had just conceded a goal to the Romanians!

Lieutenant El Fassi didn't seem to care one bit. Alpha seemed crestfallen. For the first time, the room fell silent. Ryan handed the accused a cup in a gesture of conciliation.

'Would you like a coffee, Maal?'

Suddenly, without understanding what mechanism had triggered

164

it, Julo made the connection. The light went on, as easily as if he'd flicked a switch . . . except that fumbling for it could have taken him hours.

*MAAL.*

He'd read that name before!

Julo quickly looked down at his computer, clicked on the Valioni folder, then the Bambi13 sub-folder. Double-clicking again, he opened a text file in which he'd downloaded a list of everyone called Bamby or Bambi registered in the Bouches-du-Rhône *département*. Two hundred and thirty-three names, a hundred and ninety-two if you ruled out women who were too old or little girls. He scrolled through the list. He'd spent hours the previous day scrutinising each name, searching for photos or the slightest clue about each one . . . A job he was far from having completed.

Bambi Lefebvre.

Bamby Lutz.

Bamby Maal.

*Bingo!* Julo gloated to himself. One of the hundred and ninety-two Bambys in the Bouches-du-Rhône had the same surname as the teenager currently being grilled by his colleagues! Julo continued to surf frantically, but no photo of this Bamby Maal was available online – all he could dig up was a date of birth on LinkedIn: 27 March 1995. Twenty-one years old . . . That matched!

What if the infamous Bambi13, the alleged killer, belonged to Alpha Maal's family? A relative? A cousin? His sister perhaps . . . The lieutenant tried to calm down. His heart was racing. It meant absolutely nothing. Bamby Maal was no more likely to be this Bambi13 than just about any of the hundred and ninety-one other results on the list, and the fact that her brother or cousin was being questioned in their office didn't change that . . .

Except that Julo didn't believe in coincidences! And above all, the lieutenant continued to let himself be guided by this strange intuition (you learn from your mistakes, Petar would have sneered) – he hadn't gone off to check this surname by chance, just one among a hundred and ninety-two in total, no, he had spontane- ously associated this first name, Alpha, with that of Bamby. As if his subconscious had dictated it to him, as if a second, older memory were concealing itself behind the first.

'Ryan,' said Julo, 'can you pass over his file?'

The lieutenant handed him a few printed sheets containing the boy's personal details and a brief CV. For the first time, Alpha noticed Lieutenant Flores, and studied him with a worried look. This further bolstered the lieutenant's conviction.

The guys in the squad had done a good job, even though Alpha had no criminal record. No qualifications either. Dropped out of school at sixteen. No known job since. No arrests. Fortunately, the file was backed up by other details. Alpha was the middle of three siblings. A little brother, Tidiane, ten years old. An older sister, Bamby, twenty-one.

His sister . . . *Bullseye!* Lieutenant Flores looked up, his heart still pounding. Alpha Maal was staring at him coldly. Impenetrable. No fear this time, or else the teenager had quickly learnt to hide it. Julo felt reluctant to question him head-on. *Do you have any photos of your sister? Do you have any on you? Do you know where she was last night?*

He held back.

It was too soon. He had to discuss it with Petar first. He had to find photos of Bamby Maal. Identify her formally. Then, if his instincts hadn't deceived him, they could grill the kid. They just had to keep him from escaping into the wild.

As Petar entered the room again, Julo read a few more lines from Alpha Maal's file.

Legal guardian: Leyli Maal.

Resident in Port-de-Bouc, Block H9, Les Aigues Douces.

No father?

*Port-de-Bouc.* Julo's heart was beating faster and faster. It was hard to imagine this was another coincidence.

'I've brokered a deal for you, big boy,' said Petar, directing his words at Alpha. 'If you look sharpish, you'll be able to watch the end of the match with some friends! I couldn't find you a private room, but at least there's a TV. Your carriage awaits. A nice little night in jail will do you good.'

Even though Julo wasn't as yet familiar with all the mysteries of the justice system and the police, detention like this without even a shred of evidence seemed downright illegal. No one protested, however. Not Ryan. Nor Alpha Maal.

Nor did he.

In any case, this Alpha Maal seemed keen to do everything he possibly could to get himself locked up.

The policemen left the room and Julo finally abandoned his screen. Outside, it was starting to get dark. His eyes fell on the poster of the Étang de Vaccarès and the hundreds of pink flamingos tightly packed together in the reeds of the Camargue, like an army of pastel-coloured football supporters, far nicer in his view than the others, the real ones, the noisy ones in blue and white. Julo felt he was heading for yet another sleepless night. The poster made him long to escape from the stifling heat of the city.

Another name whose secrets seemed impossible to reveal kept flitting around in his head.

*Vogelzug.*

Migratory birds.

Perhaps the wading birds would be more talkative than his boss?

A few minutes later, Julo was about to turn off his computer when an alert flashed.

New message.

Mohamed Toufik. The specialist in African history had already replied.

*Let's meet tomorrow morning. Al Islah Centre.*

The Al Islah Centre? The Koranic school attached to a mosque? Petar was going to love that!

# 28

On the dot.

This time, Leyli wasn't late. She had left the Heron more than two hours earlier, but she didn't have the heart to eat. Nor had she had the heart to prepare a meal. Since leaving Ruben's hotel, she'd gone through the motions of everyday life, out of habit, one after the other – as if you only repeated them every day so you could carry on going through them, mechanically, even when they had lost their meaning. Taking the 22. Getting off at the Littoral stop. Buying a few groceries at the Lidl, bread, eggs, crudités, pushing open the door to your block, going back up the stairs, pushing open your front door. A slow daily routine composed of trivia. Of what you just happened to find en route.

Like the salad sitting on the table, made from whatever you found at the front of a shelf and the back of the fridge. Made for nothing.

In front of her, Bamby and Tidiane hadn't touched their plates any more than she had.

Leyli felt a lump in her throat. She counted and recounted the three plates, the three glasses, the three place settings. One less than yesterday. Like when someone's died, thought Leyli, and you find yourself eating next to the empty place that once belonged to a husband, a father, a brother. You never miss them as much as you do at that moment.

The silence around the table made the atmosphere, which felt like the night before a funeral, even more oppressive. Not even the sound of a chair or a fork. *Alpha's not dead!* Leyli forced herself to think. He'll be out tomorrow. He'll be here tomorrow. Yet she couldn't shake off a terrible sense of foreboding; all she'd been thinking about for two hours had been that book she'd read before losing her sight, in her hut in Ségou, that detective novel, *And Then There Were None*, about the guests invited to dinner who vanish one by one. Ten, nine, eight, seven, six, five . . . Until there's only one left.

They were four yesterday. Three today.

The terror of ending up alone haunted Leyli. Bamby and Tidiane knew about Alpha, the arrest, being in prison, but no one dared mention it. Leyli had tried calling the police station several times, but she hadn't managed to get any information. Around 4 p.m. – too early, Alpha Maal's file wasn't registered yet. Around 5 p.m. – too late, the office was about to close. She hadn't protested. Too early, too late, not here, next door – she was well used to being shunted from counter to counter.

Bamby was surely aware of what was afoot, of what the cops were trying to pin on Alpha – he liked to confide in his elder sister. Tidiane too, perhaps; Alpha liked to show off in front of his little brother. Leyli, however, didn't ask them anything. She didn't want to embarrass them. To implicate them. Deep down, she preferred knowing nothing and having Alpha back instead.

Ever since Alpha was born, Leyli had always wondered where his natural inclination for violence would lead him. Which side he would land on. Violence always ends up tipping you permanently to one side or the other, good or bad, and how all of your qualities are perceived changes as a result. Determination becomes premeditation, strategy becomes deviousness, inventiveness becomes depravity. So many small-time kingpins would have made perfect and ruthless CEOs, so many greedy drug dealers were searching for the same adrenaline high as any intrepid firefighter. So many fathers, today placated and calm, yesterday a bundle of nerves. Alpha's father had been one of those. Alpha, if she remained vigilant, would follow his path.

Her tired eyes slid from the salad to her collection of sunglasses piled up in the basket, from the bin overflowing with laundry to the

169

display of owls. Wandered over the dust and clutter. After all, given cobblers' children are always the worst shod and teachers' children have the worst manners, why wouldn't the homes of cleaning ladies be the messiest? Leyli's gaze finally returned to rest on her children.

'Aren't you eating, Bamby?'

Leyli had broken the silence. She felt as if she'd given the signal, had given permission for conversation to begin again after a long blessing of the meal.

'Maman,' said Tidiane, 'can I watch the second half of the match with Grandpa, and extra time too, if the game isn't over?'

Thank you, Tidy, thought Leyli. It had slipped her mind. She was covering for Noura tomorrow morning. Getting up at 4.30 a.m. to be at the Heron by 6. Grandpa would be taking care of Tidiane after dinner.

'We'll see, Tidiane,' she said, without making a decision.

She addressed her daughter again:

'You're not eating, Bamby?'

'I'm going out tonight. I'm going to KFC with Chérine. I'm not having dinner twice. It's bad enough . . .'

'Bad enough you having to make the effort to be here? Is that it?'

'Just the second half, Maman?'

'No,' replied Leyli, without really knowing to whom the ban applied.

As far as Tidiane was concerned, her strictness was of no consequence since Grandpa Moussa would let him watch the game the moment her back was turned.

'Well, I'm off, Maman.'

Bamby had stood up. Her outfit was sexier than the previous day's. Short skirt. Bare legs. A little leather jacket, left open over a close-fitting white top and amply padded out by a Wonderbra which her daughter was wearing for the first time.

'Already?'

Bamby hadn't eaten a thing. Merely drained her glass and picked at the soft parts of the bread. She was hopping from one leg to the other. Nervous. Excited. In a hurry.

It was 7.52 p.m.

Leyli calculated that her daughter had stayed for just half an hour. The minimum, by trade union rules. How much longer would Leyli manage to bring her children together over a meal? How long before Bamby in turn found a good excuse?

Like Alpha. Tonight.

She smiled. Sadness was whispering horrible thoughts in her ear.

At least his big brother's absence hadn't spoilt Tidiane's appetite. Suddenly, the boy had started to wolf down his food and had finished his plate. So that he, too, could leave the table more quickly, Leyli thought with a touch of cynicism. Before the end of half-time!

Bamby went out. Leyli imagined her hurtling down each floor, the soft, melodic tapping of her ballerinas, their rapid pitter-patter resounding through the stairwell.

A violent rap beat shattered the magic. The hammering of a drum machine, before the voice of Stomy Bugsy came screaming out.

Kamila! As if she'd been waiting with her nose pressed to the door for Bamby to leave before turning on her sound system. Leyli sighed. She moved closer to Tidiane and spoke a little louder, stringing together various topics of conversation between the cheese and dessert courses – school, friends, school again – with Tidiane responding as if he were playing the Yes/No game: 'A little', 'Sometimes', 'Not bad', 'Not much'. Leyli persevered, pretending not to see her son looking up at the clock, the boy no doubt railing against his mother's obsession with never having the TV on during meals.

7.56 p.m.

Just a few more minutes before the players would emerge from the dressing room.

'Calm down, Tidy. You're just going to take your time and eat your dessert!'

And anyhow, they'd agreed that Grandpa would only be looking after Tidiane from 8 p.m., not before.

It was 7.59 p.m., and Bugsy's rhyming lyrics were still pouring out thick and fast on the floor below when there was a knock.

Leyli jumped, as she did each time this happened.

Everything had been swirling around in her head since leaving the Heron – Alpha's arrest, covering for Noura tomorrow morning, Tidiane with his head in the players' dressing room, Bamby here one minute, gone the next. She'd put down the shopping, thrown her coat on the sofa, tossed her sunglasses into the basket, without taking the time to inspect everything. Without checking meticulously, as she did every day, that she hadn't left any clues lying around.

Someone was still knocking, insistently.

Leyli tried hard to calm herself. Every time someone tried to enter her private world, she found it impossible to fight this obsession.

Her secret, her children's secret, was at risk of being discovered. It would be glaringly obvious to whoever came in.

# 29

'You're . . . You're in harmony, Faline.'

'Thanks. Thanks, Jean-Lou.'

She responded to his compliment with a smile. In harmony? In harmony with the simple, warm decor of this gourmet restaurant, Reflets, one of Michelin-starred chef Pierre Gagnaire's most celebrated establishments? In harmony with the constellation of colours on her plate – a little dish of prawns, chanterelles steeped in carrot juice, baby artichokes and ruby-red grapefruit?

Yet she had only slipped on a slim-fitting leather jacket, a Poivre Blanc top, a short flowery skirt and ballerinas. Natural. Feminine. In harmony? Just as with this plate of food composed like a work of art, everything came down to the detail. Two blue feathers as earrings, a discreet forget-me-not in her hair, a petrol-blue glint in the black around her eyes.

'Excuse me, Jean-Lou, I'll just be a second.'

She leant over to type a text on the phone in her lap. Her long black hair cascaded onto her discreet cleavage. A water pearl dangled from her neck, a pastel contrast to her honey-coloured skin, like a pendulum swinging just above her bosom.

Hello my darling
Better than KFC here!
Thanks! Keep you posted. Call you in the morning.

She shivered with excitement before sending the message. Without her dearest friend, her confidante, her *chérie*, nothing would have been possible. Neither this meal, nor the photos on her Facebook page. If she did manage to drag Jean-Lou to one of the rooms at the Red Corner tonight, it would again be thanks to her. Her loyal partner. Her ally, even though Faline hadn't owned up to her true objective. A simple little wheeze to try to pick someone up, her friend probably assumed. Better that she didn't know any more.

She sat up straight, concentrated on her plate again, on Jean-Lou. The shy fifty-something didn't seem brave enough to destroy the finely balanced beauty of the dish. He was still frozen, fork in mid-air, as if making a start on this appetiser already equated to committing adultery. Would tasting be tantamount to cheating?

Since the beginning of the meal, Jean-Lou had only touched on one subject. His son, Jonathan. His son's Down's syndrome, how he was different to other children, his innocence, the meaning he had given to Jean-Lou's life. Then he went on to talk about the T21 association, his role as president, the terrifying dilemma for parents of whether to keep their child or not, before coming back to Faline, and trying hard, above all, not to look at her as a woman, but simply as a mother carrying life in her womb, the life of a disabled child, tortured by a choice he was trying to shed light on, without judging.

Was that the sole reason they found themselves having a quiet one-to-one this evening? Because of this story she'd fabricated, and which Jean-Lou seemed to believe – or at least pretended to, so as to boost his morale? And if not, she wondered as she straightened her top, which was slipping down her bare shoulder, why had he invited her here? Out of pity?

*Jean-Lou is the nicest of all. According to Nadia, he's quite cute. She likes his puppy-dog eyes. And his wrinkles, which she finds rather moving. If I asked him not to touch me, I think he'd agree, I think he'd pay simply to look at me.*

*Besides, he makes love to me in a few minutes, and the rest of the time he just talks. He's obsessed by the birth of his child. He's afraid, especially since learning that the child's disabled.*

*I think he doesn't want to keep it.*

*I don't like it when he says that word, disabled. He says it with pity. Maybe he's going to keep this child out of pity.*

*Maybe he looks at me with pity. Maybe he makes love to me out of pity.*

*I think that's what I hate most in the world. Pity.*

A sommelier arrived to show them the wine list and reeled off a whole litany of options to consider, directing this at Jean-Lou, as if the gibberish exchanged between waiters and wine connoisseurs formed part of the mating ritual.

'That's perfect,' stammered Jean-Lou. Most probably he knew nothing about wine, and would never set foot in a Michelin-starred restaurant – let alone with a stunning girl who was thirty years younger.

Jean-Lou didn't belong here. No more than she did.

He finally fell silent and began jabbing at his ruby-red grapefruit with the tip of his fork.

Even though everything was swirling around in her head, she had to stick to the intended plan. Even though she found Jean-Lou endearing, genuinely unsettled, not at all the bastard she'd been hoping for. Not at all a scumbag like François Valioni. It had been so easy with him. She had to force herself to assume Jean-Lou was playing his cards closer to his chest, that was all.

Hadn't he invited her to this candlelit dinner which must have cost him half his salary? Jean-Lou was simply more hypocritical than the others. The only question she had to ask herself was how to make him fall into her trap. She had placed her hand conspicuously on the tablecloth, and not once had he held it, not even come anywhere close. Jean-Lou was going to be hard to tame. The kind who only kisses on the tenth date, who would run a mile from a girl who's rushing him, even if he's consumed with desire for her. Except she wasn't going to wait ten dates. She only had one chance. Only one night. Tonight.

'I have a present for you, Faline.'

Jean-Lou, increasingly ill at ease, had by now utterly wrecked the work of art on his plate, leaving his cutlery crossed to signal to the waiter – who, for his part, wasn't denying himself the chance to devour Faline with his eyes – that he had finished. He pulled a small case from his bag, the size and shape of a jewellery box.

She smiled, with sincerity, but not because of his thoughtfulness. She smiled because at last Jean-Lou was acting as predicted. He was offering her a precious gift. The message was clear: he wanted to buy her. Everything can be bought. Beauty. Women. Love.

*Jean-Lou is the most generous of all my lovers.*
*He often gives me flowers. It's the only gift that makes me happy.*
*Adil never gives me flowers.*
*Sometimes I think I can trust Jean-Lou.*

'Open it, Faline. It's not much. I found it at the airport yesterday. A souvenir.'

She opened it. Unwrapped the tissue paper and discovered the jewel inside. Surprise . . . Jean-Lou had given her a little glass pendant. A bauble that cost five euros! A trinket a kid would pester you to buy for them.

A shiver ran down her spine. That idiot Jean-Lou had touched her with his trivial gift, simple and childish, just as she would have loved it if one day a man did the same, gave her a cuddly toy at the fair, a Chupa Chups lollipop nicked from a *boulangerie*, or a pink Eiffel Tower covered in glitter – the naffest of its kind – bought just to please a pavement hawker. For a split second, a thought flitted through her mind – a thought she firmly rejected by slamming all the doors and shutters in her head.

Let him go?

The meal was dragging on and on.

*Striped red mullet, rock samphire, dog cockles and kokotxas.*

She could only understand every other word being rattled off by the waiter, whose diction remained impeccable, even as he undressed her with his eyes.

*Smoked bonito and ventrèche de thon Violine.*

This time the guy really was speaking a foreign language!

*Calamansi sabayon, lemon infusion with kaffir lime.*

Jean-Lou had barely drunk at all. Faline had barely spoken. Jean-Lou kept coming back to his association, perhaps even overdoing it a bit. The militant campaigner, the activist, practically a man of the cloth. If she hadn't been stalking him online, she might have thought he was bluffing, that he was simply wearing the holy robes of a priest to seduce her more easily. But no, he was indeed spearheading his crusade for greater recognition of Down's syndrome all year round, expending an incredible amount of energy in raising funds, and not just on the day of the annual French Telethon appeal.

A saint.

How do you steer a saint to commit a sin? And a sin of the flesh at that.

# 30

**8.22 p.m.**

Julo was railing against his own stupidity. He could see himself admiring the poster of the Étang de Vaccarès at the office, dreaming of the pink flamingos of the Camargue and increasingly overcome by the desire to flee the scorching heat of the city to admire these migratory birds. So, half an hour later, here he was, settled on a bench in the wildlife park with a splendid view of the pond. The pink reflection of the wading birds in the still water created a sublime impressionist painting, but he'd quickly become disillusioned. Dusk and the stagnant water had also attracted thousands of mosquitoes! Despite the heat, Julo had been forced to put on a long-sleeved top and a hooded jacket.

It appeared, however, that the insects were far less obsessed with sucking his blood than with surfing the internet.

As soon as he'd turned on his tablet, mosquitoes, moths and assorted fireflies had flocked towards it. No matter how often Julo brushed them away with the back of his hand, they returned as soon as he stopped moving about, fluttering around this novel halo of light as if it were a bulb glowing in the darkness – except that it was less searingly hot for their wings, and flat, like the ideal landing strip.

Julo cursed the inventor of the touch screen who must have designed it in his air-conditioned laboratory without thinking of the blatantly obvious: the screen couldn't tell the difference between a finger and the leg of a fly. For an hour now, Julo had been fighting against thousands of invisible, prankish enemies. He would try writing sentences on his screen and the night bugs would have fun adding letters, deleting others, clicking on windows and opening drop-down menus at random.

Despite all of this, he tried to filter out the swarm buzzing around him and focus on the investigation. Petar had just replied; he had accepted the appointment for the following day at the Al Islah mosque arranged by Mohamed Toufik, the scholar in African history who was to tell them about the famous cowries, the Maldivian shells also sculpted onto the walls of African banks. Petar had simply made it clear, for form's sake, that he wouldn't have time to grow a beard before the morning. Probably his way of thanking him.

When Julo had received his commandant's reply, he'd been on the Vogelzug website. This strange German-sounding name finally made sense. Migratory birds, the only border-free travellers on the planet. The organisation had branches throughout the Mediterranean basin. Its sphere of operations was extensive: housing for refugees, job hunting, legal aid, preventive measures, lobbying institutions. Vogelzug boasted several hundred employees and had established itself as a key partner for the authorities. Indeed, it was under its auspices that Frontex, the European border agency, was holding its major symposium in Marseille in two days' time. No matter how hard Julo tried to read between the lines, he found it difficult to assess where exactly the organisation positioned itself. A convenient seal of approval for states, allowing them to relax their Malthusian migration policies at the least social cost, or a real thorn in the side – both independent and militant – in the manner of Amnesty International and other agencies concerned with human rights? He lingered for a short while on the page introducing Vogelzug's founding president, Jourdain Blanc-Martin: a guy armed with local expertise, a child of Port-de-Bouc, from the Les Aigues Douces area – that was all the five lines of CV specified. The president didn't seem the type to nurture a personality cult.

The mosquitoes had calmed down a little. Perhaps the frogs had swallowed half of them. They were croaking so loudly that the wading birds woke up with a start. Lieutenant Flores abandoned the Vogelzug website and went to Bambi13's Facebook profile instead. He scrolled through the pages, ably assisted by a humming beetle – some kind of cockchafer – which was obsessed with the seductive pseudo-student's bikini.

Was Bambi13 actually Bamby Maal? Before leaving the office, Julo had tried to share his concerns with his commandant: a girl called Bamby, the sister of the rookie people smuggler arrested at midday, just happened to live in Port-de-Bouc too. In the Les Aigues Douces neighbourhood.

'That's a lot of coincidences, isn't it, boss?'

'We'll see tomorrow, kid,' Petar had replied, putting on his jacket to go home to his beloved hairdresser. 'It won't be difficult to get hold of some photos and see whether our bronze Apollo's sister matches your little sweetheart. And besides, knowing you, you're gonna spend the night there.'

'"Won't be difficult . . ."' Julo muttered to himself between two croaks. 'Won't be difficult.'

He hadn't dug up any photos of Bamby Maal online, and even if they found some tomorrow, he wasn't convinced that any certainty would emerge, given the blurred image they had from the security camera.

On Bambi13's Facebook page, Julo carried on jumping from Bodrum to Santo Domingo, from Ngapali to Lanzarote, without really knowing why since the beautiful unknown girl never once showed her face.

*Because he was in love*, Petar would have sneered.

Because something was preying on his mind, thought Julo, justifying himself.

Bambi13's Facebook profile was the polar opposite – in terms of social class – of the world in which Bamby Maal must have grown up. The Les Aigues Douces neighbourhood was classed as a deprived area, Leyli Maal was a single mother who, according to her son, hopped from one insecure job to the next. How could this underprivileged kid from the estates have turned into a globetrotting activist who leapt from hotel to hotel, each more luxurious than the last? After all, reasoned Julo, the name 'Bamby' alone proved nothing. The real murderer might have assumed this pseudonym to throw suspicion on a girl from Port-de-Bouc, having a strong hunch that investigators would make the connection. Besides, on second thoughts, why would the murderer have used her real first name as an alias, simply modifying its spelling? It made no sense at all.

'Pretty-looking girl, isn't she?' Julo surprised himself by asking aloud in the deserted park, not knowing whether he was talking to the cockchafer that was still flitting around nearby, the mosquitoes that had escaped from the frogs, or the pink flamingos returning from the tropics.

*Maal. Alpha. Bamby. Leyli.* Lieutenant Flores had checked online, this family's surname and first names were typically Fulani. He recalled that Professor Waqnine, in another strange coincidence, had told him about this ethnic group that very morning. In connection with the blood.

He pulled the table of blood group impossibilities from his pocket and unfolded it, while thinking back on what the haematologist had said: unlike other African ethnic groups, the Fulani are over-represented in group A, which itself represents 40 per cent of humanity. A+ alone accounts for a third of the world. Bamby, Leyli and Alpha's blood group was therefore probably A. That doesn't take us any further, he thought, sliding his finger along the line. No further for the moment. But he was convinced that everything was connected.

# 31

Tidiane wasn't sleeping. Even though he'd gone to bed early.

OM had conceded two goals in the first half-hour. A third before half-time. The matter had been quickly settled by the Romanians. He hadn't pestered Grandpa to let him stay up a little late to watch the end of the match. Through the window of his room, which had previously been his mother's, he could see the shadows of the orange tree dancing.

Tidiane was struggling to go to sleep. He was thinking about Alpha. About his arrest. About the sun almost within reach when he'd climbed the orange tree. About the cops. About his whistles, the ones his big brother hadn't heard. About the adults who wouldn't talk about Alpha in front of him – adults like his mother, like Bamby, like his granny and grandpa, who wouldn't answer his questions, who whispered when talking about his brother as if he'd done something stupid that was even bigger than Alpha himself. Tidiane didn't like adults being silent. Tidiane didn't like feeling left out. Feeling like a baby being protected. Feeling like a kid whom people lie to for his own good.

It was hot in the apartment. Too hot to sleep, even though Grandpa had left the window open. Through the square of night sky, Tidiane could see flames dancing. They belonged to the little scented torches that Grandpa had lit on the balcony to keep the mosquitoes away. They blinded him. He turned the other way, but the shadows were dancing on the sheets of his bed.

Tidiane tried not to look at them, but another fear was preventing him from sleeping. Ever since seeing Granny Marème and Grandpa Moussa again, he hadn't stopped thinking about that man who'd come into the apartment earlier in the evening, that man who'd kissed Maman on the cheek, that man who had a terrifying voice. He didn't like him! Grandpa had been waiting for Tidiane, he'd had to leave them alone, Maman and that man. Maman had called him Guy, but Tidiane wanted to call him Freddy, like in those horror films he'd never seen but which the older kids talked about at break time. He didn't like him. He didn't like seeing Maman with any men other than Alpha and himself anyway.

He forced himself to close his eyes so he could no longer see the cold black flames of the shadows on the sheets. He had never forgotten Grandpa Moussa's story, about how Maman had gone blind, in her hut by the river, through staring at the sun. It had made her stronger, more beautiful, more intelligent. That was why, afterwards, when she had regained her sight, she became the best mother of all. A mother who could feel everything, guess everything, read your mind. Becoming blind was like an exam you were obliged to sit.

Tidiane curled up a little and closed his eyes even tighter, wrinkling his forehead, squeezing his eyelids, making a round face. He too had to practise. Grandpa had told him how his mother had learnt to find her bearings by listening to sounds, by training her memory, by reconstructing in her head a world that was even more precise than the one seen in broad daylight.

He stood up, his eyes still closed, and tried to guess where the bedroom cupboard, the door and the window were located. He moved forward a metre and bumped into the wall. Raised his eyelids, then lowered them at once.

He would ask Granny and Grandpa for advice, he would practise every night, and during the day too; he would blindfold himself to play football, he would try to find his way to school just by the sounds of the street, to recognise each of his friends in the playground purely from the tone of their voice.

He too would become more sensitive. Quicker. More instinctive. Like Zidane. Like Barrada.

He placed his hands in front of him and walked, now unable

to see, across the room. A slight draught told him that he was approaching the window. His legs trembled slightly, but he had to force himself to walk towards the void. It was easy – you could tell exactly where the opening was from the wind on your face. There was no danger, the window ledge was high, well not very high, but still high enough not to fall. At least, he thought so. He had to remember that window without opening his eyes, visualise it in his head and keep moving, moving. He had to become as brave as Maman, so that the day she was in danger, he could save her.

Save Alpha too. Protect Bamby.

The cool air whipped across his face. The rest of his body was drenched in sweat, from his neck to the base of his spine. The evening breeze was so soft, so appealing, so good for him. He had to keep moving towards it.

He heard the owl at that very moment. The owl hidden in the big orange tree.

He didn't open his eyes, he just listened to its hooting – he knew it was heralding danger. He remembered Grandpa's stories, the mythological tales he loved, the one about the goddess Athena in particular. He imagined it was his mother who'd metamorphosed, like an Animagus in the Harry Potter books.

He stopped.

Surely he had to be right in front of the window by now? Right in front of the orange tree.

He stopped and spoke softly.

At night, owls see everything, hear everything, understand everything.

'Tell me, since you've seen everything. Tell me if Alpha's going to get out of jail. Tell me why he didn't run away . . . Tell me if Maman's going to fall in love with Freddy. Tell me if I'll find a girlfriend as beautiful as Bamby one day. Tell me everything, since you see everything. Tell me where footballs go when they fall into the hell below us. Tell me where Maman's treasure is hidden. I swear I won't steal it, I won't touch it, I just want to know if it really exists, that cursed treasure. To watch over it. You can trust me, you know. With your eyes shut.'

# 32

Leyli was standing under the shower. She closed her eyes, allowing the hot water to gently scald her skin. The bathroom was mouldy, the paint was peeling, the seals on the pipes were leaking and the pipes themselves were rusting, but it didn't matter, the water was flowing freely, as hot as in any marbled five-star hotel with gold-plated taps. She would gladly have stayed under the shower jet for hours, but Guy was waiting for her. In the next room, on the sofa. He'd come knocking on her door just under an hour before.

Two beers in his hand.

Kamila's rap music was blaring even louder in the stairwell. Leyli's first instinct had been to slam the door in his face, or at least turn him away unambiguously.

Not now, Guy. Later. Come back later.

Strangely, she hadn't dared. She'd let him in.

She had immediately regretted it. She hadn't liked Tidiane seeing Guy. She'd liked Guy seeing Tidiane even less. It hadn't lasted long, just a few minutes, just before Grandpa Moussa took charge of his grandson, but all the while Leyli had felt anxious. Guy didn't look terribly smart, but he might have discovered her secret, or suspected part of it at least. Yet he hadn't asked any questions, had simply greeted Tidiane as though everything were completely normal. Never, thought Leyli, trembling in hindsight, never had she let a stranger get so close to the truth.

Why? Because there was something about Guy that attracted her? He wasn't really handsome, apart from his two big, melancholy blue eyes, as if a seamstress had sewn them onto his big teddy-bear body. He wasn't even particularly funny. Once Tidiane had disappeared, his eyes had turned to stare at her twenty-year-old TV that was almost as squat and thick as one of those old pre-internet Minitels.

'Don't worry, I'm not going to ask you to turn it on – cheering for OM makes me depressed. If I counted the time I've spent since I was born watching European Cup matches on TV, hoping a French club might go all the way . . .'

He'd burst out laughing before adding:

'At first I thought I'd come up and see you just during half-time, but I then thought it was a bit tight to squeeze everything in.'

He'd continued to guffaw loudly. Almost all of Guy's sentences would peter away in tinny laughter – like an overwound clockwork toy – which took the place of an ellipsis when he spoke.

'I'm joking, Leyli. I'm only joking. Anyhow, you're too beautiful for me.'

This time he hadn't laughed. Leyli hadn't contradicted him. He'd cleared up the slight embarrassment by waving his two beers under Leyli's nose.

'I've brought two, but if you don't want any, I won't be offended. I'll be a martyr. Someone has to.'

Yet more screeching of metal on metal. Guy could have made a small fortune doing canned laughter for TV sitcoms. Leyli had simply smiled, unsure whether to go and make herself a tea. Guy was still looking around at the bric-a-brac in the apartment, goggle-eyed at what he saw, as if he'd mistakenly stumbled into the alley of a souk while looking for a betting shop. His gaze wandered across the books, the colourful owls, the sunset over the Niger that hung on the wall.

'It's totally nuts, your decor,' he had added while opening the beer with an expert flick of his wrist.

Before carrying on, his eyes continued to flutter around – over the African masks, the tins of green tea, the packets of spices.

'But I'll be honest, you know, me, all this exotic stuff . . .'

His eyes, still darting here and there, happened to land on Leyli just as he finished his sentence. He stood there open-mouthed, staring at her Moroccan slippers, her hair braided with beads, her ebony skin.

This time, an expletive replaced the ellipsis.

'Bloody hell, I'm such a dickhead!'

Leyli giggled uncontrollably. Guy was softening her up.

He was lugging around a face cracked by the years and a body weakened by life. He was a racist. Most likely an alcoholic. And despite everything, she liked him. Even a little more than that. She felt a strange attraction to this man. Not love at first sight. More like the opposite, even if she couldn't quite define what the opposite was. A sort of age-old feeling, weathered by time, scraped away, worn down, but obvious nevertheless.

Leyli wanted to seduce him. To let herself be seduced.

Plain and simple.

She had turned off the kettle and, without having planned any of this in advance, had told Guy that he could make himself comfortable, smoke on the balcony, put on the TV, read a book – she was going to have a shower. She stank of a mixture of patchouli and bleach. She hadn't had time to freshen up since finishing her shift at the Heron. After leaving Guy in the living room and locking her bathroom door, she had undressed and examined herself in the cracked mirror pitted with black spots.

She was better than this mirror! She was better than this mouldy bathroom, better than this dilapidated apartment, better than this derelict neighbourhood. She ran her fingers over her dark breasts, as pert and firm as before, back in the days when the men she had loved would stroke and kiss them; over the pretty outline of her waist, over her flat belly, or at least so it seemed, if you didn't feel it to search for invisible bulges.

Still beautiful. Still desirable, if she took the trouble.

Leyli finally emerged from the shower. She took a few more minutes to rub her skin with argan oil body butter, to put her make-up back on, to tie her colourful braids into an artfully disordered crown, and then, without pausing to put on any underwear, she slipped a long, slim-fitting Malian pagne over her head. It was made of blue and mauve cotton *bazin*, and gently kissed the rounded contours of her body without clinging to them. Like wrapping paper, neither too soft nor too stiff, merely hinting at the shape of the surprise hidden inside and letting your imagination do the rest. The dress slid over her dark-skinned body, slowed down a little as it passed over her breasts, and glided across her stomach before catching slightly on her buttocks and hips. Leyli tugged gently. The pagne fell away like a fisherman's net, reaching halfway down her legs.

She leant over the mirror one last time to admire her curvaceous figure, then murmured to herself:

'Let's see whether you like exotic stuff or not, shall we?'

❁

Leyli had accepted a beer, had drunk half of it. She had settled into the sofa and her head was spinning a little.

Guy was lapping her up with his eyes. A little too keenly. She was starting to regret her daring choice of clothing. She remained tightly curled up in a ball, like a cat, legs folded and arms crossed. In the apartment below, the music had faded away. No more sound drifting upstairs, suggesting Kamila had gone out. In its place, Leyli had put a Cesária Évora compilation in the CD player.

More exotic stuff! Guy hadn't made any comment.

Guy was talking, merely random banalities. Leyli listened distractedly, mostly flying off into her thoughts, fluttering around and only occasionally returning to settle on her guest's words. It was strange for her to feel beautiful and desired. It was such a distant feeling . . . Yet she had felt it twice today: tonight with Guy, and this afternoon, at the Heron, with Ruben. She could even add a third time if she counted Patrick's insistent smile – or was it Patrice, she couldn't remember now – the day before, at the FOS-HOMES offices.

The law of series? Like troubles always coming in threes? As if lovers all had to show up at the same time, without taking a ticket, without waiting their turn. Life always had to go over the top, lumbering you with both happiness and unhappiness in a single delivery, all jumbled up in a box, and leaving you to unpack the whole lot.

Sitting at the other end of the sofa, Guy was making a clumsy attempt at moving closer. He seemed to be playing at grandmother's footsteps, shuffling his buttocks a few millimetres the second Leyli looked away. An invisible, stealthy crawl. Like a wolf in the night. Or rather a crocodile. A hippopotamus. An elephant.

As soon as Guy gained a centimetre, Leyli edged back five. The message was clear: Leyli didn't want to go any further – not so fast, not tonight, even if it was the ideal evening. They were alone together, Leyli had explained the circumstances to Guy – her Alpha currently being detained by the cops, her younger son Tidiane at his grandfather's, her daughter Bamby sleeping someplace else, she wasn't sure exactly where.

Guy made her laugh. That was enough for tonight. That was already a lot.

Guy loved puns – it was his speciality, he confessed – and he'd been commenting on life in the area by messing around with Port-de-Bouc's name in all sorts of ways.

Port-de-Bouc. Port-of-the-Goat. Or *Port-of-the-Scape-Goat* more like, if you were talking about the Arabs, Italians, Portuguese and others, like the Polish, who'd arrived over the past forty years to swell the tide of the unemployed in the Étang de Berre.

Polite laughter.

. . . To the point where you couldn't even speak French any more if you went into a bar to place a bet. Makes you mad. Enough to swear, perhaps. *Port-de-Bouc-may-curse* . . .

Awkward laughter.

Guy continued his one-man show by grabbing a hardback volume from the shelf, the one full of mythological tales and stories, and making it dance along, as if bobbing on the waves.

A bookshop by the sea. *Port-de-Bouc-sailor.*

His best one!

The one-fan audience had loved it. Leyli felt good. Relaxed. The alcohol was certainly helping, so when Guy had finally exhausted his collection of cheesy puns, she was keen to carry on confiding in him.

Guy wasn't great at talking.

But there was one thing you couldn't take away from him: when he was silent, he was very good at listening.

## LEYLI'S STORY

### Chapter Five

I hope you're not shocked, Guy, to learn I was a prostitute. Because that's the right word to use, isn't it? Even though with Adil we didn't talk about clients, only about friends and meetings, even though – when everything stopped and Nadia wrote the last page of the notebook, dictated by myself – I had only three regular men who paid me. The fact that I was blind, that I agreed to sleep with men to regain my sight, or through love for Adil, or through fear of him, doesn't change that fact one bit.

I was a whore.

I hope my children never find out. I hope no one else reads that notebook but me. I won't tell you where it's hidden, Guy, you can be sure of that. You already know a lot. A lot more than anyone else.

I discovered I was pregnant on 25 July 1994 – I remember, it was the Republic Day holiday in Tunisia, they were letting off bangers all over the street and, like an idiot, I was afraid it would traumatise my child, who couldn't have been more than three weeks old in my belly.

I waited to talk to Adil about it. I counted and recounted in my head. Not the weeks before the birth, no, I was counting the money. The number of meetings, or the gifts that friends had given; they didn't always pay in dinars, francs or dollars, sometimes they also gave watches, gold, jewellery. Adil would keep everything.

Then one evening, a month later I think, after making love – we still made love almost every night – I took the plunge. I had calculated and recalculated.

'I think we have enough money, Adil. For the operation on the cornea. I think I could finish with all the meetings. Get away from here. Find a surgeon.'

Adil had replied gently. As he stroked my body, my legs, my stomach – still flat – with the same tenderness, he explained that he didn't want to take any risks, that he wanted the best doctor for me, the best hospital, a few more months wouldn't make any difference. What was the rush? So I confessed everything. In one sentence. A definitive sentence.

'I'm in a hurry, Adil. I want to have the operation before April. In the next seven months. I want . . . I want to see my baby being born.'

Adil said nothing. I just felt his body stiffen. His hand freeze. His heart beating . . . Beating . . . Beating . . .

The first blow came the next day. He'd fallen asleep without reacting. He'd woken up without asking any questions, without asking if I had any idea who the baby's father was (how could I have known?), he just kissed me as if nothing had happened while saying: 'François wants to see you tonight.' The first blow fell when I said I wouldn't go. A whack that landed me on the floor.

Then he was crying, apologising, pleading with me:

'Do you think it's easy for me, Leyli? Knowing that every night you sleep with other men, not me? But I put up with it for you, Leyli. For you!'

He never spoke to me again about the baby. I, however, could think of nothing but the child.

He carried on beating me each time I refused to sleep with others. I had marks. On my cheeks. On my arms. My lovers must have noticed them. None of them ever made the slightest comment. Even Jean-Lou. The sweetest of all. He too averted his eyes. Like the others.

Another time, he kicked me in the back with his combat boots – the only part of me he could reach, because I was huddled up in a ball on the cobbled kitchen floor to protect my belly – before sitting down beside me. It had been a long while since he'd last cried after beating me. But he still stroked my hair.

'What will you live on, my darling, if you stop the meetings? What else do you know how to do, apart from make love? If you regain your sight, do you think it'll be easier to look at the men who pay to love you, face to face?'

'I'm expecting a child, Adil,' I had the strength to reply. 'I'm expecting a child.'

'So what, Leyli? So what? What difference does it make, as long as our friends don't know?'

Three months passed. Adil had stopped beating me. He no longer had a reason. I had become docile again. I could feel my belly getting rounder. I imagined everything would work out as a matter of course. When I could no longer hide my pregnancy, when no one would agree to meetings with a girl who was six, seven, eight months pregnant . . . I was counting the weeks in my head. My baby would save me.

It was Nadia, the waitress at the Hannibal, the girl to whom I was dictating the words in my notebook, who tipped me off one evening. She had closed the door of the bar and made quite sure we were alone, except for her daughter who wasn't yet a year old and was playing with a plastic giraffe at our feet. I remember thinking how cute she must be, her chubby little girl with curly hair. That day, before Nadia revealed the secret that would turn my life upside down, I had prayed very hard – while stroking my belly – to have a daughter, a daughter as adorable as Nadia's little doll.

'Adil's going to leave you, Leyli. He's told Yan and François. He's booked a seat on the ferry to Marseille on Saturday. He wants two strong, armed men to go with him.' (She gave a wicked little laugh.) 'I think he'll be carrying all the loot with him. It's one hell of a stash, I'm telling you. I've got a hunch he doesn't intend leaving you half of it.'

Everything was crumbling around me.

I finally understood what my brain had known for years, but refused to admit. Adil had been pimping me all these years with the sole purpose of getting rich. This story of a corneal transplant was just a pipe dream, first to persuade me, then to keep hold of me; the baby was thwarting his plans, so he was getting out while there was still time.

I suppose, having listened to my story, that you knew this from the very beginning, and felt sorry – a sort of pity tinged with irritation – for the complete numbskull that I was.

Love makes you blind. But in my case, Adil didn't even need to make me love him.

'Thank you,' I said to Nadia.

'If you need anything at all . . .'

Deep down, when I think back to that day when everything fell apart, I tell myself that I never had any proof. I've never been able to rid myself of this obsession with trying to forgive everything and everyone. Sometimes I think perhaps Adil hadn't intended to leave without me, or without leaving me anything, that Nadia had made it all up. That it was all of my own making.

On Friday evening, the night before he was to leave, as I lay by his side, I took him in my arms.

'I've had enough, Adil. Enough of all these lovers. I only want to make love with you.'

My argument had surprised him. My tenderness too. I had thought that if he'd planned to leave the next day, he wouldn't refuse to make love to me. That his pride as a perverted little male would be flattered. Making me come one last time! That would be his undoing. I was riding him side-saddle, and when he'd finished thrashing around under me, I said it again:

'I only want to make love with you, Adil. I made a decision this week. I've booked myself on a boat to Tangier. I've booked into the Clinique du Soleil, in Marrakesh.' (I hadn't invented it, it really did exist!) 'I spoke to a doctor on the phone, he faxed an estimate to me at the post office, the woman who works there read it to me and—'

He cut me short.

'How did you manage it?'

I wasn't going to admit that Nadia had helped me. Thinking about it, he might have suspected. But deep inside, I knew he couldn't care less. As expected, he didn't add anything, he just said:

'Let's discuss it tomorrow.'

Adil got up in the middle of the night. I wasn't sleeping. I'd been waiting for this moment for several hours. Everything I'd told him the day before was intended purely for this: to induce a sense of urgency. To be in control of the sequence of events.

Adil was moving around in the dark, in silence, but I knew every sound in the house by heart. Outside, in the town, on the street, I was lost, vulnerable, but I'd learnt to move around at home as if I had my eyes wide open.

I listened.

I knew he was hiding the money and all the gifts from the meetings in the house, somewhere in the kitchen, somewhere secret, under one of the cobbles. But even though I'd heard him lift it dozens of times, I was unable to locate it precisely. It was perfectly sealed. Impossible to find by simply feeling around. I had to force him to take the loot out of the hiding place. And then – only then – I would act.

I heard Adil packing his bag, a big black Adidas bag we'd bought together, filling it with our memories, with anything that had even some value. Slowly, sure of himself. Proud of himself too, no doubt. He'd been executing the perfect plan ever since the day we'd met. I had made him a fortune, several tens of thousands of francs, I had calculated, and I didn't know who he was. I didn't know his face. He could abandon me, and I would never recognise him.

I stood up.

I stepped forward. I was naked. That was also part of my plan. To keep him thinking I was frailer than I actually was, despite the knife I held in my right hand. It was Nadia who'd given it to me; I'd hidden it under the mattress. An old Berber dagger, a tad rusty, with a horn handle.

I approached. He didn't utter a word.

I pretended to stab him three times in the air, staggering around like a madwoman trying to slash invisible ghosts.

He gave a cynical laugh, then stepped back far enough to enjoy my ridiculous mime show, as I chased mosquitoes in the dark with my harmless little spear. He didn't know I could pinpoint him from the mere shuffling of his feet. That I could assess every inch of this room, that I knew my position and his, and that my inner radar was able to calculate the distance with bat-like precision, that in my head I was measuring the height of my arm and the height of his neck, that I'd been practising for hours, aiming at invisible targets, swooping down like a wasp on oranges or apples placed on a sideboard.

I continued miming a few confused sleepwalking gestures, then suddenly, with all the speed and accuracy of a lunge in fencing, I took two steps forward. Two metres. The Berber dagger plunged into Adil's throat; I didn't know whether I'd pierced his carotid artery or not. He collapsed without making any sound at all.

Everything happened very fast after that. I got dressed, grabbed the Adidas bag (it was unbelievably heavy) and ran off to meet Nadia. She hid me for a few hours at her place, then helped me get to the port at the time the ferry left for Tangier.

Was Adil dead?

I don't know, I've never found out.

He had been my first love.

I don't even know if I killed him. I don't even know what he looked like.

# 33

**9.29 p.m.**

Julo was dozing in front of his screen, having no doubt hitched a ride with the migrating pink flamingos and soared off to one of the heavenly beaches where Bambi13 lay basking in the sun. Lulled into sleep by the heat, and the nocturnal song of the frogs and toads. He was walking along the edge of a lagoon towards the beautiful faceless stranger, carrying her head under his arm, reconstructed from a blurred photo and a simple 3D printer. The owl-patterned hijab fluttered against his bare chest in the trade winds.

A piercing alarm suddenly woke him up. He let out an expletive. A huge peacock butterfly – or a moth looking just like one – had just landed on his tablet!

The view of Bambi13's buttocks and lower back lying on her towel had disappeared, making way for an advert for a dating site bordering on the pornographic, blocked with a forbidding red cross. Julo swore and turned off his device. Since these bugs were refusing to leave him in peace, he might as well go back to traditional methods, which would also help him avoid nodding off.

He flipped over Waqnine's sheet of blood group impossibilities and grabbed a pen. The faint glow of the moon above the pond, elongating the reeds into long black feathers, was just enough to let him see. Deprived of a source of light, the nocturnal insects were already flying away – like those geeky types, thought Julo, who run a mile as soon as you close a computer screen and open a book instead.

He pressed the sheet against the back of the tablet. Everything's connected, he repeated to himself, picking up his train of thought from before falling asleep. The more he turned the puzzle over in his head, the more he was convinced there was a single answer to this tangle of questions.

He wrote rapidly, in nervous excitement. Starting with the obvious ones.

*Why was François Valioni murdered?*

*Why did Valioni go to Essaouira, just a few hours before his murder?*

*What's the connection between his murder and Vogelzug?*

*Why does Petar Velika refuse to talk about it?* (As soon as he'd written this line, he vigorously scored it out, lest he inadvertently pull out this memo right under his boss's nose.)

*What is the relationship between the Maal family, and in particular Leyli, the mother of the tribe, and Vogelzug's president, Jourdain Blanc-Martin, her neighbour in Port-de-Bouc, born in Les Aigues Douces?*

He continued with the questions directly relating to the murder.

*Why did the murderer take a blood sample from François Valioni, if not to determine paternity?*

*What were those shells doing in Valioni's pocket?* (The fact that they were cowries deepened the mystery more than helping to solve it.)

*What does the red band mean, the same as the ones you find in various colours, including green and blue, on the wrists of some illegal migrants?*

Julo was already at eight unanswered questions, but he could feel his intuition whispering that they could only be resolved by answering the last ones, the ones about Bamby and Bambi.

*Is Bamby Maal in fact Bambi13?*

*Why did her brother Alpha let himself be banged up so easily, as if he'd been asking for it?*

*How can Bambi13 travel round the world so easily?*

*Why did Bambi13 reveal her face, partially, to the Red Corner security camera?*

*Did Bambi13 kill François Valioni?*

*Will Bambi13 kill again?*

*When?*

*Where?*

He lifted his pen and gently closed his eyes, allowing the lullaby of the invisible frogs to soothe him once again. Bambi13's beauty fascinated him. Bamby Maal's fate intrigued him.

One and the same woman?

Two women, both trapped in the same spiral?

Two women, or more?

# 34

'That was a perfect evening, Faline.'

The waiter from the Michelin-starred restaurant had served their coffees around thirty minutes ago, not without letting his eyes hover over Faline's thighs in the process. Jean-Lou had taken the time to drain his cup, to pick at the petits fours, soufflé biscuits with Tahitian vanilla, a *déclinaison* of citrus fruit and liquorice, passion fruit *mendiants*, to talk again about the endless meetings that awaited him the next day and then, at a loss for words, had let silence take hold.

Barely a minute, then he looked at his watch, pushed back his chair and stood up.

*That was a perfect evening, Faline.*

He hadn't said 'Let's go,' mused Faline, analysing his words. Jean-Lou had left no lingering doubt as to what would happen next; the past tense 'That was' clearly meant that, for him, it was over.

Faline stood up in turn, straightening her skirt, slipping on her leather jacket, standing a few dozen centimetres away from him. He let her pass, chivalrously, making sure not to brush against her. She walked forward, assuming he was probably looking down at her buttocks, her legs and her beach-girl curves nevertheless.

She left the restaurant and lit a cigarette while Jean-Lou settled the bill at the counter. From the pavement, lit only by a streetlamp, she examined him. His trousers were a little too short, the tail of his shirt crumpled and stained. His hair was badly combed.

*Jean-Lou is the most awkward of my lovers.*

*He strokes me too hard, kisses so clumsily, comes too quickly.*

*He knows this. It makes him unhappy, I think. Sometimes it even makes him cry.*

While blowing smoke into the starry night, she calmly tried to take stock. What strategy should she adopt?

She had realised Jean-Lou wouldn't make the first move. It was up to her to be bold enough – but she sensed Jean-Lou was simply waiting for this so he could assume the role of the good guy as before, and cast her in the role of the villain. So he could admit tenderly that he found her very pretty, attractive, but that he loved his wife and son, and what's more she was the same age as his son. He would settle for a kiss on her cheek and leave with a halo around his head. Maybe he'd have a wank in his hotel room thinking about her, maybe when he got home he'd make love to his wife, his lust now heightened tenfold. A win–win situation! Fantasy with none of the hassle. A satisfied libido for the price of a Michelin-starred meal.

She took a final drag as she leant back against the brick wall, in the shadows of the alley. Her feelings were in turmoil, but it was disappointment that prevailed. Nothing to do with a bruised ego, or her powers of seduction being scorned – one random night wouldn't cast any doubt on her tried-and-tested ability to attract males with a single glance. It was a sense of failure that knotted her stomach, enough to cause violent spasms. The failure of her plan. All that for nothing? All that long, meticulous preparation, only to stop halfway?

She tossed the end of her cigarette onto the ground.

Yes, the feeling of disappointment was overwhelming her, to the point of tears, like when you screw up an exam after spending ages cramming for it . . .

And yet, a tiny flame was still burning.

A little flame of hope which had been rekindled in the darkest recesses of her mind, something she'd long since stopped believing in, as if Jean-Lou, by not allowing himself to be seduced by her, was saving not only his own life, but that of all the other men too.

She crushed her cigarette butt with her ballerina while forcing herself to imagine less noble explanations. Jean-Lou had another mistress waiting for him in his room at the Radisson Blu. Or suffered from a sexual dysfunction. Or preferred men . . . Tough, she had to go for broke. Take his hand, catch a corner of his lips during their farewell peck on the cheek. To what end? Even if she did manage to wrestle a kiss from him, the road ahead was too long to bother dragging him to the Red Corner. Tonight, at least.

Lost in her thoughts, she didn't see Jean-Lou leaving Gagnaire's.

She didn't hear him approaching.

She only sensed his shadow; they were alone in the dark street.

Jean-Lou didn't utter a word. Didn't give her time to attempt the slightest move. He merely checked no one could see them, and then, with all his weight, pressed himself against her. His mouth swallowed hers. He placed his right hand on her breast and squeezed it with almost bestial fervour. His left hand slid up her bare thigh, barely pausing against her skirt, and slipped straight under her G-string.

She let him do it. She returned his kiss. She undulated her body and opened her thighs a little so Jean-Lou's finger could worm its way inside.

She was reassured. She had won.

Jean-Lou deserved to die. Like the others.

# 35

Gérard Couturier jumped out of bed, exasperated.

At first, he'd thought a neighbour had tuned in to France Ô or RFO, or to France Culture who'd apparently lost the plot and were now broadcasting African jazz. But no, he'd had to face facts, the music wasn't coming from the room next door. The guitars and the tom-tom could be heard as loudly as if a neighbour were banging on the walls, but the sounds were coming from further away.

Gérard ventured into the corridor.

The blaring music seemed to be coming from the far end of the corridor, and more specifically from the breakfast room. Guitars were competing on the high notes with the voice of a girl singing in a language he didn't understand. Accompanied by shouts, and the sound of people dancing and clapping.

A concert?

A concert at nearly midnight? In the foyer of the Heron Port-de-Bouc?

Gérard Couturier couldn't believe his ears.

The girl was singing rather well, incidentally, but that wasn't the point. He yawned. He scratched his belly under his T-shirt, a lawn-green shirt in the brand colours of his garden centre franchise. His sales director was expecting him the next day at 8 a.m., and the figures weren't looking good. 30 per cent down on lawnmowers. Global warming, drought, scorched grass right across the south of France, grass taking longer to grow, a vicious circle . . . He felt as devastated as Ugolin when his spring dries up in *Manon des Sources*.

He paused to put on his shoes. Less than a minute later, he found himself in front of the fire door of the breakfast room. Locked. He knocked. He was tired. After a few seconds, Ruben Liberos, the hotel manager, appeared.

Gérard drew his gun first.

'What's all the bloody noise?'

The manager stared at him, wide-eyed.

'"The bloody noise?" This concert? A bloody noise? Pray enter, my friend, enter . . . These are The Whendos, the best big band on the African continent. I met them in 1994, when they played at the inauguration of my dear friend Nelson Mandela. Sharing twenty-seven years in a cell on Robben Island certainly creates some bonds! The Whendos are great friends of France. When Mitterrand gave his speech about Africa at La Baule in 1990, they were the ones who sang 'La Marseillaise'. They say Jacques Chirac's asked them to play at his funeral, it's written in his will . . .'

Gérard looked at him, dumbstruck. He was about to yell 'You're fucking taking the piss!' when the door opened again. The lawn-mower salesman had just enough time to see a guy with dreadlocks playing a guitar, a giant leaning over a djembe, and at least thirty people in the room!

A girl came out. Tall. Slim. Lots of make-up. Short skirt and leather jacket. Gorgeous. Gérard was immediately convinced it was the singer. There was no voice accompanying the music any more.

'You off already, Noura?' said Ruben.

'They're waiting for me. I won't be here before 9 a.m. tomorrow. I hope your old lady does a good job.'

She kissed him on the cheek and disappeared.

The manager opened the door wide.

'Pray enter, my friend, I beg of you.'

Gérard Couturier hesitated. He wasn't a huge fan of jazz, let alone African music. But he'd had time to eye up the demijohns of flavoured rum, lined up where the bowls of cornflakes would normally be.

Another guy was blocking his view. A giant who greeted him with a friendly pat on the back.

'Come, have a drink with us, brother. I'm Savorgnan. Have you got kids?'

Gérard nodded, feeling more and more disorientated.

'I guess you probably don't see them often, with your crazy job! Mine are arriving tomorrow. My wife Babila, my son Keyvann and my daughter Safy. Please, come in, let's celebrate.'

The music began again, even louder than before. Another girl, just as beautiful as the first, had stepped up to the mike. Well, he'd already pissed off Karl, his sales director, in any case. He wouldn't sell any fewer lawnmowers if he had a little drink before going back to bed. Tomorrow, he would leave a five-star review on Tripadvisor. He had done the rounds of half the Heron hotels in Europe, and never known such a welcome.

# 36

The guy was snoring on the bed above, causing a fine shower of dust to fall onto the one below.

Alpha consulted his watch, waited a few more minutes, then stood up. His chest was level with the upper mattress. He shook his cellmate. The man woke up in a panic, as if the prison wall had just collapsed onto him.

He stared, wide-eyed with amazement, at the figure of the black giant staring back at him, a kid who could barely have been eighteen.

'What the hell are you up to?' demanded the prisoner.

In the absence of weapons of any kind, his eyes seemed to be armed with poison.

'I need you,' said Alpha.

The man on top frowned, as if he were capable of turning his optic nerve into a blowpipe.

'Fucking hell . . . You frigging crazy or what? You wake me up for that? We'll soon teach you the rules, young lad. Bad enough being bored shitless all day, but then if you can't sleep at night because some arsehole . . .'

The guy looked a bit like Danny DeVito, the American actor. A short, highly strung guy with a round face and hair that only grew on the sides of his head, as if it were sprouting more from his ears than his skull.

Alpha spoke in a calm voice. Controlled.

'I need to see the Moneyman.'

DeVito rubbed his temples. It electrified his hair into a white crest.

'The Moneyman? Oh, is that all, kid? Well, hope you've paid top dollar, then. You'd better have gone and killed a cop, or chopped up your girlfriend with a machete, cos you need to join the queue, OK, to see the Moneyman. It can take years.'

'I'm getting out tomorrow. I need to see him before that. Tomorrow morning. Early.'

'Fancy an autograph from Ted Bundy while you're at it? And a threesome with Bonnie and Clyde?'

Alpha suddenly leant forward and, with one hand, grabbed the collar of DeVito's pyjamas. He lifted him up with the strength of his arm alone, and tightened the fabric around his cellmate's neck, causing the sheets to slide down, revealing DeVito's fat belly.

'Don't you get it? I've got a deal to offer the Moneyman! Got myself banged up just to meet him. Don't ask me why, but I knew the cops would give me some extra-special treatment. So you're gonna do what it takes to get me standing right next to him, when we go to stretch our legs tomorrow morning.'

Alpha released his grip. DeVito coughed, straightened his pyjamas, then yawned.

'You're fucking boring me stiff with your crap. If you think I'm gonna mess with the Moneyman over your bullshit—'

Alpha had to restrain himself from simply grabbing the man's neck. From squeezing harder until his round head turned scarlet. This guy would probably promise him just about anything, but then seek revenge via some third-party prisoner as soon as Alpha's back was turned. Better to appear diplomatic.

'Listen, wise guy. I've come to offer the Moneyman the deal of the century. If you don't play the go-between, if everything screws up cos of you and the Moneyman finds out, you're the one who's gonna cop it. D'you know what happened to Hitler's generals, the ones who didn't dare wake him up when the Americans were landing in Normandy? He had 'em shot! A hundred and eighteen generals. Maybe even had their heads cut off – historians don't all agree on that.'

Alpha had pulled out all the stops, but it didn't seem to have impressed DeVito.

'Never heard of your guy, this Hitler. Let alone this American dope you're saying came through Normandy.'

He'd only stumbled on the thickest inmate in the whole prison!

Alpha simply placed both hands on DeVito's arms. Almost at shoulder level. His fingers slipped easily around his skinny limbs. He debated whether to shake him, but settled for holding him a few centimetres away from his face before trying out a new tall tale.

'I'm gonna try and make you see how high the stakes are. Let's try something different. You do know that in Japan, less than a year ago, an engineer sent a file to Sony about developing a new game called Pokémon Go? The secretary didn't pass it on, the file got lost, no one thought to inform the boss, and the guy went off to knock at Nintendo's door. Sony lost three hundred billion yen in one go, and around a hundred employees committed hara-kiri.'

Apparently, DeVito was more afraid of Pokémons seeking revenge than retaliation by the Waffen-SS. Alpha slowly loosened his vice-like grip imprisoning both arms.

'You're a pain in the fucking arse, kid! Anyhow, it's none of my business. OK, I'll make sure you can talk to the Moneyman. Now time for beddy-byes – you're gonna pull up my sheet, tuck me in gently, kiss Papa's forehead and go back to sleep.'

# 37

'Hello? That you, boss? You're not sleeping?' answered Julo, surprised.

Petar's voice growled down the phone.

'Listen sunshine, I take work home with me too, you know! I had to get up from the old marital bed – I've got a question going round and round in my head.'

'Just the one? You're in luck, boss!'

'Hey, don't you be cheeky, kiddo. Never after midnight. Especially since you're the one who put the doubt in my mind.'

'What, with my academic? The one who's giving us a talk on cowries at the mosque tomorrow morning?'

'No, with your Maal family. Like you, I don't really believe in coincidences, and bumping into two Bambis in the same forest, that's one too many!'

Julo thought back to his conversation with his boss, shortly after Alpha Maal had gone off to prison. *Bambi13. Bamby Maal.* Finally, the commandant had reacted.

'I'm sorry for giving you insomnia.'

'So you should be! I'm having a lie-in tomorrow, believe me. Nadège won't like me leaving her all alone both morning and evening. You're not the first one I've called since the start of the evening – I thought I'd have it all sorted in a quarter of an hour and I pestered a few friends who're experts in IT, but there's no trace of this Bamby Maal online. No photos of her in circulation.'

'I know, I've already looked, boss.'

Julo immediately regretted his insolence, but Petar didn't react. He fell silent. Julo imagined the commandant was scratching his head, or his fat belly under his pyjamas, or his groin if he wasn't wearing any.

'Any more ideas, brainbox?' said Velika finally.

Julo answered in a flash, as if he'd been anticipating the question.

'We'll ask her mother in the morning. We've got Leyli Maal's address in the file. We just need to pull her in, and ask her to bring all the family photo albums.'

The commandant let an even longer silence slip by.

'You being serious? Did you read the file properly?'

'Yes, why?'

'Don't you see a slight impossibility?'

'Nothing insurmountable, boss! We represent the Ministry of the Interior, right? We can pull a few strings . . . Where there's a will!'

'Easy to say, kid, but it still means one hell of a tightrope act. A fucking top-notch plan, no hiccups . . . Can you see me explaining this to Serious Crime HQ?'

'You've got all night to think about it and find a way to convince them. I trust you, Commandant.'

Petar Velika's voice was now lagging slightly – more muffled, as if he'd just been hit directly in the face with a pillow full of shit.

'Mmm yeah . . . Well, give or take our Bambi homonyms, and I don't need to spell this out to you, there's a strong chance we might have to do without a one-to-one with Leyli. To convince HQ, we'd need at least another murder or two.'

'No risk of that, boss. Sergeant Taleb's keeping watch at the entrance to the Red Corner, isn't he?'

'Yeah, you're right!'

# 38

**12.47 a.m.**

Jean-Lou had never been inside a Red Corner. He'd only heard about them, like everyone else. Sitting in the taxi, he'd found the idea of setting up a supposedly romantic hideaway in the heart of a retail park particularly absurd – wedged between a garden centre, a DIY store and a Carrefour, and surrounded by a ring road, with nothing but huge concrete car parks forming a horizon and a series of red traffic lights, like a cluster of rising suns.

He had nevertheless followed Faline, like a couple of regular customers; he'd allowed himself to be led by the hand, his hand clasped in hers, had crossed the deserted automated bar in silence, climbed the dimmed staircase, slotted his business credit card into the electronic payment terminal for the Caravanserai room, then let Faline in.

Time had stood still.

Subtle Berber music greeted them. He stepped forward, sinking into straw-yellow carpet, its pile so thick he imagined he was already being sucked into quicksand. The room had no visible walls, no more than it had any ceiling. They were entering a tent, a vast *caravanier*'s pavilion, skilfully erected to fit precisely into the room and mould itself to its shape, leaving only a few gaps so you could feast on a starry *trompe-l'oeil* sky, distant dunes painted on the walls, an oasis, a clever interplay of mirrors producing endless reflections of the rugs underfoot, soft cushions, silks. Two fake torches blazed at the entrance to the tent, in front of canvas curtains which were swept back by two golden ropes.

A setting from *The Thousand and One Nights*.

A thousand nights for fantasies, thought Jean-Lou. And only one to fulfil them.

In a discreet wardrobe, clothes and accessories were provided for guests. Robes, veils, masks, turbans, belts, fans. Jean-Lou had stretched out on the cushions, feeling no urge to dress up as an Arabian prince. Faline hadn't pressured him to do so, but she'd been determined to enter into the spirit herself. She had locked herself in the bathroom for a few minutes, only to emerge . . . cocooned from head to toe. One long continuous turban, mauve with crimson and gold highlights, which began by covering Faline's face, revealing only the deep red of her mouth and the black of her eyes, then her neck and shoulders, and corseted her chest and waist before binding her legs together in a mermaid's tail, down to her bare ankles.

A mummified princess. Who was simply waiting for him to bring her back to life.

Jean-Lou closed his eyes for a few seconds, as if to check he wasn't dreaming. Everything was getting muddled up in his head. He had lost control. On leaving Gagnaire's, he had sworn to himself that this evening would be limited to a kiss, a tender farewell kiss, before dashing off. His tongue had slipped away from him, his hands too, Faline had done nothing to stop it. A single 'No' would have been enough to chase away the serpent lurking in his brain, he was convinced of that, the serpent whispering softly in his ear, filling him with the desire to know the taste of this girl's mouth, sense the weight of her breasts in the palm of his hand, feel the moistness of her vagina with the tips of his fingers.

And stop there.

With microscopic steps, like a tottering bowling pin, the mummy was moving towards him.

Jean-Lou cursed himself. He cursed this weakness in men. He cursed that bastard God and his army of creator-engineer-angels, who'd programmed men to unfailingly get a hard-on in front of a voluptuous girl, who'd injected this virus into their skulls, capable of sweeping away in a minute the defences that education and morality had taken a lifetime to construct.

Of course things hadn't stopped there.

He'd suggested that Faline follow him to his room at the Radisson Blu, but she'd had another idea.

A better idea.

Using her right arm, the only part of her body not mummified, Faline gently untied the turban wrapped around her head. Her hair cascaded in a shower of silk as the fabric she was unrolling freed her chin, her neck, her shoulders . . .

'Spin me around,' she whispered.

He grabbed the end of the turban she was holding out to him. He had understood. It was his job to strip her by tugging on the purplish cloth. This stunning girl would twirl around for him, like a shameless spinning top, until the other end of the long piece of fabric fell away and she was completely naked. He pulled on the material – gently, then more firmly. The angelic figure did not turn. The game wasn't exciting enough for her as it was; she wanted to spice things up even more. With a deft hand, she grabbed Jean-Lou's right wrist and, using the turban, tied it to one of the bars supporting the tent.

'See? This means we're both tied up. Together.'

Faline pressed the end of the turban into Jean-Lou's palm, so his tied hand could still unravel the cloth with a simple movement of his fingers. She stood up straight and, like a whirling dervish, began to revolve with each centimetre of turban released by Jean-Lou, as if guided by his endless silken arm. Hidden outside the tent, loudspeakers were playing Middle Eastern-ish music, whose beat became steadily faster and faster. A set playlist, thought Jean-Lou, whose rhythm was programmed to suit the presumed tempo of the lovers' throes of passion. His head was spinning faster than Faline's waist.

*Blandine won't know anything.* These words were pounding against the walls of his skull as his fingers continued to grip the fabric, like a drowning man at the bottom of a well clutching the rope, a rope that kept slipping away. So he pulled, and pulled, thinking of nothing else.

Faline's turban unravelled, revealing the top of her breasts.

Flattened under the tight cloth, every centimetre gained by Jean-Lou helped to liberate them. With indescribable emotion, he watched them being born under the looser fabric – hatching out, as it were, two lighter-coloured chicks sitting on a honey-coloured nest, shy to begin with, becoming rounder, filling out with each new rotation.

Blandine won't know anything. This thought was to override all the others.

Faline's belly was already half free, as flat when it was bare as when corseted, a dark plain brushing against the abyss of her navel, when the angel leant towards Jean-Lou again.

'You're still holding me, but you can't escape.'

She seized a metre of the turban that rippled across the rug, like the discarded skin of some long reptile, and used it to bind Jean-Lou's left wrist to a second bar of the tent, still letting the material run into the palm of his hand.

'Keep going, my little prince, I want to keep dancing for you.'

With his fingertips, with difficulty, awkwardly, Jean-Lou carried on. He could barely tug at the long band of cloth any more, but it didn't matter: as the sound of the violins grew louder and louder, Faline turned, deliberately slowly, the loose turban clung for a moment to her hips, whose curves seemed to have been designed to hold the silk belt in place, before it slipped down. The mauve fabric now only encircled the upper edge of her pubic mound, and was already peeling away from the rounded cheeks of her buttocks.

Jean-Lou had never been so excited, and yet he couldn't shake off his sense of guilt.

Blandine will know, Blandine will guess.

The guilty conscience that was ruining everything, that would worm its way in even when he was making love to this gorgeous creature. His squeaky-clean double, which would detach itself from his body in order to project – like a hologram – the image of Blandine alone in her bed, in love, trusting, watching over Jonathan, blurring the enchanting images swirling before his eyes. Perhaps, for the rest of his life, he'd never be able to love Blandine without thinking back to this night?

Imperceptibly, Faline had moved back. The mauve turban, in her hand, had tightened again.

Or maybe it would be the other way round, Jean-Lou forced himself to think, imagining smothering his virtuous double under a velvet cushion, he would drag this guilt around until tomorrow, until he woke up, because it was basically just a fear of being caught. Then, as soon as he'd called Blandine and Jonathan, tomorrow morning, the sky would clear up again and all that would remain of this night would be a magical interlude. The most beautiful tree in his secret garden.

At that precise moment, the two curtains framing the entrance to the tent, like twin sentries, swished together. In the seconds that followed, Jean-Lou could only make out the glow of the two torches behind the canvas, a shadow, several shadows perhaps. Then, as suddenly as the curtains had closed, the flames of the torches were blown out.

Pitch black.

'Faline? Faline? You there?'

No answer. A new game? A trap? Did they want to hurt him? Were they going to film him, photograph him, in order to destroy his family? Who? Why? It didn't make any sense.

'Faline? Faline?'

Thoughts raced through his mind. He tried pulling on the turban, but his wrists were firmly tied.

Who could hold a grudge against him? He had never cheated on Blandine. Not for twenty years at least, not since leaving Vogelzug, not since Jonathan was born. Before Jonathan, he'd made do with seeing a few prostitutes on the other side of the Mediterranean, whenever he was away for several weeks. That was all so far back.

Jean-Lou tugged frantically at the bonds securing him to the bars.

*I thought Jean-Lou could help me.*

*He knew, without us even talking about it, he'd realised a baby was sleeping in my belly.*

*He'd had doubts, of course. Perhaps he would have been ready to take responsibility? To love us? At least out of pity?*

*I believed him for a few weeks, before his wife, his real wife, became pregnant. With a disabled child.*

*Then, like the others, with even more cowardice than the others, he abandoned me. He abandoned us. Me and my baby.*

Jean-Lou couldn't tell how much time had elapsed. He could only detect a shadow moving towards him in the dark, a creature that could see at night – an owl, a cat, a bat. He had managed, by contorting himself, to loosen his tourniquets a little. Not to the point of freeing himself completely, but he could move one wrist a few centimetres, turn around. He waited. On the alert.

The creature was right next to him.

It pricked him in the arm.

Abruptly. Violently. Jean-Lou's survival instinct kicked in. He pulled with all his strength on his bonds, stretched his neck to free it and, unable to see, bit the hand that was holding the needle in his forearm.

He heard a scream, and he screamed too as the hand recoiled immediately, yanking the needle out. The sound of breaking glass was added to the commotion. Jean-Lou immediately thought of the glass pendant he had given Faline.

Faline?

His mind pictured the last images recorded by his eyes, behind the canvas of the tent, before the torches had gone out. He had thought he could make out two shadows, but perhaps that was only due to the illusion created by a double source of light. His assailant could only be Faline, but his brain refused to believe it. A stranger might have got into the room. A jealous lover. Someone who might have attacked Faline, then turned on him.

He waited some more. He tried hard to count the seconds in his head, and estimated six minutes had passed since he'd repelled his assailant – the taste of blood was beginning to fade in his mouth.

He felt the pain first in his right wrist, then in his left a second later. The blood was no longer running down his throat. It was running down his arms.

His blood.

His killer had approached silently this time. A shadow in the night, a sharp knife, a razor blade perhaps, both his wrists slashed.

'Faline? Faline, I'm begging you.'

No one answered. A few minutes later, he heard the door to the Red Corner's Caravanserai room opening, then closing again.

It was over.

He was going to die here.

Some repentant lovers confess on their deathbeds to double lives, triple lives, lives spent lying without ever being caught. He would be sentenced to death for his very first mistake. How ironic.

They were going to find him in that room in the small hours, some cleaning lady no doubt, or the next pair of guests. They would find his phone in his pocket, they would inform Blandine; she wouldn't believe it, neither his death, nor the circumstances of the crime scene, nor his infidelity.

They will puzzle over what happened, they will go to his room at the Radisson Blu to look for clues, they will rummage through his suitcases. They will find a small plane, a model of the A380. They will return his things to Blandine, who will give the plane to Jonathan, explaining that Papa has gone to heaven.

Jonathan will not be sad. When he sees the plane, his face will break into his big innocent smile; his last thought will be that his father is nice, that he always brings him surprises when he's been away. Then he will dash into the garden, lifting his plane high in the air and imitating the sound of the engine with his mouth, he will look skywards in search of Papa, to say 'Thank you'.

Then, very quickly, he will forget him.

# The Day of Wind

# 39

The Moneyman looked like Ben Kingsley.

An elongated bald head, small round glasses, a beaming, tooth-filled smile, like the keys on a piano, and wrinkles etched into his forehead, as fine as lines on a balance sheet. Indeed, it seemed to Alpha that all the guys banged up in the prison looked like Hollywood actors. He'd seen Bruce Willis coming out of the bogs, an old De Niro babbling to himself in a corner of the yard, a Robert Downey Jr. and a Hugh Jackman taking advantage of the morning walk to do some sit-ups.

Ben the Moneyman approached him, following close on his heels, walking practically side by side for a few metres along the prison wall, sheltered from the wind. He simply uttered three little words, without even looking at Alpha.

'I'm all ears.'

Alpha took a deep breath before launching into his spiel. He had to weigh his words carefully. He knew that the Moneyman, like him, had deliberately allowed himself to be locked up in prison – a few hours for Alpha, a few years for the Moneyman. Because you really need a guy on the inside to manage the business, just as multinationals need to send executives deep into Manchuria, or to Arlit in the heart of the Sahara. Some, like the Moneyman, accept, because it's temporary and well paid. Alpha set out his plan in a few words and, crucially, gave him the passwords to retrieve the file stored on Dropbox. There they would find all the details – a financial breakdown, the contacts, the deadlines. Everything was well-planned, everything was sorted and straightforward. Alpha went on to emphasise the profits, the colossal profits to be made, but they had to act quickly.

Unlike DeVito, Ben the Moneyman showed an immediate interest. He flashed him his banker's smile. They had practically shaken hands.

'I'll pass it on. We'll take a good look.'

Alpha decided to make the most of the opportunity.

'You really need to get a move on. The boat won't be available for long.'

A moment later, he regretted it. Ben was already walking away. The interview hadn't even lasted a minute. The Moneyman insisted on having the last word.

'We're not in the habit of letting things drag on. News travels fast with us. It's already gone higher up. Everything will be sorted this morning.'

# 40

*Thank you.*

These simple words, barely uttered, scarcely a whisper, one last breath, repeated themselves endlessly in Jourdain Blanc-Martin's subconscious. When he had turned on his computer at precisely 7 a.m., instead of the usual photo of the historic schooner *Marité* just off the Port-de-Bouc peninsula, his mother's face had appeared as the background. He had taken a few seconds to process this, before remembering he'd pre-programmed it several months earlier, so as not to forget the date.

Ten years earlier, to the day, his mother had fallen asleep in his arms, in the imposing bed of her house in Sausset-les-Pins, on Avenue de la Côte-Bleue, facing the Frioul Islands. Peacefully. Serenely, like a little star that fades in the morning to make way for the light. Perhaps happier than she had ever been.

*Thank you*, she had whispered to him before closing her eyes to let the darkness in.

*Thank you, Jordy.*

Those were his mother's last three words, reflected Blanc-Martin. It was also the last time a human being had called him by his real name.

*Jordy.*

Ever since his mother passed away, everyone called him Jourdain. His six hundred employees, the fifteen members of the board of directors, his three sons, his wife.

221

Blanc-Martin sent his instructions back to his secretary for the third time. Don't forget to send a wreath to Saint-Roch cemetery, and another to the mass due to be held at 11 a.m. at the Église Saint-Cézaire.

No matter how much he trawled through the deepest recesses of his memory, he retained only a few hazy impressions of his childhood with his mother. A few images and sounds from when he took part in demonstrations, when she would drag him, knee-high to a grasshopper, along the Canebière in Marseille, a mere kid marching under the flag of the CGT trade union federation. Annette Blanc was an activist, a fighter, a passion flower like Dolores Ibárruri, swept along by the mistral of social protest. A red woman! As red as his father, Bernard Martin, was colourless. Neutral. Apolitical. Abstentionist. An activist who campaigned for nothing, a nihilist who rejected everything after the Port-de-Bouc shipyards had closed. Jordy had grown up wedged between the sea and the apartment blocks of Les Aigues Douces, gone to school at the École Victor-Hugo and the Collège Frédéric-Mistral. At the parent–teacher meetings, where only his mother would turn up, to scream and shout, he was the kid no one could ever remember. *Jordy? Jordy what? Jordy Martin? Hold on . . .* The kid whose teacher would comment on his marks, which weren't that bad, without recalling the sound of his voice.

Jourdain sat staring at the portrait of his mother for a few long seconds before finally opening the Word document. All was silent at La Lavéra. He had a little time before Safietou laid out breakfast. If he focused his mind, it would be enough to lay the foundations for the speech he was to give the following day, for the opening of the Frontex symposium at the Palais du Pharo. The European agency, in order to buy itself a pristine image, had adopted the high-risk strategy of entrusting the introduction to the conference to various organisations.

Giving him carte blanche.

Blanc-Martin wasn't about to disappoint them . . .

Yet he let himself be distracted for a few moments before typing the first words on his keyboard, a wishful glance first at the pool, then over towards the teak-wood terrace and the view of the port. Jourdain liked to compare the Port-de-Bouc harbour to the jaws of a wild beast. From the top of his villa, the illusion was mind-blowing: the end of the curved jetty formed a perfect fang, while the sheltered docks at the quays and the marina to the north, and the oil tanker to the south, protruded into the half-open bay like a set of sharp teeth. The wind had picked up this morning. He remained seated, resisting the urge to go and check whether the *Escaillon*, the *Maribor* and the other boats in the port were securely moored.

His introduction would be classic in style and try to please everyone. It would delight local organisers and reassure international guests. Jourdain would recall that incident from the summer of '47 when Port-de-Bouc had made global news headlines, when four thousand five hundred Jewish refugees, survivors of the Shoah, forcibly disembarked from the *Exodus 1947*, had been confined here by the British, on three prison ships for three weeks, in inhuman conditions which would scandalise the world.

It was, however, not this page of history that Blanc-Martin would focus on, but rather the chain of spontaneous solidarity organised by the Port-de-Boucains (his mother belonging to the most active of these groups), far removed from the endless shilly-shallying between the French and British authorities. Perhaps, moreover, he had founded Vogelzug, here, in Port-de-Bouc, in remembrance of this episode, now etched in the collective memory. He would segue from this into a moral to the story – one that was a tad dewy-eyed, but which politicians who governed via opinion polls would appreciate. Often, he would go on to maintain, taking the example of the ordinary heroism of the Port-de-Boucains, men and women who claim not to want to share their territory with migrants, or refugees, are nevertheless the first to spring to their aid when these foreigners reach out in desperation, just a few metres from their promised land. As if their openly declared racism were merely a suit of armour, put on as defence against their own generosity. A lesson in humanity to kick things off. Everyone would be thrilled, from the mayor of Port-de-Bouc to the Turkish, Cypriot and Hungarian delegates.

He smiled as he reread his initial notes, then grimaced to himself. He dithered a little over the word 'racism': he would have liked to find something more suitable when referring to the fear of refugees. He was finding it hard to concentrate. This morning, the anniversary of his mother's death was taking him back, many years into the past.

Jordy Martin.

In September 1971, he had enrolled at the faculty of law at Aix-Marseille. Sitting in his first lecture in constitutional law, Jordy hadn't recognised a single young person from Port-de-Bouc among the two hundred students. It had seemed to him that all the others came from wealthy neighbourhoods and posh *communes*, from Aix or the south of Marseille, that both his name and his background condemned him to never be one of the fifteen or so students who would emerge from the funnel five years later, armed with an international master's degree or having passed the exam to become a senior civil servant. When the professor passed around the sign-up list for tutorials, Jordy simply scribbled his first name, in barely legible writing.

Jordy became Jourdain.

On that same list, he added the two surnames of his parents, who had never married, Annette Blanc and Bernard Martin. Curiously, all you had to do was put these two banal surnames together for the new double-barrelled name to sound like that of a dynasty of landed gentry.

From the start of the academic year in 1971, and for all those he would meet from then onwards, he would be Jourdain Blanc-Martin.

Jourdain became a crusader for the rights of children, victims of war and natural disasters, and illegal migrants. He swiftly convinced himself that you could become as rich by specialising in the rights of the downtrodden as you could in corporate law. A few years later, while he was still only a master's student in human rights and humanitarian law, he founded Vogelzug.

Blanc-Martin stared one last time at an imaginary point somewhere over towards the sea, then plunged back into his screen. After this formal introduction, the delegates invited by Frontex would expect him to fiercely denounce the people smugglers, the tens of billions generated by this slave trade, the fact that thousands of people perished by drowning in the Mediterranean.

He wasn't about to play them that same old tune! They didn't need him to do that – the various tables included in the delegates' conference packs offered mind-numbing, endless permutations of these statistics. Frontex enjoyed the bizarre privilege of being charged, via the European Union, with measuring the scale of migratory problems ... and solving them too. In other words, the agency itself defined the level of risk, which was used to negotiate its budget, a figure that had increased seven-fold in ten years, so as to buy a few additional planes and helicopters. He would be very careful, however, not to attack Frontex head-on; there would be dozens of activists in the hall ready to denounce its privatisation and drift towards paramilitarism. He preferred instead to catch them off guard with this statement from Stefan Zweig, one that was impossible to refute. He'd already used it many times, and it always had the desired effect:

'And indeed, perhaps nothing more graphically illustrates the monstrous relapse the world suffered after the First World War than the restrictions on personal freedom of movement and civil rights. Before 1914 the earth belonged to the entire human race. Everyone could go where he wanted and stay there as long as he liked.'

He would then carry on, seamlessly, by reminding the audience that humanity had always lived without a passport. Mankind had only invented this bit of paper at the time of the First World War, committing itself to abolishing it as soon as peace returned. This promise was debated for a long time at the League of Nations, then at the UN, before being abandoned, for good, in the 1960s. Barely fifty or so years ago, the free movement of people across the earth – that fundamental, historic, age-old right – had simply turned into a utopia in which even the most idealistic no longer believed.

A slap in the face of received wisdom! He would then hammer home his message, pointing out that the current number of migrants on the planet had been stable for years, at around 3 per cent of the world's population, namely three times less than in the nineteenth century. A paradox in a globalised society, where everything circulates much faster and more widely than in recent centuries: money, information, energy, culture. Everything. Everything except people. Except the majority of people. Democracies were now building walls. A real epidemic, ever since 11 September 2001. Walls not to barricade themselves, but to filter. To sort and select, to pass people through a sieve, separating the desired from the undesirable. No border is more militarised, more costly, more deadly than the one between the United States and Mexico, even though tens of millions of vehicles still travel back and forth between Tijuana and San Diego every year.

Jourdain read over what he'd written, and loved it. He found himself in a lyrical mood this morning. He even wondered whether he couldn't go further, proposing the abolition of borders, pure and simple. No more borders and no more illegals. Problem solved! Frontex would no longer serve any purpose. It was a fact that had been verified everywhere, especially with the fall of the Berlin Wall and the creation of the Schengen Area: the more people were free to move around, the less they settled elsewhere.

He looked up. Only he could get away with being so provocative. With Vogelzug, he had built an empire as ambiguous as Frontex. They all lived off illegal migration – his hundreds of employees, his board of directors. His family. They lived well.

On the horizon, beyond the Pointe de Carro, he could see the inlets of the Côte Bleue, the wooded hills sheltering the Provençal farmhouse in Sausset-les-Pins he'd bought for his parents in 1995. A country villa, high up by the Corniche and the coast, where the bathroom alone was bigger than their entire apartment in Les Aigues Douces. His mother had found it difficult to accept such luxury. But her little Jordy had been so proud. Turning down this excessively lavish gift would have been like pouring scorn on his success. She had remained there alone for nine years, after the death of his father, who'd collapsed from a stroke on the pontoon where he was fishing.

With the death of his parents, little Jordy had died too.

He'd started from nothing and arrived right at the top. His eyes glided over the string of apartment blocks in Les Aigues Douces, looking onto the sea but separated from the rest of the town by a maze of cul-de-sacs. An ascent that his children would never experience, even if Geoffrey inherited the presidency of the organisation, in a few months or a few years. He sat up straight in his chair and assessed with embarrassment the height of the security gates at his villa, the height of the garden walls, identical to those at his sons' homes in Éguilles, Cabriès and Carry-le-Rouet. Born at the very top. Barricaded in, so they could remain there.

Jourdain checked his watch. He was giving himself another half an hour to make progress. He still had several areas to tackle. Controversial issues to clear up. The destabilisation of French society through the arrival of a few hundred thousand refugees? The four million Lebanese had gladly welcomed one and a half million Syrians to their micro-territory, six times more densely populated than France. A disaster for public finances? All economists agreed that taking in foreign workers was an opportunity for the economy, that they brought in far more than they cost. Already trained. Not yet retired.

Jourdain Blanc-Martin was about to debunk yet another popular myth when he was interrupted by Barber's *Adagio*. He pulled his phone from his pocket.

Petar. Petar Velika.

A sense of foreboding gripped his throat. The police commandant certainly wasn't calling him at this hour to tell him that he'd nabbed François Valioni's killer. He stood up and watched the mistral shaking the hulls of the boats in Port Renaissance.

'Blanc-Martin?'

'Speaking.'

'I'll get straight to the point. We . . . We've got another body . . . Jean-Lou Courtois. Exactly the same set-up as Valioni. Tied up. Slit the veins in his wrists. Found in a hotel room, the Red Corner again. The Caravanserai room this time, and—'

'Didn't you have men stationed out front?' said Blanc-Martin, taken aback.

'Yes, of course, we *did* have guys outside the Red Cor— Look, you're not going to believe this, but—'

'In any case,' cut in the president, who couldn't care less about the police officer's excuses, 'Jean-Lou Courtois no longer worked for Vogelzug. Hadn't done for almost twenty years. That should be reason enough for my organisation not to be mixed up in all this. I'm counting on you, Velika.'

# 41

There was a gust of wind, and the window of the Caravanserai
room at the Red Corner slammed shut. Petar Velika had insisted on
opening it: the only way, according to the commandant, to avoid
thinking he'd been magically beamed up to the desert. He remained
for a moment at the third-floor window, overlooking the ring road
and the retail park, then turned back round to face the room with
its canvas ceiling and sandy walls. Serge Tisserant, the manager of
the establishment, was standing in front of him, his tie impeccably
knotted as always. Under the kitsch Arabian-style canopy, with his
feet sunk into the shifting pile of the carpet, he looked like a colo-
nial official charged with telling the Bedouins that oil had just been
discovered in the basement and they had to clear off.

'Are Red Corner rooms really exactly the same all over the world?'
asked Petar.

Tisserant nodded.

'Show me around,' said the commandant. 'If we're dealing with
a female serial killer who's leaving us a corpse in a different corner
of the planet each morning, simply by changing room each night,
I want to be able to visualise where she's going hunting tomorrow.'

He turned to Lieutenant Julo Flores, who was sitting on an em-
broidered stool, quietly awaiting instructions from his superior.

'While I'm looking round the place, can you pull together a summary of exactly what happened?'

Julo watched in dismay as the commandant walked away. Petar

had placed his hand on the manager's shoulder and was chatting to him as if he were an estate agent.

'Now then, Serge. In the Pink Lotus room, the walls are covered in erotic Japanese prints and the drawers are full of Geisha balls, are they? And in the Carioca one, there's a whole selection of G-strings, tangas and other Brazilian underwear? Give me the full tour, my friend. Show me the works.'

Petar returned half an hour later, alone. He joined Julo in the Red Corner bar, pulled up a chair, and positioned himself facing his deputy. The lieutenant had put a bottle of water on the table, a glass in front of him.

'Well?'

Julo gave a quick summary. The information was still coming through in real time. The victim, Jean-Lou Courtois, appeared to be a father, a guy who kept a low profile, closely involved with voluntary organisations, president of a support group for parents of Down's syndrome children. His only link with François Valioni was Vogelzug – he'd worked for the organisation for nearly ten years, before handing in his notice.

Petar Velika remained stony-faced.

'As for the rest,' continued Julo, 'the murder scenario's the same as for Valioni. Forensics are sending us their first report in the morning. We're busy checking the security camera tapes to see if it's the same girl or not.'

This time, Petar's eyes lit up. He turned his head towards the entrance of the Red Corner where Sergeant Taleb had dozed off. He'd been on duty, standing outside the hotel all night. For nothing. How could they have foreseen that the killer would find a way of murdering her victim, in a Caravanserai room, without even entering through this door?

'Commandant,' said Julo, raising his voice slightly. 'The crime scene did still give us a couple of nice new leads, compared to the murder of François Valioni. Do you want the details?'

'Shoot, I'm listening.'

'Well, firstly, we found bits of broken glass on the carpet, near

Courtois's body. Forensics reckon it's a little piece of jewellery, something of no value, but they've not managed to piece it together yet.'

'OK, so they'll call us as soon as they've finished their jigsaw puzzle. And your second clue?'

'Blood. Jean-Lou Courtois managed to bite his torturer. On the hand, according to forensics. They found blood on his clothes, his lips, his incisors. Mixed with his own. We'll obviously run all that through the national DNA database, but I don't really think it'll be DNA that leads us to her.'

'Oh yeah? So what are you banking on, smarty-pants?'

'Her blood group. It took less than five minutes to find out what it was.'

'And?'

'AB. One of the rarest. It runs through the veins of only 4 per cent of the world's population.'

'Brilliant . . . That leaves just a few million suspects.'

Lieutenant Flores looked at his watch, emptied his glass, took the bottle, then began to get up.

'I don't want to rush you, boss, but we've got an appointment in fifteen minutes at the Al Islah Centre. Sorry, I won't have a chance to go and get your coffee from Starbucks this time.'

'Shit,' said the commandant. 'How will I manage to get through the day without my Kati Kati from Ethiopia?'

Julo stood up with a smile. Commandant Velika trailed reluctantly behind him, clearly not thrilled about going to meet an expert on ancient Africa, let alone not being the one to decide where they would meet. Seriously, even academics were now starting to act all showbizzy, like stars in demand . . . As they walked along the pavement towards the Renault Safrane, Julo took advantage of the silence to deliver one last piece of information.

'We've already had a chance to check out Jean-Lou Courtois's phone. The procedure for making contact was the same as for Valioni. He engaged in a long conversation with his presumed killer on Facebook, over several months, using private messaging. She's the one who went looking for him.'

'Not using the nickname Bambi13, though?'

'No. This time she called herself Faline95.'

'Ninety-five? The Val-d'Oise *département*? Not exactly next door to Marseille.'

'Unless ninety-five doesn't refer to the number for a *département*, but her year of birth. Twenty-one years old, that fits.'

Petar stopped in front of the metallic-blue Safrane.

'Fits what? How can you be sure this Faline95 is the same girl as your little darling, Bambi13?'

Julo stopped in turn, in front of the car, on the passenger side, and stared at his superior.

'Do you know who Faline is, Commandant?'

'No idea . . . A singer?'

'A doe, boss.'

Velika gave Julo a strange look, and repeated as if he'd misheard: 'A doe?'

'As in deer. Faline is Bambi's sweetheart.'

'Fuck . . .'

The commandant stood still for a moment in front of the police car, then suddenly threw the keys at his deputy.

'Drive, Sherlock! We're pulling out all the stops. I'll call Ryan and ask him to launch an official search for Bamby Maal, to check if they've released her little brother Alpha yet, and more importantly to arrange a meeting for us with Leyli, the mother of these two little angels. This time HQ's sure to roll out the red carpet for us.'

# 42

**8.27 a.m.**

'Open your eyes, Tidiane!'

'Don't need to, Grandpa.'

When he had closed his eyelids, just after the roundabout, Tidiane had realised he didn't need to see to find his way to school. His brain had retained everything since he was little, without him even being aware of it. The sound of his footsteps on the gravel while crossing the park, the birdsong in the olive trees on Avenue Jean-Jaurès, even the smell of bread from the *boulangerie* on the corner of Avenue Pasteur. Waiting at the lights. Listening out for the cars stopping. Crossing over.

'Open your eyes, Tidiane!'

Tidiane had refused to let Grandpa Moussa hold his hand. In any case, he needed one hand to hold his football, and the other to sweep away the darkness in front of him, to feel his way. Nevertheless, he let Grandpa's hand rest on his shoulder to lead him across.

'Watch out for the pavement, darling!'

Tidiane lifted his foot. It was easy to walk in the dark if you paid attention to every sound. He could already hear the cries of children in the distance, in the playground. Now he just had to walk along the street, that was all. He could hear his grandpa walking beside him, imagining him with his arms outstretched ready to catch him, as you do when keeping a close eye on a baby's first steps.

A baby.

Tidiane didn't really want his friends to see him like that. When he reckoned he was a few dozen metres from the school gate, he finally opened his eyes again.

Bingo! He was bang outside number 12, the house with the bird-cage on the balcony.

This time, his grandfather held him back by the wrist.

'You cheeky little monkey, I should never have told you that story about the sun blinding your mother!'

'Thanks to you, Grandpa Moussa, I'll be as strong as her. I'll practise so I can smell things just like a sheepdog, see at night like a cat, move in the dark like a mouse.'

Grandpa straightened his grandson's shirt collar.

'And what would you use that for?'

'To find Maman's treasure. Then to protect it . . .'

You could hear shouting on the other side of the wall. The sound of a ball hitting the brickwork. Tidiane held on tight to his own football, wedged under his arm. He was desperate to join his friends now. Grandpa looked at him tenderly, but still without letting go.

'I was like you once, Tidiane. Like you, when I was your age. I had nothing but tales of buried treasure on the brain.'

Tidiane craned his neck upwards, intrigued.

'You too? Your mother had a treasure too?'

'No, not my mother. My grandfather. A treasure no one could protect. If it hadn't been stolen from us, perhaps we'd have avoided all our misfortunes.'

Screams erupted from the playground. One of the two teams had just scored. Time to go: Tidiane couldn't help dashing towards the school gate.

Eyes wide open with wonder.

'Tell me the story tonight, Grandpa Moussa!'

# 43

Noura planted herself squarely in front of Ruben.

'So, you're doubling my wages, are you?'

The manager of the Heron stared, wide-eyed, at the young African woman. As she had previously announced, this morning she'd only turned up at 9 a.m., her face drawn, frizzy hair bristling, like a witch looking for her broom. She'd fidgeted around for a quarter of an hour, before pitching up in a rage in front of the counter.

'Whoa, my diva, what's wrong?'

Noura was a curious beast. Battery-powered. By night, she sang and danced, much to the delight of the stowaways. By day, she paced the corridors and rooms of the Heron, wearing earphones, like an electrical appliance being charged. This morning, the earphones were dangling around her neck.

'What's wrong, Ruben, is that theoretically there's two of us doing the cleaning!'

Noura was a curious beast . . . and a jealous one. She complained about having too much work at the Heron, but she'd still been unable to cope with the fact he'd hired Leyli, let alone the fact that this newcomer had more experience, and her work was better. Leyli was more energetic, sharper, more efficient. And to cap it all, she was pretty and cheerful, the kind of person who could warm men's hearts without even appearing to be doing so. A solar being.

'My sweet child, Leyli's been on duty since 6 a.m. She came on foot, an hour's walk because there was no bus that early, she had to have someone look after her little boy, she—'

'I don't give a shit about her private life. If she's here, she's working, end of story.'

Noura let out a long sigh, then, as if a *Low battery* warning were flashing in her brain, pushed her earphones firmly back in and walked away, clinging to her broom.


Ruben found Leyli sitting on the bed in room 23. She was crying. At her feet, the pile of white sheets and towels made it look as if she'd gone through kilos of tissues. Before Ruben could even utter a word, Leyli turned to face him.

'I've been summoned to Port-de-Bouc police station. This afternoon. At 4 p.m.'

'What for?'

'It's about Bamby this time. They . . . they're looking for her . . .'

'What about Alpha?'

'He's sent me a text. He's been let out. Early this morning. Earlier than expected.'

'Your daughter, Bamby. Where is she?'

The tears flowed again, first slowly down Leyli's cheeks, then suddenly falling in beads onto her blue plastic apron and melting away on her thighs. Ruben didn't ask his question again, simply adding:

'If your daughter's in trouble, I can help her.'

Leyli had shown him photos of her children. Bamby was pretty, as pretty as Noura: a slender figure, a body sculpted for dancing, her curvaceous hips designed for swaying, a copper-coloured neck for a rich bass voice, peach lips as soft as velvet.

Ruben sat down beside Leyli.

'The summons is in six hours. We've got plenty of time . . . Would you like a coffee?'

Leyli nodded.

'I brought it back from the island of Halmahera, in Indonesia. Three cartloads, which the separatists presented to me after I'd given shelter to their leader, Johan Teterissa, for thirty-six months, all in the utmost secrecy. He was being hunted by all the militias in Jakarta.'

Leyli smiled. Ruben got up to fetch the Moluccan nectar from his office.

'When I come back,' he said, turning to Leyli, 'you can continue your story. Your life's far more interesting than mine.'

Leyli didn't answer, but her silence implied she wasn't convinced. Ruben looked her straight in the eye, unable to hide a tinge of wistfulness.

'At least you're not making it up.'

## LEYLI'S STORY

### Chapter Six

I landed in Tangier in September 1994. Nadia had put me in touch with Caritas Morocco, a charity that took care of pregnant women. Many sub-Saharan migrant women became pregnant even before boarding a boat for Europe. Most of them as a result of being raped, while others, on the contrary, had contrived to have sex while they were ovulating. Being pregnant was the best way to ensure men wouldn't touch them for nine months. Another advantage was that when illegal migrant ghettos were demolished by the Moroccan or Algerian authorities, social services took charge of these women as a priority, thereby avoiding body searches, beatings and yet more rapes in the prisons at the desert border posts. There was a long queue at Caritas for single mothers-to-be, but the blind, like amputees, were fortunate enough to be given precedence.

I told my story, only stopping short of revealing what was in the Adidas bag which never left my side. It contained money, lots of money, my money. But not just that. The rest, the share of the loot that belonged to Adil and which I took with me, I will never tell anyone about, not even you, Ruben. I will only say that it was as impossible for me to spend it as it was to get rid of it. That's just how it is, Ruben. There's no such thing as a treasure without a curse.

Like some woman possessed, I kept telling the nurses at Caritas that

I wanted to have a corneal operation. A transplant. I had the money. I told them my family had saved up for it. I think Caritas did some digging to verify my story. I then learnt that Adil Zairi was not the lover I thought he was. He was well known to migrant networks, and was playing a double game with his refugee aid organisation, topping up his income by smuggling illegal migrants. Other girls had ended up in his arms — all had finished up as prostitutes, then been rejected, but none had stayed as long as I had. Maybe because he'd loved me more than the others? Maybe because I'd taken longer to see the obvious? No one knew what had become of him. Whether he had survived, or whether traffickers had dumped his body into the harbour in Sousse.

I couldn't have cared less. I had only one obsession. Regaining my sight before I gave birth. *Seeing my baby being born.* I pleaded with the surgeon who was to carry out the corneal transplant. He was a guy with a brittle, high-pitched voice, like a pampered little dog. I cried, and cursed, but he only needed to say a few words to calm me down.

'It's too risky for the baby.'

He had talked about local anaesthetics, potential risks of rejection, infection, bleeding.

I had only remembered one thing.

*It's too risky for the baby.*

I gave birth on 27 March 1995, at the Bouregreg Clinic in Rabat. Dr Roquet agreed to operate on me four weeks later, once again in Rabat. The operation lasted just over an hour, less than forty minutes for each eye. If you only knew how much I yelled at the doctor when I found out. Not even a general anaesthetic, not even a week in hospital. Ninety thousand dirhams for two strokes of the scalpel!

Too dangerous for the baby, he had said.

I was so angry with Dr Roquet. My child had been sleeping next to me in her cot since birth, and I didn't know what she looked like. I would breastfeed her, change her, bathe her, kiss her, and the softness and scent of her skin would drive me crazy with happiness, without even knowing what colour it was.

The surgeon, however, was right. I only realised this after the operation.

The first thing I saw, when I opened my eyes, was Bamby.

I could then have closed them again for ever. That one image would have been enough for the rest of my life.

Bamby, my treasure, my beauty, my miracle. My beloved.

A few weeks later, I returned to live in Ségou, with my parents, my cousins, my neighbours. With some of the money I had left, I bought a little house near the river.

Bamby was growing. A flower of the sands. Delicate. As if her fair mixed-race skin made her more fragile than other girls and boys of her age. As if she lacked that ebony armour. Bamby was disgusted by the ochre water of the river, hated seeing her dress stained with clay, would be scared stiff whenever a camel passed by. The complete opposite of the tomboy I was at her age.

Bamby loved school straight away. Around fifty pupils were crammed into the one classroom, lessons only took place in the morning and were taught by an elderly teacher, a woman who spoke more Bambara than French. There was no other school within thirty kilometres.

Little by little, a crazy idea took seed.

To leave again. To cross over into Europe. To take my daughter there too.

I'd already made it to Europe, I had brushed up against it, in Marsala, in Marseille, in Almería. I had seen nothing of the other side of the Mediterranean, but I knew about it. In Ségou, we would receive letters and a little money from cousins who'd settled in Montreuil, near Paris. I had vague memories of them. Girls who weren't terribly smart, whom I used to play with as a child. According to their letters, they were employed at the town hall, they earned several thousand francs a month (I didn't even dare calculate what that was in CFA), went to libraries with their families, went to see movies at the cinema.

If those half-wits Nalo and Binetou had succeeded, if they were able to offer a bright future to their children, then why on earth should I give up trying too? I had managed to get through once, when I was blind. I would make it a second time, but now with my two eyes. If everything went well – and as I still had enough money left – I could leave Bamby with my parents and enter Europe in a few weeks. I would need time to find work, a job, and then I'd bring Bamby over with me. In France, she

239

would have a chance. My daughter was too fragile a flower to grow in the desert. Here, she would end up as a cactus. In France, she would be a rose, an iris, an orchid.

The more I thought about it, the more my decision seemed the obvious one.

I had to try and get through for Bamby's sake. To stay would be to abandon her. I would never have forgiven myself. It may seem strange to you, Ruben, to reason like that, to think that staying with your daughter is to abandon her. But since you've travelled so much, you probably understand only too well that I'm not alone, that there are thousands and thousands of mothers in the world who refuse to accept things as they are, in Africa and elsewhere, mothers who've felt the same sense of urgency as me, who've made the same sacrifice. Leaving their child behind, in order to give them the chance of a better life. Not even a better life. Another life, as straightforward as that. Give them a second chance at life.

The journey cost three thousand francs. Leaving from Timbuktu, crossing the Sahara, arriving in Nador, then camping in the Gourougou forest, in the hills a few kilometres from Melilla, the Spanish enclave in Morocco, facing the Mediterranean. In those days, they hadn't yet built the really high walls you have now, and there weren't as many Spanish soldiers. At least, that's what the guides told us. You couldn't get through via Ceuta or Gibraltar, but you could through Melilla. Once you entered Melilla, you were in Europe, you were saved.

My parents, believe it or not, Ruben, didn't even try and talk me out of it. They knew I was taking this risk on behalf of everyone. For the money I would send them from France. They knew that, one day, I could get them over there too.

I'd like to spare you the details of the desert crossing, Ruben – the four thousand kilometres of rough trail you travel in *boulboules*, the off-road vehicles they use instead of camels, piled up twelve deep under tarpaulins, the nights below freezing and the days above 50 degrees, the water rationing, the cans of petrol buried in the desert that you have to spend hours searching for, the endless wait in Gao, the gateway to the desert, then leaving for Kidal. The *boulboule* that breaks down and you have to continue your journey on foot across the Adrar des Ifoghas plateau. The companions you abandon because they're suffering from stomach ache or malaria. Of the thirty-five who set out, only nineteen of us made it to Tinzaouten to cross into Algeria.

Tinza, the republic of illegal migrants, the border town where sub-Saharan migrants pile up, day by day – those who've just arrived running into those being deported, dropped off in their hundreds by the Algerian police. Waiting for several days between lorries, paying yet more people smugglers, escaping from the soldiers who criss-cross the desert trails in helicopters, fleeing towards Tamanrasset, the capital of the desert. Sleeping there for a few nights under a roof, at last; changing vehicle for an older one, but registered in Algeria, negotiating at each checkpoint to leave town, paying each time, until the patrols become scarce. Then heading due north, the heart of the desert, two thousand kilometres without stopping, not even to drink, barely to relieve yourself, the drivers taking turns day and night. Four days of horror on top of the previous ones – only the strongest of men survive, Ruben, only the strongest of women, if only the French could understand that. Four days of torture, breaking our backs and our necks, falling asleep in our own filth and letting the wind carry away the stench of urine and bile, to finally reach Oujda, the gateway to Morocco.

Waiting, even longer than in Tinza. Paying money to strangers, getting ready every night, and suddenly being woken up. We leave, on foot, about fifteen of us, accompanied by corrupt soldiers, heading for Nador, to the south of Melilla, a hundred and fifty kilometres away. Six days of walking through the Rif Mountains, scared to death, terrified that our guides will shoot us in the back on the edge of a ravine, that we'll cross paths with Moroccan gendarmerie jeeps and everything will come to an end. The unbearable fatigue, the madness that drives us to survive, the insane hope that makes us delirious, until we finally reach the Gourougou forest, the small wooded mountain overlooking Melilla and the Mediterranean. The hotel for illegals, as the migrants call it. The dormitory-forest. The gateway to paradise. Europe is less than a kilometre away, just a three-metre-high wall to cross, but the refugees in the forest have days and days to prepare their attacks, to carve poles, to assemble ladders. You can't fail when you're that close. The thousands of migrants, almost all sub-Saharan, Nigerien, Ivorian, Congolese, Gabonese, are looking for a weak point. Waiting for the right moment. A determined army.

The gates of heaven, Ruben. I'm telling you the truth. But heaven is an enclave in hell.

There were women in the forest too. Fewer, far fewer than the men. I wasn't blind this time, Ruben. I saw. I saw those women walking away from the camp to wash, or simply to relieve themselves. I saw the men following them. I saw those women undressing, and the men undressing too. I saw those women letting men have their way, to avoid being beaten, letting themselves be taken by one man, then a second, a third, without condoms.

One evening in June, some other men, in turn, saw me leaving the camp. There were five of them.

I was more than a kilometre away from the first tent when they surrounded me. Like a herd of lions encircling an antelope. The first one, an Ivorian, spoke to me in French.

'We don't want to hurt you. If you let us do our business, everything will be fine.'

The other four were already undoing their trousers.

'You're lucky,' added the Ivorian. 'You could have run into guys a lot worse than us. We're gentlemen.'

He wasn't lying, Ruben. While the others already had their trousers round their ankles, he had produced a box of ten condoms from his pocket.

# 44

The *Sébastopol* was a thirty-metre-long yacht which had belonged to a Ukrainian billionaire. It had been moored in Monaco for a long time, and had been for sale ever since the businessman had chosen to invest in a Bulgarian football team instead. The purchase price was two and a half million euros, according to the advert on *plaisance. fr*. Gavril Boukine was paid seventy euros a day to pressure-wash the yacht for an hour, run the engine, polish the hull and portholes a bit, and show the yacht to prospective buyers, with a 150-euro bonus if the client wanted to go out to sea.

He was astonished when he spotted the morning visitors approaching. A gigantic black man in jeans, a stained T-shirt and a crumpled jacket, unshaven, the laces on his trainers barely tied, as if he'd just come out of the nick, accompanied by a gnome wearing a tie, pale as a ghost and with impeccably combed grey hair. Laurel and Hardy: the Black and White version.

Gavril gave them a tour of the boat. They barely entered the engine room, the cold room or the galley, and lingered for a long while in the vast space of the hold, nearly eighty square metres. The tall black man seemed to be making numerous mental calculations, craning his neck up towards the ceiling as if gauging its height, so as not to bump into it.

'Great, you can leave us now,' the black man finally said.

Gavril nodded and left, without turning a hair. He went back up on deck, while still keeping an eye on Laurel and Hardy. Not that he wanted to spy on them – he could only pick up snippets of the conversation they were having – but his instructions were clear: you don't leave clients alone on the boat until they've paid! Nevertheless, Gavril found it hard to imagine what there might be to steal in this shell, which had been stripped of all its furnishings by its owner. He clung to the rail and watched the stratocumulus clouds stretching out, until they disintegrated into long shreds which reminded him of the sails of a ghost ship. The wind was picking up, and he prayed they wouldn't ask him to take her out to sea for a short run.

❈

'Two and a half million euros is quite a considerable sum.'

'An investment,' corrected Alpha. 'A good investment.'

While his companion pondered, Alpha was mulling over the sequence of events since that morning. The Moneyman had been efficient. Alpha didn't know if he'd had anything to do with his release from prison that morning, but as soon as he'd been set free, a taxi had been waiting for him on the other side of the road. The taxi had headed for the port, and Alpha had found himself in the company of a guy who was most probably the equivalent of the Moneyman, but operating beyond the prison walls. Max-Olivier. A charming man in his fifties with greying hair, exactly the kind of banker you come across when you're doing the rounds to get a mortgage. A sympathetic guy, who listens carefully to your needs and explains the consequences of a thirty-year debt in detail. The understanding type, who won't think twice about calling you again the moment you can't pay any more and find yourself out on the streets: 'I did warn you.'

The banker cast a sceptical eye over the dusty hold and the wood-work consumed by cobwebs.

'Monsieur Maal, I've studied your finance plan in detail and, to tell you the truth, I still have my doubts.'

His voice echoed through the cavernous space, devoid of furniture and fittings. But Alpha simply raised his voice a little more.

'You know the rates as well as I do. Between three and five thousand euros per migrant to get them on those Zodiac inflatables which risk sinking at any minute, and will invariably be spotted

244

by the European coastguards. Three thousand euros multiplied by fifty passengers, all crammed in together, that's easy to work out: a hundred and fifty thousand euros per rubber dinghy, tax free, for a suicidal operation. What I'm proposing is a different economic model.'

The banker whistled through his teeth.

'Nothing major, then.'

'You know full well what I'm talking about. The migrant market's just like any other market, it fluctuates according to supply and demand. The better Frontex does its job, the fewer illegals it lets through, and the higher the prices. I'm not going to teach you to suck eggs, Max-Olivier. It's customs that create the smuggler, not the other way round. It was by banning alcohol that the United States allowed gangsters to make a fortune. No Prohibition, no Al Capone.'

Alpha was rather proud of his slogan – he'd been fine-tuning it for weeks – but it didn't seem to impress the banker.

'I know the border business, Maal. We both agree, it's a win–win scenario. Customs officers and smugglers. But what interests me is how you plan to make more money than the others?'

Alpha paused for a moment, to take a breath. The massive hull of the boat looked like a cathedral.

'I started with a really simple idea. To offer three guarantees to migrants. Safety, comfort and the maximum probability of getting through. In other words, everything traditional people smugglers can't promise. For these three guarantees, I'm sure loads of migrants would be willing to pay a lot, much more than the current market rate.'

'How much?'

'Ten thousand, fifteen thousand euros? Just imagine. We get the migrants on board, just off the African coast, at night, far from prying eyes. They go down into the hold. With a few alterations, we can set up around fifty beds here, without having to pack them in, toilets, showers, food and drink – and up on deck, in case the coastguards happen to come by, we plant a few blondes in mono-kinis, a black waiter with a tray of mojitos, and a burly skipper in a fisherman's jumper. No risk of sinking, or being boarded and searched. Once you're berthed, in just about any European marina – Ajaccio, Saint-Tropez or San Remo – you simply have to wait for nightfall, recruit a few guys to keep watch, and the migrants disappear one by one, like alley cats. No one sees, no one knows.'

'A racket like that can't remain a secret very long.'

'OK. But do the maths, Max-Olivier – fifteen thousand euros times fifty passengers, that makes a turnover of seven hundred and fifty thousand euros per trip. The yacht pays for itself in three crossings!'

'Fifteen thousand euros per passenger? You'll find migrants to pay that?'

Alpha became excited. The banker had no argument to counteract his.

'Have you read the file?' he replied, raising his voice even more. 'Have you read the declarations of intent? All these families from Mali, Côte d'Ivoire, Ghana, who're ready to take on more debt if we can guarantee them a result. I've got networks on both sides of the Mediterranean, I've got the idea, I've got the men, I've got the boat, I just need the cash.'

The banker fell silent for a long while, then lowered his voice by a notch, as if to temper Alpha's fervent enthusiasm.

'Understood, it's your idea. These are your networks. But if we fund you, you'll be our employee. A franchise, if you like. Completely independent, as long as you pay us back.'

'Don't worry,' said Alpha, a swagger in his voice. 'I won't pay you in shells!'

The banker gave him an ambiguous smile.

'I'll be frank, Maal, I'm not sure you can be trusted. You're too sure of yourself. My intuition tells me you're hiding something from us, but they've studied your file and given you the green light. Bravo! My prerogatives end here. I'll do whatever's needed to ensure you become the owner of this boat before the end of the week.'

The banker went back up on deck and chatted for a good quarter of an hour with the man charged with the *Sébastopol*'s maintenance and also with showing people round. Gavril had a drooping beard and thinning hair. He was missing two teeth, his right eye blinked continuously, and Alpha imagined he might be saving up to buy himself a wooden leg and a metal hook.

After the banker had walked away, Alpha approached the tooth-deficient skipper. He looked up at the tinted windows and sunroof of the *Sébastopol*'s cockpit.

'Now that everything's sorted, can we have a little test run?'

# 45

Seated on the terrace of Le Dar Zaki, opposite the Al Islah Centre, Petar Velika was cursing under his breath: five minutes had passed since the time for their appointment, and there was still no sign of the academic. The commandant was trying to spot which of the men wearing djellabas who were entering and leaving the Islamic centre might be carrying a satchel, or wearing glasses or even a Western suit. He couldn't work out whether the Al Islah Centre was a mosque, a school, a training centre, or all three combined.

Julo looked as if he couldn't care less, utterly absorbed by the screen of his phone. You could have beamed him up to Chinatown and he wouldn't have felt any more disorientated, and would have carried on surfing the internet – as if the world around him were nothing but virtual scenery, rolling by without concerning him in any way. To make matters worse, Ryan had just called from the office. Bamby Maal was still nowhere to be found. Her brother Alpha had been released early that morning before the counter-order arrived, and only their mother, Leyli Maal, had confirmed she would be present at Port-de-Bouc police station, at 4 p.m. That was something, at least! Ryan had done an incredible job of organising everything, convincing the ministry, Serious Crime HQ and Magistrate Madelin, who was taking charge of the case from this morning. Petar now hoped the day would unfold calmly, with no new corpses, no new witnesses being pulled out of Julo's hat, so as not to have to postpone the meeting.

Petar flicked his deputy's phone to attract his attention.

'Hello, hello, this is Mecca calling. So, what exactly do you know about this university guy, then?'

'Nothing! I've only read the articles he's published. You can tell he's the leading authority on the subject after just a few clicks—'

'Expert or not, I'm not wasting my morning waiting for him.'

Suddenly, a motorbike came into view, approaching slowly along the pavement just as Petar was getting up, and narrowly avoiding running him over. The biker cut the engine and kicked down the stand as he removed his helmet. A sporty-looking man in his thirties, with a beaming smile, he held out his hand while ruffling his long black hair.

'Mohamed Toufik. Sorry for being late – I was giving a tutorial at the university this morning. And at 11 a.m., I'm teaching again, with a class on pre-Islamic Arabic literature.'

Petar stared at Toufik, astounded. Not a hint of stubble on his chin. A huge diamond in his right ear. He couldn't have been more astonished if he'd noticed traces of mascara around his eyes.

'So you're the top cowrie specialist, are you?' said the commandant, with more than a hint of sarcasm.

'I'm only a PhD student. I'm in my third year, but nowadays, if you don't publish five articles a year and haven't written a book in English, another in French and a third in Arabic before defending your thesis, you've got no chance of getting a job.'

He burst out laughing. Dazzling white teeth. Eyes like Omar Sharif. A face just begging to be slapped.

'If you're in a hurry, that suits us fine – we're in a rush too. Let's get on with it. Tell us all about these famous cowries, will you.'

Mohamed Toufik realised he wouldn't have time to order a tea, smoke a cigarette or simply ask why these two cops wanted to question him. Julo, as a sign of appeasement, placed some shells on the table, identical to those found in François Valioni's pocket. Mohamed looked in turn at Petar, Julo and the shells, and then launched into a long monologue. Brilliant, precise, informative. Even Petar Velika soon forgot about the cries of the muezzin and the conversations in Arabic around him.

'Cowries are distinctive-looking shells that come almost exclusively from the Maldives, which makes them both rare and easily recognisable. These shells were used very early on as an instrument of trade between different peoples – to give you some idea, let's say from 1000 BC. You could think of them as the oldest currency in the world. Since we're in a hurry, apologies, I'm going to skip two thousand years of history and go straight to the year 1000. This was the beginning of international trade, particularly between West Africa and Asia, via Arab traders. The cowrie became the main currency used for barter between the continents. Unforgeable, easily transportable, easily weighed. The ideal currency. It developed even further during the slave trade – it's said that tens of billions of shells were transported by the Dutch, the French, the British, as bracelets, as necklaces, in baskets of more than ten thousand cowries!

'During colonisation, Europeans gradually adopted the national currency systems we know today, but cowries remained extremely popular in West Africa. As well as being the main currency of barter, they became a symbol of fertility, were used in divination and adorned clothing and ritual masks. Over time, Europeans came to see cowries as a symbol of resistance to colonisation. And then, unexpectedly, between 1890 and 1900, the French, British and Portuguese agreed to ban them altogether, as straightforward as that. Because of one simple law, cowrie shells became worthless, virtually overnight! A bloody drastic way of imposing a new social order, don't you think? A whole society collapsed. Everyone was affected equally – from the poorest, who used to be able to pay small sums with just a few cowries, to the richest, who'd spent a lifetime accumulating wealth and social prestige by hoarding tons of shells. Vendors, traders and craftsmen, previously accustomed to weighing and counting thousands of cowries in bags, vases and jars, felt lost and disorientated in the new currencies. From then on, taxes, duties and fines had to be paid in francs, pounds or reals. European capitalism managed to prevail.'

'Is there nothing left of the cowrie system today?' asked Julo.

Before replying, Toufik looked over at two girls entering the Al Islah Centre like two Islamic Marilyn Monroes, their headscarves and djellabas billowing up in the wind gusting across the esplanade.

'No. They've had no monetary value for a century. But resistance to the international market has organised itself differently. The principle of an unofficial currency has never been as topical as it is now.'

This time, it was Petar who was the first to react.

'Can you explain?'

'Well, with global migration, diasporas scattered across the world and financial exchanges between communities, informal methods of transfer can be found everywhere: the hawala in the Arab world, the hundi in India, the padala in the Philippines . . . Systems for exchanging capital without the physical circulation of money, without going through official banks, and with much lower withdrawal rates into the bargain. These transfers are said to account for almost 50 per cent of monetary exchanges across the globe, which therefore escape any form of check . . . The whole system rests on trust between brokers and intermediaries, honour and ethnic solidarity. No legal basis at all! Like cowries, these are the modern avatars of age-old practices, to avoid the risk of transporting gold by road or to markets across Africa or Asia.'

'I'm sorry,' said Petar, 'I must be as crap at economics as your ancestors who couldn't make the switch from cowries to francs, but I don't see what your hawala's got to do with our shells.'

Toufik felt the weight of the cowries lying on the table.

'It's very simple, you'll see. You could quite easily imagine that a cowrie's worth, say, a hundred dollars. But it only has that value in a closed system, and only when it's known to the initiated. If you're carrying five hundred dollars on you, especially if you have to cross Africa without any luggage, you run a high risk of being murdered. But who'd want to kill you for five shells?'

He left the two cops to reflect, without taking his eyes off the shells, as if they really were worth a hundred dollars each, and took the opportunity to get up.

'I've got to run. I've got a class.'

They watched him walking away. As soon as he passed through the door of the Al Islah Centre, they spotted a swarm of young girls following close on his heels – schoolbags in their hands or bags on their backs, wearing hijabs and buzzing with excitement. Modesty and exuberance, all in one.

Lieutenant Julo Flores stood up in turn.

'I'm going to get a tea.'

'Can you ask if they've got any beer?'

As soon as Julo returned, holding a steaming silver teapot and an engraved glass, the commandant shared his news.

'Ryan's just been on the phone. They've finished doing their jigsaw with the bits of glass they found in the Caravanserai room. Brace yourself. Guess what they've managed to piece together?'

'A dolphin? An owl? A cowrie?' replied Julo.

'A tower! The Burj Khalifa, the tallest tower in the world. Some trinket that's only sold at Dubai airport – they've checked.'

Julo pondered this detail in his head. Something to add to the model of the Emirates Airlines A380 found in Jean-Lou Courtois's suitcase. One more riddle. Since leaving Vogelzug, Jean-Lou Courtois had barely travelled at all, or as little as possible, so as not to be away from his son with Down's syndrome. Yet Dubai was now one of the factors to add to the equation. A new conundrum, much more difficult to solve than bits of glass needing to be glued back together.

He blew on his tea, wondered whether to offer to share it with his boss, burned his tongue testing the temperature, then began.

'I've got some fresh information too.'

Petar was gazing longingly at the terrace of a hotel-restaurant across the street, where they appeared to serve alcohol.

'So, beyond the routine investigations into Leyli Maal – work, criminal record, neighbourhood inquiries and so on – I went looking for her blood profile. It wasn't that hard – all I had to do was phone the only lab in Port-de-Bouc. Leyli's got a file there. As I expected, Leyli's A+.'

'A+? That's your scoop? 40 per cent of the folk on earth are A+!'

Julo dipped his lips in the scalding-hot glass, before taking Professor Waqnine's blood group impossibilities chart from his pocket.

'It's more nuanced than that, boss. We know Leyli Maal's A+,

252

and Faline95, the presumed murderer of Jean-Lou Courtois, is AB. Let's imagine this killer is Bamby Maal, Leyli's daughter. Then . . . (his fingers traced the row on the grid), her father can only be AB or B . . . there's absolutely no way he could be O or A.'

Petar stared desperately at the chart, like a secondary school pupil faced with a trigonometry table.

'Sorry, kiddo, I must be daft as a brush this morning, but I don't see what you're getting at.'

'What I'm getting at – or rather getting back to, in fact – is my initial hypothesis. This girl, let's call her Bambi13, Bamby Maal or Faline95, is looking for her father. If the guy whose veins she cuts, after taking a sample of blood, turns out to be group O or A, he can't be her father. And since 90 per cent of the world's population belongs to group O or A, that narrows the field of possibilities enormously. Let's say Bambi has a list of three or four potential fathers. According to the laws of probability, therefore, she has every chance, with a simple blood test, of identifying him.'

# 46

'Fleur?'

She simply confirmed her identity with a smile, without pointing out she'd been waiting for thirty minutes. Yan Segalen had probably turned being late into a philosophy of life. She examined him from head to toe, as he sat down beside her on the terrace of Gordon's Café. Ochre canvas trousers, a bush jacket in the same colour, a white shirt with a Mao collar, the whole *sorry-I'm-just-back-from-a-safari* caboodle. A small fortune in cutting-edge chic for the stylish explorer. Yan assessed her with his tropical-blue eyes, and combed his hands through his blondish-grey hair, which matched his impeccably uncared-for beard. A dynamic, energetic, well-groomed man in his fifties, even though his loose-fitting shirt suggested that Vogelzug's logistics manager might be a tad portly round the middle. Working out in the morning, eating out at midday.

'Sorry, Fleur, I don't have a lot of time,' Segalen had the cheek to say.

She said nothing in reply. In fact, she hadn't even noticed the half-hour passing by, as she waited for the executive who was supposed to be giving her a job interview. She had nodded off in front of her Perrier, infused with a slice of lemon, while looking up every now and then to take an interest in the activity on Rue Monnot and Place des Martyrs. Cosmopolitan activity, the kind she loved. She recalled it being the first thing that had seduced her when she'd arrived in Marseille. The mix of cultures. Djellabas, hijabs, ties, caps, pushchairs, mini-shorts, chadors, boubous, sirwals, saris, kippas, cheongsams. Of course, since then, she'd realised that everyone went back to their own neighbourhoods as soon as night fell, but the first time she'd strolled along the Canebière, this ecstatic multi-ethnic jumble had left her utterly enthralled.

'I ought to tell you,' continued Yan Segalen, 'I'm not giving you a traditional job interview. I don't give a toss why you want to work in the humanitarian field, I don't need you to give me that whole spiel you normally get from budding Florence Nightingales. So just answer this one question: why should I hire you? Why should I hire you – *you* in particular?'

*Yan is always late.*
*He makes up for it when he arrives.*
*He undresses quickly. He likes me to touch his body.*
*He thinks I do too.*
*Nadia tells me he's beautiful, more than I could ever imagine.*
*I use my imagination, even though all I know of him are the muscles he flexes to possess me.*

She pretended to think. She appreciated Yan pulling out all the stops for a three-month temporary contract in his logistics division, presumably consisting of packing boxes in a warehouse and then dispatching them to hot spots around the globe. The reason the logistics manager had come in person was probably because he'd not been indifferent to the photo on her CV, to her fringe of blonde hair contrasting with her tanned face, to her emerald eyes with their hint of insolence behind her small round glasses.

An ambiguity that Fleur had taken care to maintain for their appointment. A prim blouse, but with enough buttons undone for Yan not to miss the lace of her white bra as soon as she leant over her Perrier. A plain, straight skirt dropping down below her knees, except when she crossed them and the tight fabric rode up to the middle of her thigh.

'Well,' she simpered, 'I'm highly motivated. I like to feel useful. There's so much injustice in the world that—'

She was playing nervously with the slice of lemon in her glass, using the end of her straw. Yan suddenly grabbed her hand.

'Stop! Mademoiselle, that's exactly the kind of answer I wanted to avoid.'

He took his hand away, sliding his fingers down to her wrist and then waving to summon the waiter. Without even asking what she would like, he ordered two glasses of white wine, a Chateau Musar, then leant over to his leather satchel decorated with African motifs, and pulled out two sheets of paper.

She recognised her CV. Yan concentrated for a few minutes on her list of referees, entirely fake, then stared at her again. His eyes were no longer gliding across her thighs or her cleavage. Now he was frisking her from the inside. This man was a predator. The most dangerous of predators: he was trying to understand the woman in front of him. As if it were an absolute necessity. Stripping her naked before undressing her. She wondered if he acted like this with all the women he seduced, or whether his intuition was whispering softly in his ear, telling him something didn't quite add up in the CV provided by this *belle gazelle*.

'Sorry to disappoint you, Fleur, but you don't really look like a Mother Teresa . . . and I get ten CVs a day from girls like you, all multilingual and overeducated. It'll take more to convince me.'

The waiter brought them the two glasses of Chateau Musar. Yan offered her one, took the other, and proposed a toast.

'To adventure, Fleur. It's your move now. Seduce me.'

He looked pointedly at his watch.

'You've got five minutes.'

She thought of something. She raised her glass again and proposed another toast.

'To the unknown, Yan. To beautiful encounters. I think that's what attracts me to humanitarian work. Encounters. With women. With men. People who're different. Unsettling. Charismatic.'

Yan sucked gently on the rim of his glass, drinking her in with his eyes.

'That's better, Fleur. But it's still just talk. I need facts. Proof. Actions.'

He skimmed over her CV one last time, and pretended to put it away in his satchel. She suddenly replied, raising her voice this time:

'Yan, wait. Give me a chance! What else can I do but ask you to believe me? What if I told you that I'm braver than I look? That I'm not afraid of anything. That I'm willing to take risks . . .' (She paused and tried to catch his eye.) 'All risks.'

Yan was already on his feet, as if he'd barely been listening. A predator, she thought again. A fearsome predator.

'I have to go, Fleur. But you've won, I'm giving you another chance. Are you free for a second interview?' (He didn't even bother checking his diary.) 'Here. Does tonight work for you?'

'Yes . . .'

She'd held his gaze, without a trace of ambiguity this time. He'd added a touch of solemnity to his voice when saying 'Tonight'; she'd allowed her 'Yes' to trail off until it choked her.

He allowed the silence to linger. All of a sudden he wasn't in such a hurry any more. Once again, he stared at her as if trying to understand the mechanism which, inevitably, would lead to this ravishing girl – thirty years his junior – ending up in his bed. He seemed surprised by it himself. It was his weapon, his infallible weapon.

'I'm telling you now, Fleur, I'll be thinking about our second interview all day. I'll probably even fantasise about it, you know. About it taking a more – shall we say – intimate turn.'

'I'm ready. To take all risks. I told you already.'

She had answered without thinking twice. He reckoned he could push his luck even further.

'I prefer to be honest, Fleur. Let there be no misunderstanding between us. Even if this personal and private interview goes like a dream, that doesn't mean you'll be hired for the job. I don't work that way . . .'

She raised her glass of Chateau Musar, drained it, and looked at the logistics manager defiantly.

'Off you go, Yan, you're going to be late. And I'm telling you now, even if our intimate interview goes like a dream, which I promise it will, I'm not even sure I'll accept the job you offer me.'

He burst out laughing. Won over.

A second later, he'd already disappeared into the colourful crowds on Place des Martyrs.

She waited for a few moments, then took out her phone, which hadn't stopped vibrating in her bag during the conversation.

Well, how was the job interview?
I'm on a stopover, need to go
Take care of yourself, honeybun
Chérine

She smiled.

The interview with Yan Segalen had lasted less than fifteen minutes. Seducing him had turned out to be child's play, a mere formality compared to the lengthy groundwork required to make Jean-Lou fall into her arms.

Yan Segalen was easy prey.

Too easy.

A warning light was flashing in her brain. Everything had gone very fast, much too fast to have had time to think.

Never mind . . .

Or so much the better. She couldn't afford to wait any longer, the police were gathering the pieces of the puzzle one by one, putting them together, weaving their net.

Before getting up, she finished her glass of Perrier to get rid of the taste of the wine, tugged at her skirt, straightened her wig.

This evening, this very night, tomorrow morning, all would be over.

For her.

For Alpha too.

# 47

*My breast, drink up the wind's new drive!*
*Let's run the waves and spring from them alive*

Gavril watched, astonished, as the black giant played at being DiCaprio at the prow of the *Sébastopol*, standing facing the sea, declaiming his poetry. Who was he trying to impress? Was he practising? To be ready for when he'd bring girls down into the hold?

Gavril was holding on to the helm. They weren't on the high seas yet, but the coast hadn't been visible for a few minutes now. The black man continued to spout off at the deserted horizon.

*The wind awakes! . . . to try and live is next!*
*A breath immense opens and shuts my text*

He wasn't wrong, as it happened – the wind was rising. He wasn't going to delay turning back. If Laurel and Hardy wanted to buy his little boat, they'd seen enough. Black Laurel could reassure his friend, the guy with the chequebook: the *Sébastopol* was indeed able to float!

But before that, Gavril felt a strong urge to play his own card. He raised his voice to be heard over the sound of the engine and the waves.

'So, will reciting poetry on board be part of your future trips?'

Alpha moved closer, his hands deep in his jacket pockets. He leant his shoulder against the cabin.

'No, it's just for fun.'

Fun?

Gavril's idea of fun was rather different. Black Laurel must have understood from his gappy smile that he wasn't convinced, because he went on to explain:

'I was reciting from "The Graveyard by the Sea", by Paul Valéry. I learnt it at school, when I was really little. Don't you think the sea's one huge cemetery?'

Gavril shrugged. He started to cut the engine so the boat would slow down. The humming of the engine gradually petered out, but without the noise level actually decreasing. The impact of the waves on the hull seemed only to intensify, even though the *Sébastopol* was barely pitching at all.

Gavril coughed, as if he were about to recite a poem too.

'Was that true, what you were saying to your partner just now in the hold . . . Erm, about naked blondes?'

Caught by surprise, Alpha almost lost his balance. He saved himself from falling by grabbing hold of a lifebuoy that hung nearby.

'It's not like I was really listening to your conversation,' stammered Gavril. 'I just picked up bits and pieces of sentences, they landed in my ears, a bit like getting sea spray in your face, if you see what I mean . . . You were talking about girls in monokinis on deck, a waiter with mojitos, a guy in a fisherman's jumper at the helm. If you're buying the boat for a scheme like that, count me in. Ever since I've been a skipper on the Mediterranean, all I do is transport old fogeys who just sail up and down the coast, between an olive oil factory, a couple of restaurants and three Greek temples. I'm discreet, I know all the ropes. I could even get my teeth sorted for your clients, if you'd like.'

Alpha stepped forward, his hands wedged firmly in his pockets once more. He'd put on a woolly hat, but the wind was lashing his face.

'You don't have to answer right away,' persisted Gavril. 'In the fifteen years I've been at the helm of yachts over thirty metres,

I've not seen so much as a bloody nipple on deck! I gathered you wanted to refurbish the hold, install beds, showers . . .' (He winked at Alpha.) 'Look, if it's to stash away your high-class hookers, or shoot some pornos, that's fine with me too. Blow me down, me hearties, I'll be a grave! A Graveyard Seaman!'

The *Sébastopol* was now stationary at sea. Gavril seemed to be waiting for an answer before starting the engine again and turning the helm to return to port.

'Is there enough fuel?' said Alpha anxiously.

'Enough to go round the world!'

Gavril waited a few more seconds, but Laurel had already turned towards the sea again, fists in his pockets, hat firmly pulled down, a faraway look in his eyes.

> *Frenzied sea of such delirious spin,*
> *with thousand thousands idols of the sun,*
> *absolute Hydra drunk with your own blue flesh*
> *in such an uproar out of silence spun*

*He's taking the fucking piss!* thought the skipper. Now in a huff, he used his arm to mimic the stance of a coachman cracking his whip as he yelled out:

'Giddy up, me beauties! We're going home. We'll be there in less than an hour, you'll see just what our gutsy old *Sébastopol's* made of!'

Gavril bent down for a few seconds to operate the throttle control. When he looked up . . .

*The barrel of a revolver was pointing at him.*

The skipper began to stammer – quivering, cringing, his face contorted in fear. Enough to loosen his remaining teeth.

'I . . . I was just kidding about the hookers . . . I . . . I didn't hear anything . . . I . . .'

'Relax, buddy! If you play it cool and keep steering, everything'll be just fine. I'm simply hijacking your boat, that's all.'

Yet he was far from reassured by the quiet tone of the black man quoting Paul Valéry and armed with a handgun. This guy looked like he was straight out of a Tarantino movie! Gavril stared at him, utterly bewildered, with a growing sense of terror, as if he were dealing with a jihadist pointing a gun at him in the cockpit of a Boeing 747. He stared inanely at the deserted sea, imagining he'd suddenly see an island which he'd be ordered to crash into . . .

'Wh-where . . . where are we going?'

'Straight on. Ahead. To the other side of the Mediterranean.'

# 48

Julo had fallen under her spell.

As soon as Leyli Maal had entered Port-de-Bouc police station and walked towards the three cops, like an actress who felt slightly intimidated but was confident of her talent and strengthened by all she'd endured in life, Julo had loved her.

Nothing to do with falling in love at first sight, in the usual sense, as Leyli Maal was old enough to have been his mother, but this woman radiated an irrepressible energy – a resilience, to refer to her willpower by a highbrow word, like those ants that stubbornly follow their path come what may, that find a way round any obstacles, that lengthen their journey but always reach their destination, even while carrying a burden heavier than they are.

An ant that's not given up being pretty. Not given up perfuming itself with honey and colouring itself with primrose petals. The colours she was wearing, the mauve around her eyes, the red beads in her hair, the mandarin orange of her tunic – they seemed like a host of magic amulets, like ammunition to combat the greyness of her life.

There were three of them to question her: Petar, Julo and Commandant Toni Frediani, a cop who knew the Marseille landscape well, and in particular the mafia networks linked to immigration. Magistrate Madelin had insisted that Frediani be present at the interview. Since the discovery of a second body that morning, the Valioni-Courtois case had taken on the dimensions of an affair of state. Initiatives were streaming in thick and fast, from all directions, and it would take a few hours before the authorities, the ministry and Serious Crime HQ were able to defuse the situation and clarify responsibilities.

Leyli had taken a seat opposite the three police officers.

'I'm legally resident,' she began by saying. 'I've got a ten-year residence permit, I've got a work contract, I've—'

Petar cut her off without raising his voice.

'We know, Madame Maal, we know.'

Julo confirmed this. He'd quickly read through the file on Leyli Maal that someone had pulled together. Admittedly, she'd been illegally resident for a few years, after she first arrived in France, but she'd practically worked non-stop, and even paid her contributions. (Julo still couldn't understand how undocumented migrants, who could be deported at any moment, could nevertheless be legally employed . . . and even pay taxes.) Leyli had been granted legal status three years earlier. Had been working ever since. Had just landed a permanent contract. An exemplary record.

'Have you brought any photos of your daughter?' asked Commandant Velika.

While Leyli rummaged through her large shoulder bag, Julo allowed his thoughts to wander. He'd been combing through Faline95's Facebook profile. Just like Bambi13's, Faline95's page contained a few suggestive photos, but none of her face. Yet unlike Bambi13's album, all of Faline95's snaps had been taken in the Marseille region – on the beach at L'Estaque, facing the Frioul Islands, near the rocky inlets at Les Goudes, at the public swimming pool in La Pointe-Rouge . . .

The method of seducing Jean-Lou Courtois, however, remained the same. A virtual love parade, the kind that was now commonplace for young girls aware of how cute they were. Photos in swimsuits, the play of shadows along the curves of a naked figure, close-ups of sexy anatomical details. Faline95 and Bambi13 looked equally pretty. Twin bodies, both mixed race, both young.

Julo, like Petar, had been playing spot the difference for more than an hour. Without success.

Everything pointed to Bambi13 and Faline95 being one and the same girl. But it wasn't a certainty.

The photos had been sent to the lab, and Julo didn't know whether IT experts, simply on the basis of blurred or overexposed photos taken with a smartphone, could confirm whether two skin textures were identical, calculate the exact size of a pelvis, the length of a thigh, or the asymptote of the curve of a breast. And even if they could, there was nothing to prove that the photos on Facebook hadn't been Photoshopped. Anyone could fiddle with an image these days.

While Lieutenant Flores was lost in his thoughts, Leyli Maal circulated a few photos of her daughter. In a peculiar contrast to the images of Bambi13 and Faline95, the pictures of Bamby Maal showed a young girl as she would naturally look: barely any make-up, in trainers, jeans and a baggy jumper. Petar and Tòni spent a long time examining the photos, before turning them round to face Julo. Lieutenant Flores had the fuzzy portrait from the Red Corner security camera etched on his memory, that girl with her face partly hidden by her owl-patterned hijab. Two eyes. One mouth. He was overcome by an immediate gut reaction, something that was patently obvious.

*It was her.*

Bamby Maal was the girl filmed by the camera. That same depth in the iris of her eyes, that same defiant look coupled with indescribable melancholy. That look you'd so easily fall in love with.

*It was her.*

Julo continued to examine the three photos Leyli Maal had brought. As he lingered over them, however, doubt slowly began to creep up on him.

How could you be sure about a resemblance, almost striking in nature, but which was purely based on a look? Not even on the shape of a nose or a face, all too hazy on the video image. How could you be sure it wasn't an illusion, a clever trick using make-up, an impersonation?

Petar wasn't giving anything away either. Julo remembered the hours his superior had spent comparing this fuzzy image to those of all the prostitutes in the city, without any of them matching.

Had the commandant reached the same conclusion too? It was her, Bamby Maal! Julo was 80 per cent, even 90 per cent certain . . . But that still didn't constitute formal proof, much less answer the original question: how could this girl from a disadvantaged inner-city area also be the Bambi13 who jet-setted all over the world?

Petar spoke again. He was talking softly, as if he were apologising for bothering Leyli Maal. That just wasn't like him. Perhaps Toni Frediani's presence was making an impression.

'If you don't mind, we'll hang on to these photos of your daughter. We've been trying to contact her since this morning, on the mobile number you gave us. There's no answer. Madame Maal, when did you last see Bamby?'

Leyli answered without missing a beat.

'Yesterday evening. At 7.30 p.m. . . . Between 7.30 and 8 p.m., to be exact.'

The precision of the answer caught the three cops off guard. As did what it implied, in terms of an inconsistency surrounding the timetable of events.

If Leyli Maal was lying, she was doing it with disconcerting aplomb.

'Madame Maal,' said Petar, 'how can you be so precise?'

'My daughter had dinner with me. We have dinner every evening at 7.30 p.m. Commandant, let's cut to the chase – what's my daughter accused of?'

The policemen looked at each other. Petar made the decision. Without a word, he opened the Valioni and Courtois files and then slid them towards Leyli. They contained mainly photos of the two crime scenes, and the bodies drained of their blood, as well as portraits of the two victims. A direct and brutal way of making this mother understand what her daughter was accused of!

Julo concentrated on every gesture Leyli made, every expression on her face, when she opened each file, when she picked up the photos, one by one, when she looked at them; he saw her freeze when she closed the folders again with a trembling hand. This was not a simple reaction of surprise, nor even understandable disgust faced with the morbid pictures. Leyli Maal's face had locked solid, in a spasm of terror. It was a fraction of a second before she snapped out of it.

Petar apologised as he took the files back.

'I'm so sorry to put you through this ordeal, madame. And we still have no objective reason to believe that your daughter committed these crimes.'

Taking advantage of Petar's polite turns of phrase, as convoluted as they were unexpected, Julo revisited, in his mind's eye, the scene that had just played out. Leyli Maal's panicked expression had only lasted half a second before she'd managed to control it, but it had overwhelmed her at one specific moment. Not when she'd looked down at the photos of the corpses, nor even when she'd seen the portraits of François Valioni and Jean-Lou Courtois. After. Just after.

When she'd read their names on the file!

As if she hadn't recognised their faces. But she knew who they were.

Had Petar noticed this too? Or had he been fooled by a woman's natural emotions when confronted with such macabre photos? Julo felt a certain pride in imagining he'd been the only one to spot this crucial detail.

'Commandant,' said Leyli in a calm voice. 'I'm not stupid – if you thought my daughter had nothing to do with these murders, you wouldn't be showing me these photos. But you're barking up the wrong tree. My daughter has an alibi for last night.'

The cops looked at each other. They were waiting for Leyli to reveal all. Waiting to see.

'I'll be honest with you, I don't know where my daughter was between 8.30 p.m. and midnight. She *said* she was going to KFC with a friend, but I've got no proof of that. However, from midnight onwards, my daughter was at the Heron hotel, in the Écopolis Business Park. That's where I work.'

Petar scratched his head. The interview was taking an unexpected turn, and he no longer felt in control.

'Madame Maal, what was your daughter doing there at midnight?'

'She was singing.'

'Sorry?'

Leyli Maal appeared to waver slightly before replying. Her knuckles tightened around the straps of her bag.

'The . . . the easiest thing is to contact the hotel manager. Ruben Liberos. I suspect you're not going to believe a mother defending her daughter. But Monsieur Liberos will confirm everything.'

Commandant Tòni Frediani spoke for the first time. His Marseille accent intensified the irony in his voice.

'I'm assuming your daughter wasn't singing all alone for your boss at midnight. There must be other witnesses to her little serenade?'

'Yes,' confirmed Leyli. 'A dozen or so. Maybe more.'

Petar took out a handkerchief and mopped his brow. He jotted down the address of the Heron, questioned Leyli Maal again for a few more minutes, as a formality, then thanked her.

She had barely picked up her bag when Julo rushed over.

'I'll see you out.'

He left the office ahead of Leyli, avoiding turning to his two colleagues. Once they were alone in the corridor, he took care to close the door again and spoke to her in private.

'If you ever need anything, please call me.'

He handed her his business card. Julo couldn't work out what deep-rooted instinct had led him to do it.

'If you just need to talk. About your children. About those two murdered men. About . . . about the organisation where they worked. Vogelzug.'

Leyli took the card, and stared at him for a long time, as if to gauge whether she could trust him, then walked away without saying a word. Before pushing open the door of the police station, she put on bright red sunglasses adorned with a scarlet rose whose thorns and leaves ran along the side arms.

A curious woman, indeed . . .

As he watched her leave, as tall and proud as she had entered, as unruffled as a mother summoned because her son had forgotten to validate his ticket on the tram, he knew why he was so convinced that Bamby Maal, Bambi13 and Faline95 were simply one and the same woman. Not just because of a vague resemblance on a video image. This intuition was based on the fierce determination that radiated from every move Leyli Maal made, from every word she uttered, a resolve identical to that of the mysterious killer. A survival instinct. The instinct of someone bent on pulling through. As if, having made it back from hell, nothing could ever affect her any more.

A few seconds later, he pushed open the office door.

'Well?' said Tòni with a touch of impatience.

Julo didn't have time to answer. Petar beat him to it. He'd obviously been waiting for the three of them to be together again before setting out his conclusions.

'So,' said Petar, 'it's a no-brainer! Her daughter's our client! No doubt about it. Like peas in a pod, those photos of her little Bamby and our killer. And to top it all, this woman knew the names of both victims!'

Julo bit his lip. Petar had also spotted Leyli's fleeting expression of horror! Much as he hated the contrast between his commandant's cynical tone and the sensitivity with which he'd treated Leyli Maal, he had to admit he was a bloody good cop.

'Except,' continued Velika, 'that with her alibi, we're in fucking deep shit.'

He looked at his watch.

'We've got thirty minutes to dash over and see this Ruben Liberos at the Heron. It's barely two kilometres from here.'

Julo, still standing at the door, allowed himself a riposte.

'If Leyli Maal knew the victims, what's the connection between her and Vogelzug?'

Tòni Frediani's ears pricked up at the name Vogelzug. Petar was already on his feet.

'What exactly are you implying?'

'For Christ's sake, boss, it's bloody obvious. Leyli Maal's been in France for years without any documents. All roads lead back to them, the invisible folk, the illegals. Those bands on their wrists, like we found in Valioni's pocket, those shells that were used as African currency, Leyli's son, Alpha, the aspiring people smuggler.

Look, we're right here, in Port-de-Bouc, in the very place where one of the key refugee aid organisations was founded – the organisation where both François Valioni and Jean-Lou Courtois worked. Right here, where halfway between this police station and the Heron you'll find the home of Vogelzug's big boss, Jourdain Blanc-Martin.'

Petar walked past his deputy and stood by the door, his fingers poised on the handle.

'We'll see, kiddo. We'll find out "who" first, and we'll take care of the "why" after.'

Petar opened the door. Tòni Frediani carefully monitored the fiery exchange between his two colleagues, without intervening. Julo persisted.

'Don't you think we ought to pay Jourdain Blanc-Martin a little visit?'

The commandant had already left. Before falling into step behind, Julo watched him walking away, as he had done with Leyli Maal a few minutes earlier. He had just realised why he'd given his business card to her, without consulting his boss: because Petar hadn't asked her the right questions, hadn't questioned her about her past.

Because, if he had, Leyli Maal wouldn't have answered him.

Because Leyli Maal was afraid of him.

He sprinted off to join his superior.

Because – and he thought he was sinking into some deep form of schizophrenia as his mind formulated this theory – Leyli, Bamby, and perhaps Alpha too, needed him.

# 49

'Grandpa, grandpaaaaaa!'

Tidiane was screaming, in despair. At the foot of the orange tree.

'Grandpa, grandpaaaaaa . . .'

Grandpa Moussa's face finally appeared at the second-floor window, his hair all messy, as if he'd been yanked out of his siesta by a bad dream.

'What's wrong, darling?'

'My ball. My Morocco ball . . . It's gone! Down there . . .'

Tidiane pointed at a manhole below the gutter that went round the courtyard of the Olympus Estate. Grandpa Moussa rubbed his eyes.

'How on earth did you manage that?'

'I . . . I was playing . . . With my eyes shut . . . To practise . . . I didn't see it rolling away.'

Grandpa sighed.

'Wait for me, I'm coming down.'

A few moments later, they were both leaning over the pitch-black opening. Grandpa put his hand into the dark well, then his arm, then a stick, to no avail.

'Your ball's gone down into hell, darling.'

'Let's go and get it, then!'

'It's not that easy, Tidy. What we call hell is the basement for the whole estate – miles of corridors, cellars, one for each apartment, parking spaces too, drains, sewers.'

'But you told me Maman was busy tonight, she was coming home late. We've got time!'

'Tomorrow, Tidy. You don't have school tomorrow. Your ball won't run away. We'll have to equip ourselves. A lamp for you and one for me.'

'I don't need one, now I can see in the dark, just like Maman!'

Grandpa ran his hand through his grandson's hair. He adored it when Tidy let his imagination run wild. An imagination from which he drew boundless determination. Winning the World Cup, liberating the Moon of Endor, travelling back in time to the Wild West to save the bison. The carefree bravado that makes ten-year-old boys so endearing.

'I'll take some thread too,' added Grandpa, 'like Ariadne, so we don't get lost in the labyrinth of hell.'

'So Maman's treasure, is it hidden in hell?'

Grandpa looked down at the black hole that had swallowed the ball.

'Maybe . . .'

Tidiane suddenly stood up again, and started bouncing around like a bunny rabbit.

'What about your grandfather's treasure? You promised me this morning you'd tell me the story.'

'OK, Tidy, OK.'

❀

They walked a little further and sat down, with their backs against the trunk of the orange tree. Tidiane loved it here. Up in the sky, the wind was blowing at the clouds so fast that they were turning into confetti, but in the Olympus courtyard they were sheltered. For a moment Tidiane thought Grandpa had fallen asleep, but no, he was just thinking, as if he were downloading his grandfather's story into his head. It wasn't going very fast. There probably wasn't much storage space left in his brain. Finally, Grandpa Moussa began. Slowly. Like Maman, Grandpa was in the habit of dragging out his stories, so Tidiane would fall asleep in the middle. But he never fell asleep. Especially now that he was grown up.

'My grandfather was called Gali. He used to make jars. These

272

jars,' explained Grandpa Moussa, 'were like big earthenware pots, like vases for giant flowers. But your great-great-grandfather's vases weren't used to grow plants. They were pots for shells. Shells, in those days, replaced silver coins. Each vase could hold thousands of shells, and Gali could tell if even a single one was missing simply by weighing the jar. Tosha, your great-great grandmother, was very good at it too – she could count shells faster than anyone else. That was their job: counting shells, saving them, returning them, exchanging them for things. Your great-great-grandparents were very wealthy, but above all they were respected, because they would never have taken the liberty of stealing a single shell. On the contrary, they often gave them away to the poorest. Then, one day, a man came and said the shells were nothing more than mere shells.'

Tidiane didn't quite understand this bit of the story, so Grandpa Moussa tried to explain to him that men had strange powers, like deciding whether a shell was worth a lot of money, or nothing more than a grain of sand, or a pebble picked up in the yard.

'And that day,' continued Grandpa, 'Gali had lost everything. So he set off, travelling the roads and byways with his family, a tent and a few cows. He became a farmer, raising livestock and roaming across the desert for years, with his children and grandchildren, before settling near the great Niger River, in Ségou. That's where I was born. Where your mother was born.'

'So there's no treasure left, then?' asked Tidiane.

Grandpa Moussa made himself even more comfortable, leaning back against the trunk of the orange tree.

'Of course there is. Listen, listen to me, Tidy, and never forget what I'm going to tell you. You will find the treasure, the real treasure, in the same place as our roots.'

# 50

**5.14 p.m.**

The sign at the Littoral stop was shaking. The mistral had been gaining in strength all day long. As soon as Leyli stepped off the bus, she could feel the wind swooshing in under her tunic. Leyli seemed to have equipped herself in anticipation of the storm and was carrying a heavy bag of shopping in each hand. Milk, oranges, a chicken, potatoes . . . Three kilos on each arm!

Limping along, she followed the pavement towards the G and H buildings of Les Aigues Douces, walking past the metal shutters – now firmly pulled down – of shops that were no longer open. Nothing to do with the risk of a tidal wave: many businesses had gone bankrupt and shut for good. The grey shop fronts served as a slate for all the graffiti artists in the neighbourhood. The warm colours and primitive shapes reminded her of the Dogon rock paintings in the caves of the Cliff of Bandiagara in northern Mali. Some of it was rather well executed, just like this vast play area constructed by the council, between the sea and the apartment blocks. With water jets, rope bridges, swings, a mini boxing ring and a mini pool, the kids could play safely facing the sea, watched over by every balcony of the high-rise blocks that made up Les Aigues Douces. Eight blocks of eight columns of apartments, stacked across eight floors.

A beautiful place to grow up. Even though the buildings had been ravaged from the inside by the cancer of time – broken entryphones, mailboxes smashed to pieces – which of the residents would ever agree to moving away?

Leyli walked round the corner of Block G14. A gust of wind immediately lashed her face. At the foot of the apartment blocks, the mistral had assumed the role of a hysterical refuse collector. It was whipping up plastic bags, cardboard boxes, polystyrene, cigarette butts, cans – all the accumulated rubbish from overfilled bins and shipping containers which hadn't been properly emptied, and then took charge of scattering them everywhere. A clean-up on a huge scale, like a Kärcher power washer made of air currents. Everything would end up in the sea, and tomorrow morning it would seem as though all the concrete in the area had been purified.

Leyli, weighed down, was bent over. Head lowered.

She didn't see the Mercedes C-Class pulling up alongside the pavement, a few metres ahead of her. She didn't see the man getting out. She only saw the light from the headlamps flicker as he locked the car. A man in his sixties. Tall. Elegant. In a suit as impeccably sleek as his saloon car. The kind who only ever ventures into the neighbourhood a few months before the elections. An elected official? A civil servant? A businessman? Leyli had never come across him before.

'Leyli Maal?'

Apparently he knew who she was.

'Jourdain Blanc-Martin.'

Leyli stopped. He stepped forward and, in a gesture that seemed as natural as shaking her hand, offered to carry the two bags for her. She did not refuse.

*Jourdain Blanc-Martin.*

The boss of Vogelzug. The star pupil of the neighbourhood. Leyli knew who he was, of course.

'I've heard a lot about you, Madame Maal.'

'Really?'

There was a hint of irony in his voice.

'Can I walk you to your stair?'

'You might as well take my stuff up to the seventh floor!'

Despite her quick comeback, Leyli remained on her guard. Jourdain Blanc-Martin had not accosted her by chance. He was taking his time to lay his cards on the table. He walked beside her, charming, smiling, chivalrous, but she'd become used to being wary of hands extended in friendship.

Blanc-Martin looked up at the facade of the nearest building and stared at the towels flapping on the balconies, the wobbly satellite dishes, the drying racks falling to pieces.

'This is where I grew up,' he said. 'Block G12. École Victor-Hugo, Collège Frédéric-Mistral. Nothing's really changed in the last fifty years or so.'

'And what would you know?' replied Leyli, deliberately abrupt. 'What could you possibly know about the people who live here today?'

Blanc-Martin was silent for a long while, this time gazing out over the raging sea.

'You're quite right, Leyli. I live just a kilometre from Les Aigues Douces, and yet I think the last time I set foot here was to move out my mother, more than twenty years ago – to empty her apartment in Block G12, and settle her into a villa in the hills above Sausset-les-Pins. I'd made all the decisions for her. My mother never admitted it to me, but she always missed this neighbourhood. She'd lost interest in any form of wealth. She enjoyed that absolute luxury of being so happy that she despised money.'

They both stopped and turned around, the sea spray on their backs, dwarfed by the eight floors of the apartment blocks towering in front of them.

'What do you want from me, Monsieur Blanc-Martin?'

The Vogelzug president seemed relieved that Leyli had made the first move.

'To warn you, to help you. I know your story, every chapter in your story. I know how much you've suffered to get here. I know what ordeals you've had to endure, what sacrifices you've had to make. Your journey has been a war, Leyli.' (He took a deliberate pause, his eyes still focused on the cluttered balconies.) 'I know how many dead you've had to leave behind you.'

Leyli stared at him, unable to catch his elusive gaze. She wondered whether to take back her bags of shopping and just leave him standing there. Warning someone of danger is often nothing more than a veiled threat.

'I don't need your help.'

Blanc-Martin still wasn't looking at her, but his eyes had come to rest on the seventh floor, Block H9. Her balcony. Blanc-Martin knew exactly where she lived! He continued his soliloquy in his sugar-coated voice, which was tinged with irony again.

'You like telling people your story, Leyli. Who could blame you? It's so edifying. So exciting. What courage! What an example! Who could remain unmoved by such a fate?'

Leyli walked with a determined step towards the stairwell of Block H9, carried along by the wind. The president followed her, a metre behind, weighed down by his load. She scanned the front of the building, trying to catch a glimpse of Guy on the sixth-floor balcony, or even Kamila. No one! Everyone had barricaded themselves in, because of the mistral.

When she reached the bottom of the block, she turned around. The mistral whipped her face.

'Let me ask you again, what do you want from me, Monsieur Blanc-Martin?'

'Keep an eye on your children.'

'Sorry?'

'I've nothing against you, Leyli. But you must help us find your daughter Bamby. Your daughter Bamby and your son Alpha.'

Leyli did not reply. She was waiting desperately for someone to emerge from the stairwell. Her cardigan was flapping in the wind. She could feel Blanc-Martin's words slapping her, even harder than the mistral. She held out her hands for the president to give back her shopping bags.

'I'm in a hurry, monsieur. I've got to go and pick up my little boy.'

'Can't you see, Leyli? Bamby and Alpha are in danger.'

'My daughter's got nothing to do with these murders. No more than my son's a thug. You're not a cop! I've no idea what you're getting at.'

She seized the two plastic bags. Blanc-Martin grabbed her by the wrist.

'I'll be more precise, then. I know your secret. I know you're not who you say you are. People take your word for it, they trust you. They admire you, Leyli. They pity you. They love you. You seduce everyone. Your neighbours. Your bosses. Your parents. Your children. Your landlords. Your creditors. Even the police . . . How could they possibly suspect they're all being superbly manipulated?'

'You're insane!'

'No, Leyli. Neither you nor I are insane. You know that as well as I do. You're in complete control of your lies. But in the minds of your children, they have sown the seeds of madness.'

'You're out of your mind!'

Leyli plunged into the dark stairwell as fast as she could. Taking shelter. Not fast enough to avoid hearing Blanc-Martin's parting words.

'Think about it, Leyli. I just need to say the word, that's all. And everything you've patiently constructed will come crashing down.'

# 51

'Honourable gentlemen, pray take a seat, I beseech you, I have but this modest sofa to offer, and no beverages other than those distributed by this temperamental robot which does whatever it wants, and only adds sugar to every other coffee.'

Commandant Petar Velika and Lieutenant Julo Flores stared, dumbstruck, at the manager of the Heron Port-de-Bouc. They sat down on the bright red sofa in reception, overwhelmed by a tsunami of words.

'You remind me of David Brown and Fred Yates, two detectives from Dunwoody, to the north of Atlanta, who came to defend Goldie, an African-American woman who'd taken refuge in my motel, the poor thing, after the murder of a white farmer. The Alamo Hotel. We were surrounded by a couple of hundred guys in white hoods, all brandishing burning crosses. Based on my testimony, swearing she'd spent the night with me, Brown and Yates found Goldie innocent. In fact, I think Freddie, the short one, fell in love with her and they're still living together to this day . . .'

Ruben Liberos stared at Julo for a long while, as if he were the reincarnation of that American cop, then took out some coins and went up to the coffee machine.

Petar had gone to the trouble of verifying that the guy in front of him dressed as a tango dancer wasn't some lunatic on the run, but indeed the official manager of this shabby hotel on the outskirts of Port-de-Bouc.

'Righto, Monsieur Liberos, we're in a bit of a rush. Can you confirm that Bamby Maal, your employee's daughter, was in your establishment last night, around midnight?'

'I can confirm that. Formally.'

He slid the coins into the machine and struck it violently with the flat of his hand to make the cup drop down.

'I'm sorry, monsieur, but what was she doing in your hotel in the middle of the night? Your employee, her mother, Leyli, told us she was . . . singing?'

'Commandant, may I count on your discretion?'

Petar growled indistinctly. Neither a yes nor a no. Ruben carried on.

'You are a man of honour, Commandant. Believe me, I can recognise soldiers who only obey commands that come from the heart.'

Ruben moved closer to the two police officers and explained in a few words, with studied seriousness, that he sometimes offered rooms to illegal migrants, and organised musical evenings with them, for their benefit, and it wasn't uncommon for guests who just happened to be staying to join in too.

'Do your parties only start at midnight?' asked Petar.

Ruben Liberos handed him a cup.

'Here you go, Commandant. A cappuccino. Trust me, based on my long love affair with this capricious machine, a cappuccino is the only drinkable decoction it's capable of making for you.'

He let Petar take hold of the scalding-hot plastic cup before continuing.

'Our little *soirées* begin as soon as it gets dark. To be totally honest, I'm lucky enough to have a diva, Noura, the charming young girl you'll see appearing and disappearing behind you, sometimes riding a broom, sometimes fluttering her feather duster. But I need her to serve early-morning refreshments to those travellers who depart at the crack of dawn. So our Nightingale-Cinderella leaves us when the clock strikes midnight, and Bamby takes to the stage, even though the tone of her voice is infinitely less delicate than Noura's.' (He leant over the policemen, his eyes twinkling, and then whispered his last sentence.) 'I'm counting on you not to tell her mother.'

Julo couldn't help looking behind him. While waiting for the next princely ball, Cinderella had indeed returned to her household. An attractive mixed-race girl was making the most of the strong wind outside the entrance to shake down the bedspreads.

*Noura.*

Julo's brain made the connection even before he had time to warn it to be wary of coincidences.

Noura looked uncannily like Bamby! The same youthful figure. The same tanned skin. The same elegance in her gestures, her poses, underlined by a hint of arrogance because she was conscious of being watched and desired.

Petar, filled with dismay by Ruben Liberos's wacky tales, hadn't bothered to turn around. His hand was clenched dangerously around the cup, which was filled to the brim with a white, choco-latey, chemical foam.

Liberos had gone up to the cappuccino machine again. It was Julo's turn.

Petar looked at his watch and decided to speed things up.

'In that case, Monsieur Liberos, I assume you've got plenty of witnesses to back up your story?'

Ruben slammed his palm against the metal. A second cup dropped down.

'A few, Commandant . . . A few . . . Around twenty, at most . . . Did you know that in 1988 I assembled more than a hundred and fifty people at the Heron in Târgovişte, to listen to a Roma violinist who was being hunted by Ceausescu's Securitate? An unforgettable concert, and—'

'Twenty witnesses will do just fine,' interjected Petar. 'How can I contact them?'

The commandant's superhuman efforts to maintain his com-posure were beginning to amuse Julo. Ruben Liberos handed Julo an identical cappuccino, then headed to the reception desk, and returned with around twenty sheets of paper stapled together.

'Here you go, Commandant. The sworn statements of all the

witnesses, who claim to have heard Bamby Maal sing in my modest auditorium between midnight and 6 a.m. You'll find their surnames, first names, signatures. Nineteen in all.'

Petar glanced discreetly at the petition.

'I suppose you have the addresses of these good citizens? Phone numbers, anything at all, so we can summon them to the police station?'

Julo was going to end up with a stiff neck. He kept twisting his head around to keep tabs on Noura, who was busy airing the hotel blankets, while trying not to miss any of the manager's compelling little performance.

'Commandant, do you really think that a citizen of the world who's illegally resident in France, who could be deported at any moment, is going to come and testify of his own accord in a police station? Ask me for a video statement if these pieces of paper don't suffice, or an audio recording made under oath.'

Petar put his cappuccino down in front of him. He hadn't touched it. He'd realised he could keep going round in circles for hours like this. Ruben Liberos was playing for time. Messing around. Stringing them along. That classic guerrilla method used by activists standing in solidarity, in the face of a blind legal system.

'If this statement is too vague, Commandant, I can request those who remain in my debt to furnish you with chapter and verse: a list of pieces performed, the precise times the concert began and ended. When you're dealing with a murder charge, I suppose—'

Petar Velika seemed on the verge of bursting a blood vessel. He raised his voice abruptly.

'No need for that, Monsieur Liberos.'

'I do hope you won't think I've simply fabricated these depositions. These witnesses are all eminent people back home – these are opposition politicians being hunted by the regime, they're judges, teachers, doctors.'

The commandant could feel the last defences of his decorum crumbling away. The hotel manager would continue spouting his nonsense until Velika located the stopcock. He decided to make things abundantly clear and remove any doubt.

'We'll check your statements – trust me, we'll go through every single name. But the only thing that really matters, Monsieur Liberos, is knowing whether Mademoiselle Bamby Maal, as her mother claims and as you've confirmed, was indeed in Port-de-Bouc last night. Monsieur, are you aware of where the murder was committed? The one Bamby Maal is accused of?'

Julo had sat up straight again. He too had put down his vile cappuccino. It felt as though the draught in his back had died away; as if Noura had interrupted her work to listen to them.

'No idea,' admitted Liberos. 'Leyli simply told me that—'

'The murder of Jean-Lou Courtois, that's the name of the victim, took place in the Caravanserai room of a Red Corner hotel. Sometime between 5 and 6 a.m., according to forensics.'

'I . . . I see what you're getting at, Commandant,' stammered the manager. 'The Red Corner in Port-de-Bouc is two kilometres from here, twenty minutes on foot – God forbid I should ever find myself in charge of such an establishment. So you think Bamby Maal might have slipped away for half an hour and—'

'I was thinking nothing of the kind, Monsieur Liberos.'

The hotel was plunged into a deep silence for a few long seconds, before Commandant Velika finished what he'd been about to say.

'Jean-Lou Courtois wasn't murdered in Port-de-Bouc. There are a hundred or so Red Corners across the world, all completely identical, just like your Heron hotels.'

As Petar Velika paused again, Ruben Liberos turned towards the map of Heron hotels in France. You could count around ten in the Marseille metropolitan area alone. The commandant's next words swept him off terra firma, made his heart skip a beat, engulfed his thoughts and drowned every one of his certainties.

'Jean-Lou Courtois was murdered in the Red Corner in Dubai. Five thousand kilometres from here!'

Ruben Liberos was wide-eyed with disbelief, unable to utter a word. The commandant coughed, suddenly looked exhausted, overtaken by events, and turned to his deputy.

'Give him all the details, Julo.'

Lieutenant Flores spoke in a calm, measured voice.

'Jean-Lou Courtois was in Dubai for a conference of top-level sales representatives of SoliC@re, the multinational where he worked. He was staying for two nights at the Radisson Blu, facing the old port of Dubai, on the Dubai Creek. On the day he arrived, he did some shopping in duty-free at Dubai airport – he bought some L'Occitane en Provence products for his wife, a miniature plane for his son, and a glass pendant of the Burj Khalifa, which he probably gave to his murderer, Faline95. He had a drink with her on the first evening, in the lobby of the Radisson Blu, and dinner with her on the second night in a Michelin-starred restaurant, Reflets, one of the ten establishments across the globe run by Pierre Gagnaire. He left the restaurant with this girl around midnight, and they took a taxi to the Red Corner. The driver, a local from Dubai, is the last person to have seen Jean-Lou Courtois alive, except, of course, for Faline95. We've been working closely with the Dubai police since this morning, and more importantly with the DCI of the French embassy in the United Arab Emirates. While we were examining the local Red Corner, to see what a Caravanserai room looked like, they sent us photos of the crime scene, and the results of some blood analysis, and they're trying to put together an identikit portrait of the girl. We already know she's mixed race – we're just waiting on the rest.'

Ruben Liberos stood up. He grabbed the two cappuccinos and flung them into the nearest bin without even emptying them.

'Esteemed investigators,' he said cheerfully, 'I sincerely hope you're not *too* pressed for time – I'm off to replace this disgusting beverage with a vintage champagne right away. If five thousand kilometres separate the scene of the crime from my humble establishment, I think that clears the name of our friend Bamby Maal. Beyond a shadow of a doubt.'

# The Night of Mud

# 52

A one-to-one, thought Leyli. Her family life had been reduced to this. A one-to-one with Tidiane.

'When are Alpha and Bamby coming back?'

'I don't know, darling.'

Leyli wasn't lying. She'd had no news from her son or daughter since that morning. She had called them, left rambling messages on their voicemails, sent short texts containing more question marks than words.

No answer.

Tidiane was playing with his cold macaroni. Making brochettes with slices of Herta sausage, skewering them together with the end of his fork. Dipping them in ketchup, nibbling at them without any appetite. Leyli was trying as hard as she could to calm the ideas swimming around in her head, to make them wait in a corner, for the duration of this meal, while she was talking to her son, smiling, asking questions: 'So, how was school? And break time? Your friends?' All children around the world undergo a full-blown interrogation every evening, while adults, for their part, tell them nothing at all.

*Keep an eye on your children.*

Tonight, she couldn't manage it. Jourdain Blanc-Martin's threat continued to haunt her.

*I just need to say the word, that's all. And everything you've patiently constructed will come crashing down.*

Was Blanc-Martin bluffing?

*You must help us find your daughter Bamby.*

Blanc-Martin seemed to think Bamby had murdered those two men, both killed in a Red Corner. The three cops at the police station thought the same. Absurd! In her mind's eye, she could see Bamby again, the previous evening, leaving the table without eating a thing and telling her she'd arranged to meet Chérine at KFC. And yet while this was happening, as she had read in the file at the police station, the woman who was to murder Jean-Lou Courtois was having dinner with him in a gourmet restaurant in Dubai. That woman couldn't be Bamby, but what was a mother's testimony worth? What was Ruben's false witness statement worth? Why hadn't her daughter contacted her? Normally, she never let a day go by without sharing her news. Dark thoughts began to gather in her head, like grey clouds piling up in the sky. Sweep them aside, Leyli forced herself to respond. Sweep them aside. Look after Tidy.

'What's wrong, honey?'

'I've lost my ball . . . Alpha's ball.'

'Your cuddly-ball?'

'It's not cuddly,' said Tidiane sulkily.

Leyli cursed herself for being so tactless. Tidiane would abandon her as soon as he grew up, like Alpha, like Bamby. She'd done everything the wrong way round. She wasn't capable of being a mother.

'It . . . it rolled down a hole, Maman.'

'Grandpa Moussa will help you look for it tomorrow. Eat. Eat up, my darling.'

❀

Tidiane had fallen asleep. Leyli had read him a story, his favourite, 'The Twelve Labours of Hercules'. He had started breathing more gently at the fourth, had closed his eyes for the first time at the seventh, had woken up at the ninth, the journey to the land of the Amazons, had resisted, by rubbing his eyelids, until the eleventh, the famous theft of the golden fruit from the Garden of the Hesperides, before falling asleep just as Hercules was descending into hell for his encounter with Cerberus.

Leyli watched her boy breathing for a few long seconds. He was exhausted, overwhelmed by conflicting emotions. The blanket wasn't pulled up far enough to cover his pyjamas, and she hesitated, torn between the fear of him feeling cold and of causing him to wake up. She drew back very quietly and, with the tip of her finger, plunged the room into darkness.

As soon as she was alone, she checked her mobile. Still no messages!

As always, a drop of acid landed on her heart. She too would have liked to fall asleep like her little man – to collapse into bed, go out like a light and let the pressure subside. She walked towards the balcony. The deafening silence from Bamby and Alpha inevitably brought her back to Blanc-Martin and his threats. She felt as helpless as those mothers who are told their benefit payments will stop unless their children return to school. Only worse. So much worse.

She opened the French window and took out a cigarette.

She wanted to forget Blanc-Martin. She also wanted to banish those two names, François and Jean-Lou, those two names that had just resurfaced from the depths of her memory, two first names followed by surnames she had never known until that afternoon: François Valioni, Jean-Lou Courtois. Two old friends of Adil's, two former *clients*, despite being loath to use that word, even today. Murdered, in a hotel room.

Yet it could only be a coincidence – she hadn't told anyone about her former clients. Except Ruben or Guy perhaps, but without mentioning any specifics other than a first name. Only her red notebook, the one whose contents she had dictated to Nadia long ago, contained more details. But could you really speak of details when referring to a story told by a blind woman? No one but her had ever read it; it had lain there, hidden under her bed, for years.

A co-in-ci-dence, repeated Leyli in her head in an effort to convince herself. The police were getting nowhere, had no motive, no culprit, so they were digging into the victims' pasts in search of clues, anything whatsoever. What did she have to do with these men? All men who spent their lives in hotels probably used prostitutes. She had simply been one of them. For a few months. More than twenty years ago. In another life.

She took out her lighter and was astonished by how easily the flame stood up to the wind from the sea. The mistral which had been raging between the towers of Les Aigues Douces had finally abated. It had fled, far across the waves. In the reflection of the moon, along with the beam from the Port-de-Bouc lighthouse and the halo of the streetlamps along the quays, you could see the great black sheet of the sea, writhing and thrashing as if all the marine creatures were making love deep below – growling, sighing, amusing themselves by shaking the liners entering the port of Fos-sur-Mer in the distance.

The smoke from a cigarette was irritating her nostrils, mingling with the curls of smoke from her own.

The smell of blonde leaf tobacco. Guy was smoking, on the balcony below. Leyli leant over.

'Is it half-time?'

'I wish! I've got a choice between the World Cup of Darts or the AWBA, the American women's baseball championship.'

Guy's croaky voice could barely be heard over the sound of the waves. She leant in closer to make out what he was saying. As she often did at home, she had slipped into a pagne; tonight's was loose-fitting, very low-cut, and came down to her knees. She had no idea how much of her nakedness Guy could make out in the half-light. None, perhaps. Or almost all. She couldn't care less. She allowed the final, powerful gusts of the mistral to caress her.

'What are you up to, then?'

'Same as you, I'm looking at the sea.' (Guy fell silent for a moment, as if to give Leyli time to scan the endless panorama.) 'They've not invented a bigger plasma screen than this, not yet!'

The last breath of wind perfumed the balcony with a fine salty vapour. Her skin under the pagne felt soft and moist. Leyli was in the mood for tenderness.

'You can see it better from here. Come on up!'

'I'll bring some beers.'

'I'd rather have some wine. Lots of wine.'

Leyli was in the mood for love.

❀

Guy was like her. Bruised and battered by life.

She kissed him even before he had hung up his jacket. She let him put down his bottle. A Coteaux du Libron. Not one she knew. He was about to make a comment – about the grape variety, the tannin, the colour of the grapes – but she kissed him first.

'Come.'

She pulled him onto the bed. Guy was still wearing his denim jacket, an Aran jumper underneath, probably a shirt, a vest, a pair of cords, socks, heavy Mustang ankle boots. He could have carried on losing at strip poker all night without ever ending up stark naked. Leyli let Guy's hands venture under her pagne, let his mouth run down the hollow in her throat.

Let his palms squeeze her breasts, his mouth kiss her shoulders, his fingers roam across her belly, his mouth kiss her neck.

Let his middle finger force its way inside her, let his mouth devour hers.

She felt voluptuous. Hungry. Desperate.

'Get your things off . . .'

Sitting on the edge of the bed, Guy took for ever to undo the tight knots on his Mustangs. Excited, irritated, a six-year-old who'd forgotten how to untie his shoelaces.

Leyli was sitting curled up in a ball, her knees against her chest; she glanced over to check that Tidiane's door was firmly shut. That the computer on the shelf was turned off. That she hadn't forgotten anything. Then she turned to gaze tenderly at Guy again.

He had conquered one of his boots. He seemed to be catching his breath before tackling the second. Perhaps he wasn't in such a hurry to undress. Perhaps he was simply afraid of her looking at him. Naked. Leyli's body was throbbing. Her skin still bore the traces of Guy's almost painful caresses and slobbering kisses. It wanted more. She hadn't made love for months. Hardly ever in the last ten years.

Guy had sent his second boot flying. Everything would speed up now. Trousers. Boxer shorts. Socks.

Most of the lovers she had known had had no face . . . Until this afternoon. Before Leyli's eyes, the faces of François Valioni and Jean-Lou Courtois were superimposed on the decor of the room, like ghosts who'd finally discarded their shrouds. They were just as she'd imagined, all those times she had given herself to them: François, handsome and overconfident; Jean-Lou, so fragile, whom she found so moving.

Guy had stripped down to his waist. All three layers. Of denim, wool, cotton. He sat with his arms crossed on his belly, as if apologising for not being able to remove the last one. The layer of fat.

Flabby. Ungainly.

*I want to read in your eyes that you find me handsome.*

First the faces of François and Jean-Lou, and now Adil's words were coming back to haunt her. The first words he had uttered to make her succumb to his horrifying emotional blackmail, the odious wish she had agreed to grant him.

For which she had prostituted herself. For which she had committed murder.

The faces of François and Jean-Lou began to fade, making way for their corpses. Arousal suddenly gave way to disgust. Her senses had betrayed her. Guy's body kindled no flames of desire. His lifeless face inspired no wish to embrace him. His stooping back, the bent nape of his neck, fired no passion. Yet he was smiling at her. So sorry. Already preparing to get dressed again.

Leyli stood up. To try to save love, or what was left of it. She crossed her arms, grabbed the bottom of her pagne and lifted it, pulling it above her waist, over her shoulders, her hair, and dropped it back onto the bed, as if shedding a dead skin.

She stood there naked. Standing upright in front of him. She was conscious she was still so desirable. Her honey-coloured breasts. Her curved waist, encircling the invisible mound of her belly, its gentle slopes whittled away by the fluffy down of her bush. Out of bounds.

A woman inaccessible to a man like him.

Leyli read the desire in Guy's eyes, that uncontrollable boyish desire. That adoration.

She felt beautiful, as never before. Guy's bright eyes sparkled, just as much as they filled with tears.

In that instant, she found him handsome.

He rose to his feet. Took her in his arms. He had understood.

Two people, bruised and battered by life.

She checked one last time that Tidiane's door was properly closed, then whispered softly:

'Come.'

For a few hours, not even a night.

Together as one.

❀

Leyli had wrapped a blanket around her shoulders and was smoking on the balcony.

Guy was lying in bed; he had pulled the sheet up over his chest. They had made love too quickly, it had been more like a rough draft. He felt like doing it again. Making a fair copy. To prove to Leyli that he could do better.

Out on the balcony, Leyli was crying. Guy tried to comfort her.

'What's wrong, Leyli? You're pretty. You have three lovely children. Bamby, Alpha, Tidiane. You've done very well for yourself.'

'Done well? That's all just for show, all that. Hot air. Oh no, no, we're no perfect family. Not us. We're missing one key thing.'

'A father?'

Leyli gave a gentle laugh.

'No, no. We can easily do without a father, or even several fathers. All four of us.'

'What are you missing, then?'

Leyli half opened her eyes, like a Venetian blind letting a ray of sunshine filter through to light up a dark bedroom, turning the dust into stars.

'You're really quite inquisitive, *cher monsieur*. We barely know each other, but you still think I'll tell you my deepest secret?'

He said nothing in reply. The slatted blind in Leyli's eyes had already closed again, plunging the room back into darkness. She turned towards the sea, and blew out her smoke to blacken the clouds.

'It's more than a secret, Mr Nosy Parker. It's a wicked curse. I am a bad mother. My three children are doomed. My only hope is that one of them, maybe just one of them, will break the spell and be free.'

She closed her eyes. He continued to press her:

'Who put this terrible curse on them?'

Thunder rumbled behind the closed shutters of her eyelids.

'You. Me. The whole world. No one's innocent in this affair.'

❀

Leyli hadn't revealed any more. She had lain down in bed against Guy again, naked, cuddling him, while warning him that he couldn't stay, that her son was about to wake up, that it was out of the question that he should find Guy in the sofa bed in the living room. Guy had understood but, like the sultan from *The Arabian Nights* pleading with his Scheherazade for one more tale to prolong the night, had begged for the rest of the story.

Her story.

Leyli snuggled up against him. She couldn't have been any more than half his weight. She gently pushed back the arm that wanted to place itself on her breast, the hand that wanted to slide between her thighs.

'Be good, now! . . . You wanted to know the rest of my story?'

The words uttered by Jourdain Blanc-Martin, earlier that evening, outside the stairwell, still packed a punch.

*You like telling your story, Leyli. Who could blame you?*

*People take your word for it, they trust you. You seduce everyone.*

*Your neighbours. Your children. Even the police . . .*

*How could they possibly suspect they're all being superbly manipulated?*

She turned towards Guy. She was trembling. Guy's innocent smile restored some of her courage.

'I've not made anything up, you know. You have to believe me. It's the story of my life. My life as a migrant, an illegal one. You have to trust me, down to the very last detail. Everything I tell you is true.'

# LEYLI'S STORY

## Chapter Seven

I was doomed.

Surrounded.

Even if I screamed, even if I begged, no one would come to my rescue. In the forest of Gourougou, we were no more than animals. Sometimes one of us would leave the herd to die. The others would then hold on to each other even tighter than before.

The Ivorian carried on walking towards me, flaunting the box of condoms as if it were an anaesthetic – I would feel nothing; as if it were a talisman – they would feel nothing either. They would forget. Would start again. With another lost antelope.

I remembered Sousse, nights of love with strangers at the Hannibal Hotel. It wouldn't have been the first time I'd been raped, Guy, but it was the first time I'd seen the faces of my rapists.

The Ivorian was standing less than a metre away from me. Not so sure of himself.

'We'll give you some money, if you want.'

The four others, trousers round their ankles, looked surprised, as if they hadn't been consulted, weren't necessarily willing to contribute. I could smell their sweat – it smelt of fear, shame, loathing. Loathing of themselves as much as of me. But none of them would have given up. If one of the wolves had backed down, the others would have torn him to shreds.

'It's not me you need to give it to.'

I had answered the Ivorian with all the arrogance I could muster. As if it were inconceivable that this swine could lay a finger on me. He was amused by my look of defiance.

'Not to you? To who, then?'

'To Virgile.'

A sudden impulse. A moment of madness. The name came to me in a flash. For many nights I had listened to the stories of migrant women, especially women from Niger, who recommended finding yourself a fiancé, a friend for protection. Preferably some macho guy, someone thuggish and brutal. For a peaceful life. Becoming his meek, helpful slave, doing the washing, cooking, offering sex on tap, fetching wood and water. I was too proud to have taken their advice. Penned in by the men, I had panicked and uttered the name of the most feared man in the camp. Virgile was Liberian. A titan. Tattooed. Scarred. Respected.

The four rapists had suddenly stopped in their tracks. The Ivorian stared at me.

'You with him?'

'Go and ask him . . . Maybe he'll do you a deal.'

They hesitated, then threatened me: if I was talking a load of crap, I'd pay dearly for it. But they left me alone. They were watching out for me when I returned to the camp. I had no choice but to enter Virgile's tent.

He was sleeping. A second later, he was on top of me, a wild beast, his knife pressed to my throat.

'What do you want?'

'Protect me.'

I told him everything. He looked at me. I was beautiful, I knew; but Virgile could have any girl he wanted.

'I've already got a wife in Liberia, in Buchanan. Kids too . . .'

'She'll join you in London once you've made it across. With your family. You'll have more children. I'll look after you until you're on the other side of the gates, in Melilla.'

He took the knife away from my throat. I realised he was looking for a girl like me.

'I'm not planning on rotting here for months on end.'

'So don't waste any time. Make the most of it, Virgile. Make the most of it, while we're here.'

I slipped off the dirty rags that served as clothes and lay down on top of him. We made love. When he climbed on top of me in turn, I came loudly, loudly enough to wake up the whole camp. So that the wolves would know whom I belonged to. Once and for all.

Guy, I hope you won't be shocked by what I'm about to admit, but I wasn't faking it. I think Virgile's the only man I've ever loved. Even though there were no feelings between us, no promises, no tenderness. Purely a pact. Two lost souls, two people bruised and battered by life, that's something you'd understand, Guy. Virgile had fought in Liberia against the troops of President Taylor, the bloodiest civil war in West Africa. There was a price on his head. Virgile, for his part, was a bona fide political refugee. He had a concrete plan for when he got to England. To start work as a security guard, first in a warehouse, then at a nightclub. Virgile the Vigilant: it sounded as snappy and cool as the name of a Marvel superhero. But his secret dream was to become a bodyguard, the bodyguard for a star. He would collect photos of them like a little kid, sewn into the lining of his jacket: Madonna, Kylie Minogue, Paula Abdul, Julia Roberts . . . Virgile had the presence, the strength, he would have succeeded. I think I was proud to be his mistress. The other gang leaders, the other men who offered their protection in the forest, often took charge of several women – selling them on, by the hour, or for a night. Survival had a price. Virgile never asked me to do it. I had already paid enough.

We carried on like this for four months, in Gourougou, surviving, escaping from the Moroccan police who turned up regularly to burn everything down, as we prepared our big offensive. We launched it on 3 October 1998, when several hundred refugees attacked the wire fencing at Melilla in one co-ordinated surge. Zombies emerging from their graves to overwhelm the living. An army of beggars attacking a medieval fortress. They didn't quite pour boiling oil on us, but almost.

The army, the police had the technology; we had numbers on our side.

Nearly all would be caught; only a handful would succeed.

The others, in a few months, would start all over again. Even more of them. There were always more migrants turning up than ever managed to get through.

Virgile and I hadn't taken anything for granted. We hadn't even dared to hope that both of us would make it across the border. We refused to consider the possibility of neither of us getting through. If we were to end up on different sides of the same gate, we wouldn't have time to say farewell.

We charged forward, hand in hand for a few metres, then each of us went our own way.

That day, no one came out on top.

The Moroccan police had been forewarned, or were on the alert. They'd strengthened the teams on patrol. None of us managed to get more than ten metres from the gates: dogs, jeeps, armed guys ready to shoot as they guarded the entrance. The strongest of our down-and-out army, those carrying the battering rams intended to force open a gap, flung their wooden posts in rage. They screamed and swore at the militia, in Hausa, Igbo and every language under the sun. Then they fled, spitting as they went.

Virgile was one of them. The ones yelling abuse.

I saw the three policemen take out their pistols and fire. About twenty bullets. Five refugees were shot down that day. In cold blood.

Virgile was one of them.

I've never known why.

To set an example? To save lives, killing the strongest to avoid having to shoot the whole herd?

For the reward? Was there a price on Virgile's head?

For revenge? Adil was still alive, Adil had found me, Adil had had Virgile murdered out of jealousy. Yes, Guy, as stupid as it might sound, I've thought about it, and I still live with that terror, that Adil's ghost is haunting me, as if I had to pay for my sight with my life.

Once I'd returned to the camp, without my guardian, the wolves approached again. Wolves you can't scare away by sleeping by the fire. They only waited a few weeks. This time, I let them come near. When they were sufficiently close, I lifted my dress. So they could see my naked belly.

My belly, now already round.

Virgile's baby.

None of them would dare touch me, I knew that. An imam came to Gourougou from time to time, on Fridays, to give us a little money collected from the Muslim faithful in nearby mosques. This was one of the Koranic principles he would remind us of, in return for charity: illegal migrants had to show humanity and piety, to look after the sick and the weakest, to take care of women bearing new life.

One Friday when, despite the fear of Allah, I could sense the circle still closing in around me, I left with the imam. For the final months of my pregnancy, I stayed in a community clinic, on the Algerian border. I was sick. Exhausted. The baby was sapping all my strength.

He was born in Oujda.

He was black, and already so big. Energetic and powerful. A Hercules. He could have strangled any snake you threw into his cradle with his bare hands.

I knew he would be a force of nature, like his father whom he would never know.

I named him Alpha.

# 53

**8.32 p.m.**

'Is there wifi on the boat?'

Alpha had slipped his Tokarev TT-33 pistol into his belt. His arms, his fists, his athletic build were enough to deter Gavril from playing the hero. Alpha didn't let him out of his sight, even though the skipper of the *Sébastopol* seemed to have realised that the giant who was hijacking his boat wasn't about to shoot him and fling his body overboard. At least, not right away. Gavril was regaining some colour in his face, and a semblance of self-confidence.

'Wifi? Why? So when you've turned this old tub into a floating brothel, you wanna download porn, do you? Like lorry drivers in their cabs?'

'What about phones? Have you got reception?'

'Listen, you'd get reception on the bloody moon today. Even if you sailed to the ends of the earth, a thousand miles from Easter Island, you can't be left in peace any more.'

Gavril was right on this score. Alpha clutched his phone as if it were somehow more useful on this vessel than either a lifeboat or a lifebuoy. Today, millions of young migrants no longer had a home, didn't know where they'd be sleeping the next day or in a month's time, nor in which city, nor in which port, had no idea where their scattered families could be found – and yet they all had an address.

An address with an @ symbol! Thereby leaving a trail behind them.

He looked up at the Great Bear, Vega, Andromeda.

Becoming a tiny star. On the web.

Alpha scrolled through the contacts list on his phone and tapped on *Brazza*.

'Savorgnan? It's Alpha.'

He pressed the speaker harder against his ear. He could barely hear a thing. The sound of waves here; music, laughter, shouting at the other end.

'Can you hear me, Savorgnan?'

'Wait, I'm just going to move . . .'

Alpha continued to keep a close eye on Gavril, and motioned him to slow down the *Sébastopol*. The conversation finally became almost audible.

'I'm on my way, Savorgnan. Everything's going to plan. I'm crossing the Mediterranean, I'm arriving on the other side tomorrow. As soon as I get there, I'll need your friends.'

'Alpha . . .' (Savorgnan left a long silence hanging in the air. Alpha almost thought he had hung up.) 'The war's over.'

'What?'

'Babila, Safy and Keyvann are coming across. They've found space on a boat. They boarded yesterday. You might run into them. They'll reach Lampedusa tomorrow morning.'

'What difference does that make?'

'It makes all the difference, Alpha. It means everything. It means I can finally go and pick them up. It means that, even if it's hard, we'll stick it out. It means Babila's the sweetest, most tireless nurse in the world, and she'll end up being indispensable in a hospital here, it means I'll take Keyvann to Saint-Charles station to look at the trains, and one day he'll be the one driving them, it means my little Safy's going to grow up right here, in Marseille, and one day she'll be drop-dead gorgeous, enough to make all the local women green with envy, they'll be packing into her beauty salon, it means we'll go up to Pra-Loup to see the snow, it means I'll work my socks off for a whole year to take them to Disneyland, it means Babila and I will have another child and he'll really be French, he really will, and our grandchildren too, no one can ever take that identity away from them, it means we'll go to see the Bastille Day parade, the fireworks, and we'll make delicious *accras de niébé* and *poulet mafé* for our French friends.'

Savorgnan appeared to have been drinking. He was speaking too loudly.

'Don't abandon me, Savorgnan. We're at war. We must think of our brothers.'

'No, Alpha, sorry. I'm thinking about my family. I'm responsible for them. They're free at last, I want to welcome them. I'm not taking the risk of going to jail, not after all we've been through to get here. Reunited. All together.'

At the helm, Gavril was smiling inanely. He had practically turned off the engine. The headlights of the *Sébastopol* were flashing in the night, like a vehicle in distress stopped on the side of the road.

'We're at war, Savorgnan,' repeated Alpha, 'we must win.'

In the background, behind the Beninese, a female voice was singing. Others were accompanying her. People were applauding.

'It's not my war any more, Alpha. Happy men don't go to war.'

# 54

Most of the men passing through Rue Monnot, in front of Gordon's Café, turned around to look at her. They would peek discreetly or stare intently – from the furtive, guilt-ridden glances of boys with their girlfriends to the cruder advances of males hunting in packs.

Bamby rebuffed them all, curling her lip in scorn. Crossing her legs under her daringly short skirt, tossing a cardigan over the low-cut neckline of her blouse. Desperate for Yan to arrive. His lateness riled her more than ever. She wondered whether she'd been right to dress more sexily than she had at lunchtime. She could have turned up in a burqa and it wouldn't have made any difference to the voracious appetite of Vogelzug's logistics manager. She reflected on Yan Segalen's pathetic pick-up strategy.

*A second job interview. Which would take a more . . . intimate turn.*

What a monster of hypocrisy!

*Let there be no misunderstanding between us – that doesn't mean you'll be hired.*

The poor little darling also felt the need to ease his conscience, to protect himself from any sense of abusing his authority, while flattering his pride at the same time. *She's sleeping with me because she wants me, not because she wants the job.* Bamby was just sending a text to Chérine when Yan loomed up in front of her.

He did not emerge from Rue Monnot or Place des Martyrs, as she'd been expecting, but from the Lebanese restaurant, Em Sherif, just across from Gordon's.

'So sorry for being late, *ma belle*. I've ordered some mezze to make up for it. The chef at Em Sherif makes the best in the city.'

Bamby felt reassured. After all, Yan's tardiness suited her. Drag it out. Drag it out. As late as possible into the night. Postpone the moment when she could no longer back down, when Yan would no longer feel like acting and would fling himself at her. She had to remain in control of the tempo! A good Lebanese restaurant — well, that promised a procession of fifteen courses. She was going to relish the whole thing, going so far as to lick the bottom of the plates of houmous and aubergine caviar. Then, late in the evening, she would suggest he take her home. The perfect plan.

'Perfect, Yan,' she confirmed, fluttering her lashes as if applauding him with her eyes, 'you're just perfect.'

She stood up and stared at the Lebanese restaurant on the other side of the street, feeling nervous about cutting through the endless stream of pedestrians on the pavement and vehicles on the road. She felt so uncomfortable in her high heels and tight skirt. She could feel Yan's gaze drifting down her back, bouncing off her buttocks, sliding down her legs, as sticky as the drops of sweat running down her spine.

Game, set and match! That night, Yan Segalen would follow her wherever she wanted. Except to the Red Corner, which was clearly too risky. The entrances to Red Corners across the entire globe were probably more closely monitored than those of the Pentagon and, even if they weren't, Yan was bound to have heard about the murders of François Valioni and Jean-Lou Courtois.

'You coming?'

Yan had taken her hand; she was expecting him to help her across. But instead, the logistics manager led her towards the entrance of Gordon's Café.

'Aren't we going to Em Sherif? You've just ordered!'

'Yes, but to start off with, Fleur, I've booked a room at Gordon's. The Executive Suite, with a panoramic view of the city.'

She had to stop herself snatching her hand violently away from Segalen's.

'And the mezze?' stammered Bamby.

She immediately realised how stupid her question was. Yan had planned everything.

'The chef's a friend. He's delivering everything to my room in thirty minutes. The champagne must have arrived by now.'

Bamby followed him.

Controlling the tempo? Nothing was unfolding as she had intended. Everything was spinning out of control . . . And the evening had barely begun. In a few minutes, she would find herself alone in a suite with Yan. Without a plan. Everything had been too easy, everything had gone too fast. She hadn't been wary enough. She hadn't been prepared enough. She'd taken too many risks, because of the police, because of their ever-tightening vice.

A figure *VIII* was flashing in luminous letters on the golden panel embedded in the marble.

*VII, VI, V, IV.*

The lift would take a few seconds to come down.

*III, II, I.*

A few more seconds to go back up to the eighth floor, to the suite with champagne and a panoramic view.

A few seconds to think.

To improvise.

After all, Segalen wasn't going to rape her.

She wasn't risking anything.

Nor was Yan Segalen.

At worst, the monster would make it out alive.

# 55

Julo watched the shower of sparks illuminating the night, clinging briefly to the sky, then tumbling back onto the edge of the concrete quay. Apart from the glittering sprays of fire, he could only make out shadows, those of the three workers armed with their blow-torches, of the iron hull mounted on the slipway, of the harbour cranes. Those who love a leisurely stroll after dark, and who also love boats, are so lucky. They can switch from port to port, every single night of the week: ports used for fishing vessels on Mondays, for pleasure craft on Tuesdays, for passenger boats on Wednesdays, for the military on Thursdays. And, tonight, ports used for merchant shipping and trade. Of all of them, these were Julo's favourite, probably because no one but him would have any desire to roam around there, between the smoke from refineries bristling with flares and the stench of oil, petroleum and gas. Probably also because tonight he didn't feel like listening to teenage laughter on a beach, or watching slender figures in singlets jogging by. On the tablet sitting on his lap, the images had changed from the previous day. He had replaced the shots of Bambi13 and Faline95 with an island.

*Lampedusa.*

An Italian island, closer to the shores of Tunisia than the coast of Sicily.

Almost by chance, he had typed these nine letters into an image search engine.

LAMPEDUSA.

The contrast had left him devastated. A slide show depicting the tragicomedy of the world flashed before his eyes: turquoise water and dark skin, translucent creeks and littered corpses, tanned bodies crammed onto crescent-moon beaches or makeshift boats. The same sense of overcrowding – one in paradise, the other in hell.

He would return to Bamby and Faline later. Since that morning, since the discovery of the murder at the Red Corner in Dubai, all his certainties had been shaken to the core. Everything pointed to Bamby Maal. Everything from the identical nature of the photos to the blood found in the Caravanserai room. And yet, physically, it was impossible – how could she have committed a crime five thousand kilometres away?

*Just need to be patient*, Petar had grunted. *The DNA will speak for itself.*

Julo had left the image page and settled for reading the top results from a basic news search. LAMPEDUSA. Travel and holiday offers urging Europeans to visit the island were intermingled with stories of tragedy.

95 hotels in Lampedusa. Make the most of our special offers!
  Booking.com.
2013 Lampedusa migrant shipwreck – Wikipedia.
Lampedusa, visit the town – Up to 55 per cent off.
  www.routard.com.
Lampedusa, deadly gateway to Europe – BFMTV.

More than three thousand people had drowned off the island's coast since 2002. Twice the number of deaths from the *Titanic*, half the population of the island.

Out on the docks, a gentle breeze was whipping up the sparks from the blowtorches; they fluttered around for a few seconds, before fizzling out in the waves. Stars more ephemeral than soap bubbles. During a secondary school trip, Julo had visited Checkpoint Charlie in Berlin: the lunatics who had died crossing the wall, from east to west, had become heroes, resistance fighters, martyrs! Yet those who attempted to cross borders today, from south to north, attracted by the same West, by the same democracies, were at best outlaws, at worst terrorists.

A question of numbers? Method? Colour? Religion?

Or had the world's compass simply gone haywire?

*Their death is a declaration of love.*

Julo held his head in his hands. He had read this sentence on the Vogelzug website.

*Their death is a declaration of love.*

Illustrated with photos of migrants crammed into little dinghies, a few kilometres off the coast.

*Vogelzug.*

The Port-de-Bouc organisation where both Valioni and Courtois used to work. Julo clicked at random in its labyrinthine website, which offered explanations of the phenomenon of migration in a dozen languages, searching desperately for traces of a coloured band around a wrist, of a shell in the palm of a hand. For a connection. Any connection at all.

He surfed for many long minutes without finding anything. He split his screen into two windows, and decided to go back to the Facebook pages for Bambi13 and Faline95. To compare them, once again. If this girl *wasn't* Bamby Maal, she must be some other girl who had tried to incriminate her. And therefore a girl who knew her . . .

His phone vibrated in his pocket.

A message.

*Petar.*

Julo was unsure whether he should read it. They had fallen out on the way back from the Heron, when Julo had again insisted on hauling in Jourdain Blanc-Martin for questioning. Petar had refused. Categorically. Tempers had flared, and to cut the conversation short Petar had turned up the volume on the car radio. Renaud was singing 'As soon as the wind blows' . . .

They had been driving along the shore, not very far from Les Aigues Douces. Some kids were swimming, and Petar had eyed them with contempt before blurting out:

'The sea's disgusting. It's where all the migrants end up snuffing it.'

They had carried on driving in silence, passing in front of the

Carrefour, then the multiplex where Jack Sparrow had blanked them, the Starbucks, the Red Corner. It must have been a little after 5 p.m. by then, and a dozen or so cars were visible in the parking area of the red hotel with its pyramidal roof. Evidently, rooms at the Red Corner were in greater demand from 5 to 7 p.m. than in the middle of the night.

Julo had noticed there were no police officers on guard duty outside the building.

'So what?' Petar had replied, irritated. 'We're not going to stick officers in front of every single Red Corner in the world. There are limits to the precautionary principle, Professor Hawking!'

'Not all of them, agreed,' Julo had persisted. 'But still, surely the one in Port-de-Bouc . . .'

'And your point is? What's so special about it? No one's been murdered there!'

Julo had said nothing in return. Gobsmacked. His boss's logic went right over his head.

For a second, he had the surreal feeling that he and Petar Velika were working on the same investigation, but in two parallel universes, with two solutions to the same crime; that there was not one, but several truths.

They took a few long minutes before speaking again – as if they each had some distance to cover before they could slip back into their bodies, sitting in the same Renault Safrane crossing the bridge over the Canal de Caronte, Julo at the wheel and Petar slumped in the passenger seat, with an uninterrupted view of the pastel-coloured houses of the Île de Martigues district.

A few hours later, Petar was sending him a text. What outrageous remark was he about to come out with now?

Piqued by curiosity, Julo opened the message anyway. The text appeared on the screen.

We've got the girl.
Bamby, your little darling.
She's trapped.

# 56

**9.17 p.m.**

Noura had been singing for over an hour now. This time, the double
fire doors of the Heron's breakfast room had been left open, so all
guests could enjoy the performance. In her bewitching deep voice,
Noura was covering songs from the repertoire of Angélique Kidjo,
the Beninese diva. 'Idjé-Idjé', 'Wé-Wé', 'Batonga'.

Drawing on a host of languages and styles of music, gospel and
English, zouk and French, reggae and Fon, rumba and Bambara,
sega and Mina, Noura was blending it all together, improvising in
each verse, stretching out the choruses. Darius was trying to keep
pace on the djembe, while Whisley indulged in long solos on the
guitar which Noura accompanied by swaying her hips provocatively.
The thirty or so people who were dancing were following her, clapping, singing, thrilled to the core. Happy, joyful as never before.

Old Zahérine was telling complete strangers who'd been woken
up by the concert that his cousins were arriving, cousins from Djou-
gou whom he hadn't seen for twenty years. Whisley had slipped a
photo of Naïa, his fiancée, between the strings of his spare guitar;
she had boarded the same boat, she was a diva too and he'd learnt
to play just for her. Noura was bound to be horribly jealous, but
he'd convince them to sing as a duo. They'd be a smash hit! Darius,
the only legally resident foreigner within the small Beninese community, had donned an old, threadbare grey suit, and was talking
about going to welcome his uncle Rami – the former chief of the
village of Dogbo-Tota – and his wife Fatima as soon as they arrived.

Ruben Liberos was serving fruit juice, soft drinks and champagne. He'd been given entire crates of a special vintage by Tsar Nicholas's grandson, who had been exiled to Épernay as a reward for some obscure secret mission that no one really cared about. Savorgnan placed a hand on the hotel manager's shoulder and pulled him a little to one side, so as to enjoy a celebratory drink with him.

'Thank you, Ruben. Thank you.'

'I'm so happy. Happy for you. In a few days, in a few weeks, you'll all be together again.'

'And what about you, my brother, don't you have a family?'

Liberos emptied his glass of champagne. Too fast. Noura was undulating her body more and more, devouring Savorgnan with her eyes, singing the same lines over and over again.

'No . . . But there's no need to feel sorry for me, that's my choice. I'm a rolling stone. Nothing can grow on a rolling stone, especially if it's rolling the other way to the rest of the world.'

Ruben poured more champagne into both Savorgnan's glass and his own.

'Let us raise a toast to your families, my brother. To all your families, whether separated or reunited. When I was a child, my parents dispatched me to boarding school, in Salamanca, more than fifty kilometres from home, and I would only see them three times a year – at Christmas, Easter and in the summer. I despised them so much, back then. I'd been banished by my own parents. Today, if they were still with us, I could never thank them enough. Had it not been for them, I would have remained stuck in my village, like other children my age, raising pigs, and raising children who would raise my pigs in turn when I died. Today, my dear brethren, you have come to realise that our world is but a village. So scatter yourselves across the globe, my brothers, spread yourselves everywhere, gather sweet nectar from every flower on the planet. And the day you are all finally back together shall be a day of celebration.'

They drained their glasses once more.

'I shall reimburse you for the champagne,' said Savorgnan. 'When I win the Goncourt for my book!'

Ruben gently dismissed the Beninese's offer with a casual flick of his hand, and stared at him intently.

'How much did you pay for your family?'

'Not much.'

'Which is?'

'Three million CFA francs. Just under five thousand euros for each passenger.'

Ruben's gaze swept across the dancing crowd. Men and women who didn't even have ten euros in their pockets. Let alone a hundred euros in the bank.

'We get by,' said Savorgnan. 'Sometimes a whole village chips in. Sometimes you get into debt with a broker for the rest of your life.'

'What about you?'

'A loan. Over thirty years. In less than ten years we'll have paid it off, with my private lessons and my royalties, and Babila's salary as a nurse. We know how to save. Then we'll pay for Keyvann's studies, so he gets a job on the railways, we'll buy a beauty salon for Safy. Some folk pay a whole lot more, you know. Babila, Keyvann and Safy only have green bands.'

Ruben Liberos looked at him, wide-eyed with puzzlement. The champagne was beginning to make him feel giddy. Making the most of Noura taking a break, Whisley's guitar and Darius's djembe had embarked on a madcap race against each other.

'Our network of people smugglers uses wristbands in three different colours,' explained Savorgnan. 'Depending on what you're paying for the crossing. The same plastic bands you're made to wear in all-inclusive holiday resorts, which you can't swap or forge, which you keep on for the length of your stay, which you cut off and throw away afterwards. A green band if you pay five thousand euros, blue if you pay seven thousand, red if you pay ten thousand.'

Ruben tried clumsily to place his glass on the counter beside him. It tipped over, rolled along and fell to the floor.

'What's the point of paying ten thousand if your only goal is to get to the other side of the Mediterranean?'

'Depending on the colour of the band, you'll be crammed into the hold or sitting on deck – you'll be glued to the engines or seated by a porthole. You'll either have drinking water or you won't. You'll set off, or you'll have to wait, if there's not enough room on the boat, or if the forecast's not looking good. Does that shock you, Ruben?' (Savorgnan chuckled; he'd had too much to drink as well.) 'I was shocked too, at first, but then I thought about it. Everything works like that, doesn't it? Any form of transport, anywhere! Business or economy class. Penned in like cattle or pampered like caliphs. Why should illegal migrants be denied the same choice?'

The manager bent down with difficulty to retrieve his glass.

'Coloured wristbands to differentiate the passengers,' he muttered. 'That's one hell of an invention.'

'Hardly! It's nothing new. The millions of migrants who populated America were separated on ocean liners, even back then – on the one hand, you had those who'd paid a fortune to enjoy the incredible luxury of these floating cities, while down in steerage, the rest of the passengers were dying in their hundreds, packed in like dogs.'

Savorgnan pulled Ruben forward by the shoulder again. They edged closer to the improvised dance floor. Noura had changed her repertoire, and was now performing pop hits by the Fulani singer Inna Modja.

'I'm going to let you into a secret,' said Savorgnan, bringing his lips close to Ruben's ear. 'I didn't choose my people smuggler for the wristbands. It was for the cowries.'

'The cowries?' repeated Ruben.

'We pay in shells,' whispered the Beninese.

His eyes shone as brightly as Noura's.

'In rare shells,' said Savorgnan. 'Special cowrie shells. Within the network, a cowrie's worth a hundred euros. You can do the maths – I paid a hundred and fifty cowries for my family to cross over. To be paid in small amounts – at each stage, to each intermediary, at each border. I didn't want Babila, Keyvann and Safy crossing Africa with fifteen thousand euros stashed in the lining of their clothes. Whereas cowries, outside the network, are worth nothing at all.'

'Smart,' said Ruben, approvingly. 'Very smart.'

Noura carried on, now more suggestive, more bewitching than ever, not taking her eyes off Savorgnan for even a second.

Guests in pyjamas suddenly appeared in front of the fire door. A mother, father and two children. Tired and dishevelled, having awoken with a start. They were handed glasses of punch, fruit juice for the children, fish fritters and samosas. They accepted without batting an eye, stunned, as if they had fallen asleep in the Heron Port-de-Bouc and woken up on a different continent altogether.

Ruben let go of Savorgnan for a moment and went up to the singer. She was in a trance.

'Sing,' he whispered in her ear. 'Sing all night, *ma belle*, for your rival will not be here tonight.'

# 57

When Bamby opened the door to the Executive Suite of Gordon's Café, she thought someone was already waiting for her inside. She felt nervous about going in. Yan gave her a skilful little push in the small of her back.

No choice.

Keep moving.

The room was empty . . . but someone had got there before them. Two bedside lamps cast a soft, orangey light on the walls. Music with a hint of jazz filled the room. Rose petals lay scattered on the bed. For a bog standard job interview, Yan had certainly pulled out all the stops!

The bathroom door had been left open. On purpose. Behind a glass partition, now covered in mist, steam was rising from a jacuzzi which some unseen employee must have filled up, timed with precision just as Yan had ordered. Two champagne glasses stood delicately poised on the edge of the bubbling tub. A bottle of champagne lay cooling in an ice bucket, mounted on a stand.

Yan placed his satchel and safari jacket on the pedestal table in the hallway, and approached Bamby, intent on kissing her. She managed to evade him, playing the spellbound ingénue.

'My God, Yan . . . I didn't know the interview involved a swimming test!'

Stall for time, thought Bamby quickly. Leave enough space between them so he wouldn't kiss her. Find a way to make Yan lie

315

down on the bed without him touching her. Find a way to neutralise him. The scarf in her bag? The belt Yan was wearing? Except that Vogelzug's logistics manager had planned out a scenario that he would follow to the letter. A scenario in which the first step consisted of them undressing, before the bath bubbles cooled down and the champagne bubbles warmed up.

'You should have told me first, Yan, I'd have brought a swimsuit.'

*No need, ma belle*, replied his eyes, fixated on her breasts. Yan Segalen was sizing her up, without any inhibition whatsoever. The crude vulgarity of his gaze, trained on her, was in striking contrast to the romantic staging of the room. The twin sides, dark and bright, of the same desire.

To possess her.

Without the slightest modesty, Yan headed towards the bathroom and began to strip off. He leant over to a thermometer floating in the jacuzzi – ostensibly to check the temperature of the water, but equally to indicate that she ought to stop dithering and messing up such perfect timing.

*The timing was too perfect!* Something didn't feel quite right about this fantasy set-up, Bamby was suddenly convinced of that. Yan Segalen's attitude seemed unnatural – this eagerness to undress, this near-absence of words whereas he was normally an inveterate chatterbox. In anyone else but Yan, she would have put this down to shyness. But not in his case . . .

'You coming?'

He had hung his white linen shirt on the towel rail. He was now naked to the waist, inviting her in. Utterly confident of his appeal, despite his chubby body. He belonged to that breed of men who are born so handsome that they convince themselves that age will never diminish their charm. That breed of men who deny women the same privilege, and are always on the prowl for younger and younger prey.

Bamby sat down on the bed, and toyed absent-mindedly with the blood-red petals.

Had Yan found her out?

In the last few days, two employees or ex-employees of Vogelzug had been murdered – by a woman. Even though the protocol for approaching Yan, perfected over a number of weeks, was nothing like the methods she'd used with François and Jean-Lou, even though she'd responded to a real job advert, even though, in the end, it was Yan who'd contacted her, it was logical that he should be wary of a pretty girl . . . a pretty girl who let herself be seduced so easily.

*Yan is sly. He's the most cunning of them all.*
*He loves women the way a hunter loves game.*
*You think he's interested in them, but he's studying them.*
*I thought he was listening to me, understood me. In reality, he was watching me.*
*Lying in wait.*
*Focused. Fascinated, even.*
*To be sure of aiming straight at the heart, when he was ready to pounce.*

'You coming?' repeated Yan. 'It's a bit late to go all shy on me now.'

'What about the waiter, when he brings the mezze?'

'We'll put on some bathrobes.'

Bamby stood up.

Stall for time. A little time. Everything was about to move very fast, about to suddenly come toppling down, she could feel it. To win Yan's trust, she unbuttoned her blouse, tossed it onto the bed, got rid of her high heels. She walked towards him, barefoot, breasts swelling under her bra. She untied her hair, which tumbled like a gleaming sheaf of wheat onto her golden shoulders.

To regain the advantage. To lay her suspicions to rest.

She was standing in the bathroom, just a few centimetres from Yan, when there was a knock at the bedroom door.

'Restaurant Em Sherif!' shouted a man's voice. 'Two mezzes for Monsieur Segalen.'

'Just put them on the bed,' replied Yan, raising his voice to be heard.

Bamby heard the door opening. Then closing again. Yan was about to step forward to leave the bathroom.

She held him back.

Instinct.

No, nothing about this scene rang true. An over-rehearsed piece of theatre. A game of entrances and exits.

She placed her hand on Yan's chest.

'No, stay here,' she whispered, 'I want him to imagine what we're doing.'

Yan recoiled in surprise, but stopped when he felt Bamby's breasts pressing against him. Felt her hand slipping down to the crotch of his canvas trousers, caressing the bulge for a second, and then beginning to unfasten his belt.

Everything happened very quickly after that. Barely a few seconds.

Bamby tugged on the belt buckle with all her strength. The leather strap coiled around Yan's waist came off at once, while his trousers, the flies already undone, slid down onto his thighs. Bamby sprang backwards, without letting go of the belt. Yan, now shackled at the ankles, and unable to run, yelled into the adjoining room.

'She's coming!'

Bamby burst into the bedroom. A man was waiting for her, face like a hardened cop, shoulders broader than the wardrobe in the hallway, brandishing a club.

A trap. A skilfully laid trap. Yan had unmasked her!

The man charged with catching her allowed himself a brief pause when he saw Bamby appear. A half-naked Barbie bearing down on him. He smiled. A pretty little doll, a girl he'd take infinite pleasure in grabbing by the waist and squeezing tightly as she wriggled between his big tattooed arms.

The belt buckle whacked him on the temple, without giving him any time to react at all. Bamby had struck him hard, whirling the steel whip in her hand without even slowing down. The club dropped onto the carpet. The wardrobe-cop collapsed onto the bed. Bamby reached for the handle of the bedroom door and caught a brief glimpse of herself, half naked, in the mirror covering the wall in the corridor. In one last knee-jerk reaction, she grabbed her bag, and Yan's jacket and satchel lying on the table in the hallway, then dashed into the hotel corridor. The man with the club was left screaming 'Biiiiitch!' at her, while Yan finally emerged from the bathroom, waddling ridiculously, like a penguin.

*VIII, VII, VI, V, IV, III, II, I.*

Bamby put on the safari jacket in the lift, her heart pounding. She sprinted through the lobby of Gordon's Café, found herself on Rue Monnot, and kept on running until she reached Place des Martyrs. People were turning around to look at her. She hadn't had time to do up her jacket. Her chest rose up with every stride she took – longer and longer strides to get away more quickly, hitching her skirt even higher on her thighs as she ran.

Women in hijabs stared at her. Covered their children's eyes.

She wriggled her way between two pushchairs, and sprinted towards the boulevard along the seafront, the Corniche. Three cops, parked in front of the Mouzannar jewellery store, briefly wondered whether to abandon their post and stop her for questioning.

*Keep running.*

The concrete pavement was tearing the skin on her bare feet. Brand-spanking-new tower blocks gave way to the ruins of bombed-out buildings. She clutched Yan's satchel tightly against her, in a desperate attempt to conceal her semi-nakedness.

Panic-stricken, she crossed Rue 1.

*Let me through!*

Four lanes of cars slammed on the brakes. A woman driving a white Peugeot 504 swore at her. The young driver of a Ferrari 458 whistled at her. Bamby did not slow down. She was now running along the wide promenade of the Corniche, the sea on her right, the endless lines of traffic on her left.

A few joggers crossed her path. Four men with moustaches, sitting drinking on a bench, laughed as they watched her go by. Bamby zigzagged between the pedestrians, still running – exhausted, distraught, scanning the cars that drove past her, praying that the first one to stop would be a taxi. Anything but a police car.

She carried on running for more than three hundred metres before stopping. Out of breath. Her bag kept swinging around on her shoulder. The leather of Yan's satchel was soaked in perspiration. Her skirt was now so high that her white underpants were visible. She covered her thighs in one last-ditch attempt at modesty. Flung her blonde hairpiece onto the tarmac. Under the wig, her own hair was dripping with sweat. She brushed it aside to peer at the constant flow of vehicles through her contacts, which were burning her eyes. A yellow and white Mercedes was approaching in the right-hand lane, around a hundred metres away. Finally! Bamby planted herself in the middle of the road. The taxi screeched to a halt.

Before the driver could react, she was climbing into the back.

'*Vous parlez français?* English?'

'A little . . .'

'OK, step on it! Go!'

She stared at the cedar on the flag hanging from the car radio.

'Beirut airport,' she said. 'I have to be there in fifteen minutes!'

# 58

Jourdain Blanc-Martin was chatting with Agnese De Castro, an attractive Catalan widow who owned around a dozen vacant apartments located along the Mediterranean coast, from Barcelona to Pisa, and was willing to set aside half of them to house wealthy refugees, when the strings of Barber's *Adagio* vibrated in his right pocket. The *Adagio* was performed by the New York Philharmonic and conducted by Leonard Bernstein; only Jourdain could tell the difference between this and the 'standard' version, which was the ringtone on his work phone in the other pocket.

He apologised to his guests. His dedicated colleagues would be able to negotiate the best rate for these second homes – which were only occupied for a few weeks of the year – just as well as he could. When it came to the sharing economy, renting out your apartments to wealthy refugees was far more gratifying for the ego than topping up your income with Airbnb.

He moved away from the imposing wood-panelled reception room of the Château Calissanne, where cherished donors signed cheques whose amounts were all the higher thanks to the quality of the wine. He walked down the deserted paths, through the grounds of the chateau, before answering his phone.

Max-Olivier. His Banker.

'I'm in a meeting, Max-O.'

'Official?'

'Yes. Official. But you can talk, I'm alone.'

321

'We've got an issue with the *Kenitra*. She was meant to leave Saïdia at 9 p.m., with thirty-five red bands on board, it was all sorted, but the engine's just gone kaput. She's a fearless old lady, she's been roaming around the Mediterranean for seven years, loaded like a mule.'

'Where are you?'

'In Saïdia, at the port. The skipper's just called me.'

'Have we got another boat on the quayside?'

'Not a single one! And the red bands are screaming their heads off. The forecast says a storm's on its way in the coming weeks. Things are bad enough this evening. Not a pretty sight, out at sea.'

'You make them wait then. We've no other solution.'

'Jourdain, they'll kick up one hell of a fuss! Just imagine if they blabbed!'

Jourdain could well imagine. Even though he knew they could never trace anything back to him. Few people actually believed that crazy rumour, that the head honcho of Vogelzug owed his fortune to trafficking migrants.

'When did the last boat leave?'

'An hour ago, the *Al Berkane*. Packed to the gills, with a hundred and fifty clients on board. We're stepping up the pace, before the storm they've predicted.'

Jourdain sat down against a fountain, opposite a pretty statue of Diana the Huntress surrounded by three graceful does. He paused to reflect on the problem.

'So, we've got a hundred and fifty passengers on the *Al Berkane*. How many of those have green bands?'

'Around thirty, I'd say.'

Jourdain appreciated his quick response. His Banker was efficient. As efficient as his alter ego, the Moneyman, on the other side of the prison walls. They ought to be. They were handsomely paid for simply applying the golden rules imposed by Jourdain to the letter, or rather to the number. For example, that green bands should never represent the majority of any boatload.

'OK, so you contact the skipper of the *Al Berkane* for me, he makes the thirty green bands get off in a lifeboat, and he turns around to go back to Saïdia and fetch the others.'

Jourdain sensed Max-Olivier hesitating at the other end of the phone.

'With those waves out at sea, they wouldn't last ten minutes on a little boat.'

Jourdain was forced to adopt a harsher tone. Diana turned her head away and stared at the treetops while stroking one of the does.

'What do you suggest, then? Do you think that once they're back in Saïdia, on the quayside, you'll manage to get the thirty budget migrants off again without making a scene and waking up the Moroccan police? It'll be far more discreet in the middle of the Mediterranean. We've already done this a thousand times. The skipper comes up with some lame excuse – engine failure, customs patrol, risk of a fight – and you free up thirty seats for me. And if they don't agree, and it drags on too long, the blue and red bands will take it upon themselves to chuck the others over the side anyway.'

He could hear Max-Olivier sighing. Jourdain was insistent.

'We're not forcing anyone to come on board, Max-O. If we didn't provide them with boats, they'd still try and cross clutching a lifebuoy.'

'I get it, Jourdain. Cut it out, will you. Spare me the lecture. The skipper of the *Al Berkane* is a good soldier. He won't shy away from doing what he has to.'

Jourdain carried on regardless.

'The green bands know the risks. Everyone takes their own risks. We take our risks too. If they're lucky, a patrol will pick them up. If not, it'll serve as a lesson to others. Migrants talk among themselves, and they'll realise it's better to pay more for the crossing. Will you let me know when it's sorted?'

'OK.'

Max-O didn't hang up. As if he had something else to tell Jourdain. It had nothing to do with those thirty migrants abandoned on a flimsy boat in the middle of the Mediterranean, with more chance of perishing than surviving. Drownings in the Mediterranean were counted in the dozens every month. If it wasn't him in charge of the crossing, others would be – amateurs, with far higher casualty rates.

'Anything else, Max-O?'

'That kid from yesterday. Alpha Maal. The one looking to sell five-star crossings.'

'Yes?'

'Still no news from him, not since yesterday.'

'Fuck! But I'd asked you to keep an eye on the boy! Try and find him. Before tomorrow morning!'

It was Jourdain who hung up this time. Feeling uneasy.

He had already forgotten the business about swapping passengers. The matter would be settled quickly, and the difference in profit – thirty times five thousand euros, less than two thousand cowries – was negligible. The only thing occupying his mind was this wretched Maal family. Leyli, the mother, was stubborn. But he had her over a barrel; he knew her little secret. He had a surprise in store for her tomorrow morning. And Bamby had finally been cornered, according to texts received from both Yan Segalen and Petar Velika. About time too! That just left the issue of the little bastard to resolve.

He glanced at the stone statues one last time, put his phone away in his right pocket and headed back towards the lights of the reception room of the Château Calissanne. The wine there was excellent, and the company truly delightful.

# The Day of Stone

# 59

*Get here now!*

When Julo had received Petar's text, he'd been asleep for less than four hours. No other explanation. Just this order.

*Get here now!*

No need to specify that it was urgent. Julo was beginning to get used to his boss's restraint when it came to words. Half an hour later, he entered the main room of the office. Unshaven, his hair a mess, his clothes a right mess too. He bumped into a few colleagues roaming the corridors, who looked as bright-eyed and bushy-tailed as festival-goers who'd just spent all night at a rave.

Petar, on the contrary, seemed perfectly awake. He greeted his deputy with a spanking-new smile, one he probably only reserved for special occasions.

'Sorry to drag you out of bed, kiddo, but we've had some developments.'

Julo rubbed his eyes. Petar swung his monitor around towards his deputy, but the lieutenant, either too far away or not awake enough, was unable to decipher a single word.

'Our killer's struck again,' said Petar. 'Or at least, she tried.'

'Who?' asked Julo soberly.

'Yan Segalen. Logistics manager at Vogelzug.'

*Vogelzug*, yet again . . . Petar merely sat in awkward silence. Julo didn't press him, but waited patiently. The commandant carried on.

'Yan Segalen is stationed in Beirut. He found himself in contact with a girl who was a little too pretty and a little too, shall we say, available. He became suspicious. He arranged to meet her in a location he'd chosen himself, calling on a Vogelzug security manager to nab the girl. He should have called us first. Unlike Valioni and Courtois, he made it through alive, but the girl's on the run.'

'Did Segalen identify her? Is it definitely Bamby? Bamby Maal?'

Petar broke into another ironic smile. Clearly, he hadn't revealed everything yet, and was having fun playing cat and mouse with his deputy, whose neurons, for once, were firing more slowly than his own.

'You fretting about your little sweetheart? Be patient, it's the crack of dawn in Lebanon too, we're waking the cops up, we're checking. According to Yan Segalen's statement, the girl was blonde, green eyes, olive skin, shapely curves . . . You add a wig, some contacts, a little make-up, it all fits. Fits with Bamby, and Faline, and Fleur, that's the girl's new name – and yes, I know, I'm perfectly capable of typing five letters into Wikipedia too, that's the name of Bambi's little skunk friend. The description Yan Segalen gave us matches our girl. And heaps of other girls too . . .'

Julo was finding it hard to organise his thoughts. His brain was buzzing. He was decidedly not a morning person. The smell of coffee permeated the room. He could hear water trickling through the coffee maker; he'd seen Ryan filling it earlier, just as he was arriving. *Speed up*, begged Julo in his head, *speed up, brother*.

Petar must have drunk several litres; he was excited as never before, and seemed to take great delight in smothering his deputy's little observations under a pillow of questions-and-answers.

'So, Mr Smartarse, while you refused to give up sniffing around Vogelzug and Blanc-Martin for hours on end – no use protesting sunshine, I've looked at the browsing history on your PC – I was slogging away on that girl . . . And not just by scrolling through her bikini photos on my computer. After yesterday, and Leyli Maal's testimony, and then the statement from that raving lunatic Ruben Liberos, and his list of invisible folk ready to give evidence anonymously, we've got a bit of a problem: how do you explain Bamby Maal being in Dubai the night before last? At least Beirut's more plausible, given we haven't heard from our mysterious student-singer since yesterday morning – in other words, ever since the police began to take a little too much interest in her.'

Without really being able to explain why, since Petar was neither more nor less cynical than usual, Julo didn't like the way his superior was expressing himself. He tried to concentrate, even though everything was interfering with his thoughts – the coffee maker bubbling away noisily, the radio crackling between songs and news.

'We'll get the results of the DNA tests at some point this morning,' muttered Julo wearily. 'Once we know more about the killer's blood, from the Red Corner in Dubai, we'll have our proof.'

'Oh, for God's sake, wake up! We've got a girl on the loose. A girl who's bled two decent family men to death, and tried to slash the wrists of a third. She's probably got on a plane at Beirut airport. We've kicked everyone into gear – we're busy checking all the flights since last night. We're gonna nail this girl on arrival. We're not sitting by the phone for the lab results, believe me.'

Julo had a nasty feeling he was witnessing the beginning of a hunt. A brutal hunt with horses and hounds. That moment in an investigation when everything began to gather momentum, when Petar was undoubtedly at his very best, when you had to stop pondering and start taking action instead. When it was no longer a question of understanding how and why this girl had killed these men, but simply of stopping her doing it again. Neutralising her. Forgetting, moving on.

'My theory,' continued Petar, calming down, 'is that she might not have acted alone, and that's where I'm going to need your brain.'

Julo tried to focus once more.

'I've been working hard with Ryan and Tòni since last night. Tòni came up with a superb report on Bamby Maal's circle of contacts in just one evening. It seems the prettiest gazelles move around in herds. I've got three potential candidates to play the role of twins.'

The last wisps of fog in Julo's brain were starting to clear. Once again, Petar seemed to be a far more efficient, pragmatic and instinctive cop than he was. While Julo had been spending hours struggling desperately with unsolvable brain-teasers, the commandant had been making progress.

'The first one's called Noura Benhadda. We both met her at the Heron – a pretty, mixed-race girl who apparently sings like a goddess, legally resident, earning a cleaning lady's salary, nothing to make us suspect her except her physique, and the fact that Bamby's mother works for the same company.'

Nothing new, thought Julo.

'The second, well, it was Tòni who dug her up. Kamila Saadi, one of Bamby Maal's uni friends. She lives in the apartment just below Bamby's mother. They were very close, before they fell out. According to Tòni, when it comes to being attractive, Kamila doesn't hold a candle to Bamby, but as you've said yourself, with Photoshop, you can work wonders on Facebook . . . and you don't need to be Halle Berry to lure a fifty-year-old married guy to the local Red Corner.'

A red herring, thought Julo instinctively.

'The third will interest you more. Among Bamby Maal's contacts, we found a certain Chérine Meunier, two years older than her. They met at a Zumba class at the Centre de Danse Isadora in Marseille – two tropical vines as slender as each other. They seem to have remained very close, even though they don't see each other that often. Chérine Meunier's a flight attendant with Royal Air Maroc.'

Julo's heart leapt this time. A friend who was a flight attendant! The missing link in his reasoning. A girl who could take pictures of herself all over the planet. This was surely the explanation for Bambi13's snaps on Facebook. One less puzzle . . .

And one more question. Julo's brain immediately tempered his excitement. Was Chérine Meunier a murderer who'd assumed her friend's identity, or simply her accomplice? For the first time since Julo had arrived, Petar had stopped talking. The coffee maker had stopped too.

A jingle on the radio heralded a news flash, just as Ryan entered the office.

'Julo and Petar. Two coffees? Ready!'

Lieutenant Flores did not answer. A veil had been ripped apart. Suddenly, everything around him became a blur – Petar taking his time getting up to fetch his cup, a presenter speaking on the radio, Ryan repeating himself.

*Julo and Petar. Two coffees? Ready!*

He had finally located the memory he'd been trying to track down, deep in his subconscious, for three days now. Not an image, not a feeling – a sentence! A simple sentence, heard, filtered, stored away in some random corner of his chaotic brain, simply waiting to be sifted out again.

*Bamby and Alpha. Two coffees? Ready!*

Julo could clearly associate this sentence with a place – the Starbucks near the Red Corner – and with a precise date and time: three days earlier, just a few minutes after discovering the corpse of François Valioni.

Ryan handed him a hot cup of coffee. He accepted it in a trance, like a sleepwalker.

*Bamby and Alpha.*

Those two names, linked together.

No doubt whatsoever, Julo must have been sitting next to Bamby and Alpha Maal, at the Starbucks, less than a hundred metres from the crime scene.

His thoughts were spinning dizzily around in his head once more. As soon as one clue cleared Bamby Maal's name, yet another turned up to incriminate her. Like some unsolvable jigsaw whose pieces refused to fit together. Consequently, the previous evening he'd deliberately abandoned the task of identifying this girl to focus instead on Vogelzug, the organisation which, like the tentacles of an octopus, had wriggled its way into every nook and cranny of the investigation.

When Julo finally extricated himself from his thoughts, in order to share this bizarre coincidence with his boss, he realised no one was talking in the room any more. On the radio, between a football result and the dismal unemployment figures, the presenter was breaking news of yet another all-too-common tragedy in the Mediterranean.

Just off the Chafarinas Islands, a few kilometres from the Moroccan coast.

A flimsy lifeboat on the raging sea.

A distress message picked up by the Spanish border guards. Too late.

Around fifteen drowned bodies fished out of the water, ten other bodies washed up in the mud.

*And now let's move on to the weather.*

# 60

**6.11 a.m.**

Leyli went onto the balcony and lit a cigarette. The sun was rising incognito, shielded by a curtain of cumulus clouds obscuring the line of the horizon. The tiny wisps of grey smoke she breathed out lingered around her nose, like a mini-cloud of pollution, without a breath of wind to blow them away. No waves or any foam, only the fog, cold, damp and salty. Even the sea looked only half awake.

From her apartment on the seventh floor in Les Aigues Douces, Leyli caught sight of a few shadows walking at the foot of the tower blocks. She spotted Guy among them. Collar turned up, woolly hat pulled down tightly over his ears.

She followed his movements, watching him cross the car park and then Avenue Mistral to join his fellow morning ghosts at the stop for the 22. Towards Martigues-Figuerolles. The bus she would also be taking, in a few minutes.

One day, perhaps, they would make the journey together, would leave the same bed, take turns under the same shower, share the same breakfast table, close the front door together before going down the stairs, walk side by side to catch the bus, wait for it in silence, give each other a kiss when Guy got off at the Caravelle stop while she carried on for another five stops. Leyli always felt a tinge of melancholy watching families parting tenderly just before getting on public transport, or in a school car park, only to meet again with all the more affection in the evening.

*One day, perhaps.* Not this morning. Guy had gone back down to his apartment at around 2 a.m. She had explained that he couldn't stay over, that she had to take Tidiane to school, and he had understood. He had to go to work too. A short night, a long day.

She watched the 22 as it swallowed Guy up, in the same mouthful as a good dozen other workers, two pushchairs and a few schoolchildren. Then disappeared.

Leyli was running late; she was finding it hard to dig herself out of that early-morning torpor, when your mind keeps going round and round in circles. She checked her phone once more. Still no news from Bamby, still no news from Alpha. And yet she'd left them a message the moment she'd woken up. She was worried. She continued to brood over Jourdain Blanc-Martin's threats. Her instincts whispered that she was merely a sacrificial pawn in his vast empire. An empire constructed like a board game. Whom could she trust? In her left pocket, she felt her hand rolling up the business card of the young cop she had run into the day before, at the police station. This one, at any rate, seemed honest and genuine. Like a teacher at the start of his career. Not yet as jaded as his colleagues – the one who looked like a bulldog, and the other with a Marseille accent.

She stubbed out her cigarette. *Get a move on!* She was starting her shift at the Heron in an hour. That would really be the limit – being late, when in fact she had never been so eager to get to work. She could hardly wait to hear Ruben's ludicrous stories, to chat to Savorgnan and all the other refugees in their chamber of secrets.

She put on the cardigan that lay on one of the chairs in the living room. On the sideboard, a silent presenter was reading the news. The TV was on but the volume was turned down, its faint sound drowned out by the roars of laughter from Fun Radio which Kamila, on the floor below, was listening to at full blast. Leyli stepped forward to turn it off, indifferent to the presenter who was probably commenting on the morning rush hour, judging by the stationary queues of cars projected behind him. The rolling news banner, the sole movement on the screen, seemed to revolve endlessly, like the world on its axis. Leyli's eyes caught one of the sentences at random, reading each of the words before they disappeared to the left of the screen and were replaced by a fresh item of news.

Another tragedy in the Mediterranean. Twenty-six Beninese
migrants drowned off the Moroccan coast.

Other news continued to scroll past. The world had stopped turning.

❀

Ruben was sitting in the airy breakfast room of the Heron. Alone.
Like a guest who'd been forgotten there. Abandoned. Waiting to be
cleared away.

As she entered, Leyli met his absent gaze, his bloodshot eyes, his
trembling hands. The hotel manager had aged ten years. Noura had
sat down at a table further away, in a state of shock, hands clutching
a phone.

Everything was quiet in the hotel. A few guests were waiting
patiently at the counter to pay; they hung around for a moment,
then left. Without saying a word. Like when you come across a
funeral cortege, when you suddenly fall silent and tiptoe across to
the other pavement. Other guests, after hoping in vain that Noura
or Ruben would get up, were taking away croissants, little packets
of cereal and cups of espresso. Without daring to consume them
in the breakfast room. Hungry and embarrassed. Fleeing on empty
stomachs with their hands full, no doubt overwhelmed by a guilty
conscience thanks to their meagre haul.

Little by little, the last few guests drifted away.

Leyli took a few steps towards Ruben. In her mind, the news
banner continued to roll by, on an endless loop.

*Another tragedy in the Mediterranean. Twenty-six Beninese migrants
drowned off the Moroccan coast.*

All the way there, she'd been trying to convince herself there was
only a faint probability that this news story concerned Savorgnan,
Zahérine and the other occupants of the chamber of secrets. Benin
had ten million inhabitants, thousands of refugees and a diaspora
spread all over Europe. Why imagine the worst? Whenever the news
delivers some kind of tragedy, what morbid self-centredness always
drives you to think it might have affected someone you know?

The moment she'd entered the hotel, without Ruben there to
greet her on the doorstep, her fears had been confirmed. Leyli sat

335

down opposite Ruben. The manager seemed incapable of uttering a word. She did not press him. She looked all around her, hoping to see Savorgnan, or Zahérine, or Whisley suddenly appear from somewhere . . . But it was Noura who came towards her. She simply placed her phone on the table, then opened her inbox and clicked on an audio file attachment. Even on loudspeaker, the sound was poor, practically inaudible, broken up with static. The voice sounded weak, as if short of breath. Each word, each sentence, only followed the previous one after a long silence, as when reciting a prayer. A prayer recited too late, without hope.

*Rami . . . I'm Rami . . . former chief of the village of Dogbo-Tota . . . pass on this message . . . they took us in . . . in a military hospital . . . Isla de Isabel II . . . I think . . .*

*The boat turned over . . . almost as soon as we got on . . . the Al Berkane left us . . . we didn't last five minutes . . . waves too high . . . the phones were working . . . we called right away . . . we could see the coast . . . the Chafarinas Islands, yelled Keyvann . . . this kid knew the world map off by heart . . . a Spanish military base . . . hope . . . we called . . . we screamed . . . some clung on to the upturned boat . . . others on to nothing . . . others on to others . . . before the waves scattered us . . .*

*The Spanish guys say they arrived quickly . . . as quickly as possible . . . lo más rápido . . . rápido . . . rápido . . . They kept saying it, over and over . . . they looked shocked too . . . they were counting us as they pulled us onto the frigate . . . uno . . . dos . . . tres . . . cuatro . . . they were giving us numbers . . . they were yelling . . . cuántos? cuántos? They carried on sweeping the sea, with their searchlights . . . I was number 5 . . . Fatima, my wife, number 8 . . . cuántos? cuántos? They shouted even louder . . . I shouted back, treinta y cinco . . . after Fatima they fished out another young boy . . . number 9 . . . the last one . . . they searched again, for almost an hour . . . then they gave up . . .*

*They rescued nine survivors, out of thirty-five . . . I think they did all they could . . . it's easy for me to thank them . . . they saved me . . . my wife too . . . but you, you'll curse them for ever . . . they went back out to sea . . . when the sea had calmed down . . . as soon as the sun came up . . . looking for bodies . . . some had already been washed up . . . in the morning, the coast seemed even closer . . . barely a kilometre . . . I know it's even more cruel, saying it . . . I'm so sorry . . . I'm talking too much . . . I'm just stringing words together . . . to put off the moment when I'll have to give you their names . . . we all knew each other . . . we came from the same region . . . we'd been living together for three months, waiting to cross over . . . a community . . . you have to believe me, we held on, right to the very end . . . all of us, together . . . to the same dream . . . it was the sea that did the sorting . . . not the Spanish soldiers . . . it was the sea.*

The message then became inaudible. Staccato. Like when words turn into bullets, firing out of a gun. You could hear crying, indistinct words in Spanish and Fon. Then a female voice took over the rest of the message – Fatima, no doubt. A calm voice. Tactful.

*My friends. My dear friends. May you one day forgive me for being the messenger of death.*

She then went through each of the twenty-six names, one by one. Those of the dead. Slowly. Speaking clearly, to avoid any grim confusion.

Leyli flinched several times. Each time the pain stabbed her even deeper in the heart.

*Caimile and Ifrah.*

Two of Zahérine's cousins.

*Naia.*

Whisley's fiancée.

*Babila, Keyvann and Safy.*

Savorgnan's wife and children.

'Where are they?' Leyli asked Ruben gently. 'Where are Savorgnan, Zahérine, Darius, Whisley?'

'I don't know.'

Fatima's voice continued to list a few names, then stopped. Abruptly. The message cut off after announcing the name of the last victim, without Fatima even adding a 'God bless you'. All you could hear was a few words in Spanish behind her, most likely soldiers.

*Uno . . . dos . . . tres . . . cuatro . . .*

Without knowing whether they were counting the living or the dead.

Leyli handed the phone back to Noura. The young woman's eyes had never looked so dark. In recent days, Leyli had read jealousy, desire and anger in them. Now she read nothing but hatred.

'Sing,' whispered Leyli. 'Sing, Noura. Sing for them.'

Noura paused for a second, then began to sing – so softly you could barely hear – a soothing melody, whispering it half-heartedly in a language Leyli didn't know. A tender lullaby.

It seemed to last for hours.

It could have lasted for hours.

The soft cotton in Noura's voice had dried Ruben's tears. A few breakfast guests, the stragglers, had stopped to listen. The magic was working.

Leyli's phone rang. A knife in her back.

A piercing sound. Leyli rushed to answer.

Alpha? Bamby? Savorgnan, perhaps?

Noura, who had been singing for several long minutes with her eyes shut, opened them and glared at her. Leyli didn't care. Her screen displayed an unknown number. She answered.

'Madame Maal?' screamed a female voice, on the verge of hysteria. 'Madame Maal, come quickly!'

Leyli knew this voice, but couldn't quite place it.

'Madame Maal,' continued the voice, 'it's Kamila. Your downstairs neighbour. They're busy smashing up your whole apartment. They battered in the door, they rammed it with their shoulders, I went up to see, but there's two of them, and they're armed. I . . . I didn't want to inform the police, I've locked myself in, at home . . . I think they're going away . . . I'm scared, Madame Maal . . . Come quickly . . . I'm scared . . .'

Kamila was screaming so loudly that Ruben had heard everything. He had already got to his feet.

'I'm coming with you, Leyli. Let's go.'

❀

When Leyli and Ruben reached Les Aigues Douces, the two men had already left the scene. The neighbourhood seemed neither more nor less tense than usual. The mailboxes neither more nor less bashed up. The stairwell neither more nor less vandalised.

Kamila was waiting for them on the stairs.

'They've gone. They hardly stayed five minutes. What the—'

She was no doubt about to unleash a torrent of abuse, but caught sight of Ruben and seemed intimidated by his imposing presence. He had put on a long coat and a black felt Stetson and, like Leyli, was hiding his reddened eyes behind dark glasses.

Kamila was petrified. After the two hitmen, here was the clean-up guy.

'I didn't go in, Madame Maal. I swear. They made me stay out on the landing, I didn't see what they were up to.'

Without answering, Leyli and Ruben climbed another floor and entered the apartment. Almost immediately, Leyli realised that nothing had actually been taken. Besides, what was there to steal here, apart from the TV and the computer? The intruders hadn't laid a finger on them. Everything else had been swept aside with a few vigorous hand movements – her collection of owls, her books, her sunglasses. Strewn across the floor, just like the overturned mattresses, the children's clothes pulled out of their suitcases and scattered around . . .

'They . . . they've not stolen anything, I think.'

A few plaster owls had been smashed to pieces, but most of the objects were intact, as if the visitors couldn't even be bothered to stamp on them. It felt as though the apartment had been subjected to nothing more than a violent gust of wind.

'It's a warning,' continued Leyli, 'just a warning.'

She thought about Blanc-Martin again. His attempt at blackmail. She assumed he was the brains behind this visit. Intended to frighten her. To let her know that he was growing impatient. That if Bamby or Alpha contacted her, she had to talk.

To him. Or to the police?

Or were they all in cahoots?

Ruben sat down on the sofa and motioned to her to do the same.

'What were they looking for, Leyli?' he asked in a soothing voice.

Leyli was grateful to him for not conjuring up yet another anecdote, about some apartment burglary in Myanmar or Polynesia. For simply listening to her instead.

'My children. They're looking for the older ones.'

'They've gone, Leyli. It's over. They've gone.'

Leyli was silent for a long while. She picked up an owl which had rolled against her feet. A glass owl which, bizarrely, hadn't shattered when it fell.

'They'll be back. Not right away, but they'll be back.'

'Why?'

Leyli smiled. She picked up another owl, made of carved wood, and placed it next to the glass one.

'There's no rush now, Ruben. Would you like to hear the end of my story?'

## LEYLI'S STORY

### Final Chapter

Alpha had just been born. His father, Virgile, had been killed, shot down while trying to get through the barbed wire at Melilla. My attempt to enter Europe had turned into a fiasco. I'd heard those stories about women who still wanted to make the journey across anyway, with their babies, and ended up going mad, by dint of clinging on to a tiny corpse, a child who had died in the desert or during the sea crossing.

I went back to live in Ségou. I wanted to see Bamby again. I wanted to introduce Alpha to his grandparents. I was exhausted, Ruben. I'd survived two attempts to leave, I'd had a brush with death, I'd brushed against Europe. I no longer had the strength to carry on. I already needed so much for the journey back.

To return to Ségou was to fail. In spite of the gentleness of my mother and father, in spite of Bamby's cousins and their games, in spite of the neighbours and their endless chatter.

Long ago, my father had told me a great many stories, so many tales, to prepare me, so I could make my children believe the river was an ocean. That there was nothing beyond. That radios, books and TV screens were all lying. Can you understand that, Ruben? Of course you can. I had to find a way of giving them another life. Legal ways, like Jean-Jacques Goldman says in that song 'Fly Me Away' . . .

I was more attractive than the others, I think; I was smarter too. I loved books. Some young men liked this – the ones from the city, the ambitious ones, the ones who wouldn't remain here, the ones who'd succeed in life. I met Wa'il during the 2002 Malian presidential elections. Wa'il was campaigning in the Ségou Cercle district, part of Ségou Region, for Ibrahim Boubacar Keïta's party. He maintained IBK would be president one day, so he was campaigning while studying for a law degree and writing a thesis on democracy. Wa'il came from Kayes, from a business family much wealthier than mine. He wore tiny glasses, dressed in Western clothes, and always had a book on philosophy or economics tucked into his pocket. He would call me his little princess, his Simone when he thought of himself as Sartre, his Colette when he imagined he was Senghor, his Winnie when he fancied himself as Mandela.

I liked that.

Even though he had been elected as a town councillor in Ségou, he spent a lot of time in Bamako. With his party. He wanted to become a *député*, elected to parliament. He wanted me to come and join him. With my daughter. He wanted me to study. He was really fond of Bamby. She was already tall for her age. In three or four years, we could enrol her in secondary school, at the girls' *lycée* in Bamako. We could take an apartment in the Hippodrome district.

On condition that I left Alpha behind. The brawler. The neighbourhood terror. Wa'il didn't care much for my son, a child born of rape according to him, and the more I claimed otherwise, the angrier Wa'il would get. He hated it when I brought up my past relationship with Virgile. For even though Wa'il was a pretentious social climber, he had the intelligence to see that – of all the men who had protected me – Virgile was the only one to whom I had given everything. Wa'il would only ever have my admiration, and no more – a union based on reason, never burning passion.

I became pregnant while Wa'il was in the fourth year of his doctoral research. Our lives were split between Ségou and Bamako, and I would join him as often as I could. I did some work for the Centre Djoliba in Bamako. I sifted through the daily papers. Tidiane was born in 2006. We lived on hope. Wa'il's thesis would soon be finished, he'd soon have a job at the university, he'd soon be elected as a *député*, his parents would soon give him enough money to buy that apartment.

Soon, soon, soon, Ruben. We build whole lives with 'soons' in Bamako. Africa is the continent of the 'soon'. But in Africa, as elsewhere, men are in a hurry. One fine day, Wa'il told me he'd landed a grant from the Canadian Francophone Co-operation Agency to go off and finish his thesis in Quebec. An opportunity that was impossible to turn down. The chance of a lifetime! Wa'il hugged me, he was trembling at the very thought of it, even though it was only for a few months. Canada, Canada, he kept repeating the name like an explorer – he would arrange for me to join him over there. Soon.

I don't think I need to dwell on what happened next, Ruben. For the first few weeks, we would spend hours connected on social media. He was homesick, he missed Bamby, his baby Tidy, he felt the cold, he felt his head spinning, he dreamt of the Niger when he gazed at the St Lawrence. Then our interactions became less frequent, but Wa'il always remained visible online. I would keep up with him via the photos on his Facebook page, or those of his friends: Malians, Africans from Quebec, almost all students like him. Photos in which he no longer felt the cold, of parties where he was drinking, of nights where he was dancing.

Tidy's first words, Bamby starting her first year at secondary school, all of that interested him less. He was constantly surrounded by the same faces on Facebook. Wa'il was creating a new family for himself. They kept reappearing, always the same girls. Then, before long, always the same girl. On his lap, draped around his neck. Her name was Grace. She was an anthropology student. Wa'il didn't post any photos of her on his profile, but she uploaded some to her own page. Unambiguous pictures. The comments left no room for doubt. Wa'il and Grace were a couple. One night, I took the plunge. I sent a message to Grace.

*Leyli Maal is sending you a friend request.*

She accepted. I realised that she didn't know who I was. That she didn't even know I existed. I only realised then that Wa'il never mentioned Tidy on his page.

That same evening, I sent Grace and Wa'il a message of congratulations, along with a photo of myself holding Tidiane in my arms. They never replied. I guess they spent the night talking. Grace must have gone ballistic, freaked out with jealousy. I've no idea what Wa'il could have told her to defend himself, but he won in the end. The next day, I no longer appeared on the list of their friends.

Over the weeks and months that followed, I continued to visit their page. I still look at it sometimes, Ruben – apparently I've developed a taste for misery. They got married, they live in Montreal, they've got a child – he's two years younger than Tidiane, everything's going well. If I ever see Wa'il again one day, maybe I ought to thank him. Does that surprise you, Ruben? Let me explain.

One evening in October, I went online. It was their little Nathan's birthday, he was born the day after Halloween. He had celebrated his third birthday with his friends from Quebec, half of them white, the other half black – it didn't seem to matter, the only colours that mattered were the orange of the pumpkins and jack-o'-lanterns, the colours of the costumes you saw children wearing in their spacious homes, of showers of sweets, of a party that finished at McDonald's and then at the La Ronde amusement park. The happy parents had posted a whole photo album of this unforgettable day. My Tidiane had celebrated his own birthday just a few months earlier. But I hadn't been able to give him anything other than smiles – as many smiles as you want, my child. Smiles that resembled the worst shame of all.

I knew full well that with Tidy, Alpha and Bamby in tow, I'd never be able to smuggle myself across into Europe. That was all over now. So I hatched another plan. I sold a few pieces of jewellery from Adil's stash of loot, that curse-ridden booty I'd promised myself never to touch, and along with my whole family – my three children and my parents – we left for Morocco. For Rabat. Some distant cousins ran a restaurant there. They were looking for staff. We settled down with an official work permit. Morocco wasn't Europe, but it was a first step. My mother suffered from back pain, my father from osteoarthritis, his trade as a potter earned him practically nothing any more, and I'd convinced them that Rabat would be an El Dorado with doctors, hospitals, proper wages.

It was true. Rabat was an El Dorado, even if I had lied to them about everything else. I hadn't told them about my plans, so as not to scare them. Deep down inside, Ruben, I'll be honest with you, I'd never given up on making it across. To Europe. To France. Legally!

The cousins who ran the restaurant in Rabat, in the Kasbah des

343

Oudayas, had another one in Marrakesh, a third in Essaouira, and one more in Marseille. I'll share another little secret with you, Ruben – I'm the lousiest cook in the whole of West Africa, to my mother's eternal despair.

They say that blind people develop their other four senses. Not me! I hate smells. I've no patience for chopping up vegetables and grinding spices for hours on end, the sight of meat oozing blood, halal or not, makes me sick, and I infinitely prefer spending my nights alone – wearing earphones, cleaning supermarkets bigger than football pitches – to obeying the orders of some bossy little chef in a kitchen. And yet, I still offered my services. To the Magot Berbère, in Marseille.

They didn't need anyone. Least of all me. So I told them I could subsidise my own job. Paying myself, Ruben, just to be absolutely clear. I dipped into that damned treasure chest one last time and paid them fifteen thousand euros under the table, to finance a one-year fixed-term contract which they'd pay me back as declared income. All they had to do was to write a nicely worded employment offer letter, to the consulate, saying there was no one matching my skills along the entire southern bank of the Niger – let alone anywhere in France – to cook *fakou-ouï* and *poulet yassa*. That it was me they wanted, me and only me. For twelve months.

'And after the twelve months?' the cousin had asked. 'I won't be able to pay you any more. Your work visa will have expired. You'll have to go back to Morocco. If you stay, you'll be an illegal resident.'

'I'll find a way, cousin, I'll find a way.'

I knew my rights. The requirements for becoming legally resident were straightforward. I had read them so often, on the form issued by the Bouches-du-Rhône *préfecture*: *Three years' physical presence in France, being able to prove you had worked for twenty-four months, including eight consecutive months during the previous twelve months.*

I had to survive for three years. Three years without getting caught. Three years while working, paying taxes, proving I paid rent. It might sound Kafkaesque, Ruben, but those are the rules of the game. Illegal migrants, in reality, simply end up collecting those rules, accumulating them. Like loyalty points.

Working isn't difficult, if you accept the daily grind that goes with it.

Three years of putting up with humiliation, being hunted down, being ripped off, blackmail, slavery, but I stuck it out, since I was building up my tax and social security contributions, month by month. I even agreed to work for nothing, nothing but a scrap of paper. I finally understood that was why the state left us in peace – us, the invisible folk. We pay our contributions, we spend our money too, we abide by all the rules like every other citizen – but without demanding any rights whatsoever.

For three years.

Three years without seeing my children.

I was ticking off the days, Ruben. In hiding. I was counting the months – I had to get to thirty-six, and then I'd become a bona fide resident foreigner.

Legally!

Everything would then be simple. I could bring my children over via the family reunification procedure.

Legally!

Legally, Ruben. Do you hear me? Legally!

I was no longer being hunted. We had won, without cheating.

Nothing, no one could ever separate us any more.

# 61

Sitting on the seat by the window, Bamby pulled the safari jacket tight against her chest. It was too big for her and didn't seem designed to be buttoned. In spite of her efforts, the khaki canvas jacket kept opening with every move she made. She closed it again patiently, as much for comfort as for modesty. She was shivering with cold, the air conditioning in the plane was biting at her skin. Unless it was the pressure dropping off.

She had made it through!

Only just, but she'd made it nevertheless. She'd left on the morning flight. She had a fake passport, and she hadn't had to worry about either documents or tickets – Chérine was always able to help her out. She had taken refuge in a hotel reserved for Royal Air Maroc flight crew, two hundred metres from Beirut airport. From her room, she'd been able to book her tickets and wait for the departure time. Impossible to get changed, however. She'd been quaking with anxiety right up until the plane took off; the airports were riddled with security cameras, and she couldn't possibly have gone unnoticed by the officials who were paid to do nothing but keep a watchful eye on the passengers.

Bamby pressed her face against the window. The Airbus was flying over an archipelago that was impossible to identify. Some Greek islands, no doubt. In the next seat, a one-and-a-half-year-old baby – a little boy, maybe? – was standing on his father's lap, taking great delight in bobbing up and down while giving Bamby cheeky sideways glances. Mummy was asleep on the third seat in the row.

Bamby closed her eyes for a moment. She had bought some time. But only a little. If Yan Segalen had informed the police, the cops would have no trouble spotting her on the security cameras, following her step by step, and thereby discovering which plane she had boarded, even if she'd checked in under an assumed name. The police would simply have to wait for her in the arrivals hall, leaving them several hours to quietly weave their web.

Yes, the more Bamby thought about it, the more glaringly obvious it became: the most likely outcome of her going on the run was that everything would grind to a halt once she'd landed. Deciding to lock herself away in this plane had been such an absurd thing to do! But what other option could she have chosen? None, except for making the best possible use of the last few minutes of freedom she had left.

She unfolded the plastic tray table in front of her, and pulled out a laptop from the leather satchel lying at her feet. The one belonging to Yan Segalen, which she'd grabbed in passing before fleeing from the Executive Suite at Gordon's Café.

When she turned it on, she was surprised that the device wasn't even protected by a password. A shambolic desktop appeared: dozens of icons littered about, shortcuts to various folders. Bamby started by clicking on the Excel files. She scrolled through endless tables, deciphering names in rows, destinations in columns, amounts in cells. Each table consisted of several identical sheets, differentiated only by month. Bamby suddenly felt a warmth deep inside her, contrasting with the goosebumps prickling her skin. If the police did arrest her, she now had a bargaining chip: Vogelzug's secret accounts . . . even if it wasn't quite the revenge she had dreamt of.

Through the window, the miniature harbours and pointed mountains of an island larger than the rest were playing hide-and-seek with the clouds. That must be Crete, thought Bamby. Viewed from the sky, it resembled Australia. Next to her, the baby was having fun trying to stuff his dummy, now soaked in drool, into his father's mouth.

She sat there for a few minutes, analysing the situation. Her heart felt cold again. She carried on scrolling through the tables of names and figures, mechanically this time, not even looking at them any more. Yan Segalen had been roaming around with this computer slung over his shoulder, without any password keeping it secure. What was she thinking? That she was going to bring down Vogelzug simply by opening a file? These guys were pros! Yan Segalen, warier than a hyena. Of course there was nothing incriminating on this laptop. At least, nothing she could find on her own.

And she was indeed on her own. Cut off from the world, at a height of ten thousand metres, with no internet. She would only have a few minutes to ask for help, between the moment the plane landed on the tarmac and the moment the police apprehended her.

Whom to call? Chérine? Alpha? Maman?

Bamby clicked randomly on the icons, concentrating mainly on the PDF and JPEG files. She had navigated away from the desktop on Segalen's computer and delved into the sub-folders, selecting the oldest ones, choosing to open those neglected for years. She paused at a photo of Yan Segalen, from October 2011, posing with a cocktail in his hand, on a sunny terrace, in the company of a slim man, the kind whom old age only makes more attractive and grey hair even sexier.

Bamby shuddered. She pressed her forehead against the window again, freezing her brain.

*Jourdain Blanc-Martin.*

When he was a few years younger.

Bamby had never met the president of Vogelzug, but all you had to do was type his name into Google Images to see his face on each of his online profiles. Chérine found him so manly. Poor Chérine . . . The sweat from Bamby's brow left wet marks on the oval window. Her hazy thoughts now swooped down towards Alpha. Her little brother was floating somewhere below her, on that blue sea she was flying over. That impassable sea, over which a plane could leap in less than two hours. Two seats away, the baby had fallen asleep, wrapped in a blanket on his mother's lap. Daddy was holding her hand.

Bamby continued to burrow deep into Segalen's archives out of sheer curiosity, now convinced that Yan had left no secrets lying around. The bastard was far too well organised. As she opened various photo albums one by one, 2007, 2003, she recognised François Valioni several times, posing in a suit in front of the Vogelzug logo, sitting wearing a tie during round-table discussions, or dressed in a sirwal, inspecting huts in African villages. Jean-Lou never appeared. Had he been deleted?

She went back even further in time: 1994. A name, the mere name of an IMG file, suddenly electrified the nape of her neck, before her entire body felt the shock. Her index finger locked above the *Enter* key.

*Adil Zairi.*

She leant forward, jacket open, indifferent to the sideways looks from the father beside her who, while gently stroking his sleeping wife's hand, was staring at the lace covering the gentle curves of Bamby's breasts as intensely as a spring skier gazing lustfully at year-round snow.

*Adil Zairi.*

She had read that name so often. Especially that first name. Four letters traced in Nadia's curved handwriting. The name of a mythical demonic beast, an evil genie from a fairy tale, a faceless monster. But Adil Zairi *did* exist. He had worked for Vogelzug twenty years earlier. Yan Segalen had known him, as had Jourdain Blanc-Martin, François Valioni, Jean-Lou Courtois and all the other employees who were already working for the organisation in 1996. Warm drops of sweat formed little beads on her temples, running down from the top of her neck towards her throat, before the air conditioning froze them into tears of ice. Bamby was shivering, her finger still poised a few centimetres above the keyboard. A faceless monster, she repeated in her head. Neither she nor Maman had ever known what Adil looked like.

Before clicking on the image file, Bamby turned her head to the window one last time. They were flying over the coast of Tunisia. A fine thread of houses, specks of black and white, appeared to sew the desert to the sea.

Then she opened the file.

# 62

Leyli rose to her feet, and carried on picking up the coloured sunglasses and the owls made of plastic, cloth, wood, wool and glass lying scattered across the floor. She began to arrange them methodically on one of the shelves. It was daft, she knew. The apartment was a battlefield. Everything needed to be cleaned, sorted through, stuff thrown away, things repaired.

Ruben was still sitting on the sofa bed.

'Come and sit down, Leyli. Come and tell me the rest.'

'There is no rest, Ruben. The story's finished.'

Nevertheless, she consented to go back and sit by his side. The manager of the Heron placed a hand on her shoulder. He had slipped his dark glasses into his pocket. His eyes expressed an infinite sadness, the sadness he usually concealed behind his extraordinary stories. This morning, he didn't feel like playing any more. Or rather, he felt like playing a different game. The one where you take off your masks. Sometimes your armour too. Your armour made of cloth.

Ruben exerted a slight pressure to bring their two bodies closer together. She could sense his face turning towards her. His smoker's breath. His indefinable scent.

His eyes expressed an infinite tenderness.

'No, Ruben.'

Leyli pushed him gently away.

'No, Ruben,' she repeated.

She could read in her boss's tired eyes that he wasn't going to press her. That he was the kind of man who knows how to love in secret.

'I made love to a man, Ruben. A few hours ago. Right here.'

'Do you love him?'

'I don't know . . . Are you jealous?'

Ruben didn't answer. Or rather he did, but in his own way, by asking another question.

'Have you ever loved a man?'

'I don't know.'

The hotel manager clasped her a little tighter to his shoulder.

'Of course you have, Leyli, you have loved a man before. I'm not talking about Virgile, Alpha's father, that was just carnal passion, fuelled by the adrenaline of imminent death. I'm talking about Adil . . . Your saviour. You loved him, loved him very much, you even agreed to all his demands because of your love for him.'

'Before killing him.'

Ruben smiled.

'The ultimate proof that you loved him.'

He paused before continuing. His eyes swept across the wrecked apartment, over the books lying fallen on the floor, the creased covers, the dog-eared pages, like birds with clipped wings.

'Do you remember, Leyli? You told me you'd hidden your notebook, the one you'd dictated to Nadia, the single mother you told me about. You confessed you'd hidden it here. Under this mattress.'

Leyli was puzzled. Why bring that up now? Ruben must have noticed, and explained his train of thought.

'You haven't checked. Perhaps it was the *notebook* they were looking for, those guys who ransacked your apartment?'

They stood up.

Maybe Ruben was right? Leyli slid her hand under the mattress, searching, searching, searching.

Nothing. No book!

In a fury, she ended up pulling off the cushions, the sheets, tipping everything onto the floor of the apartment.

No notebook.

Leyli didn't have time to wonder who could have stolen it: in the place where the notebook should have been, on the bed base, lay a white envelope. She grabbed it. She remained standing. Ruben had taken a step back, far enough not to burst her bubble of privacy, not enough to resist the temptation to read over her shoulder.

The envelope was signed.

*To Leyli*
*From Guy*

*Dear Leyli,*

*I'm writing this letter in a rush, while you're having a shower. I'll slip it under your bed before you come out. You'll find it eventually. Things always happen eventually. It's easier to trust objects than people.*

*Thank you, Leyli.*

*Thank you for opening your arms to me. Thank you for accepting me as I am. As I am today. It takes a beautiful person, Leyli, to know how to love what I've become. You have to see with your heart, as the Little Prince said on his asteroid. I wish you could have seen me, twenty years ago. When I wasn't yet wrinkled by the years. When I was twenty-five kilos lighter. I used to have a nice voice too, back then.*

*I can hear you already, Leyli, brave and fatalistic. That's life, one morning after another, the grinding treadmill, grinding you down.*

*Oh no, Leyli, oh no . . . Some people grow old well. Some grow old rich. Some grow old beautiful. And others lose everything along the way, little by little, drop by drop, like an invisible leak which ends up leaving your heart as dry as a stone. That's not what happened to me, Leyli. Me, I lost everything all at once.*

*One morning. When I wasn't on my guard. I was stripped of everything. Left abandoned on the side of the road.*

*It was a woman, Leyli – it was a woman who stole my life.*

*A woman I took in, a woman I saved, a woman who, without me, would have died in a black hole, devoured by rats. A woman I also loved. It was that woman who betrayed me. Are you beginning to understand, Leyli?*

*It wasn't the asbestos from building sites that consumed my wind-pipe, to the point where my voice was nothing more than a rusty bow screeching across metal strings. It was a woman who stuck a knife in my throat.*

*Do you remember, Leyli?*

*It wasn't the financial crash, or losing my job, or God knows what other calamity that made me poor. It was a woman, who stole the treasure I'd been hoarding so patiently.*

*Apparently I'd been very blind indeed.*

*I know, Leyli, this letter will seem very long for a note written sitting on the corner of a bed. But can you imagine how many years I've been brooding over it? How long it took me to find you. To get close to you. Without you getting suspicious. Even that little weasel Nadia, twenty years ago, wouldn't tell me anything. I battered her to death, but she refused to give you away. It cost me my job at Vogelzug – I wasn't clean enough for them any more. It wasn't too bad, I set up my own little business, I carried on doing subcontracted work for them, now and again. Good traffickers are like good craftsmen, there will always be work for them.*

*But deep down, I didn't give a fuck about all that. All that mattered to me, and this will surprise you, Leyli, was winning a bet. A bet I had made, that day when I agreed to you giving yourself to other men. Do you remember? Do you remember what I'd said to you? 'Do it for me. Do it for us.' And I'd added, like an idiot: 'I want you to see my face one day. I want to read in your eyes that you find me handsome.'*

*I said that to give you courage, whereas I was scared to death. I wasn't joking, you know, that first night, when I freed you from that dungeon in Agrigento: 'If you regain your sight one day, then you'll leave me.' You were so much more beautiful than me. I was torn between the desire for you to regain your sight and the fear that then you'd no longer belong to me. Worse than that, Leyli, the fear of reading disappointment in your eyes, contempt, even disgust. If you don't call that love, then what do you call it?*

*It was so as not to lose you that I continued to introduce you to other men, to hide our treasure from you. And you, you believed what*

353

*that little whore Nadia told you, you listened to what others told you
about me afterwards – Adil Zairi, a pathetic little people smuggler,
a small-time pimp. A monster. That's what I've been for you all these
years. A monster. That's how you introduced me, in this room, on
this very bed, when you told me our story. You see, you were wrong. I
accepted your version of the facts without batting an eye. I only asked
for a measly little act of revenge.*

*The only revenge that mattered.*

*To read in your eyes that you found me handsome.*

*I've won, Leyli. I've won my bet. I read it in your eyes, before we
made love. You looked at me for the first time and you loved the man
you saw, you loved him to the point of giving yourself to him.*

*This is my revenge, Leyli. My sweet revenge. My proud Leyli, my
liberated, my rebellious Leyli, you gave yourself to your torturer of your
own free will. And you found pleasure in doing it.*

*The most brutal of rapes.*

*I'd like to have read that moment of orgasm in your eyes, to reveal
my great secret to you here on this bed, rather than in writing; all night
long, night after night, I imagined that moment when, after you'd
climaxed in my arms, I'd have revealed everything to you, then in the
small hours of the morning, before leaving, I'd have strangled you. Or
stabbed you, perhaps. I only changed my plans yesterday evening, when
I came upstairs and just happened to see Tidiane. You hadn't been
quick enough this time, or maybe you trusted me too much.*

*Then I suddenly figured it all out. I figured it out, about your little
boy. I figured it out, about Alpha too, and Bamby. I figured out your
secret. I figured out where you're hiding what's left of my treasure.*

*I need to go now, Leyli. I'm slipping this envelope under your bed.
We'll probably make love again. Then you'll shoo me away. In a few
hours you'll be looking out for me through the window, from the
balcony where you'll be smoking, you'll be watching me walking away,
and maybe imagining what kind of life we could have together, you'll
be watching me get on the bus, you'll be thinking I'm heading quietly
off to work.*

*Not suspecting that I'm leaving to take back what you stole from
me.*

*That I'm leaving to take it back from your son.*
*With all my love, for the very last time.*
*Adil*

❄

The letter slipped slowly from Leyli's hands and fluttered around for a few seconds, before ending up on the floor. Ruben hugged her, without any sort of reticence this time. Leyli was shaking all over.

'What's he talking about, Leyli? Your son's in danger. What has he figured out, Leyli? What's this secret?'

At that precise moment, Leyli realised she could trust Ruben. That in order to save Tidiane she had to reveal everything. Right now.

# 63

The hull of the *Sébastopol* bumped gently into the concrete quay without Alpha even being able to make out the seawall. A cold mist shrouded the harbour, so all that was visible was the faint beam of the lighthouse, flashing at the end of the jetty, a surreal forest of masts poking out of the fog, and pale shadows, limp flags, the faded walls of houses with closed shutters.

The orange buoys cushioned the shock. Gavril threw out a mooring rope with a confident flick of his wrist, without even asking his only passenger for help. Alpha stared around him, wide-eyed. He was finding it hard to believe he'd just crossed the Mediterranean at an average speed of more than twenty-five knots. He had struggled all night against the lullaby sung by the waves, its rhythm governed by the rolling of the yacht. Yet he had still fallen asleep, taking micro-naps for a few seconds, a few minutes perhaps, his Tokarev TT-33 dangling at the end of his arm. Gavril hadn't tried anything on. He'd remained at the helm. After all, he wasn't going to turn back having made more than half the journey. Informing the police would only have given him a shitload of hassle, whereas with this tall black man, and especially his friend with the tie who wanted to buy the boat, they could no doubt come to an arrangement.

'Last stop!' announced Gavril, imitating the signal of a steamship by whistling through his remaining teeth.

Alpha, his arm and wrist covered by a tracksuit top, kept his gun trained on the skipper. When Gavril held out his hand, Alpha

thought it was that usual gesture sailors make, helping passengers
– almost by instinct – from a boat onto the quayside. He only
realised what Gavril wanted from him when he felt the piece of
paper against his palm. A page torn from a diary. The skipper had
scribbled his name and phone number on it.

'Bear me in mind for future crossings, will you? You've seen me,
I can steer all night without a wink of sleep, as loyal to my post as a
waiter behind the bar in a club.'

Gavril winked at Alpha, then watched the young man heading
away along the quay. Alpha walked another few metres, read the
bit of paper in his hand once again, shrugged, then scrunched it up
into a little ball which he flicked into the water of the harbour. He
took a few more steps, tucking his pistol away under his belt.

In front of him, four dark figures were approaching through the
mist. Lined up, like in a western. Mute, except for the sound of
their footsteps in the cocoon-like silence.

As expected, they were waiting for Alpha.

Fifty–fifty, thought the young Malian.

Either these four shadows were coming to give him a helping
hand.

Or they were coming to kill him.

# 64

Leyli stood up. She took Ruben's hand and invited him to follow her. They walked towards the children's room. She turned to her boss.

'Look, Ruben,' said Leyli, grabbing Tidiane's football jerseys and shorts which were littered across the floor, pointing at Alpha's T-shirts, twice as big as Tidiane's, and Bamby's underwear.

She pointed out yet more things – old trainers which must have belonged to Alpha, Tidiane's football wedged under the bed, posters, books, CDs, all the traces of her three children's lives crammed into one single room. The visitors had only ransacked the beds and the wardrobes filled with clothes.

'Look, Ruben, look. A family. A lovely family, reunited. Brought back together. Legally. You might think that was the end of the story.'

She stared at Ruben, her eyes brimming with tears.

'But that's not the end of the story. Not even the beginning.'

Ruben fell silent, conscious that whatever Leyli was about to reveal might turn everything on its head.

'Listen to me, Ruben. Listen carefully.' (Leyli took a long pause.) 'My children have never lived here!'

She dropped an OM jersey on the floor. Her eyes whirled around the cluttered room.

'This is all staged. It's just for show, Ruben. The beds, the toys, the clothes. A lie. I live alone, Ruben. Alone, do you hear me! I've never managed to bring my children over. I failed, Ruben, do you understand? I failed!'

Leyli's arms thrashed around, flailing the air as if trying to grapple with ghosts. The ghosts of her children, haunting this overcrowded room. This empty room. Dark tears fell from Leyli's eyes, streaking her cheeks with mascara.

'I ran into a glass wall. Invisible. Impassable. The world's like that, Ruben, the world's like that for ordinary people born on the wrong side of the earth. You can see everything, you can hear everything, there's plenty of screens for that, plenty of satellites, signals, dishes, waves, everything's connected to everything else, everything's so close that you might even think you could touch it. Possess it. But no, you stick your hand out and you hit something, you pucker your lips and all you kiss is a transparent wall. The illusion of reality. Even more cruel than the absence of news. A virtual family. Connected, but separated. The world's become a glass palace, Ruben. Doors swing open for a chosen few, without them even having to push them, like in department stores. And everyone else remains stuck, behind solid walls of glass. Condemned to wander here and there, hunting and begging. I haven't kissed Tidiane for five years, Ruben. Haven't felt his heart beating against my chest. Haven't pulled a sheet up over him when he falls asleep. Haven't wiped away the heat of his sweat when he gets back from school or games. Alpha was twelve when I left him. Since then, he's been free to screw things up as much as he wants – he was only twelve when I slapped him for the last time. I was a head taller than him, now he's three heads taller than me. At least I think so. Only Bamby managed to get through, on a study visa, last year, for a year. Just a year. Then she left again. You understood, Ruben, you tried to help me as much as you could by telling the cops she'd been singing at the Heron last night.' (She stared at the upturned living room table, at the plates and cutlery scattered here and there.) 'But Bamby didn't have dinner here last night, no more than any other night. No more than Tidiane or Alpha. I live alone, Ruben. Alone like a mother dog who left in search of food for her children, who got lost, who never came back. Alone. Which means, you'll have realised, that Bamby doesn't have an alibi. No alibi for the murder of Jean-Lou Courtois at the Red Corner in Dubai. And neither for the murder of François Valioni. At the Red Corner in Rabat.'

# 65

The Airbus A320 was flying over the Atlas Mountains. The crest of the Amour Range blocked off the clouds, thereby allowing the passengers to better admire the wooded peaks, the pastures on the mountain slopes and the orchards at the bottom of the wadi. Bamby, however, couldn't care less about the magnificent panorama. With Yan Segalen's computer still sitting on her lap, she simply couldn't take her eyes off the photo of Adil Zairi. *Modified on 19/04/1994.* An old, long-forgotten file. The banal portrait of an elegant man posing on the ramparts of the medina in Sousse. Nothing incriminating.

When she'd opened the file, however, Bamby had stifled a scream which had shattered against the back of her throat.

She knew Adil!

He hadn't been stabbed to death by Maman. Adil had survived. Adil had found them. Adil was on the prowl.

Around them. Around Maman.

Bamby leant over to examine every detail. Since 1994, Adil Zairi had put on weight, had gone bald, had swapped his skin-tight jeans and mauve linen shirt for a shabby tracksuit, had lost that superb self-confidence he displayed in the photo, but she had no doubt whatsoever. She recognised him! She'd run into him several times, in the stairwell at Les Aigues Douces, during her year studying for a psychology degree at Aix-Marseille. He lived on the floor below. A quiet neighbour whose first name she couldn't even remember now. Thierry? Henri? A loner, not very talkative except when he was

361

mouthing off at the 'Arabs', the communist-leaning local council and the petty drug dealers. The sort of guy you'd think isn't really mean, or nasty. A bit of a dickhead, maybe, but not nasty.

Bamby closed her eyes for a few seconds to let her memories flood in, to visualise a name on a mailbox or a parcel left on the landing. Guy! His first name was Guy, she remembered now. *Guy Lerat*. Guy the Rat. That scumbag had gone so far as to choose an alias that reeked of the gutter! No, not a dickhead . . . Not a dickhead, and very nasty indeed. What was he looking for? What was he up to? What was he waiting for?

A flight attendant passed through the narrow aisle of the plane, pushing her drinks trolley. The flurry of activity among the passengers woke up the baby, who was sleeping on top of his mother two seats away. His father took him in his arms, ordering a Coke from the smiling stewardess as he did so.

'I'm fine, thanks,' muttered Bamby.

A sour taste rose in her throat, a sick feeling, setting her stomach on fire. Bamby imagined Maman alone, in her apartment. Adil Zairi twenty steps below. And she, helpless, stuck in this plane with more than half an hour of the flight still to go, half an hour before she could warn her, half an hour during which anything could happen. Even though Adil had been living in Les Aigues Douces for several months, under the name of Guy Lerat, without attempting anything at all, she had a sense of foreboding, gnawing away inside here.

Maman . . . all alone . . . Just as Bamby had left her the night before last, leaving her in such a rush, when she'd got up and claimed she was going to eat at KFC with Chérine. Without touching her plate. Without really taking part in the dinner. Yet the evening meal was all they had left. A sacred ritual. The one daily treat for ordinary families that Maman had refused to sacrifice. A way for her to defy the forces that were tearing them apart, pulling them in different directions, to every corner of the earth. The evening meal as an anchor point, like any family, anywhere in the world, gathering together at dinner after a day spent running around, experiencing separate emotions. Who meet up once again before dark to tell their stories. That same need to weave a cocoon together each night, no matter how scattered the family happens to be during the day – in the lanes of a village, the streets of a vast metropolis, or across the entire globe.

Dinner at 7.30 p.m.!

No matter where in the world Bamby was travelling with Chérine, no matter what corner of Morocco Alpha might be loafing around in, no matter what Granny Marème had cooked for Tidiane at the Olympus Estate in Rabat, at 7.30 p.m. everyone logged on, in front of their laptop screens or mobile devices, turned on their webcams, connected to Skype in conference mode. For an hour. One hour per day. One hour talking about everything and anything. One hour sharing a meal.

To miss this meal was to kill Maman.

Then between 8.15 and 8.30 p.m., without rushing too much, you could get up, clear things away, log off. Only Tidiane would stay behind. He would take his computer to his room and place it on his bedside table so Maman could tell him a story. A long story. Most of the time, Tidy would fall asleep before it was finished, and it was Granny Marème or Grandpa Moussa who would come and turn off the laptop, and pull the sheet up over him.

A little hand tugged at Bamby's jacket. Baby was bored! Daddy apologised. He had downed his Coke in one go, as the baby had been threatening to knock it over. Boy or girl? Bamby couldn't quite tell. The apple-green babygrow, the round face, the big dark eyes, the sticking-up hair and that innocent smile which pierced her heart. Bamby looked away. Acidic bile continued to devour her stomach. A vice, which carried on compressing her lungs.

Maman. Alone. At Les Aigues Douces, in Port-de-Bouc. Adil, her torturer, her tormentor, her dark angel, had survived. Had tracked her down. Had found her.

And then?

All Bamby knew about Adil Zairi was what Maman had written down. In her red notebook. Was it the notebook Adil Zairi was looking for? Had he deliberately moved onto the floor below in order to steal it, in order to get into their home, on some pretext or other?

*Tough shit, you little rat*, thought Bamby angrily. *You weren't fast enough this time!*

Bamby bent down, keeping her jacket closed with her left hand, rummaged around for a few moments in the bag lying at her feet, and pulled out a bright red notebook whose colour seemed to please the baby more than the T'choupi picture books piled up on his father's tray table.

Bamby had found it a year earlier, quite by chance, one evening when she'd lifted Leyli's mattress. She'd been looking for a place to stash her weed in that shoebox of an apartment. Maman had been working nights back then, at the head office of Banque Populaire Provençale; Bamby had carried on reading until the small hours. Before that all-night session, she had known only bits and pieces about her mother's past, just what Grandpa Moussa would tell her now and then, about Maman going blind in her youth, in Mali – a faraway story, almost a myth, of which only a few colourful traces now remained: her collection of sunglasses, her collection of owls.

Reading this notebook had turned her world upside down. At last, Bamby understood the anger that had possessed her since childhood. The notebook had explained it all. Like an object stuck in a pipe which prevents waste draining away, and makes everything rot from the inside, without anyone knowing where the stench is coming from. Finding this notebook, reading it, hanging on to it, had unblocked everything; suddenly, the sluice gates holding back her hatred had burst wide open.

The captain's voice made her jump. The Airbus was starting its descent towards Rabat. *Rabat*, Bamby repeated in her head. Where it had all begun.

Without her being able to restrain them, her thoughts also descended towards the Moroccan capital, sped through the white streets where she had strolled so often, slowed down in the western neighbourhoods, districts that had fascinated her, as a teenager, wove their way between the signs at the retail parks, the bars where they sell alcohol, the restaurants, the hotels, then finally came to a halt. Outside the Red Corner Rabat. Paused briefly, enough time to play hide-and-seek with the security camera, then entered the Scheherazade room, landed on the corpse of François Valioni, then got out very fast, ran down the steps, stopped, out of breath, in the Starbucks, just next door, the one where she'd run into that young cop, where she'd met up with Alpha, where they'd exchanged their oaths, overlaid their ebony triangles to form their black star.

Where they'd promised each other to go all the way. No matter what.

Bamby had stopped en route. Bamby hadn't succeeded.

Yan Segalen had got away with it. Adil Zairi was roaming around, on the loose.

*Rabat*, repeated Bamby again, in a whisper, enunciating each syllable. Ra-bat.

Where it had all begun. Where it all had to end?

If the police were waiting for her, ten thousand metres down below, she would have failed. Once and for all.

# 66

The Beirut–Rabat flight was confirmed as being on time. Arrivals Hall B. Gate 14.

Inside the international airport, more than thirty or so policemen stood in wait, rifles on their shoulders, looking up as if expecting to read some bad news on the arrivals board: a delayed plane, a hostage situation, a hijacked Airbus diverted to Bamako, Dubai or Marseille.

*Bloody overkill, all this panic,* thought Julo as he watched his colleagues standing on the lookout. Bamby Maal was alone on the plane, unarmed. The Lebanese police officers who'd viewed the security camera tapes over and over again had no doubt it was her, even though she was travelling under a fake identity. That hadn't prevented the Moroccan police from pulling out all the stops. Several dozen men, just to arrest a young girl of twenty!

Julo was standing a little further back, near the duty-free shops. Petar was talking to a lieutenant from the Moroccan police. The commandant loved this, lecturing the local cops, for want of being able to give them orders; collaborating with them, since he didn't have a choice, but leaving his Moroccan colleagues under no illusions as to which side possessed the technical experts, intelligence databases and forensic labs.

After all, thought Julo, that was his boss's official role.

*Attaché de Sécurité Intérieure.*

ASI, for short. He, Julo, was just a deputy, an Attaché de Sécurité Intérieure Adjoint, or ASIA.

366

France's Internal Security Service in Morocco consisted of three officers stationed in Rabat – Commandant Petar Velika, Lieutenant Julo Flores and Lieutenant Ryan El Fassi – along with three more in Tangier, Casablanca and Marrakesh.

As far as Julo knew, the Directions de la Coopération Internationale, or DCIs, had been set up in the late 2000s, bringing together officers from both the police and the gendarmerie, in total several hundred cops spread across a hundred or so embassies around the world. Their mission was to focus on threats aimed at France: terrorism, cybercrime, trafficking of all kinds, drugs, weapons and, of course, illegal migration. Over and above these perennial – and major – sources of stress for the Ministry of the Interior, there was clearly the need to protect the expatriate French community resident in the relevant country. The murder of François Valioni therefore pertained to the DCI in Rabat in three ways: a French citizen, murdered in the heart of the Moroccan capital, professionally involved in trans-Mediterranean migrant networks.

Collaboration was the operative word. Collaborating with other DCIs around the world – the one in Dubai, the one in Beirut and, more importantly, with the authorities in the local area. Petar was compelled to play by the rules, as the absolute minimum, even though he regarded the Rabat police officers as underpaid public servants who were quite detached from it all and had no real means of investigating . . . and believed that it was up to him, while handling local sensitivities tactfully, to carry out most of the work.

In the airport, passengers were becoming worried about the unusually strong show of force by the police. The commonly held fear, these days, of an imminent attack. Officers were busy trying to reassure them. Petar was playing things down, roaring with laughter and slapping his Moroccan colleagues on the back.

Julo observed the flurry of activity from a distance. His eyes drifted, lost in the reflections of the advertising signs in duty-free, identical to those in just about any airport, anywhere across the globe.

When he thought back over the investigation, he was haunted by this impression. The same places, the same shops, everywhere in the world, completely interchangeable. Brands without borders, bereft of any nationality: Starbucks, L'Occitane, Red Corner and so many more . . . Right up to the same movies being shown on planes, the same songs listened to on the radio, the same football teams followed by their fans – sub-Saharan kids wearing Barça's UNICEF jersey, Moroccan children supporting Manchester or Marseille . . .

Julo tried to rewind through the whole inquiry, reflecting back over the previous three days. He had barely half an hour left before Bamby Maal would be arrested as she got off the plane, and he had a horrible feeling he'd missed something vital.

He rapidly scrolled through his memory, pulling up those very first images: the Red Corner in Rabat, the Starbucks where he'd probably rubbed shoulders with Bamby and Alpha Maal, without knowing who they were, before lingering somewhat longer on images of the Orange Tree District, in the north of Rabat, where they had arrested Alpha, between Avenue Pasteur and Avenue Jaurès. Just like global brands, streets sometimes have universal names too. Certain streets in former French colonies, at least. He continued his journey back through his memories via the meeting with Professor Waqnine, the haematologist, in the grounds of the Avicenne Hospital, the university hospital of Rabat, named after the most celebrated Muslim doctor in the history of Islam; he then, of course, moved on to the Al Islah Centre, a prestigious institution for education and learning French, a few kilometres from Rabat, bearing almost the same name as the mosque in Marseille, the largest in the south of France, El Islah. The pace of the investigation had quickened yet further yesterday when, along with Petar, they had decided to question Leyli Maal, with the consent of the commandant of Port-de-Bouc police station, Tòni Frediani. Ryan had sorted out the administrative and logistical details, and they'd hopped on the direct Rabat–Marseille morning flight, a journey of less than two and a half hours. They'd caught the plane back in the late afternoon, after a brief stop – keeping one eye on the clock – at the Heron to listen to Ruben Liberos and his crazy testimony. In the evening, Julo had roamed around the vast Rabat-Salé seaport, mulling over the investigation, just as he'd done the previous day, sitting opposite the famous pink flamingo pond at Rabat's National Zoological Garden, or that first evening, when he'd settled himself on the beach at Salé, having wandered along the streets named after 11 January and 2 March. He had since learnt that these dates referred to the day of Morocco's proclamation of independence in 1944 and the end of the French protectorate in 1956 respectively. In short, national holidays, or commemorations, Ryan had said, trying to explain to Petar that Morocco had never been a French colony, but rather a protectorate – a simple agreement based on protection and collaboration.

Little by little, the cops were spreading out in front of Julo. The moment when the plane would touch down was fast approaching. Excitement was building. Would they go so far as to surround the tarmac, thinking Bamby Maal might escape by fleeing along the runway?

Julo felt increasingly alienated from this hunt. He had now pieced together Leyli Maal's story – her arrival in a disadvantaged urban neighbourhood in Port-de-Bouc, her children, Alpha and Tidiane, staying behind in Morocco, her daughter Bamby sailing back and forth between the two shores. Petar, along with the Moroccan cops, had spoken of a plot, of three skilfully planned murders, even though the third had failed, of a meticulously crafted chain of events, devised by a female predator concealing herself under three separate identities.

However, Julo couldn't help thinking precisely the opposite: this family, the Maals, had done nothing more than protect themselves, with their own resources, from a conspiracy that was far more dangerous, far better organised and a million times more impenetrable. But he had no proof, and every time he'd brought up the subject in front of Petar, his boss had simply referred sarcastically to Bamby's seductive eyes, eyes which had made the besotted young cop fall for her, head over heels, and to those of her mother Leyli, perhaps even more striking in her role as a 'Mother Courage who's going through hell but carries on wearing exotic flowers'. The bare facts, all of the facts, supported Petar's view. Or at least appeared to. A way of condemning Julo to silence.

He saw himself again, in the corridor of Port-de-Bouc police station, handing his card over to Leyli Maal.

*If you ever need anything, call me.*

A pathetic gesture on his part, a bit ridiculous, purely to ease his conscience. But what more could he offer?

# 67

Leyli had gone out onto the balcony, to smoke. She had never smoked so many cigarettes in one day, and the sun had only been up for a few hours. The sea opposite Les Aigues Douces was now calm again. In the distance, over towards the gantry cranes at Port-Saint-Louis-du-Rhône, a container ship was moving in slow motion, as if exhausted by a load that was too heavy for it – leaving behind a trail of slime, like a wary snail venturing out after the rain.

Ruben had joined her on the balcony. He had put on his long coat and his hat, although it wasn't cold. Leyli thought Ruben was probably getting ready to leave Port-de-Bouc; that when he seemed like this, when he'd given up telling his tall tales, it meant he was preparing to move on again. Ruben was watching the container ship, tracking its slow, almost undetectable progress.

'Why?' he asked gently. 'Why the big charade, Leyli?'

Bath towels, a child's pair of shorts, sport socks dangled from the balcony drying rack.

'Because I don't fit in. I don't tick the right boxes. It's as simple as that, Ruben.'

She took a slow drag on her cigarette.

'To bring my children over here, I need to be living in a bigger apartment. Ten square metres per person. Forty square metres minimum. That's the law. The minimum wage and decent accommodation. For three years, ever since I became legally resident, I've been trying to get one. To begin with, I thought it would be a mere formality.'

Leyli gave a nervous laugh. Ruben was still staring at the coloured cubes stacked on the container ship.

'But I don't tick the right boxes, Ruben. I'm single. I earn a pittance. The council housing people offer me studios, or one-bedroom apartments at most. *You see, Madame Maal, we reserve the two- and three-bedroom apartments for families.* It's as crazy as that, Ruben. Without children, I don't qualify for a larger apartment. And without a larger apartment, I can't bring my children over.' (She gave another bitter little laugh.) 'The guy who invented this is an absolute genius. It's a conjuring trick, like those endless Möbius strips. The authorities can force us poor beggars to go round and round in circles, indefinitely – counter A, counter B, counter C, social housing agencies, the council, the *préfecture*, OFII, ah yes, that's the office for immigration and integration, and they're each hooked on their own forms, each obsessed with their own boxes that have to be filled in.'

Leyli took another long puff. Even though most of her facial features betrayed her fatigue and weariness, her eyes continued to sparkle.

'The idea came to me three months ago. When I had to complete a new application for my housing agency, FOS-HOMES. A very simple idea.' (She paused briefly.) 'I could claim that my children had already arrived.'

Ruben abandoned the container ship for the first time, and turned towards Leyli. He squinted in the light under the brim of his hat. His line of vision now embraced the coy sun, which was beginning to shed its veil. Leyli had stuck a pair of sunglasses in her hair – a pair shaped like butterfly wings, in yellow and black – but didn't lower them over her eyes.

'The law requires decent accommodation in order for my children to join me, so why would I be denied a larger apartment if my children were already here? I simply brought forward their arrival by a few months. I rearranged the apartment to look as if my three children were living here: I hung washing at the windows, I left my door open and put on rap and techno music at full blast, I told my bosses about my childcare issues, and above all I took photos, photos to show the overcrowding, how unbearable it was. I put together a dossier for FOS-HOMES, I did everything I could to sweeten up the employee in charge of following up my case – Patrice, or Patrick, I can't remember any more . . . but I think I convinced him. I think he'll move my file to the front of the queue, I think my request for a change of accommodation will progress faster in three months than it ever has in three years. You just had to be brave enough to bluff, Ruben. Why would Patrice write to OFII or the *préfecture*, to check whether my children really were in France? The A and B counters don't even communicate with each other; I'm the one who's got to queue up each time. I've been smart enough not to give myself away when there's been surprise visits from FOS-HOMES officers or employees from the council. They do come by sometimes. Not to clean, Ruben – to deport us. But no one's ever bothered to climb as high as my floor.'

Her eyes sparkled one last time, then turned cloudy, to the point where two glistening tears began to peek through. The sun had just evaded the watchful eye of a cloud. Leyli dropped her butterfly sunglasses onto her nose.

'The plan was perfect, Ruben. In a few weeks, Patrice was going to tell me he'd found me a two-bedroom apartment. I was going to sign the papers, I was moving in. No one in the world could have made me leave it again. I simply had to open my door when the investigator from the council rang, and this time he could only give a favourable opinion regarding whether I met the conditions for family reunification.'

Leyli had put her hand on the edge of the balcony. Ruben placed his hand on hers.

'Don't say *was*, Leyli. You don't say *was* if the plan's perfect. Say *will*. It's all going to be fine.'

Leyli turned around suddenly. She lifted her dark glasses. Her eyes were red with tears, two fiery coals burnt to a crisp behind two ceramic glass lenses.

'What's going to be fine, Ruben? Can you tell me? I haven't heard from Bamby or Alpha for almost two days. I've been trying to call my mother and father for an hour now, over and over again, with no answer. I'm here, waiting, telling you my life story, while . . .'

She went back into the apartment and stared in terror at Adil's letter, still lying on the living room table.

*You'll be watching me get on the bus, you'll be thinking I'm heading quietly off to work.*

*Not suspecting that I'm leaving to take back what you stole from me.*

*That I'm leaving to take it back from your son.*

Ruben put a hand on her shoulder.

'Where's Tidiane?' he simply asked.

'At my parents'. The Olympus Estate. In Rabat. I've got no other way of contacting them. I don't have any other phone number apart from my parents'. We call each other every day. They manage everything, they've been raising Tidiane ever since I left . . . and they . . . they're not answering! It's 10 a.m., on a Saturday, and they're not picking up.'

A tremor was making Leyli's hand shake. Ruben reached out to try to steady it.

'You've no need to worry, your son's safe. He's on the other side of the Mediterranean and—'

Leyli recoiled even more violently. Her head tilted and the arms of her sunglasses caught in her hair, then suddenly came loose again. The glasses shot up into the air and then, like a butterfly whose wings are too heavy, plummeted and smashed to pieces seven floors below. Leyli didn't even bother to look. The sun, now busy polishing its shiny reflection on the surface of beached waves, car roofs and refuse bin lids, might well return to lock her in some dark dungeon, but she defied it by staring out to sea as far as her eyes could reach.

'You know full well he's not!' she yelled. 'Adil Zairi left Les Aigues Douces at first light this morning. He could have taken a direct flight from Marseille to Rabat. He might already be there by now. He's going to find them, Ruben. He's going to find them, and there's no way I can stop him.'

# 68

**10.04 a.m.**

Indifferent to the bumps and jolts of the Airbus as it made its descent towards Rabat, Bamby was concentrating on the red notebook. Yet she had read it dozens of times before, to the point where she knew the descriptions of each meeting between Maman and these unknown men by heart, these men about whom there was almost nothing she didn't know – every little mood swing, every single flaw revealed by their unconfessed secrets, each of their acts of cowardice.

Baby wanted to read as well. He was eighteen months old now, make no mistake. He pulled at Bamby's jacket to make her read him the story, just the story, even if it didn't have any pictures.

Baby liked her.

Daddy liked her too, especially when the jacket slipped down the shoulders of this girl who was roaming around in nothing more than a push-up bra. A bra as white as her skin was dark.

Mummy liked her less.

'Leave the lady alone, *ma chérie*.'

Ah, it's a little girl, thought Bamby, closing her jacket again. Already a fan of books! Baby grunted but switched arms, and Daddy buried himself back in his magazine as Bamby imagined the couple's retrospective shiver of fright when they saw her surrounded by ten armed cops on the airport concourse, dragged to the floor, handcuffed, led away. They would be told they'd been sitting next to a murderer, that their little darling had even stroked the arm of this female serial killer . . .

The cops were waiting for her in the arrivals hall, she was now convinced of that. She'd walked straight into the lion's den by rushing onto this flight to Rabat.

The Airbus continued its slow descent. During the first few flights to accompany Chérine, she had suffered from a shooting pain in her ears every time she took off, or landed, bad enough to make her want to bang her head against the tray table. Now Bamby no longer felt anything. Her eardrums had got accustomed to it. Even the worst pain can become something you get used to, something you curse at first, then accept, then forget. When Bamby was little, whenever Maman asked her if she was in pain, after a fall or when she had the flu, she always replied: 'Only when I think about it.' It was true! As a child, all she had to do was open a book to forget a headache or a poorly healed wound.

The notebook she was holding in her lap had reopened all those wounds in one fell swoop. It almost seemed as if the lines were speaking out loud, with her mother's voice mingled with her own, so often had she recited them in her head.

*He has a soft voice, he likes talking. He likes to hear himself talking, more than anything.*
*His wife is called Solène. He has a little one-year-old girl. Mélanie.*
*A little scar forms a comma under his left nipple.*

This diary was that of her birth. Of her conception, to be more precise.

A rape!

Rapes, plural. Several rapes a day, for months. Until Maman became pregnant. After Maman became pregnant. One of the men described in this notebook, with a host of details and secret revelations, was her father.

François. Jean-Lou. Yan.

One of these bastards was her father. She had read the notebook, but hadn't managed to get used to the pain, or even accept it, let alone forget it. She'd thought long and hard. In order to conquer the primeval pain tying her stomach in knots, a threefold approach had seemed both obvious and essential.

Finding them.

Making them confess.

Making them pay.

Baby-*chérie* was crying next to her, covering her ears with her chubby little hands. She hadn't yet learnt how to cope with the pain either. Her mother was rocking her desperately while Daddy held baby's hand. *You'll learn, petite chérie*, Bamby whispered to herself, *you'll learn when you've left childhood behind, you'll learn to suffer in silence. You'll learn that the only real cure for suffering is revenge.*

Just under a year earlier, after reading the notebook, Bamby had sent photocopies to Alpha. Her brother had noticed that all of Maman's clients had a link to Vogelzug, the organisation where her tormentor, Adil, happened to work. He had done some digging. Vogelzug enjoyed a good reputation, employed hundreds of people, brought together thousands of volunteers around the Mediterranean, but also included a few bad apples who took advantage of its powerful protection to get rich. Adil Zairi was one of them, along with a few of his friends. All mixed up in it, to some degree. All involved, to some extent. A vast people-trafficking racket which implied at least passive complicity at the very heart of various ministries – Foreign Affairs, Justice, Police. Officials simply turning a blind eye. Who would go and investigate a few dead migrants abandoned in the desert? A handful of refugees murdered in a forest? Drowned in the Mediterranean? Dead people without any documents. Without an identity. Like the *harragas*, the North African migrants who'd burned a path to Europe, burned their papers, even burned off their fingerprints. The perfect crime does exist, Alpha had said angrily – no need for any Machiavellian scheming, you just need to kill invisible people.

Bamby and Alpha had taken an oath, one evening, at the Olympus Estate.

She to avenge the honour of her mother.

He to avenge the honour of his brothers.

They had overlaid their two pendants, the two ebony triangles which formed the black star of their revenge. A star reminiscent of the one portrayed on the Moroccan flag.

Each of them would wear it around their neck. To the bitter end. Incidentally, although Bamby spoke of revenge, Alpha didn't like using that word. He spoke of justice. The people smugglers operated in networks, he said, like a giant octopus. You had to chop the head clean off, as straightforward as that, so the tentacles wouldn't grow back. You needed two people to succeed. Two faceless people whom no one would suspect, like Frodo and Sam facing up to Sauron in *The Lord of the Rings*.

Bamby would divert attention . . . while Alpha would strike at the head.

Through the window, Bamby could see the Atlantic coast. The Airbus was flying along the Bouregreg estuary, separating the twin cities of Rabat and Salé. The vast beach where she'd hung out so often looked like a ridiculous little sandpit, wedged under the Laalou Muslim cemetery. She closed her eyes for a moment. Tracking down François, Jean-Lou and Yan hadn't been terribly difficult, even though Bamby had neither their surnames nor any physical characteristics to go by. Maman's notebook described their habits, their families, their passions in sufficient detail. Their psychological profiles too – that was the part Maman had covered with the greatest degree of precision, and which had been the most useful to Bamby in snaring them. In putting together three fake identities for herself, each tailored to their specific needs: Bambi13, the shameless militant student; Faline95, the intimidated daughter-mother; Fleur, the determined trainee.

Divert attention, that had been Alpha's plan. Alpha had supplied her with forged documents. Her friend Chérine had helped her with plane tickets, and more importantly with the photos on her Facebook page – photos of Chérine taken pretty much all over the world, then slightly retouched. Chérine hadn't sought to know any more – Bamby had simply asked her to help track down her father, to help sift through the candidates and identify the real one.

Bamby had never mentioned, in her presence, the possibility of killing them.

When had this possibility begun to germinate in her mind? When had the loathing become so intense that the death of those swine had emerged as the only solution? As she was reading the notebook? Reading about when Maman still believed one of them could help her, love her, save her? They'd all abandoned her! Not one, not even Jean-Lou, had tried to rescue this little blind girl from Adil's clutches. All of them had continued to take advantage of her body, to the very end. With full impunity, since she'd never be able to identify them.

Or had their death sentence been pronounced later, when François Valioni had tried to rape her in a deserted alley at the kasbah in Essaouira? When Valioni had invited her for a meal, before accompanying her to the Red Corner in Rabat? When he'd kissed her, when he'd fondled her, when he'd rubbed his penis against her, even though she was the same age as his daughter, even though she could have been his daughter, even though perhaps she *was* indeed his daughter.

Or had Bamby killed purely on instinct? When the blood sample from Valioni's arm had confirmed he wasn't her father, when she'd seen that trickle of blood running down the wrist of this man who'd been stripped, blindfolded, handcuffed. This bastard who would carry on raping, allowing migrants to die, one of those tentacles of the octopus, which would grow back somewhere else anyway, even if she chopped it off. So why deny herself the opportunity?

Divert attention, Alpha had said. Little brother wasn't going to be disappointed.

She had killed François Valioni, then fled into the night. The following evening, she'd hoped Jean-Lou Courtois might be her father, in order to spare him. Until he had pinned her against that brick wall the next day, in a dark street, just after leaving Gagnaire's.

He too had abandoned her mother.

She had pierced his veins for blood.

He wasn't her father either.

He didn't deserve to survive, no more than anyone else did, even though he'd left the octopus a long time ago.

Bamby instinctively felt her pocket. The Blood Typing Kit was still there. A sampling kit which enabled you to determine a blood group instantly, in less than six minutes. She had taken it with her for Yan Segalen, but hadn't had time to use it. Could Yan be her father? A man who was attractive, a fast mover, determined, cunning. *No*, an inner voice whispered, he wasn't. No more than the others.

Through the window, the red stone of the Hassan Tower dominated the landscape, giving the illusion of a landing strip located on the esplanade of the mausoleum, supervised by a medieval control tower. The Airbus would touch down a little further to the north, in a few minutes. Baby-*chérie* had stopped crying and was sucking on her dummy with teary eyes. Daddy had abandoned his *GQ* to put away the T'choupi books.

The cops were waiting for her up ahead, surely.

She might not have accomplished her mission, but at least she had diverted attention. At least her sacrifice would help Alpha slip through the net. Slowly, she leant over towards one of the inside pockets of her canvas bag. Unperturbed by the bewitched look in her neighbour's eyes, or the furious look in his wife's, Bamby tilted her head back, stretched her neck taut and fastened an ebony triangle – hung from a simple leather thong – around her bare throat, just above her cleavage.

The gesture of a warrior.

The Airbus was now veering around, so as to position itself facing the runway. Bamby quickly grabbed her phone. Still no 4G, but she was finally picking up a signal! Taking no notice of the safety instructions reminding her that the use of all electronic devices was forbidden, she tapped the first of her contacts.

*Maman.*

Maman seemed to pick up before the phone had even had time to ring.

'Bamby, is that you?'

380

# 69

The four figures were advancing along the seawall. Alpha stopped, allowing the shadows to walk towards him. A dense mist was rising from the harbour, as if some underwater fire were boiling the water and cooking all the boats, both large and small, producing a thick cloud of steam which ended up trapped against the brick warehouses on the quay where he had docked.

Alpha wobbled around, unsteady on his legs. He convinced himself that fear had nothing to do with it, that it was a normal reaction after a day and night spent on a boat. It was the first time he'd set down his trainers outside the African continent. It wasn't he who was shaking, it was France that was trembling under his feet!

He looked beyond the fog, towards the entrance to the canal, and saw the outline of the Fort de Bouc, clearly silhouetted in the distance. The thick walls of the citadel, made of white stone, reminded him of those at the Kasbah des Oudayas in Rabat, built at the mouth of the Bouregreg valley to keep watch over the ocean, or even the less impressive ones at the kasbah in Tangier, above the medina, where he'd boarded the *Sébastopol* twenty-four hours earlier.

The four figures had stopped too, a few metres away from him, shrouded in the last veils of mist like insects trapped in a cocoon.

Cops? Heavies, tipped off by the Banker or the Moneyman?

The *Sébastopol* was hardly inconspicuous and could easily have been spotted. His feet felt around, seeking to regain their balance on the cobbles of the quay. He touched, almost superstitiously, the butt of the Tokarev tucked securely under his belt. The four men in the mist had frozen, like statues. No hint of a smile for him. No friendly gestures. Not a word.

Cold as stone. Mute as death. Pale with grief.

Alpha let go of the butt of his revolver. His welcoming party's lack of reaction had reassured him immediately. He raised his arms, walked closer, then flung them around the tallest of the figures.

'Thanks for coming, brother.'

Savorgnan said nothing in return. Alpha turned to the other three, then made time for a long, silent embrace with each of them. Zahérine the philosopher-agronomist, Whisley the guitarist, Darius the djembe player. So Savorgnan had managed to persuade three more of the illegal migrants to join him, the ones who'd crossed over from Morocco to France, two days before Alpha.

Unless fate had decided for them instead. Alpha had received the text a few minutes before docking at Port-de-Bouc, a message with news of the tragedy that had occurred off the Moroccan coast, with details of the lifeboat abandoned on the high seas by the people smugglers, listing the first names of the victims: Babila, Keyvann, Safy, Caimile, Ifrah, Naïa . . . whose bodies were perhaps already floating on the Mediterranean when he'd called Savorgnan and his friends that night, even as they were singing and dancing to celebrate their forthcoming arrival.

*Happy men don't go to war*, Savorgnan had finished by saying, before hanging up.

This morning, he was here.

The mute embraces dragged on and on, powerful and painful. Alpha took some time to break the silence, to choose words of condolence. So hollow. But he still had to express his support all the same. He was about to speak when Zahérine stopped him.

'Savorgnan convinced me to come. He persuaded Whisley and Darius too. Let's get a move on. There will be time to mourn our loved ones afterwards. Now's the time to save the others.'

They walked towards the bars and restaurants of Port Renaissance, the fog lifting as soon as they moved away from the docks.

A handful of regulars sitting on café terraces watched them passing by, before plunging their noses back in their papers and their lips back in their cups.

Alpha and his four companions stopped at the corner of Rue Papin. A few villas rose up above them, each more and more opulent, each more and more walled-and-gated as the panoramic view of the coast gradually opened up, stretching all the way to the Camargue.

Before deciding which way to go, Alpha checked his phone. His mother had called him again, as she had every quarter of an hour since the day before. She lived right here, not far away, behind the windows of one of those apartment blocks overlooking the sea, built like an army of watchtowers. She'd been living here since he was twelve, almost Tidy's age, in that apartment where she'd promised to reunite them all, so many times, for so many months now. She'd promised yet again, a week earlier: *I've got an idea, everything will be sorted, I'll have the visas in a few weeks.*

He put the phone back in his pocket. He preferred that his mother remain unaware of his flying visit. So close. Perhaps he would never return.

He wasn't here for her. Not *just* for her. He had an oath to keep first. He took one last look at the tops of the tower blocks and then, slowly, took a pendant from his pocket, a plain leather thong on which hung a pierced black triangle. He fastened it around his neck.

The gesture of a warrior.

'Let's go.'

They all looked at him, waiting for him to take the first step so they could follow.

'Are you ready?'

The four Beninese nodded.

'Are you armed?' continued Alpha.

After a brief silence, it was Zahérine who replied.

'I'm coming, Alpha, I'll follow you. But with bare hands, bare feet, a bare heart, stripped of everything. Those who've taken from us what we hold most dear have no blood on their hands, no trace of gunshot on their skin, have never held a single weapon clutched in their fists. So they'll just have to die without us having to defile ourselves either – that's the only way.'

Alpha tried to hide his anxiety. Did Zahérine and these three other lunatics realise the danger they were about to face? Alpha needed determined men, soldiers, not folk crippled by life, overwhelmed by grief, so drunk with revenge they'd end up getting shot, slaughtered as innocent victims. Two armed men guarded Jourdain Blanc-Martin's villa, La Lavéra. Day and night. Pros. Armed, and trained to kill.

There were five of them. But he felt alone in being capable of taking action. Zahérine and Darius were too old. Whisley was too frail. Only Savorgnan could help him. Perhaps.

Alpha directed his gaze at him.

'What about you, Savorgnan? What do you think?'

A look of intense pain appeared in the eyes of the Beninese. An unfathomable void. As if his life already no longer belonged to him, not completely.

'Unhappy men must go to war, Alpha. That's just how it is. So others can live in peace.'

# 70

**10.07 a.m.**

'Bamby, is that you? Bamby, where are you?'

Leyli was yelling into the phone. A distant voice, somewhat muffled, answered.

'I don't have much time, Maman . . . I can't talk very loudly . . . I'm on a plane . . .'

'A plane! What plane?'

'I'm almost there, Maman. I'm about to land in Rabat.'

Leyli let out a cry, then pulled herself together again.

*Rabat?* Had she heard right?

Her eyes suddenly lit up. Ruben, standing next to her, was trying to keep up with her surges of anguish and hope.

'It's a miracle, Bamby. You need to hurry, the moment you land, hurry, as fast as you can. Hurry home. The Olympus Estate. Tidy's in danger. You need to . . .'

'Maman, listen to me! It's you, you're in danger. *You!*'

Bamby had yelled back in turn. The whole plane must have heard. Leyli let her speak; it only took a few seconds for her daughter to explain that she'd discovered her red notebook, then that she'd recognised Adil Zairi in a photo . . . Her neighbour . . . Guy . . .

'Yes, I know,' Leyli interrupted crisply. 'I already know all that. But Adil Zairi's not here any more. He . . . Don't waste any time, Bamby, you've got to find Tidy before he does!'

At the other end of the phone, Bamby's voice seemed to break up.

'It's impossible, Maman. They won't let me through. I'm going to be stopped at customs, I won't be able to leave the airport.'

Leyli gripped the handrail of the balcony. Ruben tried to support her, thinking for a moment that she was about to topple over.

'Tell them! Tell them to send a police car to the Orange Tree District, it's only a few kilometres away.'

'They won't listen to me, Maman. I . . . I'm wanted . . . For murder . . . I'll be picked up by the cops. It'll take me hours to explain myself.'

Her daughter had lowered her voice again. She was almost whispering. Perhaps a flight attendant was approaching or her neighbours were complaining. Leyli took advantage of the brief lull to pull a card from her pocket. The last card to play.

'Contact a cop, then. Just one cop. Make the most of the minutes you've got left. He's called Julo Flores. I'll send you his phone number and his email. Just throw everything you know at him.'

'Why should we trust this guy?'

'We haven't got a choice, Bamby. We've got no other choice!'

A sudden jolt prevented Bamby from asking another question. She was thrown forward. The seat belt sliced into her stomach. The plane had just landed! Maman had hung up.

A flight attendant was passing through the aisle, telling passengers to remain seated while the plane continued to taxi down the runway.

Let it take all the time it needed!

Bamby yanked off her seat belt and placed Yan Segalen's computer on her lap again. The black bars showed a perfect 4G connection. She opened her inbox just as Maman was sending her the cop's email address. She typed feverishly, *juloflores@gmail.com*, then stuffed everything she could into attachments – photos, text files, tables, systematically excluding files that were too large. She clicked on *Send* and cursed. The email hadn't gone! An alert had appeared: 'Do you want to send this message without a subject?' Now close to hysteria, she typed three letters into the subject line of the message.

*SOS*

Then she sent it. It flew off this time.

She began again, digging through the files at random, extracting mainly photos, trying to pick out ones in which you could see Valioni, Segalen, Jourdain Blanc-Martin, Zairi, and some unknown people, unknown people with the faces of prominent figures, unknown people with the faces of cops.

Download, copy, send.

*SOS*

*SOS*

*SOS*

The plane had come to a standstill. Suddenly, all the passengers were on their feet. Including Baby-*chérie*, in the arms of her mother whom everyone was letting through first. Daddy followed. Bamby was left alone.

A few more seconds.

The last to leave.

*SOS*

*SOS*

*Create a diversion*, Alpha had told her. *Throw all the information you've got at him*, Maman had told her.

She obeyed.

Without even knowing what good it might do.

# 71

Tidiane was on his way back from the *boulangerie*, running between the olive trees, practising dribbling and step-overs along Avenue Pasteur. Grandpa Moussa had promised him that, if he ate breakfast quickly, he'd go down into hell with him. To look for his cuddly-ball, his Morocco 2015 ball, his lucky charm, the one that had rolled into the black hole the previous day while Tidiane was practising taking penalties with his eyes closed.

Tidiane stopped in the courtyard, out of breath. He leant back against the trunk of the orange tree, looking up towards his hut and the rope connecting it to the window on the second floor. Sometimes, when the weather was really nice, he would nibble at his cereal in the hut, facing Granny and Grandpa. Not this morning. The kitchen window was closed. And anyhow he didn't have time, not if he wanted to find his ball for training that afternoon.

Tidiane slammed the door of the Poseidon building and dashed up the two flights of stairs. His record was 7.08 seconds . . . He was improving almost every month, but Granny Marème said that was normal because he was a growing lad.

He touched the door of the apartment with his fingertips as he stopped the timer on his watch. *9.02 seconds.* Tidiane winced, then took on board the fact that he was carrying the bread and Grandpa's paper, whereas his record had been set hands-free on a Sunday. He considered whether he ought to work out records for each day, based on his lessons and the corresponding weight of his schoolbag, or even invent a parasport category, for when he was blindfolded. *Quick now, hop to it, no daydreaming. Sit yourself at the table, gulp down your cornflakes and drag Grandpa Moussa by the sleeve, to go down into hell.* Tidiane was desperately excited, and not just about finding his ball. He turned the handle and pushed open the door.

'I'm back!'

No answer. Not even the sound of Maroc Nostalgie which Granny Marème normally listened to all day. He walked a metre down the corridor and saw his grandparents sitting on the sofa. They never did that! Not both together. Granny didn't walk much now, and only using a stick, but she only ever sat down when she was eating, and even then . . . The TV wasn't even on. *What's going—*

'Run, Tidy!'

Grandpa Moussa had yelled at him, interrupting his stream of questions. Then Tidiane saw a man burst into the living room. He slapped his grandfather violently across the face. A trickle of blood escaped from the old man's mouth. Tidiane froze. He'd recognised the man who had just hit Grandpa.

*Freddy.*

The man who'd come to see Maman the night before last, before he'd gone to bed, the man who'd kissed Maman, the man with the spine-chilling voice, the man who was called Guy but whom Tidiane had christened Freddy. This Freddy didn't have claws instead of fingernails, but he was clutching a long knife.

Grandpa coughed, and spat, but somehow found the strength to yell again.

'Run, my darling!'

Tidiane hesitated. The door of the apartment was open behind him, he simply had to run, hurtle down the stairs – he'd be much faster than this fat old monster. What's more, Freddy made no move towards him, no attempt to catch him. He merely tugged at Granny's long grey plaits to twist her head round, and brought his knife up to her throat.

'Ru—' His grandmother was struggling to speak.

The tip of the long silver knife was already pricking the skin on Granny's neck.

'Noooo!' screamed Tidiane.

He charged forward. Straight ahead. A battering ram! There was no way he'd let Freddy hurt his grandparents. Tidiane wasn't as strong as Alpha yet, but he was fast and he . . .

With stunning agility, given how stout he was, Freddy had let go of Granny, come round the sofa, and caught Tidiane in his tracks. He let him flail his legs around in the air for a moment, before flinging him onto the rug, like some shabby old coat being tossed onto the floor. Tidiane felt a searing pain in his ankle. Freddy walked across and gently closed the door to the apartment, before returning to stand behind the sofa, at the spot where Granny was sitting. He carried on stroking her long, braided grey hair before addressing Grandpa and Tidiane in his lugubrious voice.

'You're faster than me, kid. And your grandfather might still be as quick on his feet as ever. But if either of you tries anything smart, I'll test out this pretty little Berber knife on your darling Marème. Incidentally, do you know who gave it to me?'

He was silent for a moment, then turned to Tidiane.

'*Your mother!* It was her going-away present, as it were. I've looked after it so carefully all these years.'

He ran his hand over his neck, as if his beard were hiding a deep scar, one that made his voice sound like the hissing of a snake.

'It took me a while to track you down. There's thousands of Maals . . . But I've still got some friends in the police. First I just happened to see you on-screen at your mother's, then I heard your big brother Alpha had had the brilliant idea of getting himself arrested here, and it was easy to make the connection. But I've not introduced myself: I'm an old friend of your mother's – Adil, Adil Zairi. And I'm a new friend too – Guy. You see, I'm very close to her.'

Tidiane was rubbing his ankle and crawling across the rug, which was orange with a geometric pattern. To get further away. To gain a few centimetres, one diamond at a time. Freddy, or Adil, or Guy – monsters always have several names, one for each nightmare – was staring at the jersey he was wearing. His lucky jersey. Abdelaziz Barrada's.

'So you like OM, Tidy? By the way, can I call you Tidy?'

Tidiane cowered in fear. Freddy came even closer.

'We can be friends, then. I'm a big fan too. You like OM because your mother lives right next to Marseille, correct? Just hearing that name fires your imagination. Makes your heart miss a beat. The Vélodrome stadium . . . Your mother's promised so often that you'd go and join her there. I know just how you feel.' (He examined him from head to toe, then flashed him a terrifying smile.) 'But seriously, Tidy, do you think Barrada's *really* that good?'

Tidiane didn't answer. The jersey was too big for him. He could bury his bent knees, his legs, his trainers in it. Disappear.

'Or do you like him just because he's the only player who wears both jerseys? Marseille and Morocco?'

Freddy crouched down, to be at eye level with Tidiane. He put a hand on his shoulder, glancing back regularly to keep an eye on Granny and Grandpa.

'You don't have to be afraid of me, you know. I told you, I'm a friend of your mother's. An old friend. I was with her again last night.' (He turned around to flash his vampire smile at Granny and Grandpa.) 'She sends her love. Lots of love. I think you get it now, Tidy? She's telling you fibs so as not to hurt you. When she says you'll be able to join her, that she'll soon be hugging you for real, she's just saying that so as not to make you suffer. You don't want to make her suffer either, do you Tidy?'

Tidiane shook his head.

*No . . . No . . .*

Freddy's voice suddenly speeded up, becoming almost cheerful.

'Hey, I've got an idea to make your mother happy. We'll send her a photo, shall we? A selfie. The two of us, together. Would you like that?'

He twisted round to pull a phone from his pocket, then took a few steps and stood behind Tidiane. That way he could still keep tabs on Granny and Grandpa on the sofa. Grandpa Moussa attempted a gesture of rebellion, straightening his body and raising his arm to threaten him.

'If you ever—'

'Everything's fine, Moussa. You've nothing to fear.'

Freddy held out his left hand, straight in front of Tidiane and himself. He pointed the lens of the phone at their two faces, becoming a little annoyed about the slight backlight created by the window behind them. Then slowly, with his right hand, he slid the knife up the length of Tidiane's belly, then up his chest, before stopping at his neck. He placed the steel blade on the boy's throat.

Tidiane tried not to shake, to keep his legs stiff, his back straight, but his heart seemed to have stopped pulsing blood through his veins; his hands, his arms, his face were as white as the jersey he was wearing. Grandpa bit his lips until they bled. He was forced to remain completely still, as if he were sitting on a mine and the slightest movement could trigger some irreversible catastrophe. Granny was crying, begging Adil Zairi with her eyes.

'*Voilà,*' continued Freddy, repositioning the phone to frame their faces, their necks, and the weapon. 'Maman will be surprised to see us all together – her loyal friend, her beloved son, and this lovely dagger which will bring back so many memories.'

He waited for a few more long seconds, left arm outstretched, right arm wrapped around Tidiane like a boa, steel tip pinned to the child's carotid artery. Concentrating.

Tidiane kept his eyes open, staring at the faces mirrored on the screen, watching the face of the monster stuck to his own, that cold blade like a silver necklace, convinced that Freddy would take the photo just as he stabbed him with his knife – so he'd still be seen alive in the picture, but with blood spurting from his neck, and Freddy would send a live image to Maman. That's what evil people did.

Freddy waited a little more, then pressed to take the photo. A second later, he moved the dagger away from the child's throat. He tapped his fingers on the phone's keyboard, presumably to send the picture.

'*Voilà,* it's gone . . . Maman's going to love it!'

392

Granny Marème was sobbing even more loudly. Grandpa Moussa had taken her in his arms. Tidiane's heart was pounding, fit to burst, as if, having slowed down so much, having almost stopped, it was now madly speeding up to make up for lost time.

'Speaking of your mother,' said Freddy as he stood up again, 'she borrowed a bag from me twenty years ago. A black Adidas bag. I was really fond of it. It's also kind of why I've come here. I'm guessing you know where she kept it?'

No one replied. Adil stomped heavily across the orange rug, pounding the floor.

'Come, come now, our pretty Leyli couldn't have thrown it away. And it's not exactly Versailles here. An Adidas bag . . . You give me it back, and we part as good friends.'

Tidiane looked at Grandpa, who was looking away, not looking anywhere in particular in the room, as if he were afraid of inadvertently revealing a clue by lingering too long in one particular direction, on a section of wall or a cupboard door. Freddy was walking round in circles, becoming more and more agitated.

'Fair's fair, right? I've only come to get what's mine.'

Freddy carried on moving around the room, but in smaller and smaller circles, closer and closer to Granny Marème, like a bird of prey about to swoop down on its victim. His knife still hung from the end of his arm, but Tidiane had noticed his fingers tightening around the handle – as if he were about to strike, catching her unawares.

'Well?'

Maybe he would just stab the sofa right next to Granny, plunging the blade deep into the foam? Or maybe he'd—

'I'll ask you one last time.'

Freddy's thumb and forefinger had moved – still pressed tight around the dagger – to the base of the blade.

'I know! I know where it is!'

Tidiane had practically screamed these words at him. Grandpa was about to get up to protest, but Freddy pushed him back violently with his arm as he turned to the boy.

'I know where it's hidden. Maman's treasure.'

Freddy's eyes shone. The boy had made the link, between the Adidas bag and the treasure! So this kid really *did* know.

'It . . . it's not here,' stammered Tidiane.

Freddy knitted his brow, clenching his fist around the dagger to show he wouldn't tolerate any diversionary tactics. Tidiane went on as quickly as possible.

'It's . . . it's down below . . . in the basement . . . In hell.'

# 72

## 10.12 a.m.

Through the glass wall of the airport building, Julo watched the men fanning out around the Airbus, which had come to rest about fifty metres from the terminal. They formed an almost perfect circle, gradually moving in closer and closer. The first passengers got off, one by one, and were stopped on the tarmac; searched, checked, not really surprised by the security measures, paradoxically more reassured than scared.

Petar was waiting a few metres further away, phone in hand, annoyed, his nose pressed to the glass like a child who'd been punished; he hadn't been allowed any nearer, he had to wait for the Moroccan police to question Bamby Maal, and only then could he organise an interrogation under the twin auspices of the DCI and the Moroccan authorities.

Julo checked he was alone, that no police officer could read over his shoulder, and buried himself back in his tablet. One after the other, he opened the files attached to the message he'd received three minutes earlier.

*bambymaal@hotmail.com*

*SOS*

That girl, cooped up in the plane sitting on the runway, surrounded by thirty policemen, was sending him a distress signal! To him, one of the members of the commando unit in charge of arresting her. What on earth could this surreal call for help mean?

That a countdown had begun? That this girl was going to be arrested to keep her quiet, and she was trying to protect herself by giving up her secrets?

Flinching at the slightest noise, with one eye on the screen and the other watching the arrivals hall, Julo opened the first of the downloaded files: endless spreadsheets of data whose row and column headings left no doubt whatsoever – they all came from Yan Segalen's personal computer. The DCI cops in Beirut had mentioned that Bamby had run off with the Vogelzug logistician's satchel and jacket.

Julo continued clicking on the individual tabs on each spreadsheet, unable to interpret the lists of figures. Plain old accounting entries or digital dynamite? He had no idea! He had neither the time nor the skill to check and, crucially, he was convinced there was a more pressing matter: if Bamby was sending him these files, it must be because they contained more explicit information. A revelation whose significance would leap out at him.

Lieutenant Flores decided to concentrate on the photos. He clicked at random, the pictures opened as a slide show and Yan Segalen appeared in almost all of them. Yan with François Valioni – in Africa, in Marseille, in Rabat; Yan with some men whom Julo didn't know, but had already come across on the Vogelzug site; Yan next to Jourdain Blanc-Martin, on the platform of a lecture theatre or posing at the entrance to a refugee camp. Nothing surprising. Nothing embarrassing.

Julo Flores continued to dig through the files, haphazardly, losing hope of finding any useful information at all. Bamby had sent everything she had to hand, without thinking, like a fugitive stuck on a beach who's got nothing more than fistfuls of sand to throw at her pursuers. One or two more photos, and then he would close everything before going to join Petar. He would then decide whether he was keeping these files, in order to send them straight to the examining magistrate, or whether he'd talk ab—

Julo suddenly froze. Eyes glued to a seemingly innocuous image.

The photo had captured a jeep stopped in the desert. Four passengers, drenched in sweat, had got down from the vehicle, to pose for some unknown photographer. Julo recognised – from right to left, either drinking bottles of water or passing them around – Yan Segalen, Jourdain Blanc-Martin, a bald guy who looked like Ben Kingsley . . . and Petar Velika!

Julo instinctively looked up. His commandant was scanning the last passengers getting off the plane. Still no trace of Bamby Maal! The policemen were starting to climb the aircraft steps, at the front and back of the cabin. The girl was trapped.

Julo tried to contain his excitement as best he could. This photo confirmed what he'd guessed since the beginning of the investigation: Petar knew the highest-ranking members of Vogelzug! Admittedly, there was no reason to believe he was involved in people trafficking alongside them, but this image proved his boss wasn't a neutral player in this whole business. If nothing else, he was playing a double game. Protecting friends. Allies, at least. He wouldn't rock the boat, nor be overzealous.

Julo massaged his temples, blew into his hands, and glanced through the six messages he had received one last time.

*SOS*

*SOS*

Julo was under no obligation to anyone. He would entrust them to Magistrate Madelin and his team without going through his boss. They'd comb through all the data. It wouldn't, however, prevent Bamby Maal from being arrested, from being sentenced for double murder. It probably wouldn't even help her plead extenuating circumstances, given the killings were clearly premeditated, but perhaps she'd have the consolation of not being the only one to get sent down.

*SOS*

*SOS*

*SOS*

What else could he do for this girl?

No one was hanging around the plane any more, as if it had been left abandoned in the middle of the runway. The last policemen were inside the cabin. Had Bamby tried to hide? He found himself hoping she'd managed to come up with a conjuring trick. To disappear in a puff of smoke, wriggle her way under a seat, disguise herself and get out by assuming the identity of another passenger. He was almost beginning to believe it when he saw – at the top of the steps, framed by the open back door – first one policeman coming out, then another, and finally a small group of cops surrounding Bamby Maal. Handcuffed.

It was all over.

Julo waited for a few seconds – baffled, dazed, almost shocked that the thirty policemen had managed to nab the girl so easily. Then he sighed in resignation, and prepared to walk over to join Petar.

The pocket of his trousers pinged at that precise moment. A brief notification signalling that a new email had just landed in his inbox.

One last-ditch bid for help, dispatched by this avenging angel?

He looked down, read *leylimaal@gmail.com* and thought Bamby had sent him her farewell message . . . before realising he had misread the sender's first name.

*leylimaal@gmail.com*

The message, which had no subject, had only a single attachment – just one file, which was displayed without him even having to download it.

An icy shiver ran down Julo's spine. The image revealed a scene of utter horror. He froze, stunned by what he saw. A child of about ten was staring into the lens, his eyes bulging, terrified by the blade of a knife aimed at his neck. His torturer was standing behind him, beaming.

A sick joke? Julo tried to analyse every element of the photo as quickly as possible. He recognised the orange tree outside the window, the ochre tower blocks in the background, so the photo must have been taken on the Olympus Estate, in the northern part of Rabat, where they had arrested Alpha Maal two days earlier.

The ten-year-old child could only be Alpha's little brother . . . Tidiane.

It was impossible, however, to identify the man holding the dagger – but he'd come across him, just a few minutes before.

Younger, thinner, without a beard, in the oldest photos, alongside Yan Segalen and Jourdain Blanc-Martin.

Above the photo she'd sent, Leyli Maal had written six words.

He's got my son
Save him

# 73

Freddy had taken the time to fix a long piece of sticking plaster over Granny and Grandpa's mouths, tie up their hands and feet, and then wind the cord tightly around the radiator pipe. He'd put on his leather jacket and slipped one hand inside, the one still holding the knife. Tidiane, sitting on a chair in the living room, was massaging his ankle, but it was mainly a way of trying to focus his thoughts on the most trivial of his woes. Freddy leant towards him.

'We're going to the basement. If we meet anyone in the building and you start blabbing, you're gonna get it. If you try running off down the stairs, smarty-pants, I'm coming straight back up to the apartment and I'll deal with your grandparents. Is that clear?'

They went down the two floors of the Poseidon building without running into anyone. When they reached the bottom, Tidiane pointed to a white metal door, with rusty hinges, on which an amateur urban artist had spray-painted some graffiti in red, across the entire width: 'The Door to Hell'.

Freddy produced a bunch of keys from his pocket. He'd taken them off a hook in the hallway of Grandpa Moussa's apartment. Following Tidiane's instructions, he inserted number 29 in the lock and pushed the heavy door.

'You first.'

Tidiane had never been down into hell; Grandpa had always forbidden it – it was a den of drug traffickers, dealers and junkies. But he remembered what Grandpa had said last time, when they'd leant over the black hole to look for his ball. *Miles of corridors, cellars, one for each apartment, parking spaces too, drains, sewers.*

He pressed the timer for the light. A few bulbs – one roughly every two metres, calculated Tidiane – lit up a steep, narrow staircase. He cautiously placed one foot on the first step. He'd always assumed Maman's treasure was hidden here, somewhere in hell.

Was that treasure chest one and the same as the Adidas bag Freddy was looking for? How would he find it in these miles of corridors? He wouldn't be able to keep Freddy traipsing around for terribly long. And if by some miracle he did find it, that would make things even worse. Freddy wouldn't need him any more, he'd stick his knife in his heart, then he'd go back up and do the same to Granny and Grandpa.

'What the hell are you up to?' said Freddy angrily. 'Get a bloody move on!'

Tidiane could feel the tip of the dagger in his back. A gentle pricking sensation, like a cat's claw. He tried to stay calm, without panicking, as Alpha had taught him.

*Before taking a penalty. Clear your mind. Take time. Breathe slowly.*

Grandpa had told him about his own grandfather's treasure too, the jars of shells which were no longer worth anything. Was Freddy looking for them as well? Grandpa had also told him something else, when Tidiane had asked him if the treasure was still there, something he hadn't quite understood. Something important, which he must never forget. *What was it?*

'Keep going, for fuck's sake.'

Tidiane simply went down one step.

Move calmly, Alpha had taught him. Take two steps back before you shoot, no more. Look in the wrong direction to create a distraction.

'I'm . . . I'm scared,' stammered Tidiane. 'There's rats, they said . . . Needles too, Grandpa says. Sometimes they chuck dead bodies down here.'

As he was speaking, Tidiane had closed his eyes, to get used to it. He went down another step with infinite care, blindly, while Freddy roared with laughter which echoed through the concrete stairwell. There were still a good dozen steps to go before reaching the basement. Freddy's roar of laughter ended in a throaty cough. Tidiane felt the tip of the dagger in his back again.

'OK, wise guy, now, speed—'

The timer light turned off before he could finish his sentence. As soon as the stairs were plunged into darkness, Tidiane moved forward, one foot, one step down, another foot, another step. A metre now separated him from Freddy, who hadn't moved at all. Freddy's expletives drowned out the sound of the boy's footsteps.

*Give me your strength, Maman*, prayed Tidiane in his mind. *Lend me your owl eyes.* One more foot, one step, moving almost two metres away.

He heard Freddy's heavy feet as they gingerly felt their way back up the stairs, then rush to the little red indicator light on the timer. Tidiane quickly pulled a handkerchief from his pocket, wrapped it round his clenched fist, identified a slightly darker shadow further along the wall, and struck it hard. The fabric dulled the pain caused by the broken glass, while the bulb fixed to the wall shattered into pieces.

*You've got to keep moving*, Tidiane told himself, *to smash the bulb in every wall light you happen to find.* He'd been training. He could see in the dark. Better than Freddy, at least.

He broke the next bulb less than a second after Freddy had pressed the timer. The knife-monster only just had time to glimpse Tidiane's silhouette at the bottom of the stairs before the last few steps were shrouded in darkness again. He yelled with rage. Tidiane heard the door to hell being slammed.

At first, he felt afraid for Granny and Grandpa. *If you try running off, I'll deal with them*, Freddy had threatened. Except that he was too attached to his treasure, wagered Tidiane, too attached to his Adidas bag – he'd come here specially to get it, and he was convinced that Tidiane was cornered like a rat in this maze. He just had to go back up to fetch some sort of light, come down again, catch him.

Tidiane tried to move along the corridor as fast as he could, groping his way, placing his hand on the cold, damp, slimy wall, following the thin tube of the electrical cable by touch alone. His ankle was hurting like mad. He could feel the electricity stinging the tips of his fingers. But he had to keep going – walking, walking and smashing every single bulb he came across.

Even though there was no greater chance of there being another exit from this cellar than from a cave hewn into rock.

That would be Freddy's line of reasoning.

He'd find some sort of light, he'd come down again, he'd catch him.

# 74

'Need to talk to you, Petar.'

The commandant watched the Rabat cops surrounding Bamby Maal as she walked down the steps in front of the Airbus. An escort worthy of a Hollywood star, or at least a Moroccan starlet from the famed Atlas Studios in Ouarzazate.

Forget Naples. *See Ouarzazate. And die . . .*

'Make it quick then,' replied Velika. 'As soon as that girl sets foot in this airport, I'm stepping in. I'm not too happy about being side-lined by these guys with their moustaches and fancy caps. They've just got to arrest her, that's all, given the DCI's done all the legwork.'

'Not here, boss. In private . . .'

Petar looked around the arrivals hall, unconvinced this was necessary. The nearest policemen were standing more than thirty metres away.

'Please, boss. Just for a minute. It's . . . it's a matter of life and death.'

Julo glanced over at the toilets, directly opposite. Hall B had been thoroughly swept and cordoned off by the police, from Gates 10 to 16. The facilities were bound to be deserted. Petar's eyes lingered on the policemen and their female prisoner one last time, before conceding:

'OK, kid, lead the way. But I hope it's not still about pleading your sweetheart's cause. This time, I think it's a hopeless case. If you want to propose to her, you'll have to wait a good thirty years.'

He followed the lieutenant into the toilets anyway. As Julo closed the door behind them, Petar walked up to the urinals.

'Might as well, seeing I'm here . . . Go on then, shoot, what's this super-urgent stuff you've got to tell me?'

Commandant Velika was beginning to unbutton his trousers, concentrating on his flies, content to listen to his deputy with half an ear.

'Well, what are you waiting for?' said Petar.

He finally looked round. His eyes froze in utter astonishment, while his hands, which were directing his flow, automatically rose up.

Julo was holding a SIG Sauer handgun. Pointed menacingly at him.

'You little . . . what the fuck are you up to?'

'I'm sorry, boss. I don't really think you're a bastard, I just think you're navigating as best you can through all the fucking shit around you.'

'No idea what you're bloody on about, you little prick. Put that frigging gun down and—'

'I just think you don't want any hassle, and in exchange for a cushy job at the top, you're not going to look too closely at this whole refugee business.'

Petar lowered his arms, buttoned up his flies, and risked taking a determined step towards the lieutenant.

'That's enough now – you and your bloody crap.'

'Stop right there, boss. Stop, or I'll fuck up your knee.'

Commandant Velika froze. He saw the determination in his deputy's eyes. The little dickhead was still resolute in his convictions.

'What are you planning to do?'

'I'm going to wing it . . . To save what can still be saved. It's an emergency, but I just can't trust you. I'm going to try not to let the saga of the Maal family end in tragedy. I'm going to try and save the most innocent of the siblings at least. So I'm taking your gun, and then I'm going to take a pair of handcuffs and lock you to the pipes right here, boss. Don't try and be a hero, it's not really your style. I need a five-minute head start, then you can scream and shout all you like, and your little chums from the Royal Gendarmerie will come and set you free.'

'You're gonna get yourself fired, kiddo. Why . . . why are you doing this?'

Julo took the time to look his boss straight in the eye, and then tell him a truth. A definitive one.

'Sometimes you've got to choose what side you're on.'

❈

Less than three minutes later, Julo burst into Hall B.

Deserted.

The lieutenant glanced in panic at the tarmac.

Deserted.

He sprinted. Hurtled down an escalator, ran past baggage reclaim carousels, empty and lifeless. A customs officer on duty in front of the first set of exit doors looked at him unflinchingly, as if relishing the renewed calm of the place after an intense flurry of activity.

'The girl, for fuck's sake. The girl from the Beirut Airbus? Where's she gone?'

The customs officer shrugged and answered in a detached voice.

'They've taken her away. They were parked in front of Exit 2, but they must have left by now. They're taking her to Rabat central police station.'

Julo left the customs officer without a word of thanks, running towards Exit 2. He charged down the hall, leapt over the security barriers which normally forced you to make pointless twists and turns, and then – without slowing down – slid across the polished tiles to take the final bend as tightly as possible. Behind the glass door of the exit, he glimpsed the silhouettes of policemen, flashing beacons and, even further off, buses and taxis.

He had to run before they pulled away! He sprinted so fast that the automatic door didn't open quickly enough. He had to brake at the very last moment, nearly crashing into it. The brief pause allowed him to catch his breath, as the stifling heat of the street – contrasting sharply with the air conditioning in the terminal – overwhelmed him.

A police van with tinted windows was parked in front of the exit.

Impossible to know whether Bamby was sitting inside. Julo planted himself in front of a young, arrogant-looking Moroccan officer – jacket trimmed with braid, cap screwed down as far as his eyebrows, craning his neck to see beyond the visor, like a giraffe.

'Julo Flores, I'm the ASIA with the DCI.'

The Royal Gendarmerie officer looked sceptically at the young cop with the open, crumpled-up shirt, his body covered in sweat, hair a complete mess, but the other Moroccan policemen on the pavement vouched for his identity. They knew him.

'I have instructions from the French Ministry of the Interior,' said Julo confidently. 'I have to interrogate the suspect.'

With a flick of his hand, Captain Giraffe signalled that the van would soon be driving off, which meant that Julo had to wait his turn, that France enjoyed no special privileges here, that he represented the law in this country, that they weren't living under the protectorate any more. Mr Giraffe managed to express all of this by punctuating his hand gesture with a simple look of disdain.

'It was Commandant Velika who sent me . . .'

The name of Julo's boss provoked the first sign of tension. Thanks a million, Petar. He had a rare talent for pissing them off . . . They became suspicious.

'He . . .' (Julo was flying by the seat of his pants now, with no plan in his head, merely conscious that he had to take a big gamble – a very big one – if he wanted to stand any chance.) 'They've spotted something, a trail on social media . . . A planned attack, in Marseille . . . It's . . .' (The words poured out thick and fast, of their own accord, utterly convincing.) 'It's the first day of the Frontex conference, with twenty-eight European ministers, and as many from Africa . . . Fucking hell, it's opening in less than eight hours and this girl's one of the keys to the whole bloody thing.'

Captain Giraffe was now twisting his neck anxiously – forcefully enough to fracture his cervical vertebrae – against the rigid sides of his cap. He tried stalling again, but Julo knew he had won. The Moroccan officer reflected. He had nothing to lose by letting Julo talk to this girl for a few minutes. If he refused, on the other hand . . .

He opened the door of the van.

'Yes, of course . . . Go ahead.'

This time, it was Julo who assumed the contemptuous attitude. *Thanks again, Petar!* He eyed the dozen or so Moroccan policemen scornfully, as if they might all be harbouring some radical Islamist, some distant cousin or other, then looked the Giraffe straight in the eye.

'What she's got to tell me is confidential – I don't need to spell that out.'

He twirled the keys of his team's Renault Safrane, parked a hundred metres away, around his index finger. The Giraffe seemed to dither one last time. Julo tried not to rush him, despite being terrified that Petar – or perhaps some Moroccan customs officer who'd heard his cries for help – might suddenly appear on the airport concourse. Captain Giraffe finally raised his cap with his fingertips as a sign of consent, then signalled to four policemen to escort the female passenger from the police van to the DCI car.

❀

'Who are you?'

'Lieutenant Julo Flores. Look down, pretend you're nervous when I'm speaking to you, answer in short sentences – they're watching us.'

'What are you playing at?'

Bamby Maal was sitting in the passenger seat. Her safari jacket was half open, revealing her olive skin, her long hair was in a mess. As bewitching as a fairy-tale enchantress. Her eyes, as dry and black as cold lava, flickered between rage and despair, their only make-up being a veil of energy stretched tight over endless suffering.

Julo found her even prettier in real life. For this tête-à-tête alone, he would happily have been dismissed from the National Police, sentenced by a special court and led before a firing squad.

'Your little brother's in danger. At the Olympus Estate. You've got to help me.'

Bamby was visibly shaken. Her eyes, however, despite being on the verge of tears, continued to glare at him with hostility. Discreetly, he locked the door and slid the key into the car's ignition.

'Now, you're going to speak very softly, like a GPS, and guide me to the Orange Tree District, and then to your grandparents' apartment.'

'They're not looking at us now,' said Bamby gently. 'Start the car, and at the end of the road, sharp right!'

The Safrane leapt forward before any of the ten policemen on the pavement could react. Julo slammed his foot down on the accelerator. Bamby was flung backwards and her safari jacket burst open.

'Concentrate, for fuck's sake!' yelled Bamby.

There was nothing soft about her voice any more. Julo avoided dwelling on the fact that he was clearly insane and the girl at his side was a double murderer. He turned right.

'Left, then right again, that's the quickest. They won't follow you along there.'

He obeyed. Even Petar, when Julo was driving, treated him with more respect.

'And give me a gun!'

'What?'

Julo could see the ocean at the end of Avenue Hassan II. They would be at the Olympus Estate in less than three minutes. He turned abruptly to the right and used the opportunity to admire his warrior passenger for half a second. He was crazy about this girl. No ifs or buts. Sick with love.

She delivered the lad his *coup de grâce*.

'Listen, dreamboy, I can see under your shirt too, you know! You've got two guns. Give me one!'

# 75

Using his fist, stuffed carefully into his handkerchief, Tidiane had smashed every bulb in the corridor. One after the other, all the lights on the walls of hell. He'd cut himself, he was bleeding, but he couldn't care less; he couldn't see well enough in the gloom to make out whether the white handkerchief now had dark stains, but he could feel the cloth was soaked in something sticky and damp.

No big deal. He felt no pain. He carried on walking down the unlit corridors, relying on making out the faintest shades of grey. His eyes were getting used to it; he'd practised so much. He could just pick out the frames of the cellar doors, all firmly shut, and the intersections at the ends of the long corridors, which stood out more clearly. He was moving faster and faster. For nothing.

He was going round in circles.

A few seconds after Freddy had gone back up the stairs, closing the door behind him, Tidiane had spotted his Morocco AFCON 2015 ball. It had rolled into the middle of the corridor. Tidiane had left it there, as a landmark, then continued walking to look for another way out. He'd followed every corridor, turning right, left, trying not to miss a single passageway . . . and had landed back at his ball.

The terrifying confirmation that his own intuition was right. He was going round in circles! There was no other exit.

This time, he'd picked up his leather cuddly-ball.

*

He was right at the end of the first long corridor, the one where the stairs came down, when he saw the light.

Freddy!

Tidiane pressed himself tight against the wall. In the pitch black, Freddy couldn't see him, but Tidiane could make out the knife-monster's flaming torch perfectly – the kind Grandpa Moussa used to leave on the balcony at night to keep mosquitoes away. The flames were dancing just a few centimetres from his face, like in those films set in the Middle Ages where the evil prison guards come to fetch captives from the dungeons before torturing them. Freddy was walking slowly, lighting up every little nook and corner as he passed. He must have studied a plan. He knew there was no means of escape anywhere. That his prey could try running as fast as he could, but Freddy would eventually catch him.

With or without the treasure.

All the gates of hell were padlocked. Tidiane had already wandered up and down each passageway several times, turned the handles, pushed each door without it moving.

Not the faintest trace of any bag!

He tiptoed along as the torch approached. He could see the flame, revealing Freddy's presence, from a distance; this was his chance, he could always stay one corridor ahead.

For how long? Until Freddy walked faster? Until he pricked up his ears, listening for the slightest sound of footsteps? Until he stopped, chose a different route, until they ran into each other? It was hopeless!

Tidiane clutched his ball between his arms. His only weapon. What did he hope to do with it? He turned into yet another dark corridor, and carried on walking – fearing with every step that he would see the torch suddenly appearing in front of him, or feel a hand being placed on his shoulder – while being careful to make as little noise as possible.

A cry made him jump. It came from inside the wall on his right; or maybe from the ceiling? The cry of an owl, Tidiane could have sworn.

He moved forward, and suddenly fell flat on his face.

To prevent his face being crushed on the floor, he let go of the ball at the last moment and it rolled a few metres. Tidiane hadn't uttered a sound. The soft surface here had cushioned his fall. He felt as though he'd fallen over in complete and utter silence. His foot had stumbled over something, as if someone had tripped him up. Crouching down, he brushed away the dust, and realised what it was.

A root!

He fumbled around to trace its shape, processing the information sent by his fingertips. The root continued, crawling through the corridor before running along the wall, and then climbing back up, towards the ceiling. Tidiane remembered the sound he'd just heard, the cry of the owl.

The orange tree! It had to be the orange tree, surely! Hell stretched out beneath the courtyard of the Olympus Estate – they must have constructed the cellars around the tree, but over time its roots had thrust their way into some of them. Tidiane knew the Olympus courtyard by heart, he knew there were no openings on the surface for you to slip yourself between the trunk and the tarmac, apart from those in the gutters, which were far too small. But perhaps the tree had gouged out a hole underneath, like water does in caves, a little space that was still big enough to conceal yourself in?

He continued on all fours and realised that, between the roots, some bricks had worked loose, providing a little hideout at the base of the wall, almost invisible from the corridor, but sufficiently big to wriggle into! Tidiane crawled his way through. He couldn't see any glow from the torch at either end of the corridor; he crawled in further, until he was completely inside the long, narrow hiding place. He huddled up in a corner. For the first time he felt safe. Little by little, his heartbeat began to slow. His thoughts felt better organised, even though they continued to flutter around, like the wings of a frantic butterfly.

Maybe Freddy would go straight past the hidey-hole without discovering it, just as he himself would have done if he hadn't tripped over the root? Maybe he'd manage to escape from him? Maybe . . . Grandpa Moussa's voice suddenly burst into the middle of his chaotic thoughts, like some old bit of paper you find again when you're sorting stuff out.

Every word was coming back to him now, that advice from his grandfather which he must never forget:

*You will find the treasure, the real treasure . . . in the same place as our roots.*

What if Grandpa had used that word on purpose? *Roots*. Like a weighty secret, a burden he didn't want to make his grandson bear, a sentence with a double meaning which the boy would only understand when the time came, precisely when he needed to?

Tidiane's hands scrabbled around in the dark. In front of him, the gap became narrower and narrower, leaving only just enough room to slip your arm in. He felt his way, pushing until he tore his shoulders on the razor-sharp edges of the bricks. His heart suddenly leapt, slamming into the walls of his chest as violently as his head into the roof of the tiny cave.

The tips of his fingers had felt an object!

Cold. Soft. A bag! Made of leather or plastic.

As slowly and quietly as possible, he tried pulling it towards him. The bag was heavy, stuck fast, as if it had sat there for years and years without moving. Millimetre by millimetre, Tidiane managed to dislodge it. When he finally succeeded in grabbing it with both hands, he turned on his side as best he could, grazing his back and ribs, ripping his Barrada jersey on the sharp bricks, before clutching the bag to his stomach, like a dog guarding a stolen bone.

The bag was closed. Zipped up.

Tidiane waited anxiously for a long time, listened intently to the silence, tucked his feet in even more so you couldn't see them from the corridor.

No sign of Freddy . . .

Gently, Tidiane pressed a little button on his watch. The minute source of light illuminated his hideout. He had to hold the screen right up to the bag to see anything. He moved his night light, centimetre by centimetre, until he finally saw three small blue leaves sliced by three horizontal lines. Of course, he knew this logo, he'd seen it on the OM jerseys: *Adidas!*

Going by its weight alone, the bag could easily have contained hundreds of gold coins.

Tidiane listened to the silence again, for a few seconds which seemed to last an eternity, before trying to open the zip.

It gave way easily. Without making the slightest sound, even though it felt like his heartbeat was echoing through the little cave as loudly as that of a baby during an ultrasound. He just had to take his time. He tugged delicately at the zip until the bag was fully open. Step one, breathed Tidiane.

He leant over as he inserted the watch into the bag, so as to examine the treasure minutely with his mini-laser. Its faint halo only lit up a few centimetres at a time, making it impossible to see everything contained in the bag at once. Tidiane rejected the idea of plunging his hands inside to feel the entire weight of the booty, like pirates digging up a chest and letting the coins rain down between their fingers. Too risky, too noisy. He was dying to do it, though.

The tiny trickle of light illuminated, one after the other, gold necklaces, rings, bracelets, jewellery glittering with diamonds and what seemed to be other gemstones, watches, silver pens, leather wallets. Tidiane dug his hand even deeper into the gleaming hoard. His micro-torch shone on gold-plated spectacles, jacket buttons, little ivory objects which looked like West African amulets, lighters, and trinkets which were even smaller.

Tidiane felt as though he were about to be sick. Gold teeth! He remembered that history lesson Madame Obadia had given them, about the last World War, remembered her telling them that before gassing Jews, Roma and disabled people under fake showers, the Nazis would collect all objects of any value from them. Making them believe they would give them back afterwards.

Tidiane gazed at the treasure – fascinated, disgusted. Did all these objects belong to people who'd been killed afterwards? Was that why Maman's treasure was cursed? He wished he could have seen more clearly, here in his dark little cubby-hole, so he could study it better.

Suddenly, as if his wish had been heard somewhere in the heavens, the entire hoard lit up.

All at once, in the hollow where Tidiane was hunched up, the hundreds of objects began to sparkle, all shining equally brightly.

A second later, Tidiane felt the heat behind him – a searing heat, as if someone had lit a fire under his feet. As if all the fires in hell were alight, at the entrance to the oven where he was trapped.

# 76

'Explain yourself, Velika.'

Jourdain Blanc-Martin, without even waiting for Petar's words of remorse, regretted that two thousand kilometres separated him from the commandant of Rabat DCI. He would have taken great pleasure in punching the cop's face. The commandant would have taken the blow without flinching, biting his lips and apologising humbly.

'Explain how you achieved quite such a feat, Commandant. Yan Segalen traps the girl, I hand her to you on a plate, you deploy thirty cops on the tarmac at Rabat airport, and you *still* can't catch her?'

'I couldn't have foreseen that my depu—'

'Now listen here, Velika,' interrupted Blanc-Martin. 'I'm doing my job, I'm honouring my part of the contract. I regulate the migrant market better than Frontex or the consulate. I save you a shitload of hassle, I think, and in return I just ask you to bugger off and leave me alone! OK? Don't forget – you'd never have got your cushy little number without me, Velika. If you're keen to hold on to it, find that girl. Find her quickly, whatever it takes. Let's be done with the Maal family, do you get me? You see to the kids while I see to the mother – it's really not that complicated. Is it, Commandant? Is it?'

'No,' admitted Petar Velika.

Jourdain Blanc-Martin hung up. He needed peace and quiet this morning. Serenity. The Frontex symposium was opening tonight. He had to fine-tune his speech, prepare himself to speak in front of the fifty or so ministers and heads of state. He had no time to waste on logistical concerns, any more than on that Adil Zairi, who'd suddenly reappeared out of nowhere to mop things up on his behalf, or that handful of Beninese who'd drowned last night and whom no one could give a toss about. That said, their deaths could provide him with a very moving introduction to his speech this evening. Experience had taught him that fresh corpses are the main ingredient in the recipe for humanitarian compassion.

He walked, barefoot, across the terrace, its teak planks already warm by now. He would have time to reflect on it during his morning one-kilometre swim, but first he had to root out the evil. The Maal-evolence. He took another step and buzzed the intercom.

'Ibra and Bastoun, I need you. Come up.'

The two henchmen waited at the entrance to the sunlit conservatory, between the pool and the deckchairs, motionless, arms folded over their brawny torsos, with the demeanour of patient and vigilant lifeguards. Blanc-Martin checked that Safietou wasn't hovering nearby to clear away the breakfast things, then took a few steps towards them. He looked through the French window, indicating the high-rise blocks which rose up facing the sea.

'I'm giving you permission for a little stroll. A few minutes and you'll be back. You're popping over to Les Aigues Douces again. Block H9, seventh floor. But you're doing more than just making a fucking mess this time.'

Confronted by Ibra and Bastoun's blank stares, he took another step towards them, adjusted the belt of his bathrobe, and checked once more that they were alone. His words were hissed rather than spoken.

'Kill her!'

# 77

Alpha didn't believe in miracles, nor amulets, nor all that superstitious mumbo-jumbo which generally only serves to exploit the
credulity of idiots. But that didn't stop him from wearing his ebony
triangle around his neck, from thinking of Bamby, from touching
it now and then, as if this talisman could somehow link him to his
sister and they could thereby join forces.

They'd been waiting for several long minutes at the crossroads
of Rue Papin and Rue Gambetta, under the bus shelter, keeping a
close eye on the entrance to La Lavéra.

Alpha believed only in strength combined with cunning. These
qualities had enabled him to carry out the first part of his plan,
in Morocco. He was familiar with every location, monitored the
habits of the police, the people smugglers, the networks of illegal
migrants; he'd been able to control every stage. But here, in France,
he could only trust his instinct.

He had imagined ringing at the gate of La Lavéra, taking the
guards by surprise, holding them at gunpoint, and entering. Once
he'd arrived at the villa for real, however, it had turned out to be
infinitely more complicated. Savorgnan, Zahérine and the others
were unarmed, the area around the villa was chock-full of security
cameras, and the guards wouldn't just allow themselves to be caught
unawares. Any attempt to break in would end in a fiasco. All that
effort – going on the run, crossing the sea – for nothing.

And then the miracle happened!

From their vantage point a few metres from the villa, Alpha saw the gate open . . . and remain open! Then the two guards came out. Casually, on foot, as if they were sauntering off to buy some cigarettes or have a beer on a café terrace. He watched, following their movements as far as the corner with Rue Gabriel-Péri, in the same direction as the apartment blocks at Les Aigues Douces. Perhaps they were going for a jog along the seafront? Taking a dip in the Mediterranean? Or simply going to meet some petty criminal?

Alpha was quick to react. *Now!* He motioned to the four Beninese, and they sneaked along the wall, slid through the gate, and crept softly up to the front door. The cameras were bound to have filmed them, but the guards were no longer there to view the monitor. Alpha quietly pushed open the door of the villa. The moment they slipped inside, a woman emerged from the room opposite. She was wearing an apron and a chef's hat, and holding a tea towel.

Alpha was the fastest. He rushed over, covered her mouth with his broad hand before she could cry out, and then, without any hint of violence, whispered in her ear:

'Shh . . . We're guests.'

Safietou was terrified, wide-eyed with panic as she examined each of the five intruders, calm and silent, with skin as black as her own.

'We're friends,' said Alpha. 'Old friends. Where's your boss?'

Safietou said nothing. Alpha repeated, in Bambara:

'*Min kɔrɔn i patɔrɔn?*'

She seemed astonished, still appeared too frightened to utter a single word, but looked up, towards the upper floors and the terrace. Alpha gently loosened his grip as Safietou glanced down at the gun wedged in his belt.

'We want to give him a surprise. You're not going to spoil Jourdain's little treat, are you?'

Then, silently, the five men began to climb the stairs.

# 78

**10.44 a.m.**

First, Tidiane felt the vice tightening around his ankles, then his belly scraping the floor, his arms and legs being horribly scratched by the loose bricks, violently enough to leave gashes in their skin, to make him scream with the pain. He tried clinging on, to thin air, to the dust of the cave, to the heavy bag, but he was powerless to resist the force that was dragging him out of his hole. He found himself ejected unceremoniously onto the bare concrete of the corridor.

Hell seemed to be on fire! The flames were licking at the grey walls and stretching every shadow out of proportion. Freddy's shadow in particular: he had wedged his torch between a pipe and the wall. The fire was dancing under the tunnel. The heat was warming up the air, contrasting with the coolness of the rest of the cellar.

Freddy pushed Tidiane back against the wall with one hand, and snatched the black Adidas bag from his hands with the other.

'You're a bloody smart little bastard, Tidy. Just as well I trusted you.'

He looked for a moment at the entrance to the cavity dug into the wall, under the root of the orange tree.

'If you hadn't left your ball behind, I don't think I would have stopped.'

The Morocco 2015 ball had rolled a few metres away from them. Tidiane looked at it in terror, then looked up at Freddy again.

'I'm not a thief, you know, I'm just taking back what your mother borrowed from me.' (He felt the weight of the bag in his hand.)

'Besides, it's almost as heavy as before, you'd think she's hardly dipped into it.'

Tidiane tried to get to his feet, but Freddy pinned him against the wall by ramming his foot against his chest.

'I was sure your mother would spend the money, but wouldn't touch the objects. Your mother's always been a bit superstitious.' (He opened the bag and checked its contents with a wicked smile.) 'Did you look too, you little nosy parker? So you understood then, did you, why I was anxious to find this treasure again? Not for its value, even though it represents a tidy little nest egg put away over several years, but for the ghosts to whom these objects once belonged. Invisible people who're long since dead and gone, who can never accuse anyone at all, whose dust has long since been blown away by the desert wind. But you'll learn, kid, that an object is sometimes more talkative than a person . . . A ring, a necklace, a piece of jewellery can speak, years later, on behalf of the husband who gave it as a gift, the mother who wore it. You can't kill objects, do you see? You can only hide them. Or sell them – far, far away from the place you originally found them.'

Freddy dropped the bag with a thud. The sound echoed through the corridor, while the impact sent up a cloud of starry dust. He turned to Tidiane. The monster was clutching the knife in his hand again.

'But you too, Tidy, you might talk? And you don't have anything of value that I'd like to keep as a souvenir, nothing that could tell your story one day.'

Freddy thrust his dagger into the haze. Tidiane thought the monster was going to strike the dust cloud at random, like a madman chasing fireflies, but he bent down and simply pierced the Morocco 2015 ball with his blade. Tidiane's lucky charm deflated almost immediately, like a burst balloon, with a sinister, snake-like hiss.

Tidiane exploded with rage, as sudden as it was intense. The strength he'd been lacking. He leapt up in a flash. He could see the stairs at the end of the corridor – he would be faster, he would get out, he would take his revenge.

Freddy's arm caught him by the waist. He had anticipated the boy's reaction, had stopped him as easily as you'd catch a baby who's only just starting to walk.

Freddy's burly arm then rose up and squeezed his torso, pinning the boy tight against his chest, almost preventing him from breathing. Tidiane could smell the monster puffing and panting onto his cheeks, the odour of sweat and alcohol. He saw the glint of the dagger, locked in Freddy's right hand.

'I'm sorry, Tidy, I just can't leave you to blab, and tell everyone the whole story. And more importantly, I made a promise to your mother. I've been looking for a way to make her suffer as much as I have. Looking for a long time. Stealing her own life wouldn't have held much appeal, neither for her, nor for me . . . But stealing her son's life from her . . .'

The dagger came closer to his throat again. Tidiane was no longer struggling, he'd realised the monster was too strong. The flame from the torch shimmered on the blade.

'Drop your knife!'

The cloud of dust had almost entirely disappeared. A figure was pointing a revolver at Adil, someone at the end of the corridor, at the bottom of the stairs, lit only by the exit to the ground floor whose door had been left open.

A cop, thought Adil.

'Drop your knife,' repeated the figure.

His voice was trembling. His arm was shaking. Some kid under thirty who'd never fired a shot, reasoned Adil. His stroke of luck?

Instead of loosening his fingers, curled tight around the handle of the dagger, Adil Zairi brought the knife even closer to Tidiane's carotid artery, pricking the flesh with the tip of the blade.

'If you shoot,' yelled Adil, 'I'll kill him! So you're just going to slide your gun over to me.'

The cop began to waver . . . OK, Adil, you win! He wouldn't do anything that might endanger the kid's life. A ten-year-old hostage – as good as life insurance.

'I've got nothing to lose,' insisted Adil. 'If you don't slide over your gun, I'll stab the kid. He wouldn't be the first that . . .'

Adil made a slight gesture of impatience, his features contorted with evil. The face of a sadist. Of Satan, because of the flames.

'OK, OK,' the young cop hastened to reply.

He bent down, raising his hand in surrender, then slid the revolver across the floor towards Adil.

Not enough force.

The gun came to rest around fifteen metres from the policeman, around twenty from Zairi.

*Bravo*, thought Adil, clenching his hand tighter around the knife. The young cop was trying to be clever, was he! The guy probably thought he'd be the quickest if they both rushed for the gun, especially given Adil was lumbered with the kid. But this rookie cowboy was overlooking just one key thing: firearms aren't the only weapons that can kill several times.

Adil had made up his mind: he would create a diversion and then strike by surprise, plunge the knife into the kid's chest and, a second later, use the same blood-covered blade to stab the cop who'd be sure to come charging at him. At just a few metres, almost at point-blank range, he couldn't possibly miss.

He took a deep breath. He could feel the kid tensing up in his vice-like grip. Get it over with, don't make him suffer any more.

Adil loosened his hold, as if he were consenting to let Tidiane go, and let him take a step to one side, while hiding the handle of the dagger, still tightly clenched, just by his thigh; then he suddenly whirled around, raised his arm with devastating speed, and sliced through the scorching air in order to strike, aiming straight at the boy's heart.

A bang. It rocked the whole corridor. Reverberated through the walls of hell.

Adil's final thought, at the very instant the bullet ripped through his lung, was to glance at the revolver on the floor and wonder what magic had enabled it to fire itself. As he collapsed into the dust, he noticed a second shadow, just slightly behind the policeman. A slender shadow. Female. So cold, implacable and determined that he thought he'd been killed by his own reflection.

❁

'Tidy!'

'Bamby!'

As the boy flung himself into his sister's arms, Lieutenant Julo Flores sat down on the top step of the stairs. Confused. Reassured. Proud. Overwhelmed. Incapable of sorting through a bizarre mish-mash of feelings. He would be dismissed from the police, no doubt about that. He had just saved the life of a ten-year-old kid. He was an accomplice to a murder, the third committed in three days by this girl. A girl he now had to bring to justice.

He grabbed his phone from his pocket.

'Rabat police station? Put me on to an officer, anyone at all.'

Bamby Maal turned towards him. He read no reproach in her teary eyes, no fear, no remorse. Instead, he read the answer to a question that had intrigued him since the moment he'd first come across that look, captured by a security camera. That look of defiance.

He read a simple 'Thank you'.

Bamby Maal moved closer, after planting a long kiss on Tidiane's forehead and sitting him down carefully on another step. Julo could hear cops talking in Arabic. He held the phone away from his ear.

'Please,' said Bamby. 'I'll come with you. I promise I'll come with you. But please, just give me a few minutes.'

She took a long pause, before adding:

'Six minutes. Exactly.'

# 79

**10.50 a.m.**

*Kill her*, the boss had said. At least, this time, the instructions were clear.

Ibra and Bastoun stopped for a few seconds at the corner of the street to smoke a cigarette and observe their surroundings in the Les Aigues Douces neighbourhood. There were only a few residents to be seen, dashing past in silence, heads down. No security cameras between the towers, no door codes to the entrance halls, no witnesses, not even any dealers or their accomplices keeping a lookout in the stairwells. Nothing but shops whose metal shutters were pulled down, car parks where the vehicles seemed abandoned, empty balconies you could jump off without bothering the neighbours. An open, deserted neighbourhood, where you could enter, kill and leave again with complete impunity.

Ibra lit Bastoun's cigarette with his own. They focused their eyes on Block H9 and didn't even have to search. Of the sixty or so balconies on its facade, cluttered with tables and chairs, bikes and boards, sheets and plants, only one was home to a human presence. The balcony belonging to Leyli Maal. She was staring at the sea over the handrail, like a prisoner gazing at the sky through the bars.

Like a prisoner waiting for her executioner, Ibra preferred to think. Leyli Maal was accompanied by an odd-looking man wearing a hat. An old man. Tall and thin, resembling a pastor-confessor, like the executor of your last will and testament. Tough shit for him.

Ibra and Bastoun took barely three or four puffs before crushing both of their cigarette butts under their feet, and walking in step towards Block H9.

Like them, Leyli Maal was smoking.

One last cigarette. That of a woman sentenced to death.

# 80

**10.51 a.m.**

Jourdain Blanc-Martin hadn't heard them arriving.

Alpha, Savorgnan, Zahérine, Whisley and Darius had climbed the floors of La Lavéra in complete silence, still wary even though Safietou had confirmed her boss was alone, as he was every morning, on the fifth floor, on the terrace overlooking the city. No one to disturb him.

When they'd slid open the glazed door, Jourdain Blanc-Martin hadn't heard them either. In the conservatory, which opened onto the wide teak-wood terrace, the only sound you could hear came from the gentle bubbling of the jacuzzi, next to the large pool. The one where Blanc-Martin was swimming.

The Vogelzug president was doing a series of lengths, demonstrating a perfect front crawl.

The five men moved forward. Blanc-Martin couldn't help being aware of them this time, yet he finished his length before leaning on the side and lifting his goggles. He masked his surprise admirably.

'Alpha Maal? And here was I, thinking you were still in Morocco. Well played! Remarkably well played. Crossing the Mediterranean right behind my back, while my mind's entirely occupied by your sister. And on the *Sébastopol*, I'm guessing. A yacht hired using my money, to boot. Hats off to you. I really didn't think you'd have the balls.'

Then, as if this one compliment were enough, Blanc-Martin

pulled his goggles down again and swam away in the opposite direction. Savorgnan placed a hand on Alpha's shoulder.

'Just hang back, will you, brother?'

Without uttering a single word, the four Beninese spread out, each walking in silence and taking up a position, standing, at one of the four sides of the pool. Blanc-Martin was about to reach the metal ladder which provided the only way out of the pool, in order to put on his bathrobe which was lying on a deckchair. As soon as he touched a rung to haul himself out of the water, Savorgnan, without a word, stamped on his hand. Blanc-Martin yelled at him.

'You're nuts! What the hell do you want?'

He looked all the way round. The four tall black figures stood stiffly, forming a perfect diamond controlling a rectangle of water in which Blanc-Martin was unable to touch the bottom. The president swam towards the opposite side. The moment he reached out to rest his hands, the African, a guy wearing old trainers full of holes, looked at him with scorn, and lifted his sole, ready to slam it down on his knuckles.

*Ridiculous!* thought Blanc-Martin. He swam for half an hour every morning; they'd get tired of this little game before he did. He floated in one spot for a little, then headed off again in a different direction, towards the side guarded by the youngest of the men, a curly-haired type with a dreamy, faraway look, like one of those artists with sad eyes. But he didn't let him put his hands on the side, no more than had the other two.

Even though Blanc-Martin was trying hard not to let it show, subconsciously he was starting to have doubts. How long would Ibra and Bastoun take to come back? He refused to stoop to pleading with these guys, to begging for a hand that they'd never offer him anyway. His arms, his legs were beginning to get tired. He realised that, usually, he leant against the wall after each length, always kept moving and resting, wasn't forced to practically tread water constantly.

How long could you stay in the water like this before sinking? An hour? Two hours? Much less? He'd been swimming for about twenty minutes and already felt the need to hold on to something, to put down a foot, to rest a hand. He stared at the four Africans one by one, then at the kid, Alpha, whom they'd left on the sidelines, as if he were too young to participate in Blanc-Martin's murder. This new train of thought made him anxious. He stopped swimming again, struggling to keep his head above water as he spoke.

'For God's sake, what do you want?'

He received no answer. In fact, the four Africans barely looked at him at all, except when Blanc-Martin approached one of the sides of the pool. They just stared at the Mediterranean across the terrace, as if they were searching for a ghost in its waters.

'Fine, whatever turns you on,' hissed Blanc-Martin.

On reflection, though, the silence of the five intruders reassured him. They had no intention of using a weapon against him, they would simply wait. Wait for what? And Blanc-Martin had a lifeline, for when he began to feel too tired. Floating in the middle of the pool was the large inflatable island used by the children three days earlier for his grandsons' birthday party. The treasure island, home of the mini-pirates!

In any case, Jourdain wasn't going to wait any longer, as keeping his balance without any support was becoming increasingly difficult. He flashed a smile of contempt at the four black lifeguards and then, in a few strokes, reached the shore, the shore of this plastic island where he could wait peacefully for hours for these men to get bored . . . and for Ibra and Bastoun to come and finish them off!

Blanc-Martin's hands closed around empty space. The island was nothing but an illusion. An unreachable shore, a shattered dream. It only came back to him now: during the party, the kids had used the marshmallow skewers as little harpoons, and the party hosts had been forced to clear all the kids out after twenty minutes of an aquatic treasure hunt that was descending into carnage.

Blanc-Martin persisted. He hoped that – despite this – there was enough air left to let him rest, and catch his breath. Since the island was bobbing on the surface, it therefore meant this land still existed, that it could welcome him on board, hold him up, just long enough for a brief stopover. He asked no more of it than that.

The island sank under his weight without offering him any

support whatsoever. Yet Jourdain's hands persevered, tried to cling to the flaccid coconut trees, the floppy beaches, grasped a few shiny objects stuck in the folds of the plastic sheeting, clutched them tightly for a second, before he opened his palms. The gold coins from the treasure island, left behind by the six-year-old pirates, had liquefied into a muddy slime, oozing between his fingers like sticky, stinking excrement.

Jourdain Blanc-Martin held out for a few more long minutes. Then he lost all notion of time. All that mattered was his balance. All that mattered was the deadly water line that sliced through his neck, the line he had to remain above. The line that now sliced through his chin, and ever more frequently his lips.

He tried dozens of times to get closer to the side, when he was almost drained of his strength, when hypothermia began to stiffen his movements, but each time, a foot, a sole, crushed his fingers.

He yelled, screamed, begged, he waited for Ibra and Bastoun to come back, for Safietou to come up, for his phone to ring, for Geoffrey or one of his other sons to drop by. He thought about Les Aigues Douces again (what the hell were Ibra and Bastoun up to?), he thought back to his childhood by the Mediterranean, about going to marches on the Canebière on his mother's arm, about that Frontex conference, tonight, which he would never have the chance to open, he waited for at least one of these five guys to speak, to insult him, to curse him, or to thank him, why not, because thanks to him, thousands of Africans were living in Europe, would have kids there, little coloured Europeans, a whole mixed-race lineage which wouldn't have existed without him.

One last time, he hauled himself as far as he could out of the water, using the strength of his thighs and lower back, craning his neck to catch a glimpse, beyond the terrace, of a corner of the Mediterranean. Jourdain convinced himself that he was experiencing a truly beautiful death. Real conquerors, the repopulators of new continents, the Magellans of this world, all end up drowned.

That was his final thought.

Calm again.

Exhausted, he sank below the surface.

# 81

Four minutes had passed.

Bamby was waiting, her head resting on the young cop's shoulder. He had slipped a hand around her waist, under her safari jacket, touching her skin. She'd let him do it. She knew this would be the only affectionate physical contact she'd have – the only chance to give herself to someone – for many years, until she was old, until she came out of prison one day, in an eternity, when the body that men fantasised about today would be ravaged by time.

They were alone, sitting on the last step of the staircase to hell. Tidiane had gone back up to set Granny Marème and Grandpa Moussa free. To be cuddled and made a fuss of too. Bamby had urged him to go. Adil's corpse, bathed in his own blood, was hardly the best of company.

*Five minutes.*

The moment was sweet. Perfect. This cop was tender and loving. She could have loved him. Maybe he would come to see her once in a while, before some nice, unattached girl caught him in her net. Julo's fingers were warm, his caresses seemed able to tune in to the beating of her heart, to anticipate it, to slow it down. She would have been content to fall asleep like that, huddled up against him, reassured.

*Six minutes.*

Without changing position, without even looking up, with an air of weariness, without a hint of impatience, Bamby stretched out her arm and examined the results from the Blood Typing Kit – from the absorbent cotton bud she had dipped in the blood pooling from Adil Zairi's chest, then dabbed onto the little circles on a testing card.

*AB+.*

*Probability: 90 per cent.*

So there was a 90 per cent probability that the dead man in front of her was her father.

The man she had just killed.

She snuggled up to Julo even tighter. Cocooned by his warmth. She felt empty. Pure. Liberated.

Her quest was over.

# 82

A little way back from the Les Aigues Douces block, cornered between the vehicles in the car park, Ibra and Bastoun stared at the third balcony on the seventh floor. The one that belonged to Leyli Maal. Empty. Cluttered only with a few scattered clothes.

They had done their job; you couldn't hold anything against them. They'd followed their orders.

*Kill her.*

Without a second thought, like well-disciplined soldiers.

Bastoun was biting his lips, making them bleed. Ibra was nervously kicking the gravel. Without exchanging a word.

Was it their fault that, once they entered Block H9, the stairwell was stuffed with cops? The pair of them had been caught red-handed, clutching their SIG Sauers. The boss would be furious when he found out, but what choice did they have once surrounded, apart from throwing their weapons on the floor, putting their hands up, holding out their wrists to be handcuffed and, above all, keeping their traps firmly shut?

Before getting into the police van, Ibra and Bastoun glanced discreetly into the distance, just above Port Renaissance, over towards La Lavéra. Well, the boss could at least give them due credit: they hadn't uttered a single word!

They were both convinced that their boss would have been far angrier at them for having spilt the beans than for having failed . . . and that the cops would soon turn up at his place.

❁

Commandant Tòni Frediani let the van move off towards Port-de-Bouc police station, then grabbed his phone.

The call took less than three seconds to cross the Mediterranean. It took Petar two more to pick up.

'Velika? It's Frediani. Thanks, mate. The cavalry got there in time! But next time, you'll give us just a tad more notice, right?'

'Don't complain. I was dithering for bloody ages, about whether to even call you or not.'

Tòni Frediani burst out laughing.

'I thought as much, Petar. I've only met you the once, but I'd have put you on the side of the hunters rather than the migratory birds. What made you change your mind, my friend?'

Petar was silent. In his mind's eye, Tòni Frediani replayed the film of their meeting, the previous day, at Port-de-Bouc police station – the brief questioning of Leyli Maal. That fiery little woman, that sexy ball of energy, poles apart from the sluts at the Vieux-Port.

'Leyli's beautiful eyes, maybe?' suggested Tòni.

'If only! See, I'm even more of a bloody idiot than my deputy.'

Commandant Frediani laughed loudly again, but quickly became serious once more.

'You're taking one hell of a risk, mate. You told me you'd got the heads-up straight from Blanc-Martin, to persuade me to send the whole squad charging in. The police inspectorate's going to ask how you got the tip-off. We've been trying to nab the filthy bastard for years!'

In a distant world, somewhere under the Moroccan sun, Petar Velika took a long time to reply. He could still see that crazy young Julo dashing off after handcuffing him in the toilets. Sprinting through the airport to kidnap the most beautiful girl on earth and save her little brother. Fuck it, how he'd have loved to do that! His thoughts drifted off to Nadège, his pretty stylist with snowy-white hair. Tonight, he would take her to Tajine Wa Tanjia, for the best tagine in Rabat. He'd tell her everything, and he would read the admiration in her eyes. For once.

'You still there, Petar? So, what made you decide to save our little doll?'

A silence. Before the commandant hit him with a truth. A definitive one.

'Sometimes you've got to choose what side you're on.'

435

# 83

**7.30 p.m.**

**A few evenings later**

Leyli was having dinner alone in front of a black screen when the notification arrived. A splash of colour. A flashing blue rectangle.

*You have a new message.*

Taken aback, she clicked.

*patrick-pellegrin@yahoo.fr*

She frowned, even more intrigued; she had no idea who the sender was! She didn't know any Patrick . . . A mix-up? She opened the message on autopilot, as you might tear open the envelope of a letter not intended for you, without reading the address.

Dear Leyli,

I'm emailing you from my personal account, as I didn't want to wait until tomorrow morning to give you the good news. I won! I fought really hard – I won't bore you with all the ins and outs, but your file made it to the front of the queue.

Your application for a new apartment has been successful! It's still at Les Aigues Douces – Block D7, a four-bedroom apartment, 78 square metres, facing the sea, but on the third floor, so you'll lose a bit of your scenic view, I'm afraid. It's available immediately. I've checked on the plan – when you move, you'll have to walk exactly 250 metres – you go down seven floors and up three.

I'm so happy for you, Leyli. Happy for your entire family. I'll send you an official letter tomorrow morning, from FOS-HOMES.

Yours truly,

Patrick

The cruel irony of the timing drew a smile from Leyli.

*Available immediately.*

No desperate rush, Patrick.

According to her lawyer, Bamby was likely to get between twenty years and life. Even if she could plead self-defence for the murder of Adil Zairi, it was hard to dispute premeditation in the case of the first two killings.

Alpha would be released before that, even though the charge of murdering Jourdain Blanc-Martin had been brought against him. The Vogelzug scandal had been making headlines in *La Provence* for a week now, unleashing a battle between corporate lawyers and those dealing with human rights, but that wouldn't prevent Alpha's knowledge of France being limited to the tarmac of Baumettes prison before he was extradited.

Tidiane had been placed in a children's home, in Mohammedia, seventy kilometres from Rabat. Granny Marème and Grandpa Moussa had no idea when they'd be able to have him back. Everything was going well, and they'd been able to talk to him, even though contact via social media was forbidden. The doctors wanted to conduct more psychiatric tests and, more importantly, categorically refused to let the child leave Morocco. The administrative process for family reunification would be held up until this tangled affair was sorted out by the Moroccan and French justice systems. That could take months. Even years, Ruben had predicted, despite being a born optimist.

Ruben would call her, every now and then. He had handed in his notice at the Heron Port-de-Bouc, only a few hours before his dismissal letter was signed by the general manager of the Mondor group. Ruben was somewhere in the Andaman Sea, on one of the Nicobar Islands, an Indian archipelago off the coast of Thailand, in a country where the people lived completely naked, not even permitted to carry so much as a mobile phone slung over their shoulders.

The screen in front of Leyli went black once more.

She would wait; she would have dinner alone, for as long as it took. She was about to pour herself another cup of tea when yet another message flashed up.

*patrick-pellegrin@yahoo.fr*

Him again . . .

Dear Leyli,

You'll probably think I'm a bit pushy, perhaps even inappropriate, but I only thought about it after sending you my first message.

In fact, to be perfectly honest, I'd already been thinking about it for a long time, but I didn't dare say anything to you. Voilà, I've plucked up my courage and I'm taking the plunge. Would you be free, Leyli, to celebrate the good news? Say . . . tonight? I'd love to invite you for dinner. Or just to have a drink?

Leyli reread the shy words of the FOS-HOMES officer several times. They sounded sincere, just as much as Patrick sounded kind, honest, genuinely attracted to her and perhaps even genuinely single. She stood up to reflect, taking the time to light another cigarette as she gazed at the sea. The waves were lapping at the seawall, right up to the foot of the apartment blocks. Kids were swimming where it was forbidden, above the Mediterranean-Rhône pipeline. Boats were sailing into the distance. Far away, the clouds were having fun, shaping themselves to imitate mountains.

Leyli leant on the balcony for a long time. At that moment, she found herself foolishly thinking what all people think when they stand on a shore. What people have always thought, and will always think.

No sea is impossible to cross.

The most deceptive illusion of all!

Leyli finished her cigarette and then returned to the table. She sat down in front of her plate, her glass, her napkin. Alone. She stared at the blank screen once more, and finally decided to reply.

Dear Patrick,

Thank you, but I'm afraid I'm not free. Not tonight, nor any other night. I'm having dinner with my children. They need me, as I'm sure you'll understand. I have to save whatever love I have left. For them.

Yours affectionately,

Leyli

She clicked the *Send* button. The message flew off, somewhere into a parallel universe without any borders. Then, once again, the screen in front of her turned black.

# Acknowledgements

My heartfelt thanks to Pierre Perret for his exquisite song 'Lily', which inspired both the original title of this novel, *On la trouvait plutôt jolie*, and the name of my heroine.